THE WOMAN CLOTHED WITH THE SUN

First published 2022
Rymour Books
45 Needless Road,
PERTH
PH20LE

© Stuart Campbell 2022
ISBN 978-1-7395960-2-6

A CIP record for this book is
available from the British Library
BIC Classification FA

Printed and bound by
Imprint Digital
Seychelles Farm
Upton Pyne
Exeter

The paper used in this book is approved
by the Forest Stewardship Council

THE WOMAN CLOTHED WITH THE SUN

Stuart Campbell

For Andrew,

Enjoy the pilgrimage!

Stut Camb

RYMOUR

This book is dedicated to John Aitken who first introduced me to the Buchanites, and David Raitt who traipsed with me through many sodden graveyards to find them.

ACKNOWLEDGEMENTS

Thanks to North Ayrshire Library Services, Dumfries and Galloway Library and Archeological Services, the current owner of New Cample Farm, and his neighbour, on whose land I trespassed to visit the remains of Buchan Ha', and Kerry Houston for her advice on the cover art. The cover image features a pastel by Alice Pike Barney reproduced with permission from the Smithsonian American Art Museum.

Stuart Campbell 2022

She pretends to give them the Holy Ghost by breathing on them, which she does with postures and practices that are scandalously indecent... I am personally acquainted with most of them...

From Robert Burns's account of Mrs Buchan in his letter to James Burness.

And there appeared a great wonder in heaven; a woman clothed with the sun, and the moon under her feet, and upon her head a crown of twelve stars.

Revelation 12:1

Chapter One

THE END
Crocketford, Dumfries and Galloway, December 1845

Two rodent teeth still clung to the jaw. William Charters, joiner, kneeled next to the makeshift coffin. In truth it was more of a packing case such as that used to store tools on the deck of a merchant ship. He handed the lid to his companion, Rab Little, cupped his hands and blew into them.

'Some size of a woman.' The joiner put a hand to his nose. The gesture was instinctive; there were no noxious vapours from the body which was mummified and hard to the touch. He recoiled as a wafer of brown skin detached itself from the Lord Mother's thigh bone.

'Must be six feet if she's an inch. Andra's like a midget compared wi' her.' Both men glanced at the body in the second coffin. A tiny man, thin and frail with a firm jaw and a mass of straggly hair. It occurred to Rab that he had never seen him without his hat before. It had seemed an integral part of his body.

'I'll no speak ill of the dead, but he was a strange wee man.'

'Aye,' said William shaking his hand to dislodge the flakes of skin.

'Her face has gone,' observed Rab.

'And her feet.'

'Rats likely.'

'Aye.'

Both men were troubled. They had argued for some time over the decision to honour the dying man's wishes, but Andrew Innes had been adamant. They were both to be buried in the same grave which was to be dug the day before his funeral. At cockcrow they were to place Elspeth's body at the bottom, then cover it with soil so no-one would know that she was there. He would be placed on top of her so that when she rose from the dead she would wake him and together they would ascend to paradise. It was obvious.

It was John Ewart whose farm backed onto Newhouse who

reminded them that the magistrate would likely take an interest in the matter if they followed Innes' wishes. 'There's aye rumours and loose tongues. The whole village kens he hid her body in his stair closet. She's been there for nigh on fifty years.'

'They say he washed her every day,' said William choosing a dozen or so nails. 'Aye, wi'a warm cloutie. And then,' he continued after checking that his audience was sufficiently attentive, 'he would put the auld cloth on his ain head as he sat by the fire.' He lifted the lid onto Elspeth's coffin and hammered in the first nail.

Chapter Two

THE BEGINNING
Fatmachen, Banffshire, 1744

The child rubbed the corn husks from her cheeks and looked quizzically at the red disk dropping behind the hill. Her father was still wielding his sickle at the phalanx of stalks. Elspeth was meant to be raking them into a pile so they could be bound. She dropped the rake and walked straight into the corn using both hands to clear a path with swimming motions. The corn shook momentarily and then sprung back. She was now deep in the field and completely invisible to anyone who might have missed her. No-one had. She turned sharply to the right as if dowsing for an unseen trace of water, stopped and crouched down. She lifted the rabbit and cradled it in her arms. She then balanced the dead animal on her knee and prised open its mouth with a finger. She lifted it to her own face and blew lightly. 'Faither!' she shouted. 'The beastie's living.'

Unable to see his daughter, John Simpson hurled down his flail and strode into the corn. Elspeth looked up at him and held out the rabbit as if offering it as a gift. John grabbed the animal and flung it into the far corner of the field. His hand landed heavily on his daughter's cheek. He then tucked her roughly under his arm, like an errant piglet, and hit her several times on the backside.

Instead of giving in to her tears, she asked him, 'Why, faither, did deith come to this field?' Another blow. 'I brocht the rabbit back to life, faither, I did.' Robert smacked her again.

When they entered the tavern, he dropped her onto the stone flags. She crawled on all fours until she was safely hidden against the wall under the trestle table. Although in pain, she didn't cry. She never did. Instead she looked with interest at the huge boots planted on the floor opposite her. They were dusty and there was a hole in the toe of the nearest boot. She crept forward and inserted her finger in the hole and wiggled it. The owner of the boot lifted his foot and shook it vigorously before stamping it down again. She repeated the trick. The boot moved, and a large hand probed for the source of the irritation. The hand touched Elspeth's and then firmly gripped her wrist. She was lifted out from under the table and held out for inspection.

'Mister, there's a wormie in yer shoe,' she said with an innocent certainty well beyond her five years. The company laughed. She smiled at each of the men in return. 'But I made it go awa.' The man who had brought her up from underneath the table lifted her onto his knee. She cuddled into him and closed her eyes, feigning sleep. The men grew silent like shepherds at a nativity. One of them moved to tickle her under the chin. Her eyes opened wide. Her protector dipped two fingers into his beer and put them to her mouth. She suckled on them and ignored her stepmother who placed a line of fresh tankards in front of the men. She grabbed Elspeth by the scruff of her neck, 'Get tae your bed.'

'Leave the quinie,' said Geordie. 'She's done nae herm.'

'Tak her, Geordie, I canna stand her ony mair.'

John stood watching with his arms folded. 'Since her ain mither died, we canna cope wi' her. She's wild. Feral. If she stays Jean'll maist likely kill her.'

'And that's God's honest truth,' said the new wife.

'Fit do ye ken about God's truth?' asked Elspeth. The company was taken aback. Elspeth had disentangled herself from Geordie's arms and stood facing her stepmother.

'My ain mither read the Bible and went to the kirk. No like ye. All ye wint tae dee is lie in bed wi faither, an mak daft wee noises.'

The resulting blow seemed to lift Elspeth from her feet, but she stood her ground, rubbing her face.

'At's no fair,' said Geordie.

'I've telt you, ye can tak her wi' ye fan ye leave. A present for yon barren wifey ye live wi'.'

The others looked at Geordie, waiting for his reaction.

He stared down at the table and drummed his fingers. 'For a few nichts perhaps, 'til things calm doon. Would ye like that, Elspeth Simpson, to come an bide with me an Effie for a while?' Elspeth flung her arms round Geordie's neck, and stared at the woman who had just given her away.

Effie wrung her hands with joy. Tolerated as a simpleton by her neighbours from whom she begged buttons, Effie smiled and smiled her way through the long dark days. She swept the hearth and the flags, she swept the yard, and had Geordie not restrained her, she would have taken a napkin and a pail to the cows' backsides.

'A bairn,' she said. 'A bairn.' She licked the edge of her apron and wiped it across Elspeth's face. 'Let me mak your bed.' She scuttled into a corner and emerged with a sack. 'Haud it, quine.' Elspeth stood while Effie stuffed straw into the sack before adding the spilt gleanings from the floor. She took the besom and swept the remaining dust into the hearth. 'My bairn,' she crooned, 'my bairn.'

'Just for a whiley,' said George, pleased but also a little concerned by the effect Elspeth was having on his profoundly volatile wife.

When Elspeth woke during the night, her cheeks still scorched from their proximity to the hearth, she knew that Effie was hovering close to her, emitting small whimpering sounds. She reached an arm out of the sack and touched Effie's face. 'Sleep noo,' she said. In that moment the child was older than the woman tending her.

In the morning, Geordie lifted Elspeth up onto the cart. 'Time to fetch the doggies,' he said pointing the horse in the direction of the distant sliver of sea and the smoke rising from the dwellings in Portsoy.

'Can I hiv a doggie?' asked Elspeth nestling against the large warm man. Geordie smiled.

Elspeth held her nose as the cart rattled and swayed down the brae towards the harbour. A gull swooped towards her and hovered squawking before George shooed it away. She had never been this close to the sea before and stared wide-eyed at the tangle of masts and the mountain of barrels.

After a brief negotiation with another man, Geordie manoeuvred the cart until it stood against a heap of dead fish. 'Dog fish,' he explained. Each fish was bigger than Elspeth. She touched the nearest and recoiled under the cold wet touch. 'Are they deils?' she asked. 'Is this where they wait afore they go to hell?' Geordie was taken aback by the question.

'Na quine,' he said. 'The fishermen canna sell them for food so we buy them and pit them on the land. A barrel of doggies maks the crops grow.'

The man to whom Geordie had spoken earlier stuck a pike into the nearest carcass and hoisted it into the air, then carried his dripping prize towards the cart.

Elspeth put her face inches from the fish and blew into its open jaw. 'Whit are you daeing?'

'I'll mak the fishie live again,' said Elspeth, now resting a hand on the spiny backbone while blowing even harder. 'Puir fishie.'

'You'll no mak these fishies live again,' said Geordie moving her away.

It was dusk when they arrived back at the farm. Geordie told Elspeth to go indoors while he unloaded the cart and dealt with the fish. She duly moved towards the door then paused and crept back to watch Geordie. As he lowered the side of the cart, the fish slid and slithered onto the floor of the byre. When he was up to his knees in the dead creatures, Geordie fetched a shovel, swung it above his head and brought it down hard on the fish, which, in response to the second or third blow, burst open, spilling guts and stink onto the hard earth. Backbones, jawbones, eyes and flesh mingled in a rank broth.

Elspeth howled. Geordie put down the shovel and moved to console her. 'I telt you to go inside,' he chided.

'Deith! Deith! Deith!' she shouted, pummelling her small fists into his thigh.

Effie doted on her new child and soon enveloped her in her own life of nervous ritual and superstition. She taught her to stir her broth clockwise and to put on her right shoe before the left. Elspeth soon understood that compliance was easier than rebellion and acquiesced whenever Elspeth rocked her in her arms and sang snatches of songs. She would let her new mother pick the husks from her hair and search for lice. She watched puzzled as Effie touched the Bible and then kissed the tips of her fingers every time she rose from her chair or entered the room.

One early morning, after climbing out of her sack, Elspeth hummed the tune of the lullaby her birth mother had taught her. 'Cease child, cease!' shouted Effie with her hands clamped over her ears.

'Why?'

'Auld Sandy will hear ye!'

Curious, Elspeth looked out of the window lest the devil was indeed marching towards the door to claim the family as his own.

'Wheesht! Wheesht! Never, never sing afore we have broken fast.' She rushed to touch the Holy Book.

Every night when the tallow was lit, Effie would place a small bowl of milk outside of the door. Each morning she would inspect it to see if the fairies had supped before passing by.

Geordie looked on the growing relationship between wife and this borrowed child with an air of anxious indulgence.

'Can I go to the kirk?' Elspeth wound herself round Geordie's leg and looked up at him with doe eyes. She placed a hand on his thigh. 'Please, please.'

'No quine,' he said. 'The kirk's no for bairns your age.' He patted her head and put on his coat. Elspeth left his side and slid into a corner so that she could sulk alone. Effie, sat next to the fire where small devils of flames still played, was deep into the Holy Book, pulling faces with the effort of following each word with her finger. At the end of the line, she returned to the beginning and attempted to read the words out loud hoping that, this time, they would make sense, and reveal their sacred mysteries.

'Close the door, child,' said Effie whose frustration at her inability to make any sense whatsoever of the Holy Book was compounded by the gale from the door that Geordie had left open. Elspeth rose and slipped into the yard. She caught sight of Geordie just beyond the byre. The cold bit into her as she followed him at a distance, melting into the hedges whenever he paused to adjust his coat, or on one occasion, to relieve himself. He took a short cut through the icy field. Elspeth followed before stumbling into a furrow as deep as a spade. Frozen to the marrow, and with a mouth full of mud, she stood up, brushed herself down and continued in Geordie's footsteps.

The kirk grew larger. Elspeth followed Geordie into the dark building that smelled of damp clothes and rancid soap. The water dripped from her as she squirreled into a dark corner to the side of the rear pews. Large men muttered briefly at each other before taking their places. The murmuring died, something was happening, someone was coming. Perhaps, perhaps it was the special man called the Living Christ of whom she had heard people speak. He must be a big man, bigger than her faither, he must be a kind man, as kind as Geordie. He must hate witches. He can make rabbits and fish come alive again.

Christ had a whining voice. High-pitched like Wee Jamie whose nose always dripped. If she strained upwards on tiptoe she could just see Christ's head. It was bobbing as he whined. But this Christ knew where her mother had gone. He knew.

'And there appeared a great wonder in heaven; a woman clothed with the sun, and the moon under her feet, and upon her head a crown of twelve stars… '

Elspeth moved her feet in case the moon was under them. She touched her hair and felt something, but wasn't certain it was a crown. What was a crown? She knew the proud cockerel had a crown. Red and proud. Soon she would grow one too.

'And there appeared another wonder in heaven; and behold a great red dragon, having seven heads and ten horns, and seven crowns upon his heads… '

The dragon was a beastie, and Geordie's coos had horns… She would be seven in two years. Effie aye counted to seven. God's number she said. Seven buttons, seven sticks in the hearth. Seven stirs of the broth. Seven was good.

' … and the dragon stood before the woman which was ready to be delivered, for to devour her child as soon as it was born… '

She understood now. It must have been a dragon that took Mrs Campsey's bairn. Her belly grew and then it must have burst but there was no bairn. The dragon must hae taken it. Dragons were bad and hungry beasties.

The whining Christ-man stopped. Elspeth clapped her hands together. The men all turned. Geordie came and took her out of the kirk. He was angry. He must have been enjoying the tale of the dragon.

Effie's behaviour grew increasingly erratic. She was plagued by witches. They stole her pins, curdled the milk, and put terrible thoughts into her head. Her remedies became increasingly desperate. None of her incantations worked. She heard the witches cackle as they dropped weevils into the flour. She was convinced that Geordie invited them into their bed whenever she fell asleep.

'Ye suckle their withered dugs and kiss their hurdies,' she stood defiant before her husband, hands on hips and spat in his face. Geordie wiped the spittle from his cheek and went to the byre.

Before long, Effie came to believe that Elspeth was a witch's familiar and eyed her warily. Despite Geordie's protests, she was made to eat on her own, and was not allowed to wash in the same room as her elders. Elspeth spent most of her waking hours in the surrounding countryside. She soon knew the names of all the fields. There was Toash Acre where the thistles grew, and Black Gutters where Geordie had buried the dead horse, and the Tarries where the Campsey boy had lifted her smock and touched her.

She crouched down by the tinker's fire and stared as the old man tugged the skin from the rabbit as though it were a dirty simmit. He tossed the pelt into the burn and watched as Elspeth waded in up to her knees in the cold water to retrieve it. She shook it out and placed it carefully under a bush.

'Fit are ye daein'?'

'The beastie will need its skin fan it's resurrected,' said Elspeth.

'Resurrected, eh? Yon's a big word, quine,' said the old man as he took the guts out of the small carcass and nudged the flesh onto the embers.

It was time for the lifting. The snow in the yard had been reduced to hand-sized clods clinging to the earth. In the fields beyond, the drifts still filled the ditches and lay in shrouds against the dykes. The crofters assembled in the lane, divided into convivial pairs, shared snuff and allocated the fields between them to seek out any stray cattle that might have survived the snow. Geordie went with Jamie Aitken, his nearest neighbour. Elspeth had pestered and begged to come along and find 'ony puir stooks'. Eventually, Geordie had relented, mainly because he did not want to leave her with Effie whose behaviour had become so unpredictable. If she had one of her turns, she was quite capable of striking the child and casting her out of the house. The previous night, catching sight of Elspeth by the hearth, Effie had recoiled from her, jabbering about cantrips and sorcery. Geordie had eventually persuaded his wife to lie on their bed from where she continued to point at Elspeth, gurgling incoherently as if the witch she beheld had stolen her tongue.

Elspeth walked behind the two men, singing to herself. After passing through the parishes of Ordiquhill and Fordyce they found a beast, thin and barely alive, shivering on the banks of the burn. It stared at the men with dull, mournful eyes, its troubled breath visible in the cold of the late afternoon. Jamie tugged it by the horns while Geordie slapped its haunches. The beast moaned and eventually snapped its rear legs into position while its front legs refused to cooperate. Panicking, it pulled itself forward, leaving a whirl of mud in its wake.

'The cratur's done for,' said Jamie reaching into his jacket for the knife that he would use to slice the animal's neck. Elspeth ran forward and put her tiny hands either side of the beast's head. It grew calm and stood on all four legs. The two men looked at each other. Geordie shrugged, knowing full well what suspicions were forming in Jamie's head. Rather than speaking of what they had seen, the two men picked up their staves and steered the beast back down towards the McTaggart croft. Elspeth followed, singing quietly.

When they stopped in the byway for a smoke, the men shared tales of Elspeth's gift with the cattle. Geordie eventually acquiesced to the suggestion that she take charge of the beasts that roamed the common land. He needed her out of the farm, away from Effie who repeatedly told her husband of her fears: the young girl had been sent by the devil to pluck her soul and offer it up to the moon; she visited the well and poisoned the water to make her sick; she had trained the rats to steal the bread and leave their dirt.

When night fell, Elspeth would move among her charges, running her hands over their flanks, pulling her nails through matted hair and speaking to each in turn. She bestowed on her favourites the angel names she had gleaned from the Christ-man in the grey kirk.

'Abaddon, Abaddon, my angel of the bottomless pit... One day you, Michael, the great prince who stands guard o'er the sons of your people, will arise... and you, Gabriel, one day you will bring me good news.'

She then lay among them and opened the cloth holding the cheese given to her by whichever farmer cultivated the land. When she slept, she was visited by dreams of the woman clothed with the sun with the moon under her feet and upon her head a crown of twelve stars.

With each dawn, she would stretch, rub her hands in the dew and wash her face.

If her charges were reluctant to move, she would ignore their moaning and, approaching each beast in turn, would mingle her own breath with its own until it raised its heavy head and lumbered on.

She became resigned to the teasing from the local boys who regularly followed her progress across the low hills and lay in wait for her. The pattern was well established. When the eldest gave the order, the others would emerge from the bracken waving sticks and hooting. Elspeth would run among the cattle trying in vain to calm them. The boys, for their part, would wrestle her to the ground and, when she was pinned to the earth by several pairs of knees, would daub and smear her face and hair with the hot dung. She never fought back, merely waiting until they had had their fun, before limping down to the burn and washing to the accompaniment of the ever-fainter laughter of her attackers as they ambled homewards through the twilight.

With each passing season, Elspeth grew visibly stronger; no longer was she such an easy target. But the boys would still approach her. On one occasion, the boldest walked right up to her, sucking on a piece of straw.

'Will you kiss me, Elspeth?'

'Of course,' she said. 'Fit why would I no kiss such a fine loon as yoursel'?' She wiped her hands on her smock and then held the boy's face in her hands as if he were a fallen beast. The boy was too shocked to move, and his pals were similarly affected as Elspeth gently blew on his face, then kissed him. His pals smirked with embarrassment and twisted their caps. After this the boys' sport changed completely. Less likely to hunt in a pack they would make solitary journeys into the hills to find the wild girl who always seemed pleased to see them and made them welcome. They would bring her gifts of sweet bread, and sometimes small trinkets stolen from the drunken tinker lying outside of the tavern. Jamie brought her a tiny dog that he had carved from a piece of driftwood. To his delight she made great play of placing the token between her breasts, and then gave him his kiss. When reunited with their peers, the bragging would start. Kisses became much more as the boys plumbed new imaginative depths.

Mother Nairn, a twisted figure and font of all gossip, listened as her simple son regaled her with half remembered details stolen from the braggarts. He became overexcited and, lost for words, resorted to using the forefinger of one hand and the closed fist of the other to mime the deed that his friends had gleefully described.

Mother Nairn gathered her skirts about her, grabbed her son by the lug and pulled him down the lane in the direction of Geordie's farm.

Startled by their arrival, Effie dropped the basin of hot water she was carrying from the hearth. Geordie came in from the byre, looked at the water draining between the flags, and listened as Mother Nairn invoked scripture to justify her accusations against Elspeth. He had heard similar from the men in the vicinity and was troubled.

Later that evening, he put his face in his hands, unable to bear the sight of Effie rocking backwards and forwards, keening as if she had been bereaved. He paced around the small room, glancing through the nwindow into the dusk in case this was one of the evenings when Elspeth would choose to leave her beasts and crawl into her straw-filled sack by the hearth. It was. When she entered, she seemed surprised to see Geordie who normally retired early.

'Ye've been lying wi' the boys in the fields, bringing shame into this house.' Effie's keening mutated into a low shriek. Elspeth moved her head to one side as she tried to make sense of what she was hearing.

'There was na harm in it,' she said. 'It was only kisses for the loons. Na harm.'

'Na harm? Ye'll end up a hoor, a scarlet woman... '

'A woman clothed with the sun,' whispered Elspeth.

'Nae blasphemy in my house!' Effie's shrieking reached a crescendo.

'To gie pleasure is a gift fae God. It's no a sin, it's a guid thing.'

Geordie struck her hard, then looked disbelievingly at his hand as if it had moved involuntarily. Despite the tears in her eyes, and increasingly familiar with the scriptures, Elspeth turned the other cheek towards him.

Geordie was reluctant to visit the inn at Fatmachen but there was no alternative. He would habitually nod at John Simpson if they passed on the road, but he had felt no need to visit after the brief transaction that saw Elspeth's father surrender all responsibility for her upbringing.

When he crossed the threshold the sweet smoke from a score of pipes hung in the air. The Simpson's dog growled at the stranger and then went back to extracting the marrow from a pair of sheep ribs. The locals, who knew Geordie, welcomed him and offered to buy him a dram. Elspeth's father was busy trying to ascertain whether one of the regulars was merely drunk or dead. He lifted the man's head then let it fall back to the table when he saw Geordie. 'Aye,' he said.

'Aye man,' replied Geordie. 'Can I hiv a word?'

John wiped his hands on his apron and moved Geordie towards a quieter corner.

'It's the bairn, we canna keep her ony mair.'

'I'm no surprised,' said John. 'I've heard the rumours mysel', and I've caught sight o' the lassie odd times. Aye wi the loons.'

'She's a guid girl,' said Geordie, 'but it's Effie, she's convinced the deil's living amang us.'

'Guid wi the coos I hear.'

'Will ye tak her back?'

Robert looked towards the back room where his wife was scrubbing a table.

'I canna,' he said. Neither man spoke as they searched for a way forward.

Chapter Three

LADY'S MAID
Banff, April 1752

Despite her surprise at seeing John, Annabel ushered him cordially into the parlour. He seemed far too big for the winged armchair, hunched forward, wringing his cap as if he had just retrieved it from a flooded ditch. What had her sister seen in this lumpen man that had driven her to forsake her family and become an alewife in a godforsaken corner of the parish?

Their business was soon concluded. Elspeth, apparently a strange and solitary child but a good worker, would enter into service at the Big House. She would skivvy in return for rudimentary tuition in reading, writing and the Bible.

Elspeth had never slept in a bed. On the few occasions when she forsook the company of the cattle and returned to the hearth, she would enjoy the familiar smell of the sack and the straw. Her fingers sought out the insects that shared her space. She never crushed them.

Here she felt smothered by the blankets. On her first night, she woke and shouted for her garment woven from the moon and the stars that had been wrestled from her by a gap-toothed demon. The other servants cried her to be still. Somewhere a dog barked.

Winnie, the housekeeper, hated her beyond reason. Why had she not been consulted over her appointment? She had mistrusted Elspeth on sight and was determined to break her. The first part of her scheme was to put her in charge of the stove and give her just enough instruction to ensure that her initial best efforts would be inadequate.

Elspeth was told to remove the ashes before they had properly cooled. Her arms were soon burned and scarred. When she yelped with pain, Winnie would threaten her with a beating. When the damper was insufficiently primed, and the kitchen filled with smoke, Elspeth was roundly abused. Her punishment was to spend hours on her knees rubbing the cast iron with black wax. Her arms and face turned black.

Her clothes were black. The sweat skidded from her brows and into her eyes, and her nails grew a black rind. The others would invent reasons to visit the kitchen, so they could gawk at the impish girl slowly turning into a blackamoor.

She was permitted to leave the kitchen to fetch water from the well in the yard. The handle was stiff, and it was only by standing on the very edge of the stone structure that Elspeth could make it turn at all.

Exhausted, she paused and stared into the dark well. There was suddenly a radiant light on the water. A shimmering, an incandescence. She gasped at her reflection. She was clothed with the sun as the Christman had said. She shielded her eyes from the sheer brightness of her cloak. Upon her head was a crown of stars. She started to count them. Eight, nine, twelve of them as the Christ-man had said, bright, oh so bright. Gleaming, glistening with His glory. And she felt a hundred feet tall. She could touch the heavens. And look at her garments. She was clothed with the sun. She felt faint and the blood in her head was thick and pounding at her temples.

The other servants sat round the large table and shared the bread distributed by Winnie according to the esteem in which she held them. A large piece went to Alex, the gardener. Calum, the young groom, received a smaller wedge of crust that he swallowed in one gulp.

'Where's Annie?' asked Winnie looking for the maid servant.

''Wi' the old man,' said Alex helping himself to more bread. Elspeth continued to mop the floor with long, languid strokes. She made the mistake of pausing in her labours to look up with her head cocked to one side.

'Get on with your work, lazy quine,' said Winnie. 'I'll skelp your erse if you just stand there gawping like a soul.'

'Shhh,' said Elspeth. 'There's a fire.'

This was too much for Winnie who rose from the table, rolling her sleeves up to her elbows.

Annie's scream froze them into a tableau. The banshee wails from somewhere on the upper floors grew louder. The kitchen door burst open and Annie stood howling. Alex was the first to react and pushed her aside as he climbed the stairs. Before he had reached the first landing, Elspeth had overtaken him and entered the parlour where flames were climbing the heavy curtains. The old man, stupefied in his chair, still held the candlestick that had started the conflagration. Alex stood there, uncertain what to do. Winnie too was mesmerised. Elspeth launched herself at the burning curtain and climbed hand over hand, a simian escaped from a travelling show, until the fabric tore from the brass rail and covered her in its fire. It was Winnie's turn to scream as Elspeth rolled, wrapped in flame, across the carpet. Alex stamped on the smaller flames that escaped from the tumbling mass of girl and curtain. Talons of smoke rose from the burnt material as Elspeth slowly emerged from its depths, a charred butterfly shaking off its chrysalis. The fire was out. She stood tugging at a few smouldering strands of her hair, staring impassively at her audience. Winnie and Alex took a step back. Calum moved to help her.

They were joined by Annabel, pulling her shawl across her chest to cover her semi-nakedness.

'What... ?' She took in the situation. Her drooling father, lost in his cups, had fallen asleep holding the candle and this tiny blackened girl from the kitchen had saved him. Had saved them all.

'You,' she said to Winnie. 'Bring the bath to my room.'

As Winnie poured pitcher after pitcher into the bath and tested the heat with her elbow, Annabel gently undressed Elspeth. 'Put your arms up, child.' She pulled Elspeth's smock over her head and looked at her thin body. Elspeth let herself be lowered into the bath. For a while they both breathed in the steam. Winnie was dismissed. Annabel fetched a cloth from her table and told Elspeth to close her eyes as she wiped the smudges from her face. 'There, child, there.' She poured a small vial of unction made from orange flowers and jasmine. Elspeth breathed in the heady scent.

'Thank you, mistress.'

Annabel embraced the challenge of converting Elspeth from scullery drudge to lady's maid. She had a mission, a soul to save, a mind to shape. Elspeth provided her with a welcome distraction from ministering to her increasingly truculent and querulous father now permanently wedged in his chair. Soon after her arrival, whenever the Auld Man banged his stick on the floor and shouted like a wounded animal, it was Elspeth he wanted to attend him. He seemed to have forgotten that his daughter even existed. When Elspeth entered the room, he would whine and stretch out his liver-spotted hands towards her as if beseeching her for a benediction. She ignored him and threw open the shutters and thrust the window upwards. He breathed in the cold air and gasped. She tucked the blanket into his armpits.

'Are you wanting your milk, master?'

'Aye, lass, aye.'

She held the cup to his lips as he slurped and slavered its contents down his jerkin. She cleaned his mouth with a slow wipe of his napkin. His eyes lit up with the effort of trying to communicate something long forgotten. There was a recognition, an intensity. He extricated his hand from the blanket and placed it on hers until he was claimed by sleep.

One evening, she noticed the book that had fallen to the floor, resting on its splayed pages. She picked it up. The illustrations were so vivid she touched one and looked to see if the bright red ink had stained her fingers. She gasped. The lion had three elongated, scaly necks, each with a head at the end. One belonged to a dragon with the darting salacious tongue of a salamander; the second was that of a young man, his mouth open and fear in his eyes. The third belonged to a hyena, sniffing the ground for blood. The lion sat on its haunches, supporting its weight on two spindly, old women's legs, ankle deep in slime. Its tail flailed the red air, relentlessly. Elspeth squeezed her eyes tight, then tighter still until the beast became less distinct. She could now only see it in silhouette, until that too faded but she could still hear the cry of the angry creature as it merged into nothingness. She placed the book back on the floor.

Annabel treated Elspeth like a younger friend she had not seen in ages. She eagerly showed her how to clean the combs. She showed her how to remove soap scum and fingerprints from the basin and jug.

She passed on gossip about her neighbours. She playfully corrected Elspeth's speech. She taught her to read and write and speak in English.

Elspeth stared at the spelling book and traced her finger down the curved spine of the creature with forked tongue. 'Adder,' said Annabel.

'Adder,' said Elspeth. 'Like the deil.'

'Yes, like the devil.' Annabel paused for a moment then turned the next page.

Elspeth's finger stroked the heavily inked feathers of the bird sitting in its cage formed by the upper half of the letter B. 'Bird,' she said.

'Good girl.'

'Mistress, why do birds die? Why can they no live in the sky for ever? Why does God make them fall to earth?'

'Time to lay out my clothes,' said Annabel closing the book.

After her promotion, Winnie's resentment of Elspeth intensified. She had a ready ally in Annie. A favourite trick was for both women to climb the stairs side by side as Elspeth descended each morning from Annabel's room, carrying the mistress's chamber pot. They would nudge her, apologise profusely and watch gleefully as the contents of the vessel slopped onto the stair.

Once Alex had filled the bucket with coals ready to be carried to the mistress's room, Annie would distract him. On one occasion she had found a strange beetle in the scullery and wanted Alex's opinion. While the two of them were fully occupied prodding the insect with a needle, Winnie poured water over the coals. As a predictable consequence, Elspeth struggled to make the fire catch, but Annabel, eager to help, kneeled on the hearth with her and, like children, they turned the act of lighting the fire into a game that made them both giggle.

Despite these irritations, Elspeth was happy enough in her new occupation, but she missed the animals, and when her mistress was dozing, and her immediate chores were completed, she would tie her shawl around her shoulders and cross the yard to the stables where Calum would be tending the horses. Immensely shy, the young groom would blush to his roots whenever Elspeth opened the stable door. He would nod at her as she went up to the tallest beast and placed her head against its warm flank. Her hands would move up towards its neck and she would emit the soothing noise that had served her well in the past with the cattle. It was an unearthly sound, part crooning part chant. In response, the horse would turn its head towards her and nudge her hair.

Calum was soon besotted with the wild girl who seemed to be turning into a woman before his eyes. Whenever she crossed the yard, she could tell that he watched her every step of the way. For amusement, she would suddenly stop and turn, in time to catch his pale moon face disappearing back into the shadows.

He took to leaving her gifts. Although not permitted to enter any room other than the kitchen, he would sneak up both flights of stairs and leave his love tokens outside of her door: a rabbit pelt, a small collection of seashells gathered from the foreshore. Once he left a complete nest containing a tiny injured bird. He knew that she would soon make it fly again.

These gifts were never acknowledged. His shyness precluded any such intimacy between them. Whenever she entered the barn, he would move one of the horses to the front of the stall and retreat, watching.

Eventually there came a day when he moved slowly out of the shadows and stood next to the horse as if he too was a mute animal waiting for attention. His head rested on the beast's shoulder, but his eyes were closed; he couldn't look at her. Her hands moved seamlessly from the horse's warm flank to his neck, which she massaged with the same kneading movements. Calum shuddered as if about to cry.

'How old are you, Calum?' she asked.

'Seventeen,' he whispered.

'Do you get lonely, Calum?'

'Aye Miss. Some days.' Astonished to realise that he had managed to speak, the words tumbled out. 'They say, Miss, you are a witch, a bad person but I canna believe that. You are kind wi' the horses. You never complain. You aye let Winnie treat you like dirt.'

'Do you think I'm a witch? I could always turn you into a puddock.'

'Na thanks, Miss. The horses might trample me.' Sensing that he had overstepped the mark by making a pleasantry, he blushed and turned to leave but Elspeth kept her warm hand on his neck.

'Perhaps I am a witch, Calum. I see things that are denied to other folk.'

'Ma mither was the same. She was aye seeing things. She saw the deil once; a big hairy critter wi' flames coming oot its erse. She chased it round the yard with the besom.'

'I see other things, Calum, good things. Sometimes I see this woman clothed with the sun, and the moon under her feet, and upon her head a crown of thorns.'

Calum's mouth dropped open. 'I would like to see her too. Perhaps she's a queen who will mak the world a better place. I could gi' her a horse.'

'You could, Calum, you could.'

In the dark days of winter, the howl of the wind mutated into a triumphant roar as it found the embers in the grate and blew them out of the hearth. The candles guttered and fainted, leaving tiny wraiths of smoke to drift upwards like souls ascending. From the upper windows, Elspeth stared at the distant line of sea as it heaved its bloated waves over the harbour wall.

Down below, Winnie sat huddled close to the kitchen fire, guarding her territory and barking orders at the others. When she heard Elspeth approaching to warm her chilblained hands, Winne snatched the poker from the fire and held it before her like a sword, sorely tempted to court dismissal by branding her enemy; a sharp disfiguring touch to the cheek would do. She could always claim it was a terrible accident. Annie would back her up. Elspeth stood her ground, stared at her adversary and emitted a low keening noise. After several long seconds, Winnie dropped the poker and turned away.

In any case, Elspeth had work to do, having noticed the casements rattling on the upper two stories of the house. Ignoring Winnie, she removed several crumpled pages of the *Caledonian Mercury* from the kindling bin. She rolled them into tight twists as she climbed the stairs. The Auld Man woke and muttered some semi-lucid endearments as she entered his room. 'Shhh, be at peace. I'll keep death out,' she said, forcing the rolled-up paper into the gaps beneath the windows. 'There, he'll no come for you now.'

But he did. Annabel found her father dead the following morning.

Winnie was annoyed with herself: she could have prevented it. The signs were there.

'I saw the lichts dancing in the sky,' she told Annie while scrubbing the table. 'And I heard the chap at the door. Deith came knocking, and somebody let him in.' She cast her eyes in the direction of Elspeth, then turned her attention to a wine stain on the oak.

As Annabel had taken to her bed, the arrangements were largely left to Alex. Embracing the responsibility, he gave orders for all the clocks to be stopped and the mirrors covered.

'Now mind,' he said to the company in the kitchen. 'If you want to gie the slip to ill-fortune you maun touch the corpse.' He removed his thumbs from his waistcoat. Calum said he was too feart, Annie said she would if Alex went with her, and Winnie said she had already touched the old man's forehead that morning. 'And,' she paused for effect, 'I placed a saucer of salt on his belly to stop the swelling.' The others looked at her with a new respect.

Elspeth visited the Auld Man when the others were busy. She moved the straggle of hair from his brow and kissed him on the cheek. 'Soon you will rise,' she said. 'Soon you will ascend with the band of the righteous and see Him seated in his glory. I will come for you when the time is right. Now sleep.' She kissed him again and left.

Most of the town turned out to pay their respects. Annabel met them at the door and graciously accepted their condolences.

Alex had taken it on himself to shave and dress the corpse. He propped the Auld Man up against the bedhead and placed a copy of the Bible in his lap.

After accepting a toddy and a twist of tobacco, the townsfolk took their turn to enter the room, compliment the Auld Man on his appearance, and bow before ducking out of the doorway again. As they left, Annie gave each of them a piece of dredgy bread and a cake for the journey home.

The last visitor was James Sneddon, a local landowner, recently returned from making his fortune in the tea plantations. It was rumoured that he once beat a servant to death for stealing a silver snuff box. And Annie swore that she had seen, with her own eyes, James Sneddon break his cane over the shoulders of a beggar who had approached him in the street.

He kissed Annabel's hand, and she ushered him into the parlour, closing the door behind her.

Annie fed logs to the several hearths until the heat in the house became unbearable. Stifled, Elspeth escaped into the yard and unbuttoned her blouse to let the air cool her neck. As she walked towards the barn she saw Calum moving in the shadows. And then he was gone.

'Calum, come and talk to me,' she said entering the barn. 'Come and blether.'

Eventually he emerged from behind the hay and stood before her, cap in hand.

'Why are you shaking, Calum?' She moved towards him and held him in her arms. 'Poor manie, do you have the ague? Are you unwell?' She ran her hand across his brow.

'No Miss, I jist... I jist... '

'Tell me.'

'I canna stand folks dying. It happens to us all, I ken that. I've seen horses die and all, Miss.'

'You must be a master of life, Calum, no its servant.' The grey mare in the nearest stall pawed the ground. Calum glanced in the horse's direction.'

'Calum, let me hold you a while.'

As he sobbed onto her shoulder, she told him, 'All shall be well. I will make them so. There will be no more death.' She felt him shudder like a baby who can cry no more. 'All shall be well.' As he relaxed against her, she sought out the lower buttons on his jerkin, undid them, and slid her hand down his breeches.

'Shh, Calum, shh. Be calm. This is life. Forget death. This is the joy that God intended, and I am His servant.'

When rumours of Calum's growing obsession with Elspeth reached Annabel's ears, she summoned Alex.

'The loon's bewitched, milady,' said the gardener. 'She has cast her cantrips on the poor soul. He lives in torment.'

'Then I will save her!' declared Annabel, more concerned for Elspeth than for the groom. The gardener looked disappointed. He had hoped that his words, coupled with rumours spread by Winnie, might secure the dismissal of the changeling who had come to disrupt the household.

But Annabel had a cause.

"Wives, submit yourselves to your own husbands as you do to the Lord,' Ephesians 5:22-23. Oh Elspeth, are those not the finest words in the Bible? What joy to submit, to surrender your life to another. To be guided along the paths of righteousness through subjugation to a better soul.' She paused.

'Do you think so, Miss?'

'Yes, yes,' said Annabel clutching the Bible to her chest while executing a small dance around the parlour.

'I think there are better words, Miss.'

'And what might they be?"

"And to the woman were given two wings of a great eagle, that she might fly into the wilderness, into her place, where she is nourished.' I would love the wings of an eagle, Miss. I think people need to be free, and not surrender to another.'

Annabel looked at her pupil. The lesson was not going well. She had hoped to steer the discussion from the joys and duties of marriage to Elspeth's behaviour with Calum, but the chance had gone.

'Time to make the fire.'

The reasons for Annabel's obsession with the obligations of the married state became increasingly obvious to the household as James Sneddon's visits became ever more frequent.

When he first suggested that Annabel accompany him in his carriage, she insisted that Elspeth come with them. Sneddon reluctantly agreed.

They travelled out along the bridle path to the sea. He helped Annabel down onto the foreshore and kept his arm around her shoulders as they walked on the firm sand just above the rind of seaweed. Elspeth walked behind, keeping her distance, but Sneddon would pause every so often as if to catch her out, and wave her further back to prevent her eavesdropping. Elspeth had no such intention. She was picking her way carefully to avoid standing on any of the small crabs that had been washed ashore. She then looked out at the cold sea and recited to herself, 'And the sea gave up the dead who were in it, Death and Hades gave up the dead who were in it, and they were judged, each one of them, according to what they had done.'

In that moment, she saw the corpses rising slowly from the waves, pillars of cold flesh, eyes closed with their arms at their sides, hair plastered against their heads, the water dripping from them. She ran into the water's edge, arms outspread to welcome them and help them ashore. Sensing that something was amiss, Sneddon turned around. 'Stupid girl!' he shouted, waving his stick at her. He ran to her and, ignoring the water lapping at his ankles, grabbed her and shook her violently.

'She belongs in the asylum,' he said. 'Deranged creature.' He shook her again. 'I'll talk to the superintendent.'

Annabel was more emollient. 'Poor thing,' she said. 'You must have been distracted. Look, your shoes are wet.' She placed her arm around Elspeth's shoulders. Sneddon stormed back towards the carriage. None of them spoke on the return journey to the house.

And so, a pattern was set. Whenever Sneddon visited, Elspeth kept out of his way and retired to the kitchen where she was equally unwelcome. If Annie had been a cat, she would have arched her back and hissed every time Elspeth came thought the door. Instead, she curtseyed ironically and ushered her into the room with an obsequious bowing movement. 'Welcome, Milady. Would Milady like a morsel to eat? The pickings fae my feet perhaps. Has Milady been having visions again? Will I inform Master Calum that you desire his presence?'

'You are too lax with the girl.' To emphasise his point, Sneddon tapped his cane into the open palm of his hand. 'Things are different in the Indies. Trust me.'

Elspeth would listen at the parlour door to Annabel's muted whispers interspersed with Sneddon's deeper growl. Once she was caught eavesdropping. Sneddon pinned her against the wall, put his face next to hers, and unseen by Annabel, fondled her breasts and told her how errant women were treated on the plantations. He was expecting her to resist but she stayed still and purposefully breathed into his open mouth. He relinquished his grip and returned disconcerted to Annabel, slamming the door behind him. Elspeth broke away and fled downstairs.

She was not unhappy in the Big House. She was a diligent servant. She avidly devoured her scripture lessons while not hesitating to disagree with Annabel's interpretations. She enjoyed Calum's company and, as they lay in the hay together in the shadow of the horses, she would hold him spellbound with tales of dragons splitting the heavens with the fiery wings of God's love. Whenever threatened by Sneddon, or tormented by Annie, she would retreat further into the inner world that sustained her. She knew she was different. She knew she had a purpose, a mission that God would reveal in His own good time.

Predictably, she was banished from the wedding. The other servants were permitted to follow the procession but only after the fiddler leading the party to the kirk reached the brow of the hill. Elspeth was watching from the open kitchen door when Alex beckoned her to join him. She lifted her skirts and crossed the yard to the byre where the gardener was struggling to persuade the pigs to fulfil their traditional duties by following the wedding party. 'Else the union will be barren,' Annie had explained.

'Skelp their erses,' instructed Alex slapping the backside of the nearest sow. Elspeth opened the midden gate and watched as the swine waddled and snuffled their way up the path as custom dictated.

Even before the wedding meats were cold, there were rumours that the house would soon be boarded up and the servants dismissed. Word had reached Sneddon that there had been a small mutiny among the slaves at Port Weymouth. Although the ringleaders had been executed and their families put in irons, there were fears that the unrest would spread. Sneddon and Annabel would sail from Greenock at the month's end.

Winnie wept, and Annie wrung her hands. Alex was instructed to dispose of the livestock and then stay in the shuttered house as caretaker. Calum was simply lost. He had no prospects beyond a life of vagrancy, and his beloved horses would soon be sold. Elspeth tried to console him, but he was beyond help. 'What will you do, Miss?' She stroked his hair while crooning the sound she had used to calm the cattle in her earlier life.

'My life is not my own,' she explained. 'I must bend to His will.'

Sneddon was the unlikely messenger of God's will. He grabbed Elspeth's arm tightly as she knelt lifting the still warm embers into a bucket. He raised her up until he could stare into her face. 'Good news, Missie, you will be coming with us. Strong white girls are in short supply where we are going. I will tame you.' Elspeth rubbed her forearm where the imprint of Sneddon's fingers showed no sign of fading.

'Whatever you wish, Master.'

As the carriage jolted its way down the path, Elspeth twisted her head to take one last look at the Big House. For a fleeting moment, she made eye contact with Winnie, her nemesis, who was at an upstairs window flailing her arms as if attempting to capture an escaped bird.

In the barn, Calum hand-fed each of the horses until his palm was wet with slaver. He took a coiled rope from its hook on the wall, fashioned a slip knot in one end and, at the second attempt, succeeded in tossing the rope over a large ceiling beam. He shook the bridle tools out of a small wooden box which he placed upside down on the ground. He tied the loose end of the rope around his neck, and then kicked away the box on which he was balanced

Chapter Four

THE BROTHERS
Greenock

Sneddon's mood deteriorated once they arrived in Greenock. He left Elspeth and Annabel to settle into their lodgings while he went to the customs house to investigate rumours that The Majesty had lost a mast in a tropical storm and would be delayed for at least a month. The rumours were true, and he vented his anger on the two women. 'Stuck in this Godforsaken town of drunkards when there is work to be done.' He punched the door frame then nursed his knuckles and his wrath. 'And you,' he said pointing to Elspeth. 'Clean this sty and then get out of my sight.'

Elspeth placated her hysterical mistress, unpacked her shawl and walked into the street. She had never seen so many people in the same place. She had read of great cities in the Bible and recited their names as she marvelled at the New Kirk spire emerging from the forest of wooden scaffolding. 'Tyre, Sidon, Byblos, Nineveh, Babylon.' Had she been one of the visiting angels, she could have saved Sodom and Gomorrah. There would have been no need of purgative fires. She alone could have assuaged the rage of God and set the people free to love and be kind.

She followed the rank stream of water running down the Wynd and ducked beneath the washing strung between the gables. A beggar grabbed at her elbow. He stared at her, crossed himself and slunk into a close.

At the foot of Cove Road, a long line of people stood patiently, each holding a bundle of possessions. The many children in their midst ran in and out of the adults as if they had been placed there for their amusement. A small boy cannoned into her. 'Sorry, Miss,' he said.

'What are you waiting for?'

'A ship to Canada... and *a new life*.' This last phrase, borrowed from his parents and repeated without meaning.

'Australia,' said his friend. ' ... and *anewlife.*'

At the quayside she stood back as two men, stripped to the waist, struggled to lift a hogshead between them. The shorter of the two stumbled and the barrel fell onto the cobbles. Its bung was expelled as if from a cannon and the thick black molasses spread across the road. Cursing, the larger man stepped into the cloying liquid to retrieve the bung, slipped and skidded face down into the sugar. When he managed to stop laughing, his friend fetched rags and attempted to wipe down his spluttering workmate. Without thinking, Elspeth joined them and took a rag to the man's matted chest. Surprised, he stood still and let Elspeth tend to him.

'That's fine, lass,' he said.

Soon afterwards the three of them linked arms and went into Lechie's tavern. The men introduced themselves as James and Mathew.

'Christ's disciples,' said Elspeth.

'I dinnae think so,' said James still smelling sweetly of molasses. Elspeth realised they were more boys than men but was happy to let them tease and flirt with her. They were brothers from Glasgow who had left home when their mother died. They had worked in the rope manufactory until dismissed for drunkenness, but both knew that soon, they too would join the long queue in search of new lands.

'Meantimes,' said Elspeth kissing first James, then Mathew, 'let us enjoy God's gift of life.'

As the gin flowed, James became maudlin, declared his undying love for Elspeth, and fell asleep on her shoulder. Mathew sang songs until he failed to remember any more words and hummed tunelessly.

As the night wore on, the tavern filled, and the smoke scorched Elspeth's eyes. Two men with large dogs entered. The crowd parted respectfully to let them pass, then the company rose to follow them into the back yard. James roused his sleeping brother and the three of them joined the throng. Several lanterns were hung over a pit into which the dogs were pushed. Because of her height Elspeth could easily see over the crush of men jostling for position. She elbowed herself to the front in time to witness the larger mastiff clamping its jaws round the throat of the slightly smaller animal. An arc of blood splattered into the crowd. The dogs swirled in the dust. In a snap of bone, they changed positions and rolled in a copulation of saliva and viciousness. By throwing herself along the rim of the pit, and then hoisting both legs onto the ledge, Elspeth managed to drop into the midst of the demented creatures. The male audience, arms outstretched like supplicants, apoplectic with fury and delight, bayed for the blood of this unknown woman. She stood stock-still and spoke calmly to the crowd, but her words were swallowed in the mayhem. The dogs crashed into her legs and made her stumble. John and Mathew, having fought their way to the front, hauled her back over the barrier. Her clothes were torn, and she struggled for breath as her saviours bundled her into the street.

'Well, Missis,' said Mathew. 'I think you had best come wi' us.'

'I wanted to stop the deaths.' The boys looked at her quizzically, and then at each other.

The brothers' lodgings, the attic space of a sugar store, were strewn with bedding. An old woman sat upright in a sea of rags and gestured. Two small children emerged from the same heap.

James and Mathew had commandeered the far corner under the skylight. Elspeth sat between them on the nest of sacks, taking comfort from their warmth.

'Are you sailing soon?' asked Mathew, lighting a candle.

'The ship's delayed but I'll no be going. I've got God's work to do.'

'And what work might that be?' asked James rubbing the back of his hand against her cheek.

'There's aye folks to be saved. They have to be made ready.'

'What for?'

'The second coming, what else?' She lay perfectly still between the two boys. 'Look,' she said pointing at a hole in the ceiling that framed the crescent moon. As they stared upwards, she placed a hand on each of them. Neither James nor Mathew dared breathe lest she removed her hands. They both wriggled slightly and groaned. 'Be still,' she said. 'Look at the moon.'

Mathew was the gentler lover, unhurried and solicitous of her own pleasure. James was more urgent, intense. She enjoyed them equally.

The three of them lived together in a state of companionable and sensual drunkenness for several weeks. When the boys left to find work for the day, Elspeth too would rise and wander the streets, careful not to venture too close to where Annabel and her new husband were still waiting for the arrival of their ship. Sneddon was disappointed at the minx's sudden disappearance. As the novelty of Annabel's flesh had waned, Elspeth's allure had grown. He felt cheated of the chance to teach her a real lesson.

Elspeth befriended the fish sellers on the quay; she helped the rag women sort their wares; the sailors soon trusted her to sell the silks and damask they had smuggled home, and, being blessed with a good strong voice, she made pennies by singing psalms on the street outside of the Old West Kirk.

She felt safe with her boys and brought them bread and grog. James enjoyed teasing her and would ask in a solemn voice if her God would return that night in clouds of glory.

'And smite the wicked?' echoed Mathew.

'Mock the Lord and He will aye be avenged,' she said, throwing herself onto the younger boy and forcing him onto the ground. As he relaxed beneath her weight, she kissed him hard and then bit his lip.

'Jesus!' he said, holding his mouth.

Although she shared her favours among the brothers equally, lying with each in turn, jealousy became their new companion. The boys competed for Elspeth's attention. Mathew would sing to her as she had once commented on the beauty of his voice. He had a small repertoire of hymns and shanties which he crooned close to her ear. James was always solicitous of her comfort, straightening the bedding and producing small morsels of cheese wrapped in muslin from his waistcoat pocket.

When bored, the brothers' innocent jostling mutated into full-blown wrestling. Locked together like fairground bears, they would roll across the floor, each trying to land a punch on the other. Elspeth's patience became increasingly strained.

'Boys, God's love is not possessive and nor is mine.' She interposed her body between the pair of them and intercepted a blow for her pains. Rubbing her cheek, she admonished them. 'Save your strength for the Translation. The angels will not lift His servants who fight and squabble. My body and soul belong to all who truly love Him.'

The brothers would not be assuaged. They went their separate ways during the day and kept a sullen distance from each other when they were both in the attic.

One evening, they returned to find that Elspeth had gone, taking her few possessions with her. Before leaving she had given grog and a few pennies to the old woman in the corner.

'Where is she?' demanded James, striding towards the only witness to Elspeth's departure. He knocked the cup from her hand.

'Gone to the Lord,' said the crone, laughing hysterically.

'You've driven her away!' Mathew confronted his brother, their faces inches apart.

'It was you. Ye couldnae believe it wis me she truly loved.'

'Na, it was me!'

Elspeth slept that night in a barn on the outskirts of the town. She knew her destiny was waiting elsewhere for her. This was neither the place nor the time. She was troubled, and sleep wouldn't come. As she tossed and turned, she recited aloud the words from Genesis.

'Then the Lord said to Cain, 'Why are you furious? And why are you downcast? If you do right, won't you be accepted? But if you do not do right, sin is crouching at the door. Its desire is for you, but you must master it.'

Cain said to his brother Abel, 'Let's go out into the field.'

And while they were in the field, Cain attacked his brother Abel and killed him.'

Chapter Five

THE POTTER
Langbank & Glasgow

Elspeth had left Greenock, not daring to test her premonition about the brothers. A carter had stopped for her on the road near Port Glasgow. He was a kindly man and knew not to enquire about her reasons for travel. It was no business of his. She lay back on the straw and convinced herself that with every jolt, she was shaking the devils from her body. Sometimes the potholes were so big that the breath shot from her; a torrent of small Satans, a breathy funnel of homunculi. The journey was purging her. She lay back and watched the clouds weaving shapes, spelling messages she couldn't quite fathom.

At Langbank, she thanked the carter, climbed down and stretched. She had seen the buildings from the road and knew that this was her intended destination. A blanket of ivy had partly detached itself from the walls and hung down, barely able to support its own weight. She was surprised by the loudness of the birdsong emanating from the copse that swallowed the path. Each branch held a small bird. 'And one will arise at the sound of the bird, and all the daughters of song will sing softly…' She turned back and watched a thread of smoke ambling upwards from the chimney of a conical outhouse. She walked towards its source.

As she stood in the doorway, the heat from the kiln made her cover her face. Robert had his back to her as he pushed a tray of grey pots onto a shelf. Aware of her presence, he turned around and appraised her. 'Sister,' he said, bowing slightly. Clay dust clung to his beard, a mummer's mask that accentuated his clear eyes. 'Can you make pots?'

'I have no the skill, master.' He looked at her for a moment. 'Then follow me.' He indicated the wheel in the far corner of the room. 'Sit there.' Bemused, but without hesitation, she sat astride the seat. He moved her forward until her knees almost touched the wheel and sat behind her. He slapped a lump of clay onto the centre of the wheel, doused it with water and raised it into a stumpy tower. She felt the warmth from his body, and his breath tickling her neck. He told her to hold the clay firmly while he worked the treadle. At his bidding, she pushed both thumbs into the clay which soon squirmed away from her and landed in her lap. He gently picked up the wet pieces and dropped them into a bowl adjacent to the wheel. 'That pot will no grace any table the day,' he said. He then repeated the process, this time placing his hands on hers and guiding them as if they were his own. She watched as a grey but undeniably shapely object grew from the wheel. 'Your first pot, you must make your mark on it.' He handed her a thin stick and watched as she carefully etched ES into the wet clay.

'Well, Mistress ES, will you take bread with me?' She nodded and followed him into the adjacent building that consisted of a single room with bed, chair and table.

'Do you bide in these parts? Your face is no familiar.'

'My journey has been long,' she said. 'There have been trials, but my destination is unclear.'

He seemed satisfied with her answer and prepared a simple meal for them both.

'Are you wed?'

'No.'

Robert chewed his bread.

They lay together that night.

Elspeth became Robert's shadow, watching from the doorway as he raised pots from the wheel. She sang softly under her breath. Robert picked up the tune and hummed along with her. 'I feel I am being watched by my angel,' he said.

Intrigued by this idea, he fashioned several small angels from clay and fired them without her knowing, then placed them around the room where the pair of them ate or hid them in the bed where they slept. Elspeth cried with delight when she saw another angel hiding on the hearth or sitting in a recess on the lintel.

'You see,' she said. 'Heaven is jealous of our happiness; the angels have rebelled and have chosen to live with us.'

'I don't know where they all come from,' muttered Robert, feigning annoyance at the growing host of small winged creatures.

Elspeth loved Robert. The young potter swept her obsessions aside and laughed at her delusions. Her visions were in abeyance, replaced by the joy of immersing her life in another's. The ecstasy she felt was akin to the abandon she had felt for Christ. But her new Christ was real, she breathed the same air, and they broke bread together.

She became adept at digging the soft clay from the pit in the orchard. On one occasion the cart overturned and spilt its contents. Hearing her shout, Robert left his wheel. Kneeling, he lifted the heavy clay back onto the wooden boards. Following his example, Elspeth too pushed her hands into the thick, cloying mixture. Their fingers touched, and Robert held her heavy, grey hand, and slowly lifted it up. Two hands then, swollen with clay, turning on each other, their fingers intertwined in a dumb show of strange birds trying to take wing but always held back by the other. Eventually, Robert's hand broke free and he wiped it across Elspeth's face. She shrieked and ran into the orchard.

Robert taught her to feed the clay into the pug mill, pack the tamper and turn the wooden screw until the mixture was extruded, ready to be cut and stored. He spoke to her of glazes and shared with her the secrets of cobalt and flint. He taught her to throw handfuls of salt into the kiln during firing and watched as she clapped her hands at the aura of sparks crackling towards her.

Elspeth's main task was to haggle with the tinkers who came to purchase the pots. She gave them beer, fed grain to their horses, and flattered them until they willingly left with more goods than they had intended.

As the first leaves were dropping from the trees, a stranger appeared at their door. Robert assumed from the man's bearing and dress that he was an officer of the law. Elspeth, fearing that he had been sent by Sneddon to reclaim her, stayed in the back room.

'What is your business, Sir?' asked Robert.

'Robert Buchan?'

'The same.'

'I bring you a proposal which I think will be to the liking of yourself and your good lady,' he tipped his hat in Elspeth's direction. 'I represent the Delftfield pottery in the Broomielaw in Glasgow. Mr Martin, the owner, intends offering employment and significant remuneration to this country's finest craftsmen if they will join him in his endeavour.'

Three weeks later, Elspeth helped Robert load his goods and chattels onto the Glasgow-bound cart. His new employer had agreed to pay for the removal. His agent had asked if the pair were married as this would have implications for whatever lodgings could be found.

'Man and wife,' said Robert without hesitation. Elspeth smiled.

They secured modest lodgings in the Broomielaw close to the factory, and Elspeth was soon taken into the service of Mrs Martin, the owner's wife.

Robert regaled Elspeth with his new enthusiasms. He had quickly befriended the ten or so potters who had been recruited to this new enterprise. 'They are guid folk. They work hard.' He had seen the partners when they undertook a tour of the factory under the guidance of William Martin. He had heard them discussing the possibility that soon Delftfield would produce a porcelain equal to that of the Dutch and French.

'It can be done, Elspeth, it can be done. They have had great success with the tin glaze. It's only a matter of time, and who can glean the future, my dearest? Perhaps I, Robert Buchan, will be the alchemist.' He rubbed his hands in gleeful anticipation of this future world when his star would rise. Elspeth looked as enthusiastic as the queasiness in her stomach would permit.

Each evening they would take a stroll along the Clyde. Robert would point out the gravelly shoals that broke the surface and talk about how the river would soon be dredged so that the biggest ships in the world could sail within yards of the factory. 'And then return to the four corners of the earth, loaded to the gunnels with porcelain. The porcelain that I discovered.'

As she cleaned and scurried through the Martin household, Elspeth reflected on the changes that had given her a husband, in all but name, whom she loved unreservedly; a city that continually surprised her with its noise, excitement and novelty; and social standing. Her demons had left her and she luxuriated in the space they had vacated; space in which she could dream and plan. Words from scripture still rose unbidden to her lips but they no longer held her captive.

Robert revelled in his work. He was well thought of and was encouraged to experiment with pigments and variant glazes in pursuit of his holy grail. He was always the one chosen to explain the processes and materials to visiting dignitaries.

'A young engineer, a Mr Watt, visited today,' he told Elspeth who was tugging at the skin of a rabbit freshly bought from the market. She had a flash of memory in which she was breathing into the pinched mouth of a dead rabbit, but the cameo faded, and she pictured instead Robert impressing the visitor with his talk of ochres, vermillion, and oriental blue.

'He bides in Cornwall in England where they have many clay mines. This man, Watt, is concerned with the transportation o' the pug on rails made o' steel. Can you imagine?'

Elspeth shook her head and dropped the rabbit's entrails into a bucket.

Mrs Martin paused as she passed Elspeth on the stair and looked at her servant's belly. 'Are you with child? You're but a bairn yoursel.'

Elspeth put a hand on her stomach. The thought had not occurred to her. She had attributed her cramps to the rich food they could now afford.

When she left her service, Mrs Martin gifted her a shawl and two small blankets. 'Come back,' she said, 'when the wean's grown.'

Robert showed her the tiny cups he had fired when the supervisor left for the day. 'See how thin they are. With a strong light, you can almost see though the clay.' He held one of the small vessels close to the candle and turned it in his hand. 'It's a gift for the young Buchan. He'll aye sup from that cup.'

He placed the cup on the table and stood up. He held Elspeth in his arms and then took a step back from her as she executed a pirouette beneath his raised hand. 'This child of mine will be a master potter. A porcelain merchant with his own fleet of ships.'

'This child of mine will be tall and strong,' she countered.

'This child of mine will sail the seas and return a rich man with countless loyal slaves who fight among themselves to do his bidding.' Another twirl.

'This child of mine will inherit the earth.'

'This child of mine will bring us gifts of spices and fruits unseen in this country.' A bow and a twirl.

'My son will rule all nations with a rod of iron.'

The dance stopped. He looked at his wife. 'A rod of iron?' he asked.

Elspeth intoned as if in a trance, her eyes unfocussed. 'And she, being with child, cried, travailing in birth, and pained to be delivered.' Robert lowered his hand. 'And she brought forth a man child, who was to rule all nations with a rod of iron; and her child was caught up unto God, and to His throne.' Robert laughed uneasily, but Elspeth remained motionless, staring into a distance that excluded her husband, and most of the familiar world.

The moment passed and Robert put it out of his mind. Elspeth too chose to think of the episode as an aberration, rather than a harbinger of the old troubles returning.

Her confinement passed without incident. She and Robert looked forward to the child's arrival. Robert fashioned a cot from barrel staves, and Elspeth rediscovered her knitting skills. They still entertained Robert's friends from the pottery and took supper together most nights at the window overlooking the Clyde. As they peered into the dark, they took it in turns to invent stories for each skiff and boat that toiled through the waters.

'The captain has captured a mermaid which he keeps in a cage beneath the deck. He feeds it sprats and is going to sell it to a showman.' Elspeth nodded her approval of her husband's flight of fancy.

'No,' she said. 'He's a Frenchie and his boat's full of gunpowder. He's going to destroy Glasgow… like Sodom and Gomorrah.'

'You and your Bible,' said Robert. 'Sometimes I think I'm wed to the minister.'

When her time came, Elspeth was seized with foreboding. Her sleep was troubled with premonitions of disaster. When awake, she caught sight of imps in the curtains and on one occasion, when Robert was out, she saw a single eye in a knothole on the floorboards.

The surgeon apothecary, as a favour to Mrs Martin, was in attendance for the birth. The elderly man wielded stirrups and forceps while administering reassurances and platitudes to the mother screened from him by a blanket. When he sighed to himself and muttered, Elspeth assumed that he was in conversation with the imps, seeking their advice. At the point of delivery, her scream became a cry of joy as she pulled back the blanket to see, for the first time, fresh from her womb, the Manchild that had been foretold in Revelation 12. The surgeon swaddled the tiny creature in a cloth and gave the bundle into Elspeth's outstretched arms. 'Come to me, come to me,' she pleaded.

'It's a girl, a sickly girl,' said the surgeon with a shake of his head.

The child survived for several hours after which time Robert had to unpeel Elspeth's fingers from the tiny corpse. She looked at him with despair in her eyes.

Listless and lost, Elspeth's decline was rapid. Robert had no idea how to react. Initially sympathetic, he would return from work and comfort his wife who had not stirred from her bed. He made her gruel and fed her with a spoon. He would then lie next to her and tell her what had happened during the day.

'The partners were fair pleased. Mr Martin brought them over to me. 'That's the man who will make this company a fortune with his porcelain. Isn't that right, Robert?' I said aye, what else could I say? And who knows, he may be right. And we had a right palaver when a gull found its way into the building. There's a hole in the roof. The bird flapped and fluttered, squawking all the while. And then it swoops down on Old Garvie and pecks him. The old man was fair ragin'. He started throwing clay at the gull. But it just squawked the more.' He paused, leaving a gap in his discourse for Elspeth to fill with a comment or related question. She never did, but he always acknowledged her non-existent contribution.

'Aye, that's right. It made a fair old mess.'

Big Joshua, who worked the wheel next to his, argued that Elspeth needed to be shaken out of her torpor. 'Cruel to be kind,' he said. 'She mun get over the disappointment and start to live again.'

That evening, with heavy heart but with his mind made up, Robert threw back the bedding and grabbed his wife by the arm. 'Let's be having ye, Missis.' He hauled her out of bed. 'Now put on your claes.' She stood, draped over him, her arms at her side. Eventually she shuffled to the corner of the room and looked for something to wear. Robert went over to help her. 'Guid girl, guid girl.' He helped her into her smock and sat her down in the chair by the window. 'There's that captain back with another slippery slave.'

Over the next two years Elspeth gave birth to two daughters who survived despite their mother's total indofference to their existence.

Chapter Six

THE BROTHER'S TALE
Greenock

The boys fought and wrestled in their lodgings. At first the old lady, their self-appointed concierge, turned a deaf ear to their shouts and cries. Only when blood from Mathew's gouged cheek splattered on her bedding did she complain. 'In the name o' Jesus, boys, you'll kill each other.' So tight was the headlock in which James held his brother it seemed as if he had grown an extra grimacing face under his arm. The two of them staggered the length of the attic. Both were crying. Both were ten years old again, refusing to believe that their mother had died. Her belly had swollen. They could each snuggle into her bloated flesh and seek solace there. And then she was gone. 'Dropsy,' said their father as he sobbed into his drink. And now it had happened again. Mathew was to blame. James was to blame. They were both to blame. They stood a little apart and punched each other, taking turns to administer and accept punishment. Finally, all energy and anger spent, they fell into each other's arms and sank to their knees.

'We must find her,' whispered James. Mathew nodded, wiping the snot from his face.

They visited the local taverns and the kirks. One of the ministers told how he had chased her out of the kirkyard with a broom. 'Spouting wickedness and heresy,' he said.

They stopped strangers on the quayside and asked if they had heard tell of a tall and beautiful woman with strange ideas about God. 'Only in my dreams,' said the porter wheeling a barrel of herring. 'Aye, ah merried her, and she turned intae a puddock when ah kissed her,' said his companion before spitting on the cobbles.

Chapter Seven

PELT MAN

The young man had just sold a dark brown pelt to a soldier walking along the Broomielaw. He glanced over the shoulder of his customer who was searching his tunic for coins, while muttering about the influx of Irish labourers. Something was happening on the water. A small crowd had gathered along the low wall that separated the quay from the river. He followed the direction of their pointing and saw that a woman was standing up to her waist in the Clyde some fifteen yards from the wall. The loud knot of men had been joined by others who had left the comfort of the tavern to gawk at the spectacle. It wasn't just curiosity that made him forsake the man rummaging ever deeper into his breeches for the elusive coins. His own mother had drowned herself, and the intervening years had been consumed by unmerited guilt and a need to expiate. He ran towards the crowd, pushed his way to the front and dropped into the river. The cold shocked the breath from his body. The water was red. For a moment he assumed that the woman was wounded and bleeding. 'Wait for me!' he shouted, pushing his way through the weight of water.

Elspeth turned to face him. 'Jesus' blood never failed me,' she cried before redoubling her efforts to stride deeper. He caught up with her and held her in his arms. She offered no resistance.

'Hold me, John,' she said. 'Baptise me in His name, I have been His servant all these years.' She swallowed water.

Someone from the quay threw a rope which looped towards the strange couple. The crowd laughed as they helped them over the wall. 'You'll need to take your wet claes off, missy,' said the red-faced lecher. The pelt seller ignored the taunts, retrieved his own jacket from the cart and wrapped it around Elspeth's shoulders.

'How did you know my name?' he asked, squeezing the water from his sleeves.

'John was clothed with camel's hair,' she said touching the rough texture of the coat, 'and his diet was locusts and wild honey.' She shivered.

'Oats and bread more like.'

She shivered again and touched his face. 'The waters were red. A sign of God's intent.'

No,' he said smiling. 'It was a sign that the dyers have emptied their vats into the river. The magistrates will no be pleased. I bide near here. Come with me.'

He put his arm under hers and helped her walk away from the river. A small child stamped in the puddles they left behind them, and some of the earlier spectators, disappointed that the excitement had not ended with a drowning, jeered at their cumbersome progress.

John moved the cart into the darkest corner of the vennel, and then with armfuls of heavy pelts, dragged himself up the tight stairs that led to his room. Once inside, Elspeth retrieved one of the skins that had fallen onto the steps and pulled it around her shoulders.

He crouched down and blew on the embers in the grate. His efforts were rewarded, and the flames spluttered their way towards the chimney.

'There,' he said, turning to see Elspeth naked with her arms outstretched towards him.

They stayed in the room for three days. She told her pelt-selling lover nothing about her circumstances; about her daughters and their father.

As they lay sated under a thick layer of animal skins, Elspeth sang hymns under her breath in a deep hypnotic voice. John was under her spell.

'Water woman I am your creature,' he said, lightly running a finger across her lips.

'Well, ye'll no be peeling the skin off my back, and selling it for drink in the market.'

'It would fetch a fortune, soft, covered in the finest down. They would ask what exotic animal shed its coat.'

'Ye have a fine tongue,' said Elspeth, 'but it could be put to better use.'

John shifted his position and propped himself up on an elbow. 'Dae you have a man? Ah know nothing about you.'

'A man, aye. A potter. And two girls. But they are not my mission. I see things... a different world.'

John lightly touched her lips with his forefinger then toyed with her loose curls.

'I see a world where there is no death. No gnashing of teeth. No wailing at the moon. Death is the reward for mediocrity and misery. The bonds of matrimony will strangle us; the blood red cord of childbirth becomes the dark rope that lowers us into the grave. We must embrace joy, make heaven on earth.'

Elspeth nudged his arm away and climbed onto him until she felt his arousal.

'O! O! O!' Her life-affirming cry connected Elspeth with her true mission, her reason for being. In that small moment she was heaven-bound and nothing else existed.

She lived contentedly with the innocent young man who knew nothing of childbirth, of stillborn corpses, of the drudgery of feeding gurning weans, of feigning interest in glazes and clays. A young man who had no idea of what it was like to carry the burden of a destiny unfulfilled, a life stifled by boredom. She listened to his tales about rival street traders, of the dog he used to own, of his own childhood spent beachcombing on the banks of the Tay, of the mother he missed. She ruffled his hair when his eyes filled and his words failed. Not once did he ask what had compelled her to walk into the Clyde. In return, she held him, comforted him and gave him pleasure that made him feel, as he told her, that he had died and been taken through the clouds and into heaven itself. She sat up in their bed and, looking down on his smiling face said, 'By faith Enoch was taken from this life; he did not taste death. He could not be found because God had taken him away... '

But they were both found. On the seventh day, her husband came to the door. More accurately, the door came into the room, flattened by the combined weight of Robert and two of the younger potters.

Mr Martin had released them from their duties so that they could trace Elspeth. Their initial enquiries had soon led them to the taverns that lined the Broomielaw where they heard tales of the mad woman and her rescuer. In the telling, the story was embellished: the woman was trying to walk on the water; she had taken a knife to her wrists and her blood flowed freely; the man who saved her had a reputation for taking all manner of hoors and harlots under his wing before keeping them enslaved in his room. This last falsehood ensured that Robert and his friends came armed with cudgels.

The men dragged John out from under the heap of warm pelts and beat him. Elspeth faced her husband. 'How dare you come for me who had God's mission to perform? I saw the light in this man's eyes, the light of Our Saviour who rules us all.' She moved towards him and he hit her across the face. She stood still and said nothing. Robert watched as the wheal, with marks from each of his fingers clearly visible, rose on her cheek.

He had never struck her, or indeed any living creature before this moment. 'I just wanted... I need... ' The other potters, still on their knees, paused briefly from beating John and looked up at Robert. What was he going to say?

'Come home, Elspeth,' he said. 'Come home.'

And so she returned with him to their lodgings. Although neither of them mentioned her missing days or manifest infidelity, Robert was wounded and worried. At night, he paced the floor. Elspeth lay in the adjoining room and waited for the same floorboard to creak under his weight as he crossed and crossed again. She had no wish to make things harder for him. He just didn't understand. He worked ever longer hours but never again shared his hopes with her. The dream of becoming Glasgow's finest potter had died. Elspeth, for her part, felt no guilt. She accepted that, on occasions, her life was not her own. He too must understand that a greater power was shaping her. It was as simple as that.

Being born just a year apart, Annie and Maggie compensated for their mother's distraction by becoming inseparable. Even in the crib they clung to each other. As infants, self-preservation taught them to stay still when their mother approached. They developed a tiny clucking sound that served to warn the other when they heard her footsteps. But where was the Manchild she had been promised? Why was God testing her in this way?

Elspeth had dared to hope when pregnant again, that having endured God's will with fortitude, this time He would reward her. And so it came to pass. When the wriggling infant was placed on her breast she knew that this was he: the one who was destined to rule all nations with a rod of iron.

Robert, worn down by his wife's lassitude, was cheered to see her spirits rise after the birth of their son. He chose the child's name. 'James,' he said. 'From the Gaelic. It means a gift from God.'

Elspeth looked at him oddly. Perhaps he had understood all along. In his heart, he knew about her mission. Joseph too, a simple carpenter, must have known that he was to play a part in a foretold pageant of greatness. And now it was the turn of a humble potter.

Their life together improved. When the children slept, she would weave simple clothes for them. She listened intently as Robert repeated verbatim the conversations he had overheard between the managers. They would need to take on more men, but Joshua would have to go: his hands shook all the time and his work was not up to standard. The business was thriving despite competition from the Frenchies. 'Inferior pots,' he told her, shaking his head. 'Too heavy, too coarse.' Eventually she returned to his bed and lavished on him the attention that had marked their first days together.

They lay in the early morning light, before the children woke, listening to the sounds from the Clyde: shrieking gulls, ships' bells, stevedores' cries. 'Look,' he said, 'we make two esses, your body curled round mine. I wonder what word we are making.'

'HappineSS,' she said.

'My mark. On the pots.'

'What do you mean, my dear?'

'I'm going to change it to SS. Big letters, bold and proud! The best pots in the world.'

It was an innocent remark from Maggie that ushered in the next period of darkness.

'Mama, James's got skelly eyes. The one points to the sky, and the other to the flair.' Elspeth hadn't noticed before, but her daughter spoke the truth. There was something disconcerting about her Manchild's eyes. In short, these were not the eyes of a prophet destined to bring the righteous to the throne of God and smite the wicked. These eyes belonged to a fool, a charlatan. She looked askance at the grizzling infant.

Robert noticed the change in Elspeth. She reverted to her monosyllabic self and forsook his bed. She became obsessed with her child's deformity. As she stared at her son, his features seemed to melt like wax, and then reform as a grotesque, smirking mask. She was tempted to take the boy and dash his brains on the cobbles, but she knew that would only play into the devil's hands. No, this was her biggest trial yet. She must hold firm and prove that she was worthy of the task for which she had been chosen. Accordingly, she forced herself to tend to her son's needs and tried to ignore her inner voice urging his destruction.

In the days that followed, she argued with God, presenting Him with irrefutable evidence that His behaviour to her had been unreasonable. These discussions occupied most of her waking hours. Simple questions from the children were met with incomprehensible gibberish interspersed with scriptural references. Eventually she understood what God was saying to her. His view was that Robert's seed could never bring forth the promised Manchild.

As she walked towards Trongate, she loosened the top buttons of her blouse and removed the pins from her hair. She had frequently looked through the door of The Black Boy when shopping at the market, and had been overwhelmed by the waves of boisterous, bawdy male laughter and the smell of drink. Heads turned when she walked in. The landlady paused from mopping a puddle, briefly looked Elspeth up and down, and then carried on with the task in hand. Elspeth entered as if she were on urgent business and approached a man standing on his own. He gawped at his new and very beautiful companion.

'Will you no buy a lady a drink?' she asked, pinching the roll of flesh that protruded above his waist. 'It's been a long day and I've a drouth.'

'Ah'll help you slake it,' he said, beckoning the landlady who put down her mop.

The farmer was soon captivated by this wild stranger who sparkled with life and the promise of pleasure. She whispered teasing, salacious words into his ears until the evening took an inevitable turn. The landlady readily agreed to rent them an upstairs room for a few hours.

She slowly removed her clothes and stood with her arms above her head. On tiptoe she stretched until she touched the ceiling. 'Heaven is pressing down,' she said, 'waiting to envelop us in its joyous pleasures.' She smiled at the dumbstruck farmer who let himself be undressed like a grateful child about to receive a new set of clothes.

After their lovemaking she traced a scar that ran from her companion's chest to his navel.

'A bull,' he said. 'The critter carried me the length of the field on its horns.'

She lowered her head and licked the red marks left by the crudely sewn stiches. Her tongue lingered on the small raised wheals of flesh then worked its way down his body. 'Soon you will be whole again, your skin will grow anew.'

'And how will I explain that to my woman?'

'Tell her you were cured by a holy witch.'

When she returned home smelling of drink and strangers, she thought that Robert would strike her. He raised his hand then caught it in the other as if it belonged to an impetuous enemy who needed to be restrained.

'For Jesus' sake, woman,' he said. 'What is wrang wi' ye? What demon possesses your soul? Why do you do this to me who has only ever loved you?'

Elspeth looked at him as if startled out of a dream.

'It's God's path…' she started but suddenly lost all conviction. She felt deserted but by whom or why, she didn't know. Robert came over and held her with a tenderness that surprised them both.

Her aura of vulnerability gave them both comfort in the weeks that followed. Elspeth became the lost, sometimes errant child being nurtured by a forgiving parent. The two older children, taking the lead from their father, fetched and carried for Elspeth, and looked after their infant sibling as best they could.

'The deed is done,' said Robert the moment he entered the lodgings. Elspeth looked at him, surprised by this unexpected air of certainty. He slapped some papers onto the table.

'It's this city,' he continued, ruffling Maggie's hair as she wrapped herself round his legs. He walked awkwardly into the room, his daughter still holding on. 'You've no been yourself since we left Langbank. Life was fine then with the fields and the birds. We must leave this place of noise and stink. We must start again. We must go north, back to your ain country.'

Chapter Eight

ADVENTURES IN A NORTHERN PARISH
Banff, March 1764

Angus Cook looked back at The Prince of Wales lying at anchor. He had been loath to forsake his ship and crew, but felt obliged to visit his sick wife and, if necessary, beat some sense into her. Letters waiting for him in Inverness had confirmed his worst fears. The mad woman from Glasgow had driven his wife to distraction with her rantings and talk of sin.

'Visions, my airse!' he thumped his fist against the gunnel. The sailor, rowing hard against the retreating tide, and knowing better than to question the captain in this mood, bent further over his oars and focussed on the outer harbour, the walls of which were, thankfully, gradually drawing closer.

'Let me see her!' he shouted as he entered the house. He thrust aside the servant standing at the door of her chamber. Hearing the commotion, the physician stuck his thumbs into his waistcoat pockets and rose unsteadily.

'Angus, it's yoursel'.'

Ignoring him, the captain dragged his wife into a sitting position. 'In Christ's name, look at the state of you.'

'Has He come? Is that you, Jesus?' asked his wide-eyed wife.

Angus Cook stormed out of the house and marched up the hill towards the pottery. Rumours of the captain's return, and speculation concerning his likely course of action, had spread through the neighbourhood. As a result, a small flurry of townsfolk followed his progress, determined not to miss what promised to be a significant meeting.

Robert was bent over his wheel, steadying his hand as he incised the wet clay and dragged a symmetrical fir cone pattern across its surface. It was a technique he had latterly perfected at the Broomielaw, which partly explained why his decision to leave the Glasgow factory had been resisted by the owners. By varying the depth of incision, he created an effect of continuous movement, especially when the glazed pots were seen in sunlight. It had been a good day so far: twenty pots were ready for firing.

With one smooth movement, Angus Cook swept them onto the floor. Robert stared at the grey heap of clay in which the pots were now gently reverting to their original state.

'Why did you do that?' he asked.

'Why did the lunatic woman you live wi' cast her spells on my wife, and infect her with lies and blasphemies?'

'I will thank you, Sir, to leave these premises.' Robert stood. He was well above the common height, and towered over the porky captain who, deciding that cowardice was the wisest course, turned to leave, kicking over and breaking another line of biscuit-fired hand bowls in the process. The onlookers who had crammed into the doorway also ran back down the hill so that they could share their own exaggerated version of events with any neighbours who had not had the good fortune to witness the commotion.

Although mild-mannered, and in his own way, unworldly, Robert had become increasingly impatient with the constant stream of townsfolk who came to the pottery with the express intention of talking to Elspeth on a huge variety of religious topics, or if they were husbands, accuse him of corrupting their wives.

Soon after their arrival in Banff, Elspeth had taken to holding court in the kirkyard after the Sabbath service. All the townsfolk would be there. While the children played among the leaning stones, the youths flirted and stole kisses. The men, in their blue serge coats and knee breeches, would talk about the price of cattle or the latest unreasonable edict from the harbour master. The women congregated separately and gossiped as they appraised each other's attire.

From her very first appearance, Elspeth had been the candle that attracted the moths. Her soft, deep voice entranced all who heard her. She knew her scriptures better than the minister. She could embellish the psalms in a way that made them relevant to the lives of her audience. She exuded a teasing sensuality that drew in both the men and the women. When someone seemed uncertain, she would rub her index finger under their chin as if they were puppies. If the minister had earlier castigated the entire congregation for its sinfulness, sloth and moral turpitude, Elspeth would merely shrug and ask what use God would have with perfect human beings. Sitting on a fallen gravestone, she would absentmindedly point her toe towards the daisies and suggest that The Creator would soon become bored with perfection. She even boldly stated that it was sin alone that showed that we were all His creatures, with the human blood of life and temptation coursing in our veins.

A collective unease gripped the parish as the day of the sacrament of the Lord's Supper approached. All members of the congregation knew that they would be summoned individually and questioned about the shorter catechism and the paraphrases of the psalms. And so they made their way to the pottery, each bringing small tokens: neat posies tied with twine or tasty bites for the children.

Elspeth listened patiently to their faltering replies.

'Did God leave all mankind to perish in the estate of sin and misery?'

Bruce twisted his cap in his hands and looked as if he was about to wet himself. He was all of 17.

'It's coming, missis, on the tip o' my tongue. I ken this one... God having... out of his sheer guid pleasure... '

'Mere good pleasure, Bruce, mere.' Robert, who had been leaning in the doorway, sighed and walked back through to the pottery.

' ... mere good pleasure, from all eternity, elected some... elected some... I canna mind it, miss.'

Elspeth put her hand around Bruce's chin and pulled him towards her. 'Open your mouth, Bruce.'

He did so, and Elspeth gently blew into his mouth. He stepped back startled. ' ... elected some to everlasting life, did enter into a covenant of grace, to deliver them out of the estate of sin and misery, and to bring them into an estate of salvation by a redeemer!'

'Well done, Bruce, well done.'

The minister was wary, but the parishioners had no such doubts. They competed among themselves to invite Elspeth to their homes where she would interpret the scriptures with a smile.

She paced around Elizabeth Sloan's parlour, pausing to flick away a moth immolating itself against the glass of the oil lamp. The insect settled briefly on her hair. That too was interpreted as a sign of her greatness. Seeing that she was preparing to speak, the murmuring ceased. All eyes were on her.

'There be many that believe it is the revealed will of God that all men and women without distinction, should embrace salvation. And yet, by the same teachers, they are instructed, that God's secret will is, that a certain number only should be saved. These are two wills surely contrary and contradictory; the one expressing a desire to see all men happy, and another only inclinable to the happiness of a small select number. But is anything more absurd than to speak of a secret will in God?'

Leaving her question hanging in the air, she moved towards Gibby the cooper, who was sitting next to the hearth. Putting her hand beneath his shirt, she rubbed his back, as if she was administering embrocation to a rheumy child. He smiled with pleasure.

'Ah dreadful! What a dreadful tyrannical being this deluded world takes God to be… '

She kept up her daily round of visits, consoling the needy and comforting the confused. She even took to teasing the Reverend McBain whose severe demeanour revealed a growing animosity towards this woman usurping his authority. Red in the face, and with spittle on his chin, he made a habit of interrupting Elspeth.

'This is heresy. May you rot in hell with all the demons of carnality and delusion.'

Elspeth smiled indulgently at him which infuriated him further.

'Satan has sent you among us to corrupt the good folk of Banff. He is waiting with his sulphur-tipped lash to beat your nakedness.' With the subtlety of a courtesan, Elspeth made a slight adjustment to the hem of her dress and winked at the apoplectic clergyman who left slamming the door behind him.

For a while at least, all was indeed comparatively well. Their life resumed its rhythm. Despite the absence of customers, Robert continued to make pots which each evening he added to the toppling heap that had spread into their living quarters. 'Soon they will come,' he said staring into the square, looking for the itinerant merchants who would, after gentle persuasion and a generous discount, fill their carts with second-rate cracked stoneware. But they never came.

Elspeth would fill a bag with pots and leave the house to hawk her wares around the surrounding farms and crofts. Few of the folk she approached had the wherewithal to purchase anything. Instead they offered company and refreshments. The women who knew her from her impromptu sermons in the kirkyard, greeted her as the prophetess she increasingly believed she was.

'My man is seik,' said Margo guiding her towards the truckle bed crammed into the alcove. Elspeth approached the figure hidden under sacking and animal skins.

'Do not fear,' she intoned. 'I am with you. Do not be dismayed. I will strengthen and help you.' Margo covered her mouth with her hand as if preparing herself to witness a miracle. 'I will uphold you with my righteous right hand.' She slid her righteous right hand under the bedding until she found the hot, fevered body of Margo's husband, and restored his strength.

She also ministered to the labourers toiling in the fields. She walked through the stubble to the rick against which Damon was resting. He raised himself onto an elbow to watch her approach. She lay down her bag of pots.

'Welcome, Mistress,' he said holding a bottle towards her. She drank, wiped her lips and then put them on his.

They lay back and squinted into the sun. 'A rare day,' said Damon breathing heavily.

'Aye, it is that,' said Elspeth. 'Do you believe in angels, Damon?'

'I think one has just visited me.'

They watched a lark dwindling into the haze.

Robert was waiting for her on her return. He glanced at the bag of unsold pots. He knew how she had spent her day. 'Why do you treat me this way?' he asked more in resignation than anger. 'Why do you do this?'

'It's just who I am,' she said.

Robert listened to the children playing in the yard. They were fighting over the metal hoop he had found discarded at the harbour. Although uneasy with his wife's reputation, he took pleasure in her enthusiasms and looked forward to her return from the fellowship meetings as she dubbed them. She glowed with energy and took some persuading to stop pacing and sit at the table. They had certainly known worse times. Even Angus Cook had abandoned his efforts to have her arrested for witchcraft. Perhaps the decision to leave Glasgow had been the right one. He broke the bread, freshly taken from the kiln, and divided it between them.

'I tried that new glaze today,' he said. 'It looks promising. There's an emerald hue to it. A hint of the sea.'

Elspeth stared at her plate.

'I'm a little vexed though. Turner, the merchant, didn't keep his appointment. There are rumours that he's taken up wi' a potter from Whitehills.'

Elspeth stared at her plate.

'Perhaps I should make more cider jars, the big ones.'

Elspeth threw the plate to the floor.

'What's the matter with you? Are you unwell? No again, Elspeth, no again.'

Her chair clattered to the floor as she clutched her head as if to tug it from her shoulders. Robert rose to comfort her, but she pushed him away.

'Don't you see? Don't you see?'

Young Maggie came in from the yard. 'What's wrong wi mama?'

'And David fasted and went and lay all night on the ground. And the elders of his house stood beside him, to raise him from the ground, but he would not, nor did he eat food with them,' she declaimed looking through the window at the sea beyond.

And so it came to pass. Elspeth refused to eat. Despite Robert's entreaties and the pleadings of her children, Elspeth kept rigidly to her fast. Initially her spirits were high. Gradually her self-denial took its toll. Missing her frequent visits, her admirers took to dropping into the pottery at all hours of the day. Robert's patience was wearing thin.

'Mrs Cook,' he said as the woman bustled her way through the pottery and into their bedroom. 'Does your man know you're here? This will no end well.'

She ignored him and went to Elspeth who was lying still under the covers. 'Oh, my dear,' she said. 'I've brought you a tiny piece of chicken, will you no tak it, just to please me?'

Elspeth shook her head and stared at her guest. Mrs Cook was startled by the brightness of Elspeth's eyes. 'Fit are you trying to say my dear? Fit message do you have for us?'

The bedpan remained untouched. Prayers were offered at her bedside. Tempting morsels of food were left within arm's reach: the flesher's wife brought a small parcel of calf tongues wrapped in newspaper; Bruce, still grateful for his tuition in the Small Catechism, brought a rabbit from which he picked off the maggots before laying it on top of the bed. The landlord of the Ship Inn brought a flagon of port which he opened and held under her nose. As she showed not a flicker of interest, he shrugged and drank the contents himself.

Elspeth was giving birth to snakes. With each contraction she forced more of the creatures through her ring of black hair and into the world. She pulled at them until they tumbled into her lap like scarfs from a conjurer's mouth. Each serpent held another's tail. Her heavy breasts, tipped with steel, pointed downwards at the venomous brood cascading, cartwheeling, slithering into existence.

Her nightmares frightened her. She understood that her joyous insights came at a cost. Satan, furious with her for peddling views of simple happiness must kill her and claim her soul. She remained oblivious of all attention and turned her head to the wall. Maggie, having failed to get her mother's attention, ran to her father. 'Is mama dying? Is she going to the Lord?'

'No lass,' said Robert, although he was far from certain that his wife's fast wouldn't prove fatal.

He persuaded the barber surgeon to visit during his monthly circuit of the county. The elderly man took a vial of blood from her thin wrist. He inspected the liquid by holding it up to the light. 'Leeches are your only hope. Leeches and Almighty God.'

After feeding the children, Robert returned to his wheel. No other activity served to calm his mind. Although the business was failing, he continued to add to the small mountain of carefully stacked pitchers and plates. Things would change for the better. 'Trust in the Lord,' Elspeth would say before this latest episode. The seam of clay in which he had invested so much hope, and which had sustained his early efforts, was running thin. Many of the pots didn't survive firing and cracked when he removed them from the cooling kiln. The pottery, thick with broken shards, increasingly resembled a white, frozen seascape.

With heavy heart, he climbed the stairs to see if Elspeth's situation had changed. Sometimes he wanted to shake her; shake out whatever devil had wormed its way into her head and destroyed their happiness. The bed was empty. She wasn't there. Robert looked beneath it, clutching at the hope that his wife had somehow slipped onto the floor and rolled away. He opened the curtains lest she was hiding there. It was already dark when he looked through the open door swinging in the night breeze. He ran down the Vennel. 'Have you seen her?' he shouted at an amorous couple wrapped around each other in the shadows. 'My wife, has she been this way?' he asked Old Billy, the idiot man who slept on the quay.

'Naked! Naked! Nae claes!' said Billy pointing towards the headland that stretched beyond the village.

Robert climbed over the bracken and stones that marked the ascent onto the cliff. He stood at the top and briefly cursed whatever God had done this to him, then set off along the path. The occupants of a gull's nest screamed into his face before he brushed them aside. At that moment, the moon appeared through the clouds and he saw Elspeth standing with her arms outstretched on the cliff edge in the distance. Stumbling, he ran towards her. As Billy had indicated, she was completely naked, with her face upturned to the night sky. He wrapped her in his arms. He felt her ribs in their taut cage of skin. He felt her heart, a trapped pulsating sparrow. He breathed in her bitter breath of starvation. He took off his jacket to cover her lest the frail construct of bones that passed as a body might disconnect and clatter to the ground.

'I thought my time had come. The time of Translation. The angels were gathering in the clouds to pull me towards them, to the seat of His throne. I saw them, Robert, I saw them. I heard their singing.' She shrugged herself free from Robert's jacket. 'There they are again.' She pointed to a spot on the horizon and walked towards the edge of the cliff. 'Wait for me, I'm coming.'

Chapter Nine

THE BROTHERS' TALE
Gourock

The brothers cried and held onto each other. 'Your hair's grey,' said James.

'It's gey dark in the jail.'

Before his imprisonment, Mathew had suggested they should widen their search for Elspeth. He reminded his brother of how she had earned pennies singing psalms outside of the local kirks. 'She's likely moved further doon the Clyde.'

They first looked for Elspeth in Gourock where the ministers shared their concerns about the two drunken ruffians who regularly stood in their kirkyards intimidating the innocent, god-fearing worshippers. The consensus view was that they were part of a Glasgow gang which had been looting local kirks of their sacred ornaments. When the constables arrived to apprehend the villains, James, the fitter of the two, was able to escape into the maze of cobbled streets while Mathew was apprehended and imprisoned.

'Ah'm starvin'. The food was shite. Have you no found her yet?'

'Na, but I'm aye askin' aboot her.'

'The thing is, brither, wi' every turn o' that fuckin' treadmill, ah heard her words: 'All shall be well. All shall be well.''

'And all manner of thing shall be well,' finished James.

Chapter Ten

SEPARATION AND REUNION

A fortnight had passed since Robert returned to Glasgow to beg his employers to take him back. He had told Elspeth that he could take no more.

She had rallied in his absence. She knew he was a good man, but the angels had reminded her in a dream that marriage was an abomination; an unnatural yoking that bred only misery. In a second dream, God himself appeared. His message lit up the firmament. 'This is my daughter in whom I am well pleased.' As the lightning cracked, He pulled back a veil revealing a tableau in which the pottery had been transformed into a dame school. This was to be the next stage on Elspeth's journey to paradise.

Mary Pirie rounded up the children and led them up the brae to the pottery. They walked in pairs and held hands. They were excited at the thought of going to school. They would learn to read and write; they would then become lords and ladies. They would sail the seas and keep lots of rabbits. Elspeth greeted them at the door. 'Suffer little children to come unto me,' she said smiling as they stood wide-eyed before running their hands over the clay coated furniture. Hamish smeared the white dust on his face. 'Ah'm a ghostie,' he said.

Each day the children fought and squabbled. Wee fat Hennie from Whitehills was the first to creep into the pot store on all fours when Elspeth's back was turned. Placing her feet carefully, she climbed the unstable hill of broken pots. Once on the summit she tried to stand and instantly fell down the moving stack. Howling, and covered with blood, snot and her own small shroud of powder, she burst back into the main room where Maggie, Elspeth's eldest, was demonstrating how to draw a pot hook without removing the pen from the page. Frightened by the apparition, no longer recognisable as one of their own, the others burst into tears. 'Mama Buchan,' they said, between wails. 'Save us.' Elspeth roused herself and surveyed the chaos.

'I can't save you,' she said. 'You have no souls. You have no souls…' Struck by the words that had emerged unbidden from her mouth, she retired to her bed in the alcove and started to write.

In nothing are the people in this world more deluded than in their views concerning the generation of children. They think that God put a soul in every child that comes into the world. They fail to understand that God only bestows His gift of soul when that child understands His will and embraces selfless joy…'

She put down the paper and whirled through the room. Her brain was on fire. She felt exhilarated, exalted, chosen.

The lamps were burning low and the air was thick with the sickly scent of over-powdered women and the ale-laden breath of the men. This was the fellowship meeting that Elspeth valued the most. The Reverend McCrae was young and unconventional but had recognised at their first encounter that Elspeth was different from any other woman he had ever met. He was in love with his newest and most unruly of parishioners, and frequently woke from dreams in which she had breathed the spirit of God into his mouth before surrendering herself to him. He stood, quietened the room, and invited Elspeth to finish her address. She waited until the last conversation had died, sipped water from a cup proffered by the minister as if it were a communion chalice, and, standing tall and elegant, resumed her discourse.

'Only the truly courageous can embrace the challenge of joy. We are made to fear happiness and choose to see it as the harbinger of doom. The naysayers and miserabilists poison our souls and strangle our contentment. Look into your hearts. What sorrows burden you? What shadows cast darkness into your lives? Do you lie abed and think on the failing harvest? Do you hoard every penny against the days of famine and want? Do you fear the bailiff? Do you fear your minister when the tithe is due?' McCrae shrugged. They both knew that he would never harass his god-fearing parishioners. 'Do you want to be free of care? Do you wish your souls to dance with joy?'

STUART CAMPBELL

She paused as the room resounded with rapturous shouts of 'Amen!' She smiled at McCrae who seemed particularly eager for the assembled throng to disperse so that he could talk more intimately with the extraordinary woman who cast light on the most impenetrable biblical tracts.

To his annoyance, Mrs Cook was reluctant to leave and stayed behind after the others had left. Ignoring McCrae, who was pointedly holding open the door, she approached Elspeth and placed a thin hand on her arm. 'Beware my husband,' she said. 'I bring you warning that he intends you harm.' With that she curtseyed to the minister and left.

After hearing the gate close, Elspeth pulled McCrae towards her, tore the shirt from his back, clawed at his chest and tugged at his breeches.

Elspeth had no fears for her safety and took no extra precautions. Her door was never locked. She let her children roam as free as the wind. After all, Christ was vigilant on her behalf.

Once, after returning to the pottery after a fellowship meeting to find her chickens decapitated, and her children cowering in an outhouse.

'Twa men wi beards and rings in their ears,' said James between sobs. 'They said we were Satan's spawn.'

'The puir beasties still ran about the yard wi' nae heads. One ran into my leg,' said Maggie.

Elspeth was vexed. Cook was influential and had sought to persuade the ministers of Banffshire that the deil was alive and living in their midst. According to him, her fanaticism was infecting the hysterically inclined, such as his own feeble wife whose head had not been formed to detect theological falsehoods. Furthermore, she was corrupting the young who would return to their own hearths having imbued the most preposterous notions from the Buchan wife. His neighbours' children now regularly listened for the souls of the dead moaning in the inglenooks and urged their parents to leave milk for the lost angels who limped sadly through the countryside looking for forgiveness.

For his part, the Reverend McCrae was thrilled that God had sent a prophetess into his parish. He paced the bedroom at night, repeating Elspeth's sacred pronouncements. Mrs McCrae listened as she lovingly sewed the buttons back onto his shirt, still concerned that a parishioner's demented cat had attacked her husband, tearing his clothes and scratching his skin. She watched dotingly as he flicked at the spots of hot wax that had fallen from his candle onto the Holy Book. She must not interrupt him as he sought for scriptural confirmation that he had been chosen for a special mission.

The words blurred: all McCrae could think about was the next private interview with Elspeth.

After the next fellowship meeting, once the last of the faithful had left, they sat in silence at the back of the quiet kirk. When the last vestiges of light dropped away from the window, she took his hand.

'Do you not see, Stephen, that there is nothing more absurd than to speak of a secret will in God?' As she asked the question, she made small, circular movements with her forefinger on his wrist.

'No, indeed not. It is a nonsense.' He had been hoping for rather more than a spiritual discourse.

'How can God have a will, called secret, and yet every teacher and writer informs us what the secret will is?'

To his delight she moved her hand onto his knee and continued the circular movements. They were both startled as the kirk door slammed shut. The echo shook the darkness. McCrae stood and stared. 'Cook's spies,' he said.

The town was soon alive with rumours like fleas on a dog's back: she was the devil's mistress; she had a monkey's arse; she bewitched innocent folk by breathing sulphur into their mouths; she stole babies; she could burn holes in the Holy Book by merely touching the pages. Predictably, the regular attendees at the fellowship meetings appeared less often. If they encountered Elspeth in the street, they would lower their gaze and pass quickly by. Gradually too, the children stopped attending the dame school. Initially the mothers sent apologies. 'Tam has the ague... Nancy has nightmares and I canna persuade her to return.'

For a while Elspeth carried on as if nothing had changed. She still instructed her own children, and it was Maggie who eventually said, 'Mama, I miss the others... will they no come back?'

'Soon dear, soon.'

James too, showed signs of increasing boredom. 'Will papa come back and stay wi' us? I want to be a potter. You dinna need letters for pots.' He sat on his haunches and mimed bringing his hands carefully up the sides of an imaginary pot. He wiped his fingers on his shirt when he had finished.

As the school died, so too did the family's only source of income. Elspeth sent her children, under cover of dusk, to forage for whatever vegetables they could find on the edges of the fields. For her part, she would visit the harbour after the market had closed to gather up any fish heads which still dripped slivers of flesh.

Her belief that God would provide was amply demonstrated when the Reverend McCrae gave her the broaches bequeathed to his wife from her mother. 'Take them,' he said. 'See them as tokens of my love... and God's,' he added hastily.

Although grateful, Elspeth knew that her flirtation with penury was evidence that she was still behaving and thinking like the ordinary folk whom it was her mission to save. She needed to escape the stagnation that was smothering her. She also needed a larger stage if she was to rid the world of greed and unhappiness. It had never been God's intention that the woman clothed with the moon and the stars would confine her mission to Banffshire.

She sold the broaches to the tinker, who had previously bought their pots, and asked him to carry a message to her husband in Glasgow.

Robert, I hope you are well and safe in God's keeping. If it be His will that we must starve to show Him our love, then we will meet our fate in joyful expectation of rising in glory. The bairns miss you. James wants to be a potter. Your loving wife, Elspeth.

Within days of receiving his single word reply: COME, she and her three children stepped aboard the Edinburgh-bound brig, as it strained against its anchor in the swell of the harbour. They huddled down against the mast and pulled a tarpaulin over their heads. The children shivered from both the chill March wind, and dread of the journey ahead.

All four were restless during the night. James twitched involuntarily, and Annie seemed trapped in a dream about decapitated chickens. 'Catch them, mama, catch them before they leave circles of blood.'

Maggie woke to be sick from the alternate plunging and climbing of the vessel, and then let her head fall onto her mother's shoulder. At first Elspeth enjoyed the thought of being dragged through a dark universe of sea towards an unknown destiny. She thought of the Reverend McCrae, she thought of Robert, she thought of John and his cart of pelts. She saw movement on the deck and thought of Cook who was, perhaps, at this very moment, waiting for her to fall asleep, before emerging from the shadows to drag a knife across her neck. But Christ would protect her.

She became aware of a low, rumbling sound, quite distinct from the lash of the spray and the clatter of sail ropes. It grew in intensity until she covered her ears, but it wouldn't go away. Louder and louder, it invaded her senses. She opened her eyes and saw lights dancing in the darkness; pinpricks that grew into balls of fire plunging into the sea. She had the strength to challenge this phantasmagoria; she of all people could confront and confound this demonic apparition that had come in the night to claim her soul and devour her children.

Striding across the tipping deck, her arms outstretched to aid her balance, she moved towards the wooden rail at the deck's edge, and there she saw her nemesis, the monster dripping water and blood, rising from the depths as foretold in Revelations:

THE BEAST ROSE UP OUT OF THE SEA, HAVING SEVEN HEADS AND TEN HORNS, AND UPON HIS HORNS TEN CROWNS, AND UPON HIS HEADS THE NAME OF BLASPHEMY.

Leaning towards the deep swell, she shouted her defiance as the beast rose from the waves and enveloped her in its stinking breath.

Annie woke and saw her mother leaning against the rail. She heard her screaming at the darkness. Alarmed, she made her way to the hatch on the deck, lifted the heavy door and shouted down into the warm square of light. A man's head appeared in the gap. Growling with annoyance at having been disturbed from his grog and cards, he hauled himself onto the deck, and quickly moved to drag Elspeth out of danger. She was limp in his arms, all strength spent as he took her below deck and tied her to a bunk with ropes.

Robert had borrowed a cart from his employers and had taken a day and a half to travel from Glasgow to Leith. He stood next to the horse pawing at the cobbles on the quay and watched the few passengers disembark. His children saw him and ran down the gangplank and into his arms. 'Where's your mother?' he asked, looking above their heads towards the ship.

'She's no well,' said Annie. 'The sailors took her away.'

'Stay there.'

The captain, annoyed at having had to restrain a lunatic when he could have been drinking, insisted on payment before he would release Elspeth into her husband's care. He assisted her off the vessel and onto the quay. They looked at each other. Robert saw nothing but emptiness in her eyes. He had hoped that their time apart would have wrought changes; that his wife might be returning to him as the woman he first knew and loved. With heavy heart, he helped her into the cart.

Robert's trade had flourished after leaving his failed venture in Banff. His former employers had accepted him back with an alacrity that showed the faith they had in the young potter. He had also moved up in the world and now lodged in the Saltmarket, still within walking distance of his place of work. The pleasure he derived from being reunited with his children almost compensated for the challenge of renewing acquaintance with his wife.

Elspeth, having been her own mistress in the dame school, was reluctant to seek work in service. Instead, she used every hour of the day to make the acquaintance of the local ministers and infiltrate their parishes. As news of her behaviour in Banff had not travelled south, she was able to enjoy the pleasure of reinvention. The minister at the Tron was delighted by her scriptural knowledge and took pleasure in testing his new prodigy. 'Deuteronomy 17?' he challenged after she had chosen a private moment to congratulate him on his sermon.

'Ah,' she replied, touching her forefinger to her chin, her eyes sparkling at her inquisitor. 'Thou shalt not sacrifice unto the Lord thy God, any bullock, or sheep, wherein is blemish, or any evilfavouredness.'

'Well done, my dear. If I'm honest,' he continued in a light-hearted vein, quite at odds with his pulpit demeanour, 'I find the idea of God entertaining views on the ugliness or otherwise of sheep a bit challenging.' Elspeth smiled at his witticism.

The minister at St Georges presented more of a challenge. A tiny man, he managed to combine a general disdain for his parishioners with a more specific hatred for all women.

'Let a woman learn quietly with all submissiveness. I do not permit a woman to teach or to exercise authority over a man; rather she is to remain quiet. 1 Timothy 2: 11 – 15. This is my text for today.'

The congregation, men and women alike, nodded sagely.

During his next inflammatory sermon about the fickleness and carnality of womankind, she rose to her feet and stood silently in the middle of the congregation, staring at the bigot in the pulpit. For a moment, he forgot his words and could only stare back at the tall, thin woman who dared to challenge his authority. He was completely confused. He pointed a long claw at her as he framed the words of a withering rebuke, but then let his arm drop back onto the rail of the pulpit. The other parishioners murmured their disquiet. He stammered, scratched his head and thumbed the pages of the Bible looking for the passage he knew was there somewhere, which would tell him how to confront such a brazen challenge to his authority. Not finding the verses he was looking for, he sought refuge in a prayer intoned with as much authority as he could inject into his habitually nasal whine.

After the service, the congregation spilled out into the yard. Several husbands firmly steered their wives out of the gates, as they tried to look back over their shoulders at the remarkable woman who had appeared from nowhere. She was soon surrounded by a circle of widows, spinsters and those women strong enough to ignore the entreaties of their spouses to return meekly to the domestic hearth.

'Where do you bide, Mistress?' asked one.

'Will you come again?' asked another.

Elspeth touched each of them reassuringly on the arm. 'I will return,' she said, 'like He who will descend from heaven, and the dead in Christ will rise first. Then we who are alive, who are left, will be caught up in the clouds together with them to meet the Lord in the air.'

'Amen,' said the woman whose hand Elspeth touched.

'Amen,' repeated the others. The minister, chilpit and mean-featured, stood on the kirk steps. He pulled himself up to his full diminutive height, stamped his foot, turned on his heel and exited stage left, pursued by the bear of his own anger.

Pleased with the impression she had made, Elspeth was in better spirits when she returned home. Robert watched her as she removed her bonnet and untangled her ringlets, while young Maggie tried to interest her mother in the finger puppet she had fashioned.

'Will things be good between us?' he asked. 'Now that you are back.'

'Of course, my dearest, of course.'

For a while Elspeth enjoyed the company of the women who brought her small gifts: fans fashioned from sticks and thin silk, and gingerbread cakes, as they vied with each other for her attention. Afterwards her supplicants would scurry homewards to seek out their neighbours to whom they would eagerly repeat Elspeth's words, proving that they alone were the custodians of the prophetess' pronouncements.

But Elspeth was restless. Reluctantly she accepted that her time had not yet come. Craving excitement, she frequently returned to the Black Boy in the Trongate. Whenever she crossed the threshold, the hubbub ceased as her aura filled the room like ectoplasm. Conversations faltered as all eyes focussed on the tall, sensual woman in their midst: an apparition exuding the promise of carnal pleasure. The landlady, anticipating an increase in trade once news of her return spread, rushed upstairs to prepare the room to which she knew Elspeth would soon retire in the company of her chosen companion.

She was a gentle lover. She never chided the men for their overeagerness. She never drew attention to their shortcomings. She flattered them, put them at ease, and when necessary, assuaged whatever guilt threatened to compromise their pleasure with her. She sang to them, crooning long-forgotten hymns that frequently evoked memories of their more innocent boyhoods, and which, on occasions reduced them to tears. She revelled in their strength and ameliorated their weaknesses. She enjoyed their tales and encouraged them to talk of their families. Old George had survived several shipwrecks and swore that he had heard siren voices on a voyage to the South Seas. Jamie, having lost a leg in the war with France, was coaxed away from his inhibitions and persuaded to pirouette at great speed on his wooden limb. Elspeth clapped and laughed as the show ended with him losing his balance and falling heavily on top of her.

Peter, the tar merchant, self-conscious about the black muck under his nails, was unable to perform. She held his shrinking manhood in one hand as if it were a wounded sparrow and soothed his brow with the other.

'What ails you?' she asked.

'It's no right,' said Peter. 'I'm a married man. Jenny is a good soul to me and the bairns. She's a fine cook and looked after me when I had the accident.'

'What do you think of marriage, Peter?'

'It's a holy state ordained by God. All fornicators and adulterers will roast in the reddest pit of hell.'

'Do you really think so?' She gave the sparrow an extra squeeze. 'Only non-believers, tainted by doubt and racked by guilt, will roast in hell. God wants us to live and enjoy the gifts He has given us. He wants us to be strong and overthrow this bondage, this tyranny that yokes people together in misery.'

Suddenly he relaxed, and the sparrow was transformed into a bird of a completely different feather.

When not providing charitable solace to lost men, Elspeth would visit the homes of her many female admirers who she had met at the kirk.

After chapping Mrs Jamieson's door, she was ushered into her parlour and introduced to a tiny, bright-eyed man perched on a chair by the grate. His legs, being too short to rest on the hearth, were stuck out in front of him. He compensated for his lack of height by wearing a tall hat that squatted on his head like a chimney.

'This is Andrew Innes,' said Mrs Jamieson. 'He's come all the way from Muthill for the Sacremental this Sunday.' She raised her eyes heavenwards indicating that her new lodger was either irremediably boring or completely mad.

As Andrew was not inclined to forsake his perch, Elspeth, curious, knelt next to him. 'Muthill,' she said, 'is that the place with the holy wells?'

Andrew stared at this remarkable woman who somehow understood that the wells of Muthill were his sole reason for living. He stammered and swallowed. 'The minister, he cries me a heretic.' He had now swivelled round completely, though his legs still failed to touch the floor. 'He disnae understand. I've seen the miracles with my ain eyes.' Disconcertingly, he pulled down one of his eyelids. 'Yon woman wi' the whooping cough, she was cured after I telt her to drink the water after the sun sets out of a horn taken from a live cow. And she was cured.'

'Tell me more.'

'I was sore afflicted with the strangury, I couldnae piss, if you ken what I mean… so I put baith elbows into the waters of St Serf's Well. Cold, it was. But I was cured! But the ministers, they say it's the work of the deil. This wee woman from my ain parish was taken before the Kirk session for putting pins and head laces down the well at St Conwalls. Injustice!'

After Andrew had taken a moment to nurse his indignation, Elspeth said that she needed some air and asked if the small man would walk with her on Glasgow Green.

The odd couple attracted attention as they strolled towards the long line of women bleaching their linen on the banks of the Clyde.

Elspeth, having recently antagonised the minister at the Tron Kirk by arguing that Jehovah ultimately forgave David for his adultery, wanted to rehearse her evolving argument with her new acquaintance.

'If Uriah, summoned home from the battlefield, had agreed to sleep with his wife, then he would have raised the child as his own and no harm would have been done. Furthermore, he would not have been sent back to fight, and he would not have been killed.'

Andrew jumped up and down with excitement. 'It is clear to me now. Mrs Buchan, you take the shades from my eyes.' Being momentarily deprived of his shades didn't stop him from colliding with a tree in his enthusiasm. Elspeth steered him back onto the path and treated him to several of her more unorthodox biblical interpretations.

They walked back through the booths. A juggler, seeing them approach, hurled his diabolo into the air. With the startled excitement of a child, Andrew watched its progress into the clouds then gasped as the tinker caught it neatly on the string and doffed his hat.

Elspeth touched her small acolyte on the shoulder. 'When we climb through the clouds we will not fall back to earth.' Andrew looked at her quizzically. The next stall provided her with another metaphor. The puppet master towered above the gaudy box where the marionettes responded to each subtle tug on their strings. The female figure fell to the floor under the onslaught of blows from her assailant. In an instant, the roles were reversed, and she sprang back into life and bludgeoned the man whose stick limbs collapsed under him.

'Our enemies too will be confounded.' Andrew nodded vigorously, though he had not a clue what he was agreeing to. 'And our lives will not be our own. The Lord God will pull our strings and make our limbs bend to his will.' Andrew joyfully pictured himself as a marionette being manipulated by his newly discovered prophetess.

The low sun was reflecting off the river when they parted. Andrew stood upright like a small soldier preparing to salute, declared his gratitude to Elspeth for sharing her insights and promised to return to Muthill and spread word of her wisdom. She watched the small figure shuffling towards the Gallowgate and felt suddenly lost. It was growing dark and cold. This odd wee man was not her Manchild. Where was her companion as foreseen in Revelations? How could she possibly give birth to a Manchild? What did the words mean? She was floundering in a dark void waiting for God to reveal His purpose. 'All shall be well,' she muttered under her breath, without any real conviction.

Chapter Eleven

THE BROTHERS' TALE
Dalmellington

Rumours of an approaching press gang had terrified the community. Along with a dozen other men, James and Mathew had spent a week hiding in a barn in the hills. The farmer's spies had reported that the King's recruiters had only met with moderate success in Ardrossan and had been forced to retreat after an encounter with the regulars in the Fox's Heid. One of the recruiters had his eye gouged out by a ferocious woman who had taken exception to her new young lover being prised from her ample arms. Next to suffer was the unfortunate purse carrier who was upended and shaken until at least twenty shillings, property of the king, tumbled from his pockets. He was then carried and dropped headfirst into the harbour. But quotas had to be met and Greenock could be relied on to fill a skiff of men who would be conveyed to the man o' war waiting in the estuary.

Despite the dangers, hiding behind a false wall of straw held few attractions for the brothers who were desperate to resume their search for the Mother.

During a fitful sleep, Mathew dreamed of Elspeth. She was tugging at his arm, nudging him. 'Boys,' she urged, 'you must flee.'

Jerking awake, Mathew smelt burning and heard the crackle of fire on dry straw. He woke his brother and then the others. Blinded and coughing, they struggled into the yard where they were set upon by the press gang. One of their companions ran shrieking into the night, his hair on fire. The manhunters had stretched a rope in front of the main door. The men fell like tavern skittles, tumbling on top of each other. Gasping for air, James realised he had been tied back to back with Mathew. In the foreground the farmer protested in vain as he watched his barn destroyed by fire.

'The Mother will save us,' said Mathew.

Chapter Twelve

THE MANCHILD AND A SPY

Andrew Innes was hyperventilating with excitement. Unable to retrieve any words, he stamped his feet on the floor and flapped his hands as he tried to dispel the mist of confusion that had robbed him of his senses. 'It's fae an angel,' he said at last. 'One o' they cherubims. It floated doon during the preaching.' He opened his fist to show the holy relic. 'And then they a' started dancin' in the aisles. Auld yins wi' sticks that coudnae walk before. Wimen reelin' aboot the kirk... dancing, singin', praising the Lord... and, and he'e coming tae Glasgae to preach!'

Elspeth had heard rumours about Hugh White, the charismatic preacher who had left a theology college in Baltimore to assume charge of the Relief Kirk in Irvine. After the tedium and irrelevance of the Glasgow ministers, she was intrigued by Innes' tales of the Shaker ways White had introduced. She wanted to see him in the flesh. She wanted to hear his smooth, yankee tongue.

The kirk was packed. The congregation was swaying in a loud wave of expectation. The clamour comprised spontaneous prayer and gossip in equal measure. The door at the back of the kirk opened and the crowd caught its collective breath. The groundlings gawked open-mouthed, and then he appeared. Tall, with the flowing mane of an Old Testament prophet, he swept towards the pulpit which he climbed two steps at a time. He stood arms outstretched, aping the spread wings of the wooden eagle beneath him on the lectern. 'Dearest people,' he declaimed, 'Christ is in our midst. He will brook no denial. He will sunder your hearts with his bare hands and enter in. The blood from His sacred wounds will mingle with yours. Bathe in His holy crimson blood... ' He raised both fists, and, in that moment, saw the tall woman in the middle of the crowd, smiling slightly as if she recognised him. He paused, lost for words. The moment's silence was filled with the echo of his own voice sweeping back towards him.

After the service, he sought her in vain. She had melted away.

Perhaps she was a figment sent by Satan to tempt him. Perhaps she was an emissary from the Messiah. Either way, there was no sign of her.

Robert Buchan and the three children looked up from the table when Elspeth came into the room. She said nothing as she dropped her coat on the floor and went into the bedroom. Sighing, Robert left the table to pick up the discarded garment which he placed over the back of a chair. He had long given up trying to understand the woman who shared neither his bed nor his interests. His sole source of comfort remained his alchemist's dream of mixing a clay so transparent that the sun's rays would pass through it, and he would be a rich man.

A drop of ink fell onto the page as the nib circled above it, waiting for the first words to form in Elspeth's head. And then they came.

Glasgow, 17th January 1783
Dear Sir, whom I love in our sweet Lord Jesus.
I write to you as a friend. I have met with many disappointments from ministers who were neither strangers nor pilgrims on the earth, and I can say by sad experience that I have been more stumbled by ministers than by all the men in the world, or by all the devils in hell. On Saturday night when your discourse was ended, an acquaintance says to me – 'what do you think of Mr White?' I answered – 'What do you think of Jesus Christ?' for I have lost sight of the minister and myself...

Flattered and roused by the letter, Hugh White invited Elspeth to visit Irvine and stay with his family. White's wife, Margaret, pregnant with their second child, embraced Elspeth as she crossed the threshold in Seagate. She was still in denial about the scandals that had dogged their lives in America and precipitated their retreat across the Atlantic. She had ignored the women who turned up at their door claiming that her husband had fathered their children. They were frauds. Similarly, the rumours of financial mismanagement spread by those lesser mortals who made their parish a poisonous place. She had long grown used to her husband's fads and enthusiasms. Not an especially sensual creature, she had been happy enough to turn a blind eye to his philandering in America under the guise of 'escaping the tyranny of marriage'. She had herself enjoyed a brief dalliance with a baker from Boston before losing interest and reverting to a celibate life only temporarily compromised by her husband's need for a son. Nevertheless, she was soon wary of Elspeth who seemed to have bewitched her husband more than any of his other women. She watched them walking down the brae from the Relief Kirk to the river. She shook her head; he was at least ten years younger than his latest spiritual muse.

'It's not just the laws of marriage, ma'am, that stifle our flock,' said White, prudently removing his arm from Elspeth's waist as a parishioner passed by. 'It's the spurious notion of ownership. The idea that goods and chattels hewed from God's own earth should belong to the strongest and the loudest is beyond comprehension.'

They paused for a moment to watch a coracle struggle against the tide on the River Irvine. It seemed a metaphor for the challenges they would face together.

They lay that night on the truckle bed moved into the parlour. Margaret had not said a word. Their lovemaking alternated with enthusiastic recitation of biblical passages, each trying to outdo the other in a competition that successfully combined the carnal with the theological.

'Song of Solomon,' said White as he lay back, sated.

Elspeth rose to the challenge: 'Let him kiss me with the kisses of his mouth! For your love is better than wine… ' White cupped her breast. 'With great delight I sat in his shadow, and his fruit was sweet to my taste.'

'Is that why you bit me?' asked White.

'Your anointing oils are fragrant, your name is perfume, therefore the maidens love you.'

'All the maidens of Irvine love me,' said White. Elspeth squeezed his genitals. He lay his head between her breasts and counted his good fortune. Her visions of paradise were increasingly sensual. She spoke in tongues. In bed, she was gratifyingly demanding; her sexual appetite threatened to overwhelm them both.

'Oh, my America, my new found land… ' The rhythm of his words fitted the act perfectly. 'Shush,' he urged as she shouted out in passion. 'They will think the end of the world has come.'

'Perhaps it has,' she murmured. 'Perhaps it has.'

In the morning, as Margaret moved about the house, Elspeth propped herself up on one elbow and gently woke her new lover. 'You are my Manchild,' she said.

'What are you saying?'

'My Manchild. I understand it now. Listen to me. 'And she brought forth a Manchild who was to rule all nations with a rod of iron: and her child was caught up unto God, and to his throne."

'I've heard it called many things, but rod of iron... '

'This is not a jest. The passage has haunted me from my childhood. At the age of six, when toiling in the fields on a hot day, I heard those very words spoken from the clouds. The sky turned dark and the air was cold.'

White sat up and faced her.

'I was feart. What sin had I committed so great that Jehovah himself would speak to me from the heavens? I ran home, feart and shaking. The words stayed with me. I have aye known I was chosen for His work. I believed the Manchild so prophesied would come forth from my own loins. I would give birth to the Manchild. I had not understood the will of the Lord. He spoke in a riddle that only now reveals its meaning.'

After the service on the following Sabbath, Mary Bennet, a simple woman, broken by rheumatism and a drunken husband, reached out to Elspeth as she passed down the aisle. 'Let me touch you, mother,' she wailed. Elspeth paused, uncertain how to proceed. At her side, White nodded, as if giving her permission to pause while Mary pressed the hem of her coat to her lips. A rattling noise came from the old woman's throat as she sank back in a faint, into the arms of her fellow parishioners.

Details of Elspeth's intervention were greatly exaggerated. Mary was reportedly seen running from the kirkyard, kicking up her knees like a young foul; she was also reported to have been laughing, a phenomenon never before witnessed by her astonished friends and neighbours.

In response to endless requests, White convened a series of special 'diets of examination' during which Elspeth held court in the minister's front room while his wife dispensed monkey bread 'as favoured in Boston' and cups of elderflower cordial. As the moths threw themselves against the glass of the oil lamps, so Elspeth threw herself into theological debates.

'Do you believe that Enoch was translated that he might not see death?' asked a small, middle-aged man in a black frock coat whom nobody recognised. Impressed by the stranger's apparent erudition, the assembly murmured their approval.

'Not only Enoch, but Elijah too,' said Elspeth. 'Remember, he was taken into heaven by a whirlwind.'

'There's a mighty wind tonight, missus,' said Davy before he was shushed by those nearest and cuffed around the head by his mother.

'All who believe in Him and the true interpretation of His laws, uncorrupted by man, shall also enjoy a glorious Translation.'

This news was well received by all apart from the man in the frock coat who barged through the crowd and left, banging the door behind him.

My Lordships,

It is with heavy heart that I pen this epistle, but I must warn you that infamy and wickedness are come in our midst. Such calumnies against Christ our Redeemer cannot be tolerated. Your Lordships asked me to make a visitation to one of the services conducted by the Reverend Hugh White that I might bear witness to the heresies that spew from his mouth. I must inform your Lordships that the situation is worse than we feared: he has been joined by a female devil called — I can barely write her name lest my hand withers — Elspeth Buchan. A tall, some would say handsome, hussy, whose demeanour bewitches all who see her. The ignorant hang on her every word as she spouts Satan's own gospel. To compound matters, this harridan prefaces her sermons with 'O! O! O!' Her eyes become those of a basilisk, and the ignorant congregation all chant 'O! O! O!' It is a palpable nonsense. She claims that all who follow her will never die; they will be lifted into the heavens by the angels. Such heresy I have never heard. And yet she casts her cantrips on the simpletons who beg for a hair from her head that they might join her on her infernal journey. Like a travelling mountebank she produced a frog from a woman's ear, saying that her deafness was now cured; she seized the crutch from a cripple boy and bade him walk. And White, that deluded charlatan from the colonies, follows her like a salivating dog. I understand your Lordships will be astonished to read of these things. I would urge that as a matter of extreme urgency you scour this canker in our midst and ensure that both blasphemers are summoned before the presbytery. May God smite them! (and shine on your Good Selves!) Meanwhile I will continue to gather intelligence and report my findings to your Lordships as befits,

Your Humble Servant in Christ,

Alexander Gillespie.

The session was packed as it was common knowledge that charges of heresy were often brought to hide a variety of much more interesting transgressions. The loyal parishioners from Irvine had borrowed two hay carts and travelled east to lend their vociferous support to their traduced minister. Humphy Hunter, so named because of his deformity, waved a thick bundle of papers at the presiding officer. It was a technique that he frequently employed to great effect in his capacity as depute Town Clerk.

'Yer oot o' order, ye dinnae ken yer erse fae yer elbow! Who dae ye think ye are? Wi' yer fancy ways, stickin' snuff up yer neb sos ye cannae smell the common folk.'

Mrs Muir was dressed as the lady of the Manor, as well she might, given her occupation as a milliner with a considerable stock of dresses reserved for special occasions. One of the session lackeys placed a hand on each of her shoulders and pushed her back down into her seat.

'Get yer hauns aff o' me, ye servant o' Satan!'

Andrew Innes forced his way to the front and glared at the black-clad figures frowning back at him from behind a large oak desk. Elspeth had contacted her new acolyte and asked him if he would travel from Fife and provide her with a reliable account of the proceedings. He told her he would willingly travel to the ends of the earth, which he assured her were much further away than Glasgow, if that was her bidding.

In the early evening, Robert Buchan wearily opened the door, and having assumed it had been chapped by mischievous bairns who had then run away, looked down and saw Innes.

'They couldnae charge him with onything, just.... a troupe of ignorant weevils; a lair of hypercritical puddocks! They've barred him fae the pulpit for seventeen months. And he wi' a wife and bairns.' Elspeth thanked him, gave him a bun for his journey, patted him on the head and sent him on his way.

There was a finality about her next departure from Glasgow. Robert had thrown in the towel. His house was not his own. A constant stream of visitors trod their way upstairs hoping for an audience with the Lord Mother who always received them graciously. On one occasion, having made his way to the latrine during the night, he opened the door and disturbed a family of three who were sheltering there so that they could be the first to pay their respects in the morning. Robert stood, his breeches unlaced, 'Pray God, let this end,' he said before relieving himself in the yard.

The end came soon enough. Elspeth, singing hymns, swept her few belongings into a bag, kissed her children and placed her hand on the door. She paused, looked over her shoulder at Robert, shrugged and left.

Her return to Irvine created a commotion. News spread rapidly. Three of her more unhinged followers swept the path before her with rushes pulled from the riverbank. They were roundly abused by the townsfolk who watched the procession. She stood on the threshold of the Whites' house in Seagate and spoke to the small crowd. 'Let us celebrate the word of the Lord at eight o'clock tonight.'

Margaret, with a child hanging from her breast, looked at her with resignation before stepping aside to let her pass through. White, leaped from his seat and embraced her. 'Oh, Great Mother!' he declared.

'Manchild with the rod of iron,' she returned with a smile.

The house was not big enough to accommodate the throng, many of whom had to wait outside in the pouring rain while straining to hear the sacred truths being uttered inside. The air was rank with candle smoke, damp clothes and expectation.

As Elspeth spoke softly, the hard of hearing pushed their way to the front.

'Brothers and sisters in Christ, our time will come. We will leave this place and walk the earth until we find our Eden. The righteous will be free to live and love as He intended.' Her voice grew stronger, mesmeric. White stood at her side basking in the rapt adulation as if he, and not the Lord Mother, was the intended recipient.

Humphy Hunter was the first to succumb. Like an echo, he repeated her words: 'His will... blessed Translation... realms of pleasure.' The others followed suit until the babel was deafening; a cacophony of reprise and repetition which transmuted into hard, guttural sounds from another language. Incomprehensible words tumbled from many mouths. Jumbled phrases, imbued with the cadences of prayer, merged with cabalistic chants. Those outside pressed their faces against the windows in a dumb show of frustration. As rapture made its masterpiece in the room, the congregation swayed in unison. A plate fell to the floor and broke. The younger White child toddled into the room and grizzled, unable to find his parents. Mrs Muir fainted but was held upright by the crush of the others.

Eventually the spell was broken. An uneasy, embarrassed silence descended in the room. Murmuring their apologies, the worshipers nodded at White, bowed before Elspeth and took their leave.

White and Elspeth stood in silence at opposite sides of the room. He was the first to speak. 'What happened here?'

'I don't know.' She moved to White and held him close. 'We have been chosen,' she said.

'Ma'am, our destiny is being shaped.'

To accommodate the crowds that now regularly descended at dusk, White arranged for a tent to be erected in the garden. Several sails, purchased at no small expense from the chandlers, were spread over the repositioned drying poles. The expectant crowd crushed into the tent. However, having rained for two days without respite, the water collected in the sails which bulged downwards until the heads of the taller members of the flock touched the swollen cloth. Elspeth improvised and wove several homilies around appropriate biblical references. Once more, the old testament came to her rescue, 'Now Elijah, the Tishbite, said to Ahab, 'I serve the God of Israel, as surely as the Lord lives, no rain will fall unless I command it." Remarkably, and to the predictable astonishment of those assembled, the drumming on the roof ceased.

'Praise the Lord, praise the Lord!' shouted Humphy Hunter.

'Praise the Lord!' echoed Alexander Gillespie. A new convert, he had approached White after one of his sermons, declared his undying loyalty, and asked if he could throw in his lot with him and the Lord Mother. White had welcomed the stranger into the fold. He was clearly intelligent and could prove useful in the future. Elspeth was less certain. He had flinched when she first approached him and had a coughing fit when she attempted to blow into his mouth by way of initiation into the ranks of the saved. 'Give him time,' urged White. 'There is a natural reserve about the man. He has integrity.'

Again, rumours spread about witchcraft. There were reports of demonic and licentious practices. There was talk of wives refusing to honour their husbands once they returned home from a preaching.

The magistrates met secretly in a High Street tavern, discussing how best to quell the insurrection and discord in their midst. Alexander Gillespie left the company in no doubt. 'We must lance the boil; we must purge the puss from the brains of these cavorting hoors!' Intrigued, the landlady spent a little longer mopping the table than the task demanded.

Money changed hands as a suitable gang of ne'er-do-wells was recruited to disrupt proceedings in Seagate. The mob eagerly embraced its task. A ladder, requisitioned from a stone mason's yard, was used to access the roofs of adjacent properties. Half bricks, bottles and stones were arranged with military precision on the tiles. When the order to attack was issued, the barrage commenced. The shouts of praise mutated into screams as the tent ruptured and exposed the worshippers. Hugh White led the retreat, sheltering under a hefty Bible that deflected the heaviest of the missiles. The second offensive line had positioned itself overlooking the close that ran along the side of White's house.

These guardians of the moral law were armed with softer weapons: buckets of excrement, bovine, canine and human, which they gleefully tipped onto the howling procession below.

'Shit for shit! Pit some holy turds oon yer parritch!'

Elspeth was the last to leave, walking slowly in pursuit of the others, ignoring the taunts while calmly brushing the filth from her clothes.

It was Humphy Hunter who, several days after the commotion had subsided, nobly offered his own capacious dwelling in the Glasgow Vennel as an alternative, and more easily defended meeting place. Mrs Hunter, fearful for her husband's sanity, was less amenable to this arrangement and scowled as the entire ground floor of her house quickly filled with undesirables from the lower parts of the town. She at least recognised Hugh White and nodded a reluctant greeting as he crossed her threshold. She looked daggers at Elspeth who positioned herself next to the disgraced preacher.

After reading a passage from Revelations, Elspeth closed the holy book and stared in silence at her expectant congregation. 'O! O! O! Beloved friends, soon you must make a choice. You can continue in your old ways, enchained by the blasphemous tyranny of matrimony and by the love of earthly possessions, or... ' She paused for effect. 'Embrace a life of freedom and happiness. Those of you who renounce this human world and its manifold attachments in favour of the Lord will join me in rapture. We will inherit not the earth but heavenly realms. You will gaze on Christ's face when He chooses to lift us from this veil of tears. And you will not die. Death is the province of disbelievers. We will join hands at the appointed time and in the appointed place, many miles from here. You, with songs in your heart, will be raised by the angels; the world will never have witnessed such a Translation. As we ascend, all other eyes will be raised in disbelief, envy and wonder... '

'Envy and wonder.'

There will be the gnashing of teeth and wailing from those left behind to face the conflagration on their own. We will gaze down as flames from the east engulf these poisoned lands. The rank stench of burning will not reach us.'

'Will not reach us.'

'And we will know peace. We will know happiness.'

Aware that he might appear a peripheral figure to the crowded room, White raised Elspeth's hand as if she were a victorious prize fighter. 'Behold the third person of the trinity!'

There were gasps and cries from the congregation.

'Be not afraid, my children in Christ,' said Elspeth smiling. 'Those of you who wish to join me in this sacred covenant, step forwards.'

At first no-one moved, then Jean Gardner, a neighbour of White's, moved to the front and stood before Elspeth, head bowed and trembling.

'Open your mouth and receive the breath of Christ.' The young woman closed her eyes and opened her mouth as if to receive the sacrament. Elspeth stroked her convert's face, ran her finger over her lips and blew gently into her mouth. The others jostled to be the next to receive this intimate blessing. Men and women, young and old, were treated similarly. White was the last to step forward. She breathed in his mouth before moving her lips onto his.

'You are all now brothers and sisters in Christ. You must embrace each other. Husbands and wives, do not hold each other, remember our precepts. Our love is for all.'

Initially shy, the couples separated and found others in the group whom they held joyfully.

Emily Turnpike and Kitty Buckie, inseparable friends for over sixty years, clung to each other and waddled in a tight circle.

'Mair fun than sex,' said Emily.

'Ah'll tak your word for it,' said Kitty.

'You didnae ken ma William.'

'Well, only the once… ' said Kitty.

They cackled and embraced once more.

The evening meetings grew in popularity. The prospect of holding, and perhaps fondling whichever girl took their fancy was sufficient incentive for many of the young lads of the parish to endure strange speeches and blessings before they could get to grips with their loved ones. It was no surprise that the men employed scutching the flax in the heckling shed adjacent to Humphy Hunter's house were among the newest visitors. As they toiled through the night, they listened to the groans and gasps of delight emanating from their neighbour's house. 'That's yon minister gien a length tae one of they lassies,' said Rab.

'Na, it's God who's tickling their fancies.'

It was Rab, the youngest, constantly teased by the others because of his claims to be a poet, who first plucked up the courage to visit the group. After telling the others he was 'gain' for a piss,' he crossed the lane to the Hunter's cottage. If he stood on tiptoe and wiped the dust from the window, he might catch sight of Jean Gardner, the small, dark-haired lassie who had stolen his heart and roused his lust.

'Oh she was fair. At kirk or market to be seen, When a' our fairest maids were met, The fairest maid was bonnie Jean.' Blushing, he handed over the poem. 'It's no finished,' he stammered. She smoothed the paper with her hand and smiled at the gawky youth, smelling of flax, who, when he should have been praying, just stared at her. She knew that when the time came for the embracing, he would be the first to wrap her in his arms. She liked him, but she was not ready for courting.

Among the new recruits were Alan, a gangly lad who was apprenticed to a dry stane dyker employed to enclose the Dreghorn road, and Elizabeth, only daughter of the McKenzies who owned the big estate. Rumour had it that, on discovering his daughter in flagrante with Alan, the laird horsewhipped the boy, then forced his head into the ditch to dissuade him from ever returning. Here they were safe. Despite her preference that couples should separate during the blessing, Elspeth made an exception with Alan and Elizabeth. When they finally drew breath after a prolonged embrace, she moved towards them. They both looked at the carpet, embarrassed. 'Feel no shame,' she said. 'When they enjoyed God's favour, our forebears in the garden felt no need to hide their nakedness.' Alan glanced down nervously lest he had suddenly become naked. 'They revelled in the sun beneath the trees heavy with fruit, and worshipped Our Saviour with their hearts, minds and bodies. Do the same and be free.' Elizabeth caught Alan's eye, smiled briefly then looked away.

They were not the only lovers who were welcomed into the Hunter's front room by the Lord Mother. Initially, Agnes and Ann had pretended to be sisters when they arrived from Kilmarnock to raise goats on the edge of Irvine. The Reverend Flockhart, the minister of the free kirk, loudly voiced his misgivings. 'In our midst are living the false sisters,' he declared from the pulpit after a particularly insipid sermon. For the first time in three hours he could feel that the audience was listening to him. 'Harlots, flaunting God's immutable laws in this very parish, whores of Satan.' Yes, he had their attention now. 'Foul perpetrators of unnatural acts, eschewing the male member in favour of... ' He had no idea how to finish the sentence on which he had embarked, much to the annoyance of his now, exceedingly alert congregation.

'Welcome both,' said Elspeth, kissing one then the other. 'Here we love our neighbours better than we love ourselves. Welcome.'

The magistrate's first attempt at intimidating the Buchanites, as they now called themselves, had failed. They needed men not boys to do their bidding. Fortunately, the town was awash with idle sailors who, having been plied with ale, were encouraged to abuse and pinch the arses of anyone attempting to enter the Hunter house. One of them was heard to declare that this was by far the best employ he had ever known.

Elspeth stood at the door and checked that every member of her flock was unharmed as they entered. If they were bleeding from a well-aimed stone, she would staunch their wounds.

A small man, clutching a bag as big as himself, crossed the threshold, rubbing his head.

'Andrew,' she said. 'You have returned.'

'Aye, Mother. The Lord has directed my feet tae this place.' She lifted Innes from the ground and hugged him before finding him a seat in the front row so that his view of the proceedings wouldn't be obscured by the taller members of the congregation.

Andrew Innes had little time to bask in the friendship and welcome afforded to him by the Lord Mother. Unbeknown to him, his real mother, on learning that her son had been bewitched by the mad woman from Irvine, had left Muthill and set out in pursuit. She burst into the room.

'Ye feckless wee man... ye hondless cretin wi' no a brain in your heid.' The others watched as the large woman berated her son, who cowered under the onslaught. 'And as for the rest of you...' she turned her attention on those who were looking sympathetically at Andrew. 'No a brain amang you. All sleeping thegether in a nest of sin and wickedness. Corrupting ma puir laddie wi' all yer nonsense. May you all roast in the darkest pit of hell.' She turned towards Elspeth. 'Ah, if it isnae the deil's ain concubine...' Elspeth paused in her recitation of a particularly ecstatic passage from the book she was compiling with Hugh White with the working title, *The Divine Dictionary*. Mrs Innes waved her fist at White who assumed the air of someone who was not easily intimidated by an escaped lunatic from Fife. At that moment, a brick shattered the window.

Chapter Thirteen

THE BROTHERS' TALE
Greenock

The brothers had been taken, along with twelve others, back to the port that had been their home. The prisoners, chained together, were marched to the edge of the wooden dock, slippery from spillages. Two of the men operating the winch recognised the brothers but knew better than to interfere: the guard, armed with cudgel and musket, might welcome an excuse to swell the numbers already pressed into the service of His Majesty's fleet. As there was no sign of the skiff to take them to HMS Hercules waiting beyond the mist, the men were given permission to sit. The brothers slouched despondently against each other and listened to the tide lapping against the pillars. As the sun burned through the heat, the captives visibly wilted.

'All will be well,' said Mathew inserting a finger between the tender flesh of his ankle and the manacle.

'Aye, mebbe,' said James who had been enjoying his fantasy of Elspeth emerging from nowhere to seduce each of the guards in turn, so distracting them from their duties.

Mathew noticed that the man to whom he was also chained was sobbing. He wasn't really a man, more a boy, prematurely grown. His young face was creased with tears. Mathew, struggling to summon any words of comfort, squeezed the boy's forearm. 'At least they'll feed us,' he said. 'And it's no a bad life in the navy, so I hear.' James grunted ironically, and the boy's sobbing grew louder. As the heat was oppressive, the guards removed their hats and used them to fan themselves. When word arrived from the harbour master that their wait would be protracted, they muttered briefly before deciding to secure their charges while they visited the tavern. Despite their protests, the men were chained in a tight circle around the metal pole used to tether the larger vessels.

'It's a fuckin' totem pole,' said a man marked with scrofula. His less well travelled companions looked at him quizzically. 'And ah need a pish.' He unbuttoned his breeches and urinated onto the pole, splashing those nearest to him.

'For Christ's sake!'

James noticed that all the guards, save one, had slouched towards the tavern.

'We need to bring him closer,' said Mathew.

As if on cue, his brother started to convulse like a demented puppet. As his arms jerked as far as the chains would permit, he involved the others in an involuntary wave of movement. As he shook and writhed, he emitted demonic sounds. Alerted by the unearthly noise, the guard approached, holding his musket by the barrel. As he came close with his weapon raised to deliver a crushing blow, Mathew jerked his elbow into the guard's stomach. He groaned, dropped his musket and was quickly overpowered by the frenzied circle. Mathew removed the key from the man's belt and after releasing himself, did the same for the others. Rubbing their ankles, the men glanced at the prostrate guard. Four of them took a limb each and after swinging their human ballast until they had both rhythm and momentum, hurled him over the edge and into the water. One of them threw his musket after him. 'Shoot some fishes for yer supper.'

The prisoners scattered in all directions to the delight of the winch operator who applauded their escape.

'All will be well,' said James.

Chapter Fourteen

THE ATTACK

The twilight attack was well coordinated. A local reprobate who had been drummed out of the dragoons for drunkenness and indecent practices took it on himself to coordinate the others. When he gave the order, the drink-addled recruits released a salvo of bricks. In an instant, the windows were broken. The wind gusted into the room and snuffed out the candles, leaving clumps of acrid smoke. The Lord Mother stood still and composed, emitting a high-pitched hum inaudible in the chaos. Several of the worshippers, wrenched from their intense contemplation of God's mercies and His tolerance of fornication, screamed and fell over in their rush to escape. Agnes and Ann clung to each other; Andrew Innes hugged his mother; Hugh White fled into the back room; Rab climbed out of a window and returned to the sanctuary of the huckling shed; Humphy Hunter wrapped his sleeve around a shard of glass and led the counterattack.

'Let's be having ye, lackeys o' Satan, lickspittle turds…   ' His invective was curtailed by a well-aimed punch in the mouth. As the mob were wielding cudgels, the Buchanites were easily overpowered. Davy McConville, the Irvine blacksmith and a colossus of a man, who had fallen deeply asleep during an earlier theological discourse between Mother Buchan and White, roused himself and gradually assimilated the scene playing out before his eyes. Grunting, he strode towards Elspeth whom he grabbed round the middle, tucked under his arm as if she were a milk churn, and barged his way through the mob and out into the street. A late recruit to the riot, having stepped into a doorway for a drink, saw his chance, stuck out his leg and tripped Davy and his prize. Elspeth was still sprawled, groping her way in the mud when the mob caught up with her.

'Hang the hoor!'

'Tak oot her eyes and flail the ugly skin fae her body.'

'Get the kindling and burn the witch. Mak her flesh melt and drip into the flames.'

Droun her in the river, gie her a good ducking.'

'Gie her a good seeing to first.'

Inspired by this last exhortation, one of the younger lads tore at her bodice. Elspeth stumbled back onto her feet, hiding her nakedness as best she could. The carnival procession grew as the shopkeepers abandoned their wares and joined in the excitement. Infants were dragged along by their mothers, eager to embrace this respite from their chores; the old men loitering outside the tavern hobbled as fast as they could so as not to be left behind. The flesher on Seagate had the foresight to bring along a tray of offal which the youths threw at their victim. One of them sunk his hands up to the wrists in the lights and livers before catching up with Elspeth and smearing the entrails on her face.

Distracted by the furore, the tinker had failed to notice a light-fingered lad removing a kettle from his pack. The thief ran to the front of the mob where he assumed the role of drummer boy, leading the unruly regiment collectively intent on disembowelling the blasphemer in their midst.

Jeering and taunting, the mob kicked Elspeth whenever she faltered. Still walking with her head held high, she stared though unseeing eyes at the road ahead. After all, this had been foretold. It was her destiny. 'Beware of men, for they will hand you over to the courts and scourge you... Then they will deliver you to tribulation, and will kill you, and ye shall be hated by all nations because of My name... '

There was some debate within the mob about the wisdom of killing Elspeth, whether in His name or not. Although the magistrates wanted rid of her, there was no guarantee that her killers would be treated with leniency. But they would have their sport with her.

The miller from Auchendells, who spent his days hoisting sacks of flour onto wagons, lifted Elspeth bodily from the ground and flung her into the air. 'Let's see if ye can flee to heaven! Up you go lassie, say good day from me to that God of yours.' She fell heavily, much to the delight of the crowd who insisted that he try again. This he did many times until his strength gave out.

Farmers came to their doors to gawk at the procession, labourers left off milking to see what was happening, and the bedridden strained to see who or what was passing by their doors. Several dogs happily attached themselves to the group.

As they neared Stewarton Bridge the clamour grew for her to be tossed into the river. Surely the authorities could be persuaded that it was the devil himself who ordered Mrs Buchan to plunge headfirst from the parapet and dash her brains on the rocks below.

Hugh White, who had been following the crowd at a safe distance, almost intervened at this point but his courage failed him, and he sank back into the throng baying for her blood.

Torch flames danced on the faces of the mob, picking out angry eyes, and spittle-flecked mouths. The drumbeat became louder and faster, moving inexorably to a climax that boded ill for Elspeth.

'Hang her! Hang her! Hang her!'

The crowd had swelled, forcing those on the edges into the ditch. As they approached the prow of the hill, a strong gust of wind snuffed out the torches. The air was rent with cries of frustration as the mob floundered in darkness and confusion.

'Christ Almichty, ah' cannae see!'

'The deil's poked his finger in my een!'

Elspeth, felled in the crush, crawled through the sea of legs until she tumbled into a ditch at the side of the road. From there she pulled herself into the adjacent field.

The mob became subdued. Something had happened. The mood changed from one of righteous anger and bloody revenge to one of fear. Like children lost in a wood, they held onto one another. Had Satan saved the witch by plucking her from their midst? Was the Prince of Darkness still among them, eager to torment and kill them also?

'There's a reek o' sulphur!' shouted a petrified woman. The cry was taken up by the others. Now panicking, they rushed blindly down the road back towards Irvine. Hugh White, who had kept his distance, chose his moment to infiltrate the retreating army which eventually slowed as the frailer succumbed to exhaustion.

There were beasts in the field. Elspeth heard their lowing and moved towards them. She still had an infinity with cattle and leaned heavily against the hot flank of the nearest animal. The others moved closer until she was supported by them. As the moon made an appearance through a gap in the clouds, she saw their misty breath and felt their comfort.

She moved down the slope towards the copse that hid the burn. Her progress was slow as she was snarled by thickets and pierced with thorns. The branches tore at her clothes and ripped what remnants of clothing remained on her back. She caught her foot in the root of a tree and fell heavily. She slumped against the trunk and closed her eyes. The visions possessed her.

The devil was sitting on a rock tearing pages from the Bible. He then tore each page into strips and shreds that he dropped into the burn. As the holy words floated downstream they reconfigured themselves into blasphemous sentences full of death and horror. Hugh White appeared, priapic, hands on hips, flaunting his nakedness at her. She saw her children, holding hands and weeping as they walked away from her down an endless road until they grew tiny and disappeared into an insinuating cloud of dust. Robert was sitting at his wheel on which she spun like a lump of clay that he shaped and raised with his fingers. Wet and slippery, the pot rose between his palms until it folded in on itself and collapsed. He swept the clay onto the spoil pile and wiped his hands on a cloth. Tired of casting sentences onto the water, Satan approached, held her jaw and blew his stinking breath into her mouth. She was choking, suffocating in the foulness.

Shivering, she opened her eyes. The first rays of dawn picked out the ripples on the burn. The leaves on a thin branch, swaying next to her, were heavy with dew; minute perfectly formed droplets balanced on the purest of green. She rubbed her elbow, sore from where she had fallen and breathed in the scents of musk and ripeness from the vegetation. She revelled in the songs of the birds welcoming the new, fresh day. She was alive, she had survived. She had work to do.

Many of the Buchanites returned to Hunter's front room, where his wife, despite her anger at Humphy for welcoming them to her house, offered comfort to the exhausted followers. All eyes were on White when he came through the door in the early hours.

'What news?' asked Andrew Innes.

'Great joy has come amongst us,' proclaimed White embracing Mrs Hunter. The others roused themselves and listened intently. 'Mother Buchan has risen!' Mrs Innes spat into the hearth.

White knew that this was a slightly dangerous gambit, but he had already hatched a contingency plan should events prove him wrong. 'The Lord rescued her from the pernicious mob, He reached down from the dark clouds and took up His daughter.'

'God be praised!'

'Hallelujah!' Agnes and Ann danced a jig together, knocking over several cups. Andrew Innes ran on the spot like an excited toddler, until his mother stepped forward and slapped him. The others hugged each other and wept with joy.

When Elspeth appeared in the doorway the mood of rejoicing had mellowed into one of quiet reflection. Those nearest stepped back in awe. Had the Lord Mother returned to collect her followers? Had she had a quick word with God and then taken her leave again? Alan and Elizabeth held hands tightly so that they would not be separated at the point of Translation. Otherwise, they might have to wander through God's many mansions looking for each other.

As the morning light filtered into the room, Elspeth stood tall before them, bruised and bloodied, her torn clothes barely covering her breasts. Seeing her condition, Davy McConville decided that being dragged through the clouds by muscular angels must be more painful than he had thought.

Although disconcerted, this was the moment that White had prepared for. In any case, his plans to become the leader on earth of his new movement were not yet fully formed. He threw himself on his knees, 'Oh great merciful God,' he proclaimed. 'You, in your infinite mercy, have returned the Lord Mother to us. Her work is not yet done.'

'Did you see my William?' asked Emily before Kitty poked her in the ribs.

Elspeth accepted a drink from Mrs Gibson. She was shaking, wishing that God had left her alone and not chosen her for His purposes. White took advantage of her vulnerability and claimed the moral high ground. 'We must protect this wonderful woman in our midst; we must give her our strength. We must prevail against the forces of darkness. Tomorrow belongs to us!' Mrs Innes shook her head and left to retrieve her belongings. Wee Andra could rot in the pit of hell for all she cared.

Several days later Hugh White and Elspeth Buchan wandered through the graveyard of the Old Kirk. They had been observed by Luckie Minnie, the parish simpleton who, ignoring White's attempts to shoo her away, approached Elspeth and pinched her cheek. Shaking her head in disappointment, Luckie ran back shrieking through the overgrown graves. Elspeth shrugged and picked at the moss on a particularly illegible inscription.

'If John, faithful husband of Agnes, loving father of David, Sarah, George and Helen had lived well and loved where his heart had led him, he would not now be lying under this stone. If he had grasped the gift of life with both hands, he would not have had it snatched from him by frailty and disease. If he had not married Agnes, if he had not gathered his goods and children about him like a miser, he would have inherited the earth; he would have been taken whole into Christ's sacred realm. As will be our fate.'

White looked at her and shielded his eyes. Against the strong sun he could not make out her features, he could only see the aura that clung to her silhouette. 'The woman clothed with the sun,' he murmured.

My Lordships,

Please accept my apologies for the illegible nature of this epistle. My hand shakes as it prepares to summon the words to adequately describe the depravity I have witnessed with my own eyes. Despite your Lordships' best efforts to confound the wicked heretics and drive them from the Reverend White's abode, they were offered sanctuary by Patrick Hunter, a humpy-backed toad of a man whose deformity can be attributed to his carrying the devil on his back. In that very house I witnessed scenes of carnal turpitude that beggar description. In short, I saw women kissing women. I realise your Lordships may have never heard of such an abominable practice. But worse is to follow: Elspeth Buchan, (May God forgive me for mentioning her name), went among the men encouraging them to take out their pintles and wander through the room like wanton satyrs. All this in the name of a pagan God who deplores the sacred bonds of matrimony. Their lust sated, the pernicious company came together to worship (I assure your Lordships I took no part in the proceedings despite the unwanted attention from several of the women present). This diabolic prayer consisted of incomprehensible words which they uttered in a trance-like state. I sat to one side and with pen and ink captured the exact sounds emanating from the deranged worshippers which I now transcribe for the benefit of verisimilitude.

Bobobobobo, ah ah ah ah yoki yoki yoki, canha canha canha bobo bobo yik hor gug jug jug…

(at this point Buchan and White engaged in the foulest of embraces)

… modi modi modi…

There was much more of this ilk but I have no wish to try your Lordships' patience.

I commend your Lordships for the prompt action that saw Satan's own mother pursued as far as the Stewarton Bridge. However, with heavy heart I must report that she was aided and abetted by the forces of darkness to escape the clutches of the law and reappeared by some demonic sleight of hand at the Hunters' house once more.

Rest assured, I will leave no stone unturned in my attempts to scour this vile abomination from our midst. Your Lordships will be gratified to hear that I have assumed the cloak of a Buchanite that I might gain more intelligence.

May the Good Lord above guide my steps.

I await further instructions,

Your servant,

Alexander Gillespie.

Chapter Fifteen

THE EXODUS

Elspeth told Andrew Innes to spread the word. The sacred hour had arrived for their departure from Irvine. They must travel the earth until they found the sacred place chosen by God for their glorious Translation into His kingdom.

Katie Gardner was among the first to arrive. She looked for Jean, her older sister, who had told her that she just wanted to see her poet for one last time. The two girls were markedly different in temperament. Jean was vivacious and handsome, while Katie was shy and, in the eyes of some, ill-featured by comparison. Having spent all eighteen years of her life in her sister's shadow, Katie was secretly hoping that she would not have to share this, the greatest adventure of all, with her sibling.

In fact Jean and Rab had been enjoying a quiet moment on the banks of the Irvine, poignant with the sweet pain of parting.

'Fare thee weel, thou first and fairest!

Fare thee weel, thou best and dearest!

Thine be ilka joy and… '

Rab slapped his pockets. Where had he put his commonplace book? 'Treasure,' he said, scribbling the words in the margin of a new page. Jean looked at this earnest young man who had offered to marry her if she stayed.

'I'll maybe bide a bit longer,' she said taking the book out of his hand and kissing him. The pilgrimage to heaven could wait.

Mrs Muir was the next to arrive, having finally closed her drapery shop. Because of unwanted attention from the town's self-appointed vigilantes, she had not sold so much as a handkerchief for a month. Stepping out of her shop, she had skidded on a shit left on her doorstep and decided, there and then, that she would move to her sisters in Kilwinning. She was struggling to load her three remaining bales of muslin onto a rented cart when word reached her that Mistress Buchan had summoned her followers. Joyfully, she pulled on the reins and propelled the old nag towards Seagate.

Humphy Hunter was anxious as his wife was nowhere to be found. They had endured many challenges over the years: bankruptcy, stillbirths, accusations of a rigged election, and he wanted them to face this new one together. Apart from anything else, he had been relieved of his duties as depute Town Clerk and felt that he owed the town nothing.

Many of the unruly youths of Irvine and the surrounding district were also in attendance. Their motivation was less the lure of being bodily grabbed into heaven than a continuance of the excitement they experienced in the company of the mad woman. Endless skirmishes with the neighbours, fist fights with the law keepers, and joyous, sensual trysts with whomever their hearts desired were not pleasures to be surrendered on a whim.

Elspeth addressed the crowded room. 'Brethren, dear friends, loyal servants, the time has arrived when we must leave this place and follow the word of Christ our Saviour. We must be strong. We will endure vicissitudes. We must cross the wilderness until we find the place and time of our glorious Translation... '

Andrew Innes was spread-eagled against the door when it was forced open by the constables who had accompanied the magistrate.

'Elspeth Buchan, it being the 1st May 1784, you are hereby... '

But she wasn't listening. She bid several quick farewells to her tearful followers, and willingly surrendered herself to the nearest constable whom she remembered from an earlier affray at the Hunters' house.

'We're no leaving you, Mother,' said Mrs Gibson marching behind Elspeth. Declaiming their undying loyalty, the others fell in behind and tumbled into the street. As it was Cow Fair day, they made little progress. A herd of bellowing cattle was blocking the path. The spooked animals strained and moaned as they were funnelled down Bridgegate. The youngest of the White's children fell under the hooves of a bullock before being plucked to safety. One of the many drunks, sensing sport, barged into the Lord Mother and sent her sprawling across the back of a frightened beast. She was lifted to her feet by Ann and Agnes, late arrivals to the commotion. Now in the middle of a small stampede, the

Buchanites were tossed onto the Porthead cobbles and held onto each other as best they could. The constables, assiduous in the pursuit of their duty, used their night sticks to prod the Buchanites towards the Kilmarnock road.

'Get tae fuck!' said Tam, a passing drunk who had been caught up in the crowd.

Elspeth turned to speak to her man handler whose face was inches from hers. For a moment it looked as if he was going to kiss her. Instead, he gleefully bit her cheek, a gesture seen and appreciated by his fellow upholders of the law. As they turned the corner, the flesher at his stall raised his cleaver and waved it above the frightened band of men, women and children.

'Butcher them! Butcher them! Cut off their ears and gie them to the dugs!'

'Gie us a slice of yon fat buttock. It'll feed ma weans for weeks.'

An urchin tugged at Elspeth's bonnet until the tightening strings were about to slice her head from her shoulders.

Clutching her throat and struggling for breath, Elspeth looked in vain for White who was nowhere to be seen.

After punching, kicking and abusing the stragglers as they staggered the first mile out of the town, the mob tired. Although still jeering and gesturing, they forsook the chase and returned to the day's main business which they had to admit, had got off to a fine start.

The band of a dozen or so Buchanites lay exhausted on the edges of the field. No-one spoke. Bruises were probed, and distressed children reassured. Elspeth lay back and stared at the sky. In that instant, she saw a face in the clouds: a huge, radiant, triumphant face. She rose unsteadily to her knees. 'The Lord God is smiling at us,' she declared pointing upwards. The others followed the direction of her arm but struggled to see anything of note, apart from two rooks floating on the current.

A distressed woman ran up the lane towards them. 'You've taken my son,' she mouthed, completely out of breath. Ann and Agnes recognised Mrs Galt, a neighbour. At that moment, a small boy emerged from behind a tree, rubbing his eyes.

'John, John,' said his relieved mother who shot a last venomous look at the Buchanites, and with her arm tightly round her son, steered him back towards the town.

They first heard, then saw, several small handcarts being pushed over the brow of the hill. Any fears that their attackers were returning were soon allayed by the sound of hymn singing.

'Though many do press us,
We ne'er look about:
Though Satan distress us,
We still keep our rout.'

Elspeth recognised the tune as the one to which White attached whatever words seemed apposite at any given time. She knew that her Manchild would not forsake her. The reinforcements were led by Mrs Hunter who had been visiting her sister-in-law in the next village. On her return she initially assumed that Elspeth and her followers had been lifted bodily into the heaven of which she frequently spoke. After picking up the chairs that littered their front room, she spoke to a neighbour who pointed out the direction of the Buchanites' departure. Others too had missed the great event and begged Mrs Hunter to lead them to the Lord Mother.

As she closed her front door for the last time, she was approached by a dishevelled man who pushed three children in her direction. 'Take them,' he said. 'They won't bide with me. They miss their mother.' With that Robert Buchan turned and left.

Elspeth was surprised to see her children and welcomed them uncertainly.

The new arrivals rushed forward to embrace the Lord Mother and declare their unqualified devotion. White, who was pleased to see some of Irvine's more wealthy residents among the newcomers, was less than delighted to recognise two of Andrew Innes' siblings. One member of the family was more than enough.

White took charge of the situation. After a brief word with Elspeth, who was plainly exhausted, he addressed the assembly. 'Brethren,' he said, 'I've spoken to the Lord Mother, and it is our wish that we move towards the east, the direction that the prophets and Christ himself, chose when cast in the wilderness.'

The two score or so of adherents cheered, shouted several hallelujahs and resolutely marched towards Dreghorn, and from there towards Dundonald.

The sun shone, and the larks soared. When the younger children tired, they were helped onto one of the handcarts. Labourers paused in the fields and leant on their scythes to watch the rag-taggle army wind its way through the byways in the afternoon heat. At each hamlet, doors opened, and the locals gawked. Some offered bread and water, some offered insults. Three young women emerged from a byre and bared their backsides at the convoy before running away shrieking with delight. A shrivelled minister stood at the door of his kirk, fulminating as they passed. He pointed a bony finger at the Lord Mother. Elspeth turned to look at him whereupon he clutched his chest and staggered against a gravestone.

Feeling inspired, White improvised a hymn incorporating several incoherent references to a rod of iron and the evils of matrimony. The youngest Gibson child, riding on the broad shoulders of Davy McConville, clutched at thin air in a vain attempt to capture an elusive dragonfly. 'It's a wee angel,' he said.

'A bit like yoursel' then,' said the blacksmith.

Ann and Agnes held hands tighter and tighter as they wordlessly communicated the sheer joy they felt at the prospect of being together for all eternity. This was an adventure like no other. The pilgrims were joined by various farmyard dogs, and at one point by a piglet which Amy Johnson tucked under her arm and stowed under a blanket in her cart when nobody was watching.

A mad woman emerged from a wayside hovel, clawed at the flowers growing at the roadside and, cackling as she held up her skirt, thrust the blossoms into Elspeth's arms. 'Flooers for a queen.' Elspeth acknowledged the gesture graciously then moved down the procession, giving one to each of her followers, braiding a single foxglove through Emily's hair, then putting a bluebell behind Alan's ear and kissing him on the cheek much to the delight of Elizabeth who held his hand even tighter.

As night fell, the company marched through the darkness towards whatever destiny awaited them. They had their faith to light their way, and the Lord Mother was their guide. Despite their enthusiasm, several of the older Buchanites were limping and their pace slowed. At Elspeth's bidding, Humphy Hunter took a lantern and wandered into the adjacent fields until he found a sheltered spot where they could rest. White too was done with walking and wanted to be alone with Elspeth.

Ignoring his entreaties to follow him, Elspeth sat on a large rock with her skirt up to her knees, took out her pipe and tapped the bowl into the palm of her other hand. She held up the thin white pipe until she caught Innes' attention. He ran towards her and fumbled in his bag for the twist of Lurgan that he knew was his mistress's favourite. He took pride in his appointment as unofficial tobacco carrier and always had the tinderbox at hand.

Before the Buchanites settled down for the night, White stood in their midst, waited in vain for complete silence and then, despite being largely ignored, led them in an improvised hymn.

Alexander Gillespie begged a candle that he might transcribe the inspired words from White's latest composition for the benefit of posterity.

'No again,' muttered Kitty whose rheumatism had not been improved by a hard day's walking.

'Stick yer fingers in yer lugs' whispered Emily who was already following her own advice.

The younger of the Gibson children howled. His mother clipped his ears, making him cry louder. White abandoned the hymn in mid verse and scowled at the ingrates who surrounded him. Apart from any other consideration, his inspiration had failed to supply him with a phrase to rhyme with 'sacred mission'.

Elspeth moved among her sleepy followers with a word of encouragement for each of them.

'This day was foretold... ' She hugged both Ann and Agnes.

'His will is our will... ' She touched the face of a man she did not recognise. Wincing at his breath, she remembered that it was Tam, the town drunkard who had unwittingly joined the exodus.

As the dawn crept over the fields, the Wifies shared their dreams. Emily had been reunited with William; she had returned home to find him waiting for her in his favourite chair. Kitty had been a young girl again learning her letters.

Something was happening. The Lord Mother was running through the early morning mist flapping her hands at the corbies swooping down on her. One of them hovered briefly above her head then darted towards her face. She shielded herself with her arm until the creature squawked and rose. Eventually the birds spied a dead sheep near a copse and flew away to circle it instead. By now most of the group had wandered towards the source of the commotion and waited for the Lord Mother to speak to them of crows and God's wishes. They were not disappointed.

'Brothers and sisters. We are the enemies of death. Satan, smarting in his sulphury lair, has sent his familiars to peck out the eyes of faith. But it is he who shall be blinded by the bright flame of our mission. We will never know death, not like the wicked blasphemers squirming in their apostasy.' She clenched her fist for emphasis, and those nearest to her shrank back lest they, and not the unbelievers, were about to feel the full weight of her righteous anger.

'Praise be to the Lord Mother!' declared White as he approached her with his arms outstretched. The others followed suit, a phalanx of guardians saluting and protecting their prophetess.

Striding to the head of the group, Elspeth, despite her call to arms against Satan, still flapped intermittently at non-existent crows. Her brain was addled by apocalyptic visions. The crows were sucking the life out of her brain, filling it with a dark broth of beak, feathers and eyes. The birds started devouring each other, ripping at bone and black flesh, thin scaly legs flailed, obscuring her sight.

Maggie, older than her ten years, and long attuned to detecting these changes in her mother, moved to the front of the group.

'Mother, are you no weil? Will I hold you for a while?' At first Elspeth resisted her daughter's approach but then let herself be wrapped in her arms. She continued to walk.

'It will pass,' she said. 'In God's good time.'

'Mother, you need to rest. Let's return to Glasgow, faither will take you back. The others will understand. They will wait for you.'

Elspeth broke away from her daughter. 'It is my destiny. I'll no fight it.'

Her daughter's words haunted her as Satan changed tack and smothered her in the warm cloak of nostalgia and remorse. She remembered the snuggle of Robert's body as they made plans and laughed together about his fellow potters at the Broomielaw. She remembered his magical tales of mermaids; she could smell his sweet breath as he whispered endearments. 'No!' she shouted, shaking herself like a dog emerging from a pond. 'Be gone, phantoms!'

Recognising that things were amiss with the Lord Mother, White approached her, making soothing noises and offering her water.

'Sometimes,' she said, 'the deil attacks me when I am least expecting him. It is the price I pay. If he can turn me from the road of human happiness, then I will become no better than the others. If I embrace misery, then I too will be claimed by death.'

White placed his arm around her. His concern however was far from altruistic. At this stage on his spiritual odyssey, he needed Elspeth to be strong. He knew that in the fullness of time it was his destiny to succeed her and assume her raiment of divinity. But not yet.

The prospect of another day's wandering did very little to improve the spirits of the group. Margaret White started a desultory hymn that soon died on the lips of communal exhaustion. The Hunter and Gibson children were grizzling and hungry. Some of the group shared doubts about the haste with which they had departed from Irvine.

'I left the broth on the stove,' said Kitty. 'The whole hoose will ha' burned doon by now.'

'I didnae feed the coo,' said Emily. 'Poor critter will soon be deid.'

'I didnae lock the door.'

'Dinna fass yersel, ye've naething worth stealin.'

'I have so.'

'Whit?'

'Ma jewels.'

'Whit jewels?'

'Ah'm no tellin' ye, Emily Turnpike. Ye'll pockle them yoursel' if you ken aboot them.'

Elspeth summoned the energy to rally her followers. She placed her hands lightly on each of them in turn. 'Soon, we will leave this veil of tears and be free. Soon, we will see the angels who have been watching us on every step of our journey. You may have heard them... '

'I heard one the other day, Mistress, down by the... ' The older Gibson child received a clip on the ear from whoever was standing closest.

'They watch our every step; they are beautiful beyond imagining.'

Tam made a mental note to be on the lookout for these fine sounding creatures.

'They watch us when we sleep.' Agnes glanced at Ann and smiled. 'They hold us when we lean into the brook to wash our faces. Sometimes you may glimpse their smiles in the water. They hold our hearts when they are heavy, they gather our sighs when we are downcast. At dawn, you can catch the scent of their breath mingled with the new day as they spread the dew before us.'

The group swayed in rapture.

'O! O! O! We must be ready. We must be vigilant for that precious moment when they wrap us in their wings and stroke our faces with their soft down. And when the trumpet sounds – Oh how we wish for that celestial sound – they will lift us through the clouds of this troubled world into the realm of our glorious father.'

Several of her audience looked upwards for any hint of angels descending, a stray feather perhaps or an angelic foot poking through the clouds. 'And now the blessing.' All eyes returned to Elspeth who had already moved towards White. 'Embrace not the person of whom your heart is most fond, but someone you do not yet know well. God does not want our love to be confined in narrow bonds. We must shake free from the yoke of attachment.'

Agnes and Ann separated from each other only reluctantly.

An outdoor blessing was something of a novelty but one that was universally welcomed. Andrew Innes made a beeline for Katie Gardner, who, although not best pleased to be his chosen one, acquiesced to the extent of removing his hat and kissing him on the top of his head. Andrew purred with delight. Emily, who now realised that Davy McConville reminded her of her dead husband, let him hoist her up in his blacksmith's arms. He lifted her off the ground with consummate ease, prompting the hope that if her good fortune held, this wonderful man might soon be her guardian angel in the life to come.

Amy Johnson had fallen for the mysterious Alexander Gillespie. She was attracted by his quiet demeanour and his erudition. He had recently shared with her a lewd poem he had penned in an idle moment. Emboldened, she approached him and kissed him lightly on the lips.

White felt inspired; he felt on fire with the rapture that filled his heart, but he must direct their attention back to himself – their true leader. He would use all his old Shaker tricks: pregnant pauses, repetition, and wait for that blissful moment when the words would flow unbidden from his mouth and the more vulnerable women in the company would swoon before the torrent of his holy wisdom. Elspeth too would be in awe of her Manchild who would rule with a rod of iron. And she would show her appreciation later that night when he wrapped her in his arms.

'Those of you who do not bow to her oracles will be destroyed in the ferocious fires that will engulf you all.'

There were grumblings of discontent as the Buchanites reluctantly disentangled themselves from whatever pleasing embrace they had chosen. They didn't need to be preached at, at least not now. They just wanted a little longer to fondle their new partners.

'Follow the old ways and feel the bitter taste of death on your tongue.' He let the last phrase hang in the air for effect. One of the younger men idly licked his teeth, and wondered what death tasted like. He had, for a wager with his neighbour, once swallowed several maggots. Surely that had been the taste of death. And no, it wasn't a taste he wanted to experience again.

'In God's mansion, love is never mean-spirited or possessive. There are no forbidden fruits… ' There are in my orchard, thought Ricketts Jamieson, whose trees had recently been stripped of their fruit by tinkers.

'Furthermore, when we move to a better place and wait in glorious expectation for the moment of Translation, we will take no possessions with us. No goods or chattels, no coins, no keepsakes. All we own will be held in common. Wealth will not distinguish us in the eyes of the Lord.' He had stolen the concept from Elspeth and corrupted it for his own purposes.

This thought more than any of White's previous pronouncements, caught his audience's attention. It was one thing to lie with your neighbour's wife, indeed there might be much to be said for it, but to relinquish all possessions? This was true blasphemy. The Buchanites muttered among themselves and shook their heads.

Annoyed by his failure to make the impact he had hoped, White found some solace when he saw Alexander Gillespie unpacking his writing implements to record these latest words of wisdom.

Chapter Sixteen

THE BROTHERS
Kirkcudbright

Having escaped from the clutches of the press gang, the brothers had wandered aimlessly in their search for Elspeth. An amenable landlord had offered them accommodation in exchange for clearing his blocked drains. The flooding had left an appalling smell and the departure of previously loyal customers. The brothers were also promised drink if they would guddle in the rank water and solve the problem. They had drawn straws to see which of them would duck into the culvert. James insisted on the best of three after the coin span briefly on the cobbles before landing heads up. Mathew's benign acquiescence saw him lose the wager. 'Shite,' he said removing his shirt. 'Shite, shite.'

'Jist dinnae swallow,' said James.

The culprit was a dead cat which Mathew dragged out by its back legs and tossed in the general direction of his brother. James successfully executed a neat pas de deux. 'Ye stinkin' mockit fart catcher,' he said.

The landlord, pleased to see the noxious water subside, kept his promise.

The man who joined the brothers at their table had returned from navvying on the River Irwell in Manchester. 'Lots of Irish folk,' he said. 'Good workers, mind.' He paused and looked at Mathew whose teeth were chattering from the cold. 'Is yer pal no well?' he asked.

Na, he's fine,' said James. 'He went doukin' in the stank.'

'Ah thought he was one o' they shakers... ' The brothers were interested. 'Aye, mad folk. Shaking wi' God's ain love. Manchester's houchin' wi them. There's this woman, see. They cry her Mother, and heng on her every word. There's a wee chapel in Toad Lane, near to where ah was staying. God speaks to her, they say. Visions.'

It took the brothers five days to reach Manchester. The innkeeper arranged for them to travel in a wagon bound for Carlisle. The driver, fully aware that his cargo of wood was unstable, welcomed their presence. If they both lay across the load, they should prevent it from toppling. His hopes were ill-founded, and the three of them spent several hours reloading the cart. Once they took their leave of the wagoner, they settled into an easy rhythm, walking for the most part in companionable silence. The thought of being reunited with Elspeth sustained them equally. Their fantasies were identical: she would throw her arms around them both and kiss them until their hearts could take no more; she would smile knowingly and beckon them to her room where she would remove her clothes until she stood proud and naked in front of them; they would lie in the throes of passion; she would bestow a blessing on every part of their bodies, saving the best until last.

The smell of drink from the Carlisle taverns and the come-on smiles from the streetwalkers almost persuaded them to abandon their mission, but the lure of the Mother proved stronger and they trudged onwards. One of the women followed them for at least a mile down the road. Whenever they turned to see if she was still there, she would open her bodice and flaunt her breasts at them.

The recent storms had washed away the bridge at Penrith and they were obliged to make a lengthy detour. The same had happened at Threshfield and they had no alternative but to pay an exorbitant fee to the ferryman whose coracle showed little inclination to reach the opposite bank, preferring to loiter in the treacherous eddies. Once on dry land, James suggested they toss their guide into the river and set his craft adrift, but Mathew said they should just walk away. At Ilkley the winds returned, and they took shelter in a sheep pen. At Brighouse they saw a band of beggars on the road ahead and kept their distance until the mendicants had gone their separate ways. The strangers who greeted them did so in incomprehensible accents. At Rochdale they were forced to hug the hedgerows as a seemingly interminable line of soot-coated packhorses passed them. Their owners seemed to derive pleasure from barging into the brothers.

'They're carrying coal,' said James.

'Manchester,' said Mathew

Chapter Seventeen

THE APOCALYSE AND A HANGING

White's frame of mind found its echo in the storm clouds that had rolled in from over the hills. The skies grew dark and the group looked up anxiously wondering where they might find shelter. White was still sulking when four men on horseback emerged from around the corner of a barn and blocked their passage.

Elspeth froze, then threw back her head and screamed. The unearthly primeval sound stopped the others in their tracks. The first horse, a large white beast, was spooked by the Gibson's dog running between its legs. The horse reared above Elspeth at the front of the procession. Refusing to flinch beneath the hooves thrashing near her face, she shouted her defiance, 'Behold the evil conqueror!' Her eyes bulged, and her lips flecked with spittle. Those closest to the confusion turned and ran into those behind; a cart was overturned; bags were dropped; and the Wifies fell into a ditch. Only Davy McConville was unmoved. He had tamed enough horses in his time not to be intimidated by those whose mission was apparently to announce the Apocalypse. He calmly reached into his tool sack and withdrew his hammer.

Surprised at being identified as the Antichrist, the horseman stared at the mad woman in his path.

Now utterly convinced that the Last Day had arrived, albeit a little sooner than she had anticipated, Elspeth brushed past the first horse and confronted the second, an elderly russet nag. Its startled owner raised his stick ready to strike the fury approaching him.

'Go wage your wars in hell!' she told the bemused rider. 'We will not be subdued by Satan's sword.' The constable shook his head and gripped his night stick more tightly.

Elspeth grabbed the third horse, a thin black animal, by its bridle and shouted into its face, 'Famine holds no fears. We will feast on manna from heaven's kitchen!' The horse whinnied and, tossing its head, shook itself free of Elspeth's grip. She smacked a fist into its thin ribs before moving towards the fourth horse, a pale dun-coloured creature.

All courage forsook her. Her hands dropped to her sides. She closed her eyes and muttered, 'I looked, and before me was a pale horse. Its rider was named death.' She slumped to the ground.

White ran forward to lift her up. 'The Lord Mother is exhausted. She needs to rest.' He entrusted her limp form to John Gibson who put his arm around her and led her away.

'What business do you have with us?' he asked the leader of the posse. White took strength from the proximity of Davy McConville who was tapping his hammer into the palm of his hand. The first heavy drops of rain fell.

'We hereby issue a fugie warrant for the apprehension of Patrick Hunter on behalf of his creditors in the Royal Burgh of Irvine.' The messenger-at-arms handed down the document to White who read it quickly.

'You have no power over my people. We recognise only the authority of our Lord God.' The Buchanites murmured their approval and crowded closely around the horsemen.

'Step back or my constables will convey you to the nearest magistrate.' Reluctantly the crowd backed away, apart from Davy McConville who raised his hammer. It was rumoured that he had once punched three horses and their riders to the ground when confronted by robbers at his forge.

'Step away!' ordered the messenger-at-arms. Further confrontation was avoided as Mrs Hunter pushed her husband into the space vacated by the shrinking crowd. White had noticed how she had recently taken to criticising the primitive conditions in which her family were now living. Whose side was she on? She was another one he would have to watch.

'Face it like a man,' she said, 'and when you return, bring with you what is mine.' Humphy Hunter nodded, understanding the allusion to the trove of money that they had secreted under the hearth in case of difficulties. She was right. If this wasn't a difficulty, what was? Furthermore, if he could placate his wife, he could give his own share of their wealth to the society. The Reverend White would thank him, and the Lord Mother might reward him with a special blessing.

'I will come wi' you,' he said offering both wrists up to the constable who had climbed down from his horse with a rope.

A small commotion ensued as five or six of the Buchanites pushed their way to the front. Their spokesman looked at the ground and mumbled something at White.

'Speak up, man.'

'We also need to return and settle our affairs. We left in great haste and had no time to bid farewell to our friends or pay our debts.'

White grabbed him. 'How dare you forsake us now? How dare you betray our Lord Mother?' He pushed the man to the earth which was already turning to mud in the downpour. One of the women stepped forward and looked at White, defying him to treat her similarly. 'I left my beasts locked in the byre, I cannae sleep at night for hearing their bellowing. I must return and give them to my neighbour.'

'They are only cattle!' shouted White in complete exasperation. 'Do you think the Living Christ cares about your beasts?' He looked at the larger group for their approval. It was not forthcoming.

'Remember your psalms, Minister. 'For every beast of the forest is Mine, the cattle on a thousand hills.''

'Go back. Go to hell for all I care!' Defeated and furious, White turned away.

The party receded into the distance. One or two of them stopped to look at those they were leaving behind. Someone waved.

Elspeth, who had been given water by Mrs Gibson, felt that she was waking from a bad dream. 'He attacked me again,' she said. 'Satan saw that my guard was down. He knows that only those with truly contented minds can enter paradise without passing through the gates of death.' Mrs Gibson nodded as if she understood what the Lord Mother was saying. Gradually the horsemen of the apocalypse were replaced by more mundane objects: the handcart that had earlier impeded their progress, and a scarecrow in the adjacent field tilting towards her as if concerned for her wellbeing. Her children were at her side looking anxious. She placed a hand on each of their heads in turn. 'All shall be well.'

'And all manner of thing shall be well,' they duly intoned, long used to playing their part in this ritual exchange.

Mrs Gibson explained to the Lord Mother that their party was now diminished in number. Elspeth saw Hugh White pacing and went to console him.

'They will return, my love. They will return.' White ignored her. He was still stunned by the departures and took the betrayal personally. How dare they flout his authority? They needed the strong leadership that only he could provide. Let the Mother tend to their spiritual needs and their dreams; his plans were more firmly rooted in the pursuit of temporal power.

'Thon Humphy's a thrawn soul,' said Emily. 'His missus will be pleased he's gone.'

'A sleekit wee man,' said Kitty hunching one shoulder into her neck and treating her friend to her best hunchback impersonation.

As the Buchanites trudged on in silence, the sun sank beneath the hills, casting into sharp relief the gibbet that marked their entry into a new barony. Elspeth glanced back to check that there had been no more deserters and saw that Thomas Neil had climbed the slope and was now standing close to the gibbet. She told White to keep the party moving towards Thornhill while she stepped into the field and walked towards the solitary figure.

'My son. My son.' Neil stared into the past. Elspeth held him, but he stayed rigid, staring at the black frame. 'I saw him in the cairt, his hands tied. He saw me and spoke but I couldnae hear his words.'

'Eli Eli Lama Sabachthani,' said Elspeth beneath her breath.

'The chaplain mannie said some prayers. I had a knife. I was going to cut my boy down and help him escape but the crowd was too big. I couldnae get near him. Then they whipped the horses and the cairt moved away.'

Neil broke away from Elspeth and stood underneath the scaffold with his arms wrapped around the shape his son's twitching body would have filled, had it been there.

'I tried to buy his claes but I had nae money and the hangman laughed saying he fancied the breeches for himsel'. I just wanted a minding, you understand.'

Elspeth lifted him up and after wiping his cheeks with an edge of her shawl, blew into his mouth. 'There will be no more death,' she said. 'We have been chosen to escape the tyranny of death. His cold fingers will never tighten round our necks. His stink will never fill our nostrils. No more bodies on carts, no more craws picking at the eyes of soldiers on the field where they fell, no more widows crying into the night. Never again will the black death do Satan's work.'

'Look!' said Elspeth pointing at the darkening sky where the last of the light played with the clouds. 'There! Your son! He's waiting for you.' At that moment, the clouds altered shape.

'My son! Wait for me. I will see you soon!' Neil embraced Elspeth. 'Thank you, Mother, thank you.'

Elspeth led him back down the field towards the others. 'Soon we will find a better hill,' she said. 'A hill of life, not death. The hill where our destiny will be fulfilled. We are close. Very close.'

White had taken advantage of Elspeth's temporary absence to address the company. The travellers sat on the ground or leaned against the carts, patiently expecting, at best another homily, at worst, a new hymn.

When he had their full attention, White moved towards Ann who was picking corn husks from Agnes' shawl. She had started to irritate him with her apparent indifference to his sermons. He placed a hand round her throat and propelled her backwards. The others gasped. 'Yea, I say unto you… ' His victim flailed hopelessly. 'Let me remind you that your covenant is with the Lord Mother and her Manchild. Remember, I can see into your souls. I will smell the rank odour of treachery if any one of you even thinks of leaving before the glorious Translation that is our destiny.' Ann tripped and fell onto her back but White kept his hand on her throat. Leaning above her he continued, 'I will rip out your entrails and throw them in the flames of the Lord Mother's wrath!' Eventually he stood, and quietly told the group that not a word of what had passed would reach the Lord Mother's ears.

'All is well!' Elspeth opened her arms wide and beamed at her followers.

'And all shall be well,' they replied, deadened. Agnes moved to console Ann.

Chapter Eighteen

A NEW HOME

'New Cample Farm,' said a breathless Gibson. 'I have secured accommodation. The farmer, Davidson, will let us rest in his barn in exchange for labour in his fields.'

'Well done, man,' said White shaking his hand. Elspeth too kissed him on the cheek. Gibson was disappointed, having hoped for a more intimate display of the Lord Mother's gratitude. Perhaps later.

Davidson ran a hand through his whiskers as he watched the long line of pilgrims snaking down the track towards his land. He could make out several large men in the company who could easily lift the coping stones out of the burn where they had toppled during the recent storm. He was surprised though at the number of young women in the company. He supposed they could tend the cattle and feed the hens. He looked askance at the small man, almost a dwarf, who doffed his hat to him as the group assembled in his yard. He had no idea what employment could be found for him, unless it was sorting through the box of buttons that his late sister had guarded all her days.

'Welcome,' he said. 'I think the Good Lord has sent you.'

'He has indeed,' said Elspeth greeting their new landlord. Davidson had never seen a woman like her, tall and upright with eyes that made him feel as if he was standing naked before her. Indeed, he placed both hands over his groin, then self-consciously moved them to his sides. She had only spoken three words, but he was already in her thrall.

'Follow me.' He led the way into the empty barn. Elspeth brushed against him in the doorway.

'Perfect,' she said. 'Perfect.'

White issued orders and delegated tasks. He negotiated a supply of hay and twine from Davidson and put the women to work making bundles for bedding. 'There are forty of us,' he reminded them. 'Smaller ones for the children. And the best for the Lord Mother and her Manchild. Quickly now.'

Davidson invited some of their number into his kitchen for a meal of potatoes and salt herring. He listened mesmerised as Elspeth spoke a grace that incorporated a lengthy description of the paradise that awaited them. Their bodies would be rendered perfect by the process of Translation through the clouds. They would gasp with wonder on beholding themselves lithe and young once more, then gaze down at the flames devouring the wicked. They would see the dragons of Christ's ire stamping through the charred bodies of the damned.

William Lindsay remembered finding the burnt remains of two calves after a fire at his farm.

Then silence, total blissful silence, as they ascend through the ether. They would touch the stars; they would brush against the filigree wings of angels. And then, at the end of their journey, the gold burnished gates of paradise would swing open onto a beautiful land from which pain, suffering and guilt had been banished. The air would be scented with jasmine.

'Amen, amen. Praise to the Lord Mother.'

'And her Manchild,' said Mrs White who remained resolutely fond of her husband, and still protected his interests, despite his having long forsaken her bed.

Andrew Innes popped a potato into his mouth and sighed contentedly.

After the meal, and while the others decided who was sleeping where, Elspeth and White walked around the farmstead. She was feeling strong again after her unwanted encounter with the four horsemen. White was revelling in the possibility of lining his pockets with the fruits of others' labours. While he explained at length his theories of delegation, he realised that Elspeth was no longer at his side. He turned and saw her several yards back staring at the skyline. Annoyed that she had not heard his wise thoughts on utilising Mrs Muir's dressmaking skills, he retraced his steps.

'What do you see?'

'The hill.'

'What hill?'

'The one we have been seeking. The one chosen by God for our

Translation.'

He followed her gaze and took in the shallow promontory that fringed the farm to the south. He looked at the woman at his side. She was beyond radiant. Consumed with desire, he embraced her and taking her hand, led her to a spot away from the disputatious clamour of voices emanating from the barn.

'This is our corner!' declared Kitty on behalf of the Wifies. 'We're the oldest so we get tae choose.' They stood together, intransient in the face of demands from Mrs Hunter who wanted to protect her children from the draughts that were already lifting the eaves.

'You wait until my man returns… '

'They say a wee lassie in Irvine has turned his head,' said Kitty. 'He'll no be back.'

Mrs Hunter looked daggers, but not having one to hand, retreated to the far corner of the barn. The Wifies smiled at each other in their small triumph.

Agnes and Ann were less than happy that Tam was watching their every move, ready to place his bundle of hay close to wherever the young women placed theirs. Agnes removed a pin from her hair and made as if to poke him in the eye with it. Tam grunted and placed his bundle on the floor just out of eye-stabbing range.

'Nae snoring,' said Agnes who was aware that Ann had not slept since her encounter with White.

For his part, Andrew Innes alarmed Katie Gardner by suggesting that they sleep side by side so that he could protect her should the need arise.

Alan and Elizabeth had sensibly placed their bedding against the far wall, as far away from the door as they could manage.

Andrew Innes stood on a milking stool and fastened a curtain made from sacking across the far end of the barn. 'For the Lord Mother and her Shepherd,' he explained. He had overheard a conversation between Elspeth and White during which she referred to her Manchild as Shepherd. He subsequently took great pleasure in spreading White's new name among the others. Initially, White had been uneasy when he was so addressed, not seeing his position as analogous to that of a stinking peasant roaming the hills for stray animals, but he quickly reminded himself that Christ had entertained no such reservations.

Mrs Muir and Mrs Stewart took it on themselves to smooth the bedding beyond the curtain and then cover the straw with rose petals.

When Elspeth and White entered the barn, the Buchanites rose to acclaim the couple who bowed graciously as they picked their way through the improvised mattresses.

In the dark centre of the night, Elspeth moved closer to her companion. 'Our great adventure begins,' she whispered. White grunted and turned away from her.

Their slumber was disturbed by a commotion. The women were screaming, and the men were shouting. The turmoil was compounded by the collective confusion experienced by those who, waking in complete darkness, had no idea where they were. White fumbled for the tinderbox. He swore as he first dropped the flint, then accidently extinguished the first hint of a spark. Finally, he lit the tallow and moved the curtain to one side. The flickering light revealed a scene of chaos. Some were standing, some were crouching, while Satan's familiar ran amok among them.

'Be still, in God's name!'

The lesser culprit was easily identified, not as Satan's pet, but as Amy Johnson's piglet, which she had smuggled into bed with her.

The major culprit was Tam whose shamefaced expression betrayed his guilt. 'Ah meant nae harm,' he pleaded. 'I wanted a pish and was going outside when I stumbled and found that my hand was touching a bare erse. It was soft, so I gave it a wee kiss. I didnae ken it was a pig.'

Only now did White realise this was the same man who had been frequently expelled from Irvine for harassing young women. According to his victims, he would follow them through the dark vennels barking like a dog. What on earth was this man doing in the company of those chosen by God to ascend to heaven without tasting death? He had no idea when he had joined the exodus. White told him he would be dealt with in the morning and told the others to go back to sleep.

White negotiated long and hard with Davidson.

'Food and shelter is all I can gi' you,' said Davidson eventually. 'I am no a rich man.'

'My people are not slaves,' said White disdainfully. Davidson lit his pipe. 'I can manage two pence a day for your strongest workers. Half for the women.'

'And ale.'

'As you wish,' said Davidson.

As he hurried back to the barn, White thought over his own reference to slaves. In truth he had always supported slavery and had no time for those who saw it as an evil. The firmament itself was hierarchical. Just as God was superior to all men, so it followed some men were superior to others. Apart from this noble theological truth, he had experienced at first hand the pleasures of slavery. He thought fondly of his visits to the slave house in Charleston, sanctioned by his friend Abe Philip. 'Help yourself,' Abe would say pointing in the direction of the fortified living quarters. 'If any little missis proves difficult, I will personally string her up.'

Elspeth was concluding the morning prayer when White took her aside and explained that thanks to his bargaining skills, money would flow into the society.

'No, my dearest, you don't understand.'

'What?'

'We take no reward for our labours. We serve the Lord in all we do.'

'We have to live.'

'Trust me. He will provide.'

White grabbed her by the arm, then quickly released her as Mrs Hunter was looking in their direction. He forced a smile but spoke between clenched lips. 'This is madness. Are you becoming unwell again?'

Elspeth stepped back from him. 'You forget that I am Christ's sister.'

'Ah, have the angels spoken to you again? You have a new title!'

Elspeth was taken aback, stung by White's reference to her unwellness. 'You, above all others should know that I have a divine illness. I control it not. It is both a blessing and a curse. I see sights that would freeze your blood. I have seen the rebellious angels tumbling through the firmament, screaming for mercy, and tearing out the feathers from their wings as they plunge into the roasting pit of hell. I have walked with Christ in the wilderness. I have held firm to the stinking mane of the tempter as he took the Son of God to the high mountain… '

That night things remained strained between them.

At first light, White beckoned Tam to follow him out of the barn. As the older man scratched his head, White took hold of a cudgel-sized log and hit him hard across the back. And again. And again. Tam howled and called out to the Lord Mother. White kicked him as he lay on the ground. 'Don't you ever, ever do that again.' Tam had survived many beatings in the back wynds of Irvine. He had been thrashed by a passing band of army deserters who wanted the sport. He had been punched and pummelled by a tinker for stealing his bread. His earliest memory was of his own father taking a rod to his back. The secret of survival was to curl up in a ball and keep the body clenched and taut. White lifted Tam's head by the hair and landed several short, hard punches on his face.

'And where do you find the drink? Eh? Who gives it to you? Is it Davidson?' Each question was punctuated by a blow. Tam, on the point of betraying his benefactor, opened his mouth to speak but the combination of blood and broken teeth stole his words, and after groaning for several minutes, he kept his silence.

My Lordships,

You will be pleased to learn that my decision to don the hypercritical mantle of a true Buchanite is proving wise indeed. Daily I gather intelligence that will damn the pernicious and dangerous army of deluded souls. I'm sure your Lordships will appreciate the personal sacrifices that I willingly endure in the valiant pursuit of justice. Of necessity I bite my tongue and feign loyalty to the demonic leaders of this satanic crusade. I must confess, however, that in the interests of perpetuating the grand deception, I lay one night with one of the younger hussies who has become fixated with your humble servant. Your Lordships will be relieved to learn that I resisted her overtures, feigning a gripe in the bowel. As a consequence of this and similar actions I have gained the trust of White, the arch villain. So convincing is my character that I am the only member of the foul tribe who is permitted to convey missives penned by the Buchan witch to the outside world. I am a trusted messenger!

I have much to report! With my own eyes I have witnessed many unnatural couplings and carnal excesses. An accurate description of these revolting acts would be better fitted to the pages of a salacious fiction (not that your Lordships will be familiar with such productions of the gutter).

Furthermore, oblivious of the rightful strictures placed on her gender by men of discernment (in which number I include your Lordships), Elspeth Buchan persists in addressing her followers as if she were a minister in his pulpit. To fully express the abhorrence of this act, I seek refuge in the words of a man more gifted than myself: 'Sir, a woman preaching is like a dog walking on his hind legs. It is not done well but you are surprised to see it done at all.'

I must congratulate your Lordships for the speed with which you executed my suggestion regarding the issue of a fugie warrant. The stratagem has seriously weakened the society as several members have returned to Irvine under a variety of excuses. However, because of their defections White has sealed the windows and bolted the door. They are all his prisoners now.

I must close now as the charlatan White has returned. He still labours under the misconception that, when writing, I am compiling a book of the turgid hymns that he composes daily.

Yours in haste,
Alexander Gillespie

Chapter Nineteen

GOODS, CHATTELS AND TURNIPS

The Wifies were scrabbling on the floor. On all fours, they could have been sheep rooting for neeps. White watched them, bemused.

'She's lost her ring,' explained Emily. 'Her man gave it her. Mind you, I think he filched it.'

'He didnae,' said Kitty, not looking up. 'He found it in the fields.'

'There it is!' squealed Emily, darting towards the far corner of the barn. She retrieved it and held it up.

'You're a pyot!' said Kitty, snatching it from her and sliding it back onto her finger which she held up for the others to admire. 'A holy pyot.'

White had recently noticed that several of the women wore jewellery. Mrs Hunter played with her necklace when agitated, and Mrs Muir proudly wore a broach that served to remind her of past times when business was thriving. Her reputation as dressmaker to the great, and intermittently good of Irvine, had been second to none. Davy McConville too, took great pride in producing a half hunter from his waistcoat when he felt a pause from working was in order, and pronounced the time as if it was a sacred truth entrusted to him alone.

White approached the blacksmith under the pretext of wanting to know the hour. 'Davy,' he said, 'how come you have such a fine watch?'

'A gift,' said Davy, closing the lid. 'Ah wis fixin' a gate on Auld Turner's ferm when these twa horses came oot o' the mist. One o' the beasts wis limpin'. His rider wore the plaid and had a wound tae his face. But there was something aboot him, he wis no an ordinary man, if ye ken whit ah mean. Anyways, ah shod his horse, and he was so pleased he gave me his timepiece. It wis him, ken: the Prince.'

White grunted and decided to have a word with the Lord Mother.

Elspeth was surprisingly amenable and agreed that she would again speak to her followers about material possessions after the evening meal.

Davidson, in response to complaints whispered to him when White was out of earshot, was prepared to vary the Buchanites' diet. He agreed that although the potato was a fine vegetable, once the supply of salted herring was exhausted, it needed to be augmented with something else. He offered to introduce cabbage onto the bill of fare. Tam, who had barely recovered from his beating, had been the only one to object, 'Ah cannae bide cabbage. It aye makes me fart.'

As the plates were being cleared from the table, Elspeth stepped out into the yard and filled her pipe. It had been a good day. She had been mercifully free from unwanted visions for some time now. The pain in her back troubled her but it was as nothing compared to the apocalypse of suffering that the deluded residents of Irvine would have to endure once the dragons of hell were unleashed on them for their perfidy. Amy Johnson, who some still thought of as a witch, had offered her an ointment made from calf bladder and oatmeal. Perhaps her Manchild could rub it into her spine later. She was pleased that he had readily agreed that they should work for free. He was indeed a pillar of strength despite his occasional failure to understand the nature of her mission. And he was right about the need to pool their wealth in the interests of the larger group. She would find the words to explain. Her pipe had gone out. She knocked it against the wall and rejoined the others.

The words came readily enough. 'Davy McConville,' she said. Davy shuffled to his feet hoping that the Lord Mother was not going to ask him about his biblical knowledge. He could recite the commandments, all eight of them. Yes, eight, he remembered that the ones about honouring parents and adultery had been Moses' mistake.

'What is the hour?'

'Half past eight, Mother,' he closed the lid of the hunter with his forefinger and returned it to his pocket.

'And who owns that fine watch, Davy?'

'I do, Mother.' He was aware that all eyes were on him. He hated being the centre of attention.

'And what about God, Davy?'

'I dinnae think God needs a timepiece, Mother. He made all the time that there is in the world.' He was pleased with his answer and dared to make eye contact with those sitting closest to him.

'Give me the watch, Davy,' His mouth fell, and he shuffled like a small child who has been caught stealing.

'We all own this watch, Davy.'

'Yes, Mother,' he said. With head bowed, he handed over the watch. Elspeth passed it to White.

'Mrs Muir,' she pointed to the brooch prominent on her dress. Agnes Muir quickly covered it with her hand. Surely she wasn't going to take her brooch?

When they had all surrendered rings, coins and jewellery, the mood in the room was sombre. Elspeth knew she would have to give them something in return.

'The Holy Spirit is pleased and wishes to enter each of your souls.' She moved quickly through the room, embracing everyone in turn, then kissing them full on the mouth, young and old, men and women.

White was more than happy to continue the good work started by Elspeth. 'All that we own is ours in common,' he said picking his way through the straw mattresses while shaking a wooden box that had previously held nails. Even Tam eventually parted with the penny he had found at the far end of the barn close to where Mrs Gibson kept her clothes.

'How will you fly through the clouds with your souls weighed down by the things of this earth, and your pockets lined with riches? Leave your coins and baubles for Satan to play with; a poor consolation for having to watch you rise towards the seat of the Father.'

Emily Turnpike fidgeted, convinced that Elspeth, despite not staring at her directly, knew her secret: she had not surrendered the sovereign she had brought with her when they escaped from Irvine. If God in His wisdom, at the time of the Great Translation, were to decide that she was insufficiently good to merit salvation, then she would need money to get her home. She would need a horse and cart; she was far too old to walk. She put a hand down to check that the coin was still in its secret hiding place.

'Our goods and chattels, our clothes, our tools… '

It was Davy's turn to look uneasy; his chisel and mallet had belonged to his father and now belonged to him, and him alone. He had earlier resisted White's attempt to forcibly remove them from him.

With heavy heart, James Stewart parted with the ring that he had prised from the swollen finger of his late mother. White shook the box as if it were a tambourine. He then beckoned to Alexander Gillespie to join him outside. They walked together across the yard, White with one arm around the other man's shoulder, the other clutching the box.

'The Lord Mother has great faith in you, Alexander. I know that she would want you to be custodian of our shared wealth. When the chance presents itself, travel to the nearest town and exchange these trinkets for the money we will need to support our vigil.' Gillespie nodded his assent and placed the box under his coat for safekeeping.

The Buchanites had all been allocated tasks on the farm. The fittest men were to toil on the banks of the Linn under the supervision of Davy McConville whose formidable strength meant that he could easily lift the stones needed to shore up the collapsed sections of the bank. The women, children and Andrew Innes were required to harvest the neeps. So long as they could bask in the approval of the Lord Mother, the Buchanites were happy to labour and sweat for no reward. Even White's tyranny was supportable so long as the Mother was with them in spirit. They would have all of eternity to rest.

Elspeth approached the stooped circle of women. They paused from their labours, stretched and greeted the Lord Mother. As Davidson possessed only a limited number of tools, the women were for the most part obliged to prise the vegetables from the hard soil with their fingers and any implement they could find. Mrs Muir tried to hide her bleeding hands from Elspeth, but it was too late. She stepped forward and took the blood and earth-caked hands in her own and stroked them gently.

'Thank you, Mother,' said Mrs Muir, grateful for the attention. It was true, she thought, the Lord Mother has the power to cure the flesh and sooth the fevered breast. 'Thank you.'

Elspeth looked at the raw centre of Mrs Muir's right palm and the mark made by the stick she had been using to dig into the unyielding soil. 'This is a sign of the sacred cross,' she said. 'This is our Calvary.' The women bowed their heads and muttered their gratitude.

She turned away from the group and glanced at the growing heap of vegetables, testimony to the women's labours. She stood transfixed in front of the pile, then removed the highest turnip. Holding it at arm's length, she pronounced, 'And this is the place of the skull.'

As the vision enveloped her, the women became uncomfortable. They understood that communing with God was not an easy task and one that frequently made her a target for Satan himself. As Elspeth stared, the ridges in the field became the bones of everyone who had ever lived. She heard the wailing and gnashing of teeth. The deep, dark eye sockets showed nothing. No life, no hope, no resurrection. Nothing. The women saw that she was shaking and ran to hold her.

'This is the sly fiend's work,' she sobbed. 'He wishes to unnerve me and deflect me from my mission.' Andrew Innes also abandoned his furrow and rushed to her aid. He looked around anxiously lest Auld Hornie was hiding behind a rick. Not seeing him, he took Elspeth by the hand and led her back to the barn where White was holding forth to a visiting delegation of local ministers.

White was annoyed at Elspeth's demeanour. Her gift of prophesy had been the prime object of their discourse. The Reverend Foulis, a man riddled with scepticism, stroked his chin as he inspected the distressed woman in front of him. He raised his eyebrows several times to communicate his suspicions to his companion, the Reverend Maitland, a rotund man with a rubicund face. The clergymen rose to their feet, perfunctorily thanked White, collected their hats, and left. White heard both the creak of the farm gate, and the sound of their laughter. He gestured at Innes to leave them.

'What is the matter with you?' he shouted. Elspeth stood expressionless. 'Why do you do this to me?'

'I stood in the field of death.'

'What nonsense is this?'

'My breath and all my strength were sucked from me. There was only despair and sadness.'

White was annoyed. Weakness in any form could undermine all his plans. If he was to flourish and accumulate riches, then he needed Elspeth to play her part. It was crucial that the malleable simpletons believed unreservedly in her powers.

'You must be strong,' he urged with a more conciliatory edge to his voice.

'I was shown the oxen and the plough. The turned earth was pitted with white stones and the skulls of children.' She slumped onto a bench. Thomas Neil approached, concerned for the Lord Mother. White's clenched fists left him in no doubt that his company was not required.

The nightmare vision of the skulls took a while to fade. In a variant dream, Elspeth was in a future time. The plough was being pulled by a machine that belched smoke and made a noise like all the devils. There were no horses. The man stopped his infernal machine and picked up one of the small skulls. Childish gibberish poured out of its mouth and eye sockets.

Chapter Twenty

THE BROTHERS
Manchester

Toad Lane proved almost impossible to find. The strangers they approached for directions invariably contradicted each other, gleefully pointing in opposite directions. An urchin, dripping snot, said he would show them the way for a penny. Despite their misgivings, they followed him as he weaved his way between buildings whose upper floors were propped on staves to prevent them tumbling into the street. After leading them through a labyrinth of alleys, the boy indicated that they should duck through a hole in the brick wall. James peered into the opening and saw several men and dogs waiting for them on a wasteland of twisted metal and broken bottles. 'Ah dinnae think so,' he said.

They next approached two young men smoking pipes on a street corner. At the mention of Toad Lane and a chapel, the men glanced at each other, tapped out the contents of their pipes on the adjacent wall, and started to shake and jibber. They jerked and convulsed; they threw their arms about as if they had no control over their limbs. After contorting his mouth as if he were stricken with palsy, one of them spoke. 'SSSatan help mmme... someone has cut off my ccock... I must shake off my balls. I am a shaker! I shake for Christ!'

His friend became momentarily still and stared into the distance. 'Great Mother, save me! I promise never to fuck my neighbour again, or my mistress... '

'Or my dddog.'

The men roared with laughter and pointed towards a building further down the lane.

Bemused, James and Mathew watched the two men lurching their way towards the public house. 'Perhaps they're all mad in Manchester,' said James.

'They mebbe escaped fae the asylum.'

'Aye. Dae you think we're about to see her again? Will she recognise us?'

'Of course, man. We'll gie her a surprise. And she'll gie us a special blessing.'

The brothers walked towards the small chapel and joined the queue. 'We ken the Mother,' said James.

'From way back,' said his brother.

The custodian put a finger to his lips. 'Shhh, the Mother is speaking.'

The room was crowded and hot. Someone was speaking but it wasn't the Mother. The small dumpy woman was barely visible above the throng. 'It's no her,' said James.

'Perhaps she's changed. She was aye performing tricks... miracles,' said his brother.

'Dinnae be daft. Yon's a wee wifie wi' a whining voice.'

' ... and in this dream God told me that the evil sin perpetrated in the sacred Garden of Eden was craven sexual indulgence. Men and women who seek pleasure and gratification from their own and others' bodies will never be saved. Their concupiscence will lead to their damnation. Satan will roast their genitals... '

'That's no oor Elspeth. That's no her way of thinking at all.'

'She's a fraud.'

'Leave this sacred place now,' hissed the man who turned around to confront the blasphemers in their midst. 'Do not speak ill of our blessed Mother Lee.'

'Who?' asked Mathew, rising to leave. As they walked out of the town it was an age before either of them spoke.

'Ah cannae believe we went a' that way to see an auld crone,' said Mathew.

'A shrivelled witch wi' hengin' dugs and nae teeth,' said James. 'Mother Lee.'

'The wrang mither.'

Chapter Twenty-One

THEY HAVE NO SOULS

Despite the warm summer air, the water was freezing. Davy McConville stood up to his knees rocking a stone that was half submerged in the riverbed. The pain in his legs was intense. He had never known cold like it in his life. The other men shouted encouragement. With a final effort accompanied by much grunting, he lifted the stone and heaved it onto the bank. He lay back, resting on his elbows. One of the men started humming. The others, recognising the tune, joined in and incrementally supplied the words.

Elspeth lifted her skirt and stepped through the long grass towards the banks of the Linn. She heard them singing one of the hymns that Hugh had devised on their first night in New Cample Farm. She remembered how pleased he had been when he realised that 'sin' could be used to rhyme with 'cherubim'. He was a clever man and she was lucky to have him at her side.

The men stood and doffed their hats when they saw her approach.

'Ah,' she said, touching each of the men in turn on the shoulder. 'The river that flowed out of Eden to water the garden.'

'I doubt there were stanes in that river,' said Thomas Neil.

'True, Neil, true.' The men relaxed. The Lord Mother was in good humour which was a relief. Recently some of them had noticed that being a member of the Holy Trinity seemed to be taking its toll.

'Mother, when will the angels come for us?' asked Neil, relieved that his comment had not provoked a storm.

'We are not yet ready,' replied the Lord Mother. 'Only when we live as he intended will he let us enter His home. We must surrender all the old ways and embrace the new.'

Davy McConville thought briefly about asking if he would be united with his half hunter in paradise but thought better of it. He noticed the flash of a kingfisher above the river. Perhaps it was an angel. He must try harder to believe.

White had been thinking about the children in the party. Barely an hour passed without one of them squabbling or complaining. How could he ever finish *The Divine Dictionary* if he was constantly being disturbed? His own progeny were the worst. Ruth had been caught stealing food, and Will persisted in tormenting Amy Johnson's pig-child with a lighted taper. While Margaret worried obsessively about their offspring, as far as White was concerned, his children simply didn't exist. The younger, a thin, puny child, suffered from nightmares and would wake everyone with her screaming. The boy, who had, in the words of his father, a face pocked with sores like the devil's arse, grizzled and gurned constantly. He had recently taken to attaching himself like a limpet to his leg, a small human calliper, an overgrown leach. Whenever White left the barn, his son would cling to him.

The Hunter children were little better. Convinced that Amy Johnson was a witch, they took it in turns to sprinkle her with salt leaving the poor woman choking and furious.

In the early days of their relationship White and Elspeth would, after their lovemaking, discuss theological matters. He remembered that she had been particularly preoccupied by God's intention regarding the precise moment when children received their souls. She would agonise over the fate of soulless children when the moment of Translation arrived. White would reinforce the notion that children were an obstacle to fulfilling God's plans. They must talk of such matters again.

Elspeth, still in awe of her Manchild, willingly agreed to pray for guidance.

The fruits of her discussion with God were shared with her followers after the evening meal. The Lord Mother's established practice was to ask someone to stand and serve as the empty vessel into which she would pour her exhortations, praise, or most recent insights depending on how the Spirit moved her. This approach had the benefit of enabling the others to digest her true meaning without fear of being singled out. However, it was not unknown for the chosen one to wilt under the weight of Elspeth's intensity and become unwell. This evening, Mrs

Kerr, an elderly biddy who had welcomed the chance to embrace a new life and escape from her violent husband in Irvine, was the chosen one.

'Do you have any bairns, Mrs Kerr?'

'No Mither. It wasnae God's will.'

'Do you think, Mrs Kerr, that any one bairn is more important than any other?'

'No Mither, we are all equal in Christ's eyes.'

'And what say you to those folk who give more attention to one bairn than any other.'

Mrs Kerr, knowing that she was being manipulated into a particular response, hesitated.

'Come now, speak.'

'I would say, Mither, that those folk were wrang.'

Someone coughed. Someone else scraped their chair across the floor. Andrew Gillespie started writing in his ledger.

'And I say to you that often those folk go by the name of father and mother. Their false thoughts make them believe that the squirming fruit of their coupling is more important, more blessed, more well favoured than their neighbour's bairn. What say you to that, Mrs Kerr?'

'I say, Mither, they are wrang.'

'Indeed, they are wrong. These are the ways of unbelievers. For so long as they entertain these delusions, they will never be taken into the arms of Christ, but will wander the earth with their sickly bairns, and will never know the joy of salvation.'

Hugh White, uncomfortable with Elspeth's train of thought, tapped his forehead with irritation. This was not quite what they had agreed.

'All that we hold, we hold in common. We own nothing on our own.'

'Our food and drink, the cup we fill from the well, the straw on which we sleep, all these things we hold in common. Just as we cannot be weighed down by trinkets and baubles and finery when the hour of our ascent arrives, so too we cannot be pulled back to the earth by the children we have selfishly nurtured.'

White sat open-mouthed. Surely the Lord Mother was not going to evict the society's children? However, Elspeth's final pronouncement on the matter, although difficult, was not quite as bad as he had feared.

'Henceforth all our children are to be held in common. I instruct you who are father or mother, to sever the ties that bind you unnaturally to your children and surrender your offspring to all of us. Together we will share the burden of raising the children in our midst to accept and fear the Lord God.'

White realised that he should have had more faith in the Lord Mother. Nevertheless, murmurs of unrest spread through the room.

'We will all be parents to the bairns in the name of the Lord God.'

White found it surprisingly easy to lead the chorus of 'amens' that started quietly and then grew in volume. Margaret looked to her husband but found no comfort in his eyes. Having surrendered Hugh to Elspeth, in accord with the Lord's wishes, she could not bear the thought of her offspring seeking food from others or nestling into strangers at night. What would be the point of anything?

Mrs Hunter too knew in her heart that she could never forsake her children. Why had that foolish husband of hers got himself arrested just when she needed him?

An incident later the same evening confirmed that the Lord approved of Elspeth's innate wisdom in all matters spiritual. As White pulled up his breeches having relieved himself in the field, he saw smoke issuing from the barn. Moments later, Davy McConville appeared at the door, almost obscured by a bed of burning straw; a satanic apparition.

'The bairns,' he said, tramping on the dying flames. He explained how the Whites' younger child, scared of the dark, had begged her mother to let her light a candle which she had then dropped with predictable results.

White held his daughter upside down with one hand while he skelped her backside. She howled, and Margaret tried to intervene before being brushed aside.

'Did you no hear the Lord Mother? Are you stupid or deaf? You must heed her words!' He dropped his daughter onto the floor. 'She is no longer our child. She belongs to all of you.' He gestured at the others, who averted their eyes, then picked up the child by the scruff of the neck and, striding across several occupied beds, dropped her between Ann and Agnes. 'You look after her.' The two women looked awkwardly at each other before comforting their new child who sobbed some more then fell fast asleep. At the other end of the barn, Margaret cried silently.

Elspeth had witnessed the brief fire and then the real conflagration of Hugh White's fury. When he joined her in the alcove, his anger was unabated. 'It's your fault,' he said turning away from her.

She lay still in the dark, not wanting to disturb him.

It was difficult, but she knew she was right. After all, God had spoken to her and opened her eyes to the errors of parenthood.

Squabbles among the group were not uncommon. The unchanging diet, the perceived unfairness of the allocation of tasks in the fields, and Mrs Muir's custodianship of clothing, all provoked annoyance and minor jealousies. It was John Gibson who usually prevented the pot of resentment from boiling over. He was proving to be a skilful arbiter, deciding that the Wifies need only work for half a day because of their age, and successfully negotiating with Davidson over the thinness of the soup.

There were sexual tensions too. All four apprentices from the huckling shed had joined the exodus from Irvine. Their motivation was less the lure of spiritual rapture than the promise of carnal pleasures, and the knowledge that at least two of the town's beauties were part of Elspeth's entourage. The Dowie sisters, Rowan and Meg, were free with their favours. The boys had all lain at some point with one or both of the girls and took it in turns to follow them with a dog-like loyalty wherever they went.

The two Wifies, unable to sleep owing to the sounds of fumbling and merriment from the corner where the younger folk lay, took matters into their own hands. Having carried two full pails of water from the well, they tiptoed the length of the barn, and emptied their contents over the squirming fornicators.

'Ye shrivelled auld witches!'

'Yer scabbie auld whores!'

The company woke. The barn was awash with water and complaints from those whose nocturnal endeavours extended no further than dreaming of friends and family members whose company they were missing. Hugh White, in nightgown, and holding a taper, strode towards the source of the disturbance. 'What in God's holy… ?' He paused, having caught sight of Meg's nudity, and made a mental note to pay her more attention. 'Back to sleep,' he said. 'And you two,' he looked at Emily and Kitty who were standing, their eyes lowered like naughty school children, 'if you repeat this folly, I will flay the wrinkled skin from your backs and feed your withered dugs to the beasts.' Kitty put a protective arm over her breasts.

Yes, he had overlooked Meg's considerable charms.

Despite these occasional crises, most of the Buchanites still believed implicitly in their imminent translation to a better place and enjoyed the pleasure this knowledge brought with it. They would lie in the fields in the heat of the midday sun, sharing food, memories and hopes for the future. Their love of the Lord Mother was unconditional and made bearable their treatment at the hands of Hugh White.

'I'll see my man soon,' said Emily who was struggling to dislodge a shard of corn stuck in her teeth. 'Mind you, I'll gie him a piece of my mind for leaving me like that. Without a word o' farewell. Jist went and died for nae reason. Mind, I'll want all the gossip frae heaven. Who are the maist important angels? And which ones tae avoid. My man'll see me right. And what do you say when in God's presence? I'll no say anything until I'm spoken tae.'

'I think you should bow as low as you can,' suggested Kitty.

'What, wi my knees the way they are?'

'No, we'll have our young bodies back, mind what we were telt by the Lord Mother.'

'If I've got my young body back, my man may have to wait his turn. Think of all they handsome young angels.'

'They're no men,' said Kitty.

'What do you mean?'

'What I'm saying. I've seen pictures. They're no anything. Neither men nor women.'

'I dinnae like the sound of that… '

William Lindsay and Davy McConville sat against a tree and shared a pipe.

'I'll no beat about the bush, Davy, I'll miss my beasts. If you think about it, they apostles were all fishermen, no farmers.'

'And tax collectors.'

'That's what I mean. Nae farmers.'

'And I dinnae mind if there's ony blacksmiths in the Bible.'

'They must have horses, Davy. Tae pull a' they chariots. You'll no get many sermons without a mention of chariots.'

'True, William, true.'

The young apprentices sat in a circle playing dice while the Dowie sisters watched. The boys had been pleasantly surprised to learn that gambling was not forbidden by either the Lord Mother or her Manchild. Indeed, Hugh White had once joined them, using each throw of the dice to flaunt his biblical knowledge. 'The lot is cast in the lap, but its every decision is from the Lord,' he reminded them, before adding with a smirk, 'Proverbs 16:33.'

Meg Dowie, increasingly unable to decide on which of the apprentices she should bestow her favours, even considered that she might have to decide the matter with a throw of the dice.

Ann and Agnes were floating sticks down the burn much to the delight of the White's child – she liked her new parents. Two mothers were much better than one. The foremost stick became caught in an eddy until Ann thrust her hand deep into the water to release it. The young girl squealed with delight.

That evening White watched as Meg undressed. He was provoked by her modesty. He was provoked still further by the brief glimpse of her breasts in the flickering candlelight. He waited until Elspeth's rhythmic breathing confirmed that she was asleep and left their bed.

Meg started when he approached and pulled the blanket to her chin. So far, unlike the other young women, she had avoided White's attentions. She assumed this was because of her unattractiveness and had felt oddly grateful for the nose she considered too large for her face, and her untameable hair. She closed her eyes and feigned sleep, but she knew that he was not fooled. He pulled back the blanket. 'Come to me,' he said, but she held herself rigid. 'Help me,' she whispered in the direction of the apprentice boys, none of whom woke.

'Relax,' said White.

Your Lordships,

I crave your indulgence for sending you this letter hot on the tail of my preceding communication but matters here have continued at a pace, and it is vital that you are appraised of the latest heresy to spew from the mouths of those who rule this demonic tribe. I must remain calm; my pen shakes as it prepares to transmit a blasphemy almost beyond imagining.

I am now composed.

Suffice it to say, in defiance of natural law, Buchan and her 'Manchild'(!) now openly advocate that all goods should be held in common; personal property has been abolished! I can only imagine how your Lordships shudder at this particular piece of intelligence. If unchallenged, such astonishing ideas will destroy our society and progressively erode all human happiness.

Please think kindly of the messenger who brings this appalling news,
He is still,
Your most humble of servants,
Alexander Gillespie

Chapter Twenty-Two

A NEAR DROWNING
AND A HINT OF MURDER

Andrew Innes, who had once declared to the Lord Mother that he would walk through fire and flood to do her sacred will, had the opportunity to put the latter boast to the test. The heavens had opened hours after he left Thornhill with a clutch of letters destined for Humphy Hunter and other friends still in Irvine.

Elspeth had become increasingly anxious at the lack of news from those followers who had felt obliged to leave and settle their affairs. On one intolerably warm night, she had stood fretting next to the insect-infected pond in Davidson's yard, irritated by the murmur of the dragonflies and the insistent whine of the gnats. Her mission too had grown stagnant, and she felt listless. Had Christ forsaken her? Like her Manchild, He had undeniably been keeping His distance from her. Why was He withholding the visions from her? Although they left her weak with either joy or dread, and pierced her very heart, they were her lifeline; a reminder that she had been chosen above all others to lead the righteous out of this veil of tears and into paradise. Perhaps He was annoyed that she had let some of her followers desert her. Why had she not urged her people to dash out the brains of the constables who stole Hunter from her? They should have clawed at the flesh of the horses that led him away. She must make amends. Christ would forgive her if they returned. She would not fail Him again.

She wrote through the entire night. Sheaves of paper littered the floor, and she burned her hand lighting a new candle from the hot stub of the old one. The letters were riddled with pleadings and entreaties; they were tear-stained, passionate. They held promises of joy unbounded if only they would return.

She closed her eyes and the last letter fell from her hand. The dream that claimed her had its origins in the bestiary she had glimpsed as a child in the big house. The naked dancing figure approached, a hermaphrodite with hanging breasts and a penis. It ran through the darkness holding a severed head, a token of victory. A torch flamed in the being's other hand. His body is wound with a snake which is headwear, then necklace, then castrator. She jerked awake. 'Why do you torment me?' she cried. Slowly the vision faded, and she dared to hope that it had passed like a whirling funnel of storm.

White's instinct was to destroy the letters and claim they had gone astray. The defectors could rot in hell. There was no room for traitors in the camp. On reflection he realised that he could exploit their return for his own purposes. They must all of course repent their error. He could pick on one of them and make a public flogging the cost of their return. He could impose fines on them and swell his coffers. Yes, let them come. Although Alexander Gillespie was the obvious person to convey the letters, he needed his calm wisdom and his undying loyalty. Let the wee man go, let Andrew Innes be the messenger.

Innes listened to the distant thunder. It was the sound of God signalling His approval. His chest swelled, and he ignored the heavy drops falling on his hat until the wind snatched it from his head and deposited it in the rapidly swelling river blocking his way. Muttering, he strode into the water. His hat bobbed out of his reach, and he overbalanced into the flood. The effort of keeping the satchel containing the precious words of the Lord Mother out of the water caused him to lose his footing. He grabbed at the vegetation on the bank, but it came away in his hands. Fully submerged, he swallowed water and choked. He was swept powerless on the torrent rolling like a babe in the womb. In the eye of his panic, he found a moment of calm; an acceptance that he would not see the Great Translation. He was a sinner who deserved to be crushed by the weight of water and God's righteous wrath. 'Forgive me, Mother.' The words formed in his head and his torso shot out of the water.

Dribbling and droukit, he lay on the bank. He had been tested. It was a warning that he must redouble his faith and the fealty he owed to the sacred Mother. Stuffing the wet bag inside his jacket, he walked on, barely pausing for two days until, exhausted, he reached the outskirts of Irvine.

Hunter greeted him. 'Andra! Come away inside for a few locusts and some wild honey!'

'As long as it's no a ploy to put my heid on a platter.' The men embraced.

Unable to resume his duties as depute Town Clerk, and still subject to derision from the locals, Humphy Hunter had found little pleasure on his forced return to Irvine. What was the point? One moment he was marching proudly towards paradise, the next he was a virtual prisoner in his empty home. The terms of the fugie warrant specified that he remain in the confines of the parish. Unable to sleep, he spent most nights pacing, haunted by memories of Elspeth Buchan. He missed the camaraderie of those friends who had willingly forsaken their previous lives to follow the Lord Mother. He missed the communal meals. He even missed the apprentice boys who delighted in mimicking his lopsided gait. On balance, he even missed his wife and children. And so, when Andrew Innes presented himself at his door, he smothered him in an eager embrace. Once Innes had extricated himself, and regained his breath, he handed over the missives from Elspeth. Hunter read them avidly, reading key sections aloud and clenching his fist by way of emphasis at other points.

'I shall return,' he declared, punching Innes enthusiastically in the shoulder. 'Take me to that sacred woman. The magistrates can shit on their warrant. Lead me to her.'

Andrew's face crumpled. 'Let me rest a while. I am still tired. I need to eat, then we can leave.'

The time spent eating the mildewed broth gave them both time to think more clearly.

'What about the others?' Andrew removed something particularly unpalatable from his bowl and dropped it on the floor. 'Will they come too?'

'Yes. I forgot. Agnes Wyllie and Mrs Young will join us, without a doubt. They have settled their affairs. And Jean Gardner.'

Andrew raised an eyebrow at the mention of Katie's wild sister. He well remembered her flirtation with Rab, the man who claimed to be a poet. It was no more than an excuse to bed the women. He had seen through his shallow ways. He had heard rumours that they had agreed to wed, but then the Lord Mother had told the young woman in no uncertain terms that matrimony was the devil's business and would never be permitted in the New Order. Jean had cried. Later that evening the imposter poet had arrived and attempted to take his Jean away from 'that mad hoor of a simpleton who is no more the third person of the holy trinity than my erse.' Innes shuddered at the recollection and hoped that God would forgive him for repeating those heretical words, even inside the privacy of his own head. Yes, she would be an interesting addition to the society.

Once the others had joined them, Humphy Hunter led the small band of Buchanites through the Dumfries hills. Andrew Innes attempted to entertain them with the latest hymn laboriously improvised by Hugh White. 'Follow the trumpet of Gabriel / Away from the gates of hell / Follow the Lord / and all shall be well.' He elongated this final syllable until it became indistinguishable from the whine of a distressed animal. One of the women looked at him quizzically.

'Wheesht!' she said.

As they approached the neighbourhood of Tarbolton, Jean Gardner became agitated. She pulled up her headscarf and holding it tightly over her face, ran ahead of the others. Innes eventually caught up with her. 'What is the matter?' he asked with a hand on his chest to prevent his over-exercised heart from failing completely.

'It's him. His house is over there.' She pointed towards a cottage that backed onto the road. 'What if he sees me? What will I do? I love him, yet I don't.'

'Who?'

'Rab, my poet.' Innes put an arm round her waist and comforted her. Her warmth aroused him and for a fleeting guilty moment he entertained the thought of lying between both Gardner sisters.

Their return revived Elspeth's spirits. 'My prodigal son,' she declared, embracing Humphy Hunter who blushed. She was euphoric. God was giving her a second chance; one she would not squander. She declared that the evening meal would be followed by a special blessing. The group murmured their approval. White scowled.

Once the bowls had been cleared, Elspeth made James Stewart, the cobbler, the focus of her rapturous outpourings. Embarrassed at being the centre of attention, he fidgeted and moved the weight from one foot to the other.

'James, we both deal in souls.' Laughter mixed with relief rippled through the group who relaxed knowing that the Lord Mother was in fine fettle. 'The last is your tool, and we too will last with fortitude and courage until the sacred day arrives when we will shed the shackles of this tired earth and rise in glory and unimagined splendour into the perfumed realms of eternity. We will use the awl to prick the hide of the unbelievers, and the hammer to break their heretical views.' She beat an imaginary hammer on the table. The others mimicked her.

'All rise!' she ordered. The benches were moved back while the followers waited their instructions. She chose one of the apprentice boys and held his face between her hands, kissing him as if only she could suck out the devil of lust hiding within. A murmur of approval from the others. She turned to the next young lad and did likewise, pushing her groin into his. All the men and several of the women received the same treatment. The atmosphere was charged with sensual anticipation. After receiving their benediction, many of the followers gravitated to whomever they felt most attracted. Margaret White glanced towards Hugh just in case they could be together again for one last time, but he was already wrapped in the willing arms of Rowan Dowie. What on earth had he seen in her sister? Mrs Hunter, more pleased at seeing her husband again than she thought would be the case, held his hand. Kitty and Emily, after feigning disapproval, surrendered to the mood in the room and waddled towards Davy McConville. The children, aping the behaviour of their elders, snatched kisses from each other then ran away shrieking. Many of the couples spilled into the warm darkness where their laughter mingled with the distant lowing of the cattle.

As the morning sun sneaked into the barn through the many knotholes and gaps between the planks, the mood was more subdued. Several of the younger men stretched and made their way back to their own mattresses, while Emily Turnpike lit the fire under the pot to heat the porridge.

Hugh, who had returned to Elspeth's bed after his encounter with Rowan Dowie, had risen early for an arranged meeting with Davidson.

He seemed jubilant on his return, standing in the open doorway, dark against the light. 'Great news,' he announced. Elspeth pulled back the curtain to listen, then propped herself on one elbow. 'We have been given land to build our own home. Davidson needs the barn for the harvest, but we can build in the field to the north.' He rubbed his hands together. 'We will build Buchan Hall. The temple in which we will wait for the end of time.'

The Wifies looked at each other and shrugged. 'He can build it himsel',' muttered Kitty.

White walked across the sea of mattresses, administering a kick to Amy Johnson's pig as he passed. 'Solomon built the house of the Lord. Its length was sixty cubits and its width twenty cubits and its height thirty cubits... He covered the house with planks and beams of cedar, and he overlaid the floor of the house with boards of cypress, and he overlaid the inner sanctuary with gold... '

Davy McConville nudged John Gibson who was lacing his boots. 'How lang's a cubit?'

'It's the distance fae the elbow to the tip of your longest finger,' whispered the former master builder.

'No very big then,' said Davy. 'No for all these folk.' Gibson nodded. 'And cedar's no an easy wood to work wi'. And where's he getting the gold?'

White, seduced by the intensity of his own vision, continued to stride through the barn flaunting his architectural knowledge.

The Buchanites were enthused by the thought of leaving the barn and building their own house, which was either to be a temple, a mansion or a fortified tower, depending on who you listened to.

The Wifies, both of whom were permanently cold, no matter the weather, insisted that there be several hearths. Mrs Muir, who had embraced her role as custodian of all clothing, suggested that larger wardrobes be incorporated in the design. The apprentice boys and the younger women asked for more separation from their elders, not all of whom approved of their promiscuous lifestyle. There was a consensus too that Tam, increasingly perceived as a voyeuristic menace, should be given a separate outhouse. Amy Johnson asked if her pig could possibly have its own sty, or if that was not possible, it could perhaps share with Tam. Davy McConville and James Stewart made a case for a separate building that could function as a workshop. John Gibson took to obsessively laying his forearm and extending his fingers along any available surface so that he could more readily think in cubits. Ann and Agnes, relishing their role as surrogate parents to the community's children, raised the possibility of the young ones being housed separately. The idea was not dismissed out of hand, although Margaret White left the barn in tears.

Hugh White was in his element. Kneeling over a patch of dry earth outside of the barn with several of the men, he sketched an outline of the proposed building with his finger in the dust.

Elspeth didn't share her Manchild's enthusiasm and irritated him by asking what was the point of building a new temporary home on this sinful earth when they would soon be dwelling in Christ's own celestial palaces? 'In our new home the air will be suffused with glorious perfumes beyond imagining as petals rain from on high and lie deep on the pavements of gold and diamonds...'

William Lindsay, who had frequently listened to this description of the paradise that awaited him, had developed a profound aversion to flowers. Everyone knew they strangled the corn and attracted the birds. If he was honest, he far preferred the smell of dung. Fresh of course.

'Mother, will there be dung in heaven?' The moment the question escaped his lips he knew it was a mistake. Hugh White rose and dragged him by the collar out of the barn while Ruth looked on concerned.

Some of the others also needed his especial attention. A freckled apprentice boy had been behaving strangely. He avoided the others and was frequently in tears. The Lord Mother had tried to console him but to no avail. He had blurted out that although he loved the Lord Mother with all his heart, he was petrified of being dragged through the clouds.

'Ah cannae staun heights. Ah couldnae even cross the Stewarton brig. Ah feel that ma heart is aboot tae burst oot o' ma chest. Ah get the skitters and ah'm seik.'

Elspeth told him that the angels would cover his eyes with their wings, but he was inconsolable. He wanted to leave.

It was Andrew Innes who stumbled across his body in the yard. He must have fallen after relieving himself and hit his head on a stone. 'A thin skull,' said Innes, who frequently claimed medical knowledge after witnessing a barber surgeon letting blood from one of his siblings.

Chapter Twenty-Three

THE BROTHERS
Innerleithen

After their disappointment, the brothers felt no wish to remain in the vicinity of Manchester and so set out on their return journey. They subsisted by scavenging in the fields for food, and on one occasion, by stealing from the kitchen of a large house.

Unbeknown to the brothers, their return journey north took them agonisingly close to the Buchanites. But the residents of Tarbolton closed their doors as they passed. Had the locals been more forthcoming, they would have imparted tales of the mad woman and her indecent ways who had moved into the next parish; the gossips would have shaken their heads and pointed them in the direction of New Cample Farm, but it wasn't to be.

'No very friendly, are they?' observed James as a young girl stopped playing with her spinning top and ran away.

'But we will find her,' replied Mathew.

Several days later on the outskirts of Innerleithen they met the tinker. He was festooned with cages and surrounded by feathers.

'I didnae recognise ye at first,' said Mathew.

'Ye ken this man?' asked James.

'It's Birdman, he aye looked after me in the jail.'

The man nodded. 'Ah ken ye too.'

'Ye put crumbs o' breid by the bars. And they always came.'

'It's a gift ah dinnae understand mysel', and 'it's no jist the birds,' said the tinker. 'Ah can catch rabbits better than any man in the county. 'If yous wid gie us a hand pushing the cairt, ah'll be your cook and guide… and birdman.'

'Aye, we need one of them,' said Mathew, already resigned to accepting their new travelling companion.

As they explained their mission, Birdman nodded enthusiastically. 'A' the mad folk bide up the coast. She'll be in the Far North.'

THE WOMAN CLOTHED WITH THE SUN

As the three of them followed the road to Edinburgh, James had a strange sense that they were walking beneath an invisible canopy of bird song.

Chapter Twenty-Four

BUILDING BUCHAN HA'

The other apprentice boys were inconsolable and howled piteously when the body was discovered. They had their suspicions about the true cause of his death but were too frightened to speak their thoughts aloud. They had also heard rumours that the Lord Mother could bring dead animals back to life by breathing into their mouths, but Elspeth was prevented by White from approaching the fallen boy. 'Save your miracles for the deserving.'

Only when Alexander Gillespie and Andrew Innes had been ordered to watch for potential escapees, did White agree to the boy's burial. The society traipsed over the fields and watched as his coffin, made in great haste by Duncan Robertson, was lowered into the ground. Kitty and Emily held each other. The Dowie sisters sobbed and blew kisses as Davy McConville shovelled the earth onto the crude box. A sudden gust of wind removed Andrew Innes' hat and sent him scurrying over the heather to retrieve it. The Lord Mother stepped forward. 'Then we who are alive shall be caught up together with those in the clouds to meet the Lord in the air. Therefore comfort one another with these words.'

The Buchanites embraced sorrowfully and returned to the barn.

White, irritated by the lost hours, made plans, and issued orders. The loan of an ox was negotiated with Davidson and it was deployed to drag the stones from both the surrounding fields and the riverbed. To his annoyance, Davy McConville tore a muscle in his back during the first day and, no longer able to contribute his prodigious strength to the enterprise, took to organising the cartloads of red sandstone.

Andrew Innes, having dispatched John Gibson to purchase some stone dressing tools from Thornhill, eagerly embraced his former profession, willingly sharing his skills with two of the more sensible youths in the party. He enjoyed seeing the callouses return to his hands and simpered with pleasure whenever Katie Gardner paused to admire his handiwork.

On the second day of building, Emily Turnpike lay down her pail on returning from the well, stretched, and watched Innes manhandle a particularly large stone into position. As his mallet connected with the head of the chisel, a splinter flew into the air and embedded itself in her eye. She ran howling into the barn where Elspeth had been disputing with a local minister. The Lord Mother, growing bored of the man's pomposity, welcomed the distraction. She excused herself and consoled the old woman. 'Hush, Emily, hush, all shall be well.' She used the corner of her apron to clean the blood and blew gently onto Emily's eye. 'And the Lord opened the servant's eyes and he saw; and behold, the mountain was full of horses and chariots of fire all around Elisha.' Emily blinked and looked anxiously lest her problems were about to be compounded by stampeding horses. On seeing neither horses nor chariots, she thanked Elspeth and hurried to share her tale of healing with the others.

Once the disputatious minister had taken his leave none too graciously, Elspeth went into the yard, sat on a bench, and lit her pipe, but she was not at ease. She still viewed the new building with indifference. They were not meant to stay, to become comfortable. She looked above the pile of stones and wooden scaffolding at the small, rounded hill on the opposite side of the farm. Its contours suggested a sleeping person, a woman. A woman clothed with the moon and the stars under her feet. She was even more certain that this was the designated place from which she and the chosen ones would rise from their slumbers and ascend to glory. How she yearned to see His face and lose herself in His love. She knew she must be patient; she must endure.

She felt dissatisfied but couldn't identify the cause. And then she remembered. When Innes returned with Hunter and the others, he brought news that Robert Buchan had raised a petition of divorce against her. Why did this rankle? Matrimony counted for not a spit. It was a delusion that spread unhappiness and was directly counter to

God's wishes. And yet, and yet she was still visited by the memory of the blissful few weeks she had spent in Langside. She could still feel the warmth from the kiln and saw the line of small pottery angels fashioned for her by the man who had shown her nothing but kindness, and who had tolerated her ways that must have seen incomprehensible to him. She must stop these thoughts. They were no more than temptations; small worms of doubt dropped into her ears by the Prince of Darkness who never rested, never paused from his mission to subvert the word of God. She knocked her pipe out against the side of the bench.

Hugh White decreed that the one storey building was to be twelve ells long and six wide. The dimensions were largely dictated not by biblical precedent but by the number of stones that remained in the neighbouring fields. Davidson was delighted at the prospect of an increase in his arable land.

'No much of a temple then,' muttered Kitty, hoping that White had not heard her sacrilegious words.

The building was roofed with heather and consisted of a long garret running from end to end which was to serve as a communal bedroom for the society, accessed by a trap ladder fixed in the middle of the house. It was decreed that the lower space would be used for eating and for religious ceremonies. It was furnished with two rough deal tables, benches, a meal chest, a dresser, and a few cutty stools. There were two small closets partitioned off at one end for the use of Elspeth and White.

Elspeth declared that there would be a special blessing to mark their first night in Buchan Ha'. John Gibson was prevailed on to loosen the purse strings and Andrew Gillespie was despatched to purchase mutton and ale. The Wifies assumed responsibility for cooking the poultry gifted by Davidson who was eager to ingratiate himself with Jean Gardner whom he considered a most welcome addition to the society. His wife, assuming his interests were theological and not carnal, had grown accustomed to his absence from the family hearth. 'It's a special prayer meeting the night,' he would tell her on leaving the house.

'Again?'

The women waited patiently for Mrs Muir to mend and sew the

clothes they eagerly brought to her.

One of the apprentice boys reported that Tam had been seen washing in the burn, but this ridiculous idea was dismissed out of hand.

Emily asked Andrew Innes if he could fasten her a pin so that she could tie back her hair. 'Of course,' he said.

White pulled across the curtain separating him and Elspeth from the excited throng on the other side.

'Well, Lord Mother,' he whispered in her ear while running his hand down her breasts.

'Well, my shepherd.'

After the meal Mrs Gibson took the initiative and sang White's latest composition. This was not difficult as the tune never varied, and the words were endlessly interchangeable. Gradually the others joined in until Amy Johnson's pig, now fully grown and tethered outside, contributed his own discordant accompaniment. The menfolk banged their tankards on the table in as close an approximation to the rhythm as they could manage.

Elspeth moved among them, whispering words of encouragement, and hugging each in turn. 'Soon we will see His glory... He will wash away your aches and pains... His radiance will fill your heart... Yes, Neil, you will see your son again... We must be patient... '

White watched and wondered. Did they not understand that he, and not Elspeth, was the chosen one? While God may be using her as His conduit, it was his strength that would prevail.

Eventually the dishes were cleared, and the table pushed against the wall. This would be a blessing like no other. Tam wiped his lips lecherously. Emily stole a glance at Davy, remembering his smile when she had offered to rub ointment into his back.

White took Elspeth's hand and steered her into the middle of the room as if they were newlyweds and this was their first celebration among friends. Assuming this was the opening move in a dance, the others found partners and sufficient space to execute a turn or two. Kitty danced on her own, her arms outstretched, embracing the space once filled by her dead husband. Andrew Innes couldn't see Katie and wondered for a moment if she was hiding from him.

White moved Elspeth's hand from around his waist and pushed down on her shoulders until she was kneeling in front of him. Understanding what was expected, Elspeth undid the buttons on his breeches.

'Oh! Oh! Oh!'

Your Most Revered Lordships,

Please excuse my tardiness in communicating with you. In truth, that foul man White has grown over curious when he sees me with my pen in hand and, believing that I loyally transcribe his every pronouncement in addition to his facetious musical compositions, asks to read my journal. Accordingly, I am obliged to hide my epistles to you under a transcription of his nonsensical words.

O blasphemy has made its masterpiece! Of all the heresies perpetuated by this most wicked of societies, none is so demonic as the edict that all children in the society are to be raised in common. The sacred bonds between parent and child have been torn asunder. This most fundamental tenet of our sacred religion has been thrown to the devil. Your Lordships will recoil with horror when I tell you that some of the children are being raised by TWO mothers; women who enjoy carnal knowledge of each other! Such practices are anathema to even the most ignorant tribes who live in the jungles of Borneo.

To compound this folly, the 'Buchanites' have forsaken their barn and built a new temple, a monument to Beelzebub and his ways. O despair!

Their debauchery runs unchecked. Suffice it to say, I have witnessed White and his witch commit a public act of such indecency that it would make blush the depraved scribbler who chronicles the lewd and lascivious proceedings of the hell fire club of Anstruther, a publication of which I have heard BUT NEVER READ.

Your Lordships can no longer sit idly by. I strongly urge that you marshal all forces at your disposal and mount an assault on Buchan Hall; a true monument to shame.

Your faithful servant,
Alexander Gillespie

Chapter Twenty-Five

THE BROTHERS
Fraserburgh

'Shelfies,' said Birdman pausing in front of a bush alive with birds. 'Ye can tell by the white flash on the wing. And see, there's a wee pipit. There are no many this far north.' Thanks to their tutor, the brothers were getting better at identifying the wild birds that accompanied them on their journey north.

'And there's a huidie craw to scare it awa,' said James, tracing the predator's flight from the roof of the neighbouring cottage to the bush.

'Is this the place?' asked Mathew, eager to see if this was the abode of the mad woman who spoke of angels.

'Mebbe, mebbe,' said James.

They had endured several disappointments during the previous two months. An innkeeper in Kirkcaldy confirmed that Elspeth Buchan was alive and well in the neighbouring parish. The shrivelled crone in question barely looked up as the superintendent introduced the brothers to one of his more difficult residents. It wasn't Elspeth.

The minister from Cults had much to say about the female heretic who had been banished from his parish for declaring her love for a large dog she had found wandering by the Dee. 'She asked me to call the bans. She was aye crawling on all fours.' It wasn't Elspeth.

'Nae smoke fae the lum,' said Birdman. The brothers, not daring to hope, waited at the gate while their companion pushed his way through the door hanging off its hinges. He emerged seconds later holding a hand over his face. He shook his head. 'Deid.'

'For the love of Jesus,' said Mathew as he looked at the cadaver lying on the truckle bed, its emaciated hand resting on the floor.

'Poor soul,' said his brother, 'But it's nae Elspeth.'

Chapter Twenty-Six

A SICK CHILD

This was the first public display of intimacy between the Lord Mother and her Shepherd that any of the society had witnessed. They all knew full well what had passed between them behind the curtains in the barn, but this was different.

'Rod of iron!' murmured Kitty until Emily jabbed her in the ribs. Ann and Agnes looked at each other, relieved that the children were already sleeping in their heather beds.

Outside of the hall, Robert Burns stood on tiptoe and gawked through the window as the tableau of debauchery unfolded. This was not the first time he had indulged his voyeuristic instincts. Irritated by his mother's insistence that he get a real job and stop 'footling wi' a' these daft wee poems,' he would frequently escape her nagging by visiting Closeburn, hoping to glimpse his Jean through the windows of Buchan Ha'. He had been pleased to note how over time the blessings had grown even more intimate than he had remembered them from his days in Irvine. He was delighted too by the indiscriminate nature of the couplings, and the palpable joy of those involved. On one occasion he had been astonished to see two completely naked old women wrestling happily with a man big enough to be a blacksmith. He had even considered ripping off his breeches and bursting through the door to join in the happy endeavours but had lacked the courage. But rarely had he seen anything like this.

Jean Gardner screamed. White opened his eyes and looked in the direction of the window at which she was pointing. Annoyed, he pulled up his breeches.

'His face!' she shrieked. Relieved by this distraction from their mounting embarrassment, several of the men ran to the door and set off in pursuit of a figure running across the fields in the direction of Thornhill.

Jean was inconsolable. 'It was him,' she panted.

'Who, dear?' asked Margaret White. She had especially welcomed the interruption to the business between her husband and the Lord Mother.

'Him. The poet, wi' his white face and mad, staring eyes.'

The men returned, their quarry having eluded them.

For several, the memories of the previous evening were hazy at best. A popular idea spread by Humphy Hunter was that the publican had sold Alexander Gillespie contaminated beer. 'We're no popular in the village,' he explained. 'It's because we freely give of our labour.'

'It had a tint o' nightshade,' said Davy McConville. 'Left a nasty taste.'

'Mebbe a rat had died in the cask,' suggested James Stewart.

'Or a craw... '

The comparative comfort of their new accommodation proved a welcome distraction from the practicalities of the Great Translation whenever it might come to pass. Buchan Ha', as it was dubbed, was warmer and more spacious than Davidson's barn. Elspeth gave assurances to the Wifies that their journey to the heavens was not imminent; they would have time enough to enjoy their new home. White complimented James Stewart on the quality of the shoes he was making and asked if he too might be measured for a pair. Elspeth once more told Ann and Agnes that God would not separate them when the end of the world came; of course they could hold onto one another when they heard the last trump. White had a quiet word with John Gibson and thanked him for his assiduous management of the society's finances. He also revised the work schedule to ensure that no-one was required to toil for an entire day without rest or refreshment. Elspeth, having persuaded Jean Gardner to use her charms on Davidson and secure a quantity of pigs' blood, promised that there would be a surfeit of puddings that evening.

The new building soon attracted the interest of the locals who had for several months been eagerly spreading rumours of satanic practices and ritual slaughter based on innuendos attributable to the various ministers who had visited Elspeth. The Reverend Timms shook his head when he described the sleeping accommodation to his curious parishioners. 'The beds a' touch each other,' he declared, 'and when I visited, I heard sounds of… ' – he could barely bring himself to utter the words, but so charged was the expectation of his audience that he eventually overcame his reluctance – ' … of copulation!' An elderly spinster of the parish who held the minister in unqualified awe, could not for the life of her imagine what these sounds might be; somewhere between a fart and the noise the devil might make when grinding his teeth, she assumed.

The young boys of the parish would dare each other to hurl stones and abuse at the Buchanites working in the fields. One particularly well aimed rock found its mark. Davy McConville, now fully recovered from his back complaint, strode through the corn like a man-of-war ploughing the sea. Grabbing two urchins by the ears, he soundly thrashed their backsides and sent them home to their mothers. The others voiced their approval then bent again to their tasks.

Jean Gardner, still disturbed by the face she had glimpsed at the window, persuaded Mrs Muir to make curtains for the main room. After an evening spent writing to her friend in Irvine, she found a note on the elevated end of the mattress that served as her pillow. She reached for the candle, and read:

'I couldna say How much, how dear I love thee, I see thee dancing o'er the green, Thy waist sae jimp, thy limbs sae clean, Thy tempting lips… ' She crumpled the note and held it to the flame until she burned her fingers. She would ask the men to be more vigilant for the scrawny, tallow faced, black-haired man who was besotted with her. He must have returned when they were working in the fields.

Only the Wifies were spared the harvest. White had asked the men to build him a wooden dais in the middle field from which he could supervise his labourers and spot defectors. Despite the late summer sun, Andrew Innes refused to abandon his stovepipe hat. At least it made it easier to observe his progress as he toiled among the stalks that matched him in height. Davy McConville could be seen moving among the workers, sharpening any blunted sickles. Having applied the stone to a blade, he would run it along his forearm until he drew a thin line of blood, testimony to his skill. The Buchanites, working in teams of three, swung their implements in a shared rhythm, their blades glinting through a flurry of dust and insects. When one paused, the others followed suit, stretching and wiping the sweat from their eyes. Humphy Hunter made the mistake of glancing at the sun during one of these breaks and had to wait several minutes before the motes cleared and his sight returned. Elspeth made it her duty to engage with each knot of workers. Eager to hear the Lord Mother, and indeed to rest a while, they bowed as she approached. Innes even removed his hat.

After touching each of them on the shoulder or face, she spoke, 'And behold, I saw sitting on a white cloud one who resembled the Son of man, with a crown of gold on His head and a sharp scythe in His hand...' She took Jamie's scythe and held it up to the sun. 'And another angel came out of the temple, calling with a mighty voice to Him who was sitting upon the cloud. "Thrust in your sickle and reap for the time is come for thee to reap; for the time to reap for the harvest of the earth is ripe." The men smiled self-consciously.

Apart from a dwindling succession of curious ministers of the cloth, there were few visitors to Buchan Ha'. Understandably then, the urgent knock at the door late one night was a cause for alarm. John Gibson armed himself with a cudgel before opening the door to a young couple, shivering with the cold, holding a bundle.

'Can the holy woman cure our bairn?' asked the young man, holding out the sick child. Gibson grunted and went to wake Elspeth. The Lord Mother soon appeared in her night attire, followed by White who made no effort to hide his annoyance at being woken.

'We have no shelter for tinkers,' he said, while wondering if he couldn't make an exception for the child's comely mother whose baleful eyes roused him.

'He's seik,' said the father who, in the light of the lantern produced by Gibson, looked no more than sixteen years of age. 'Folk say you have powers denied to the rest of us. Make him weil again. Please.'

'Please, ma'am,' echoed the young woman who had lowered her eyes under White's unwanted scrutiny.

As Elspeth moved to take the child, White intervened and pushed the strangers towards the door. 'Don't you see?' he hissed. 'They are spies sent by our enemies to destroy us.'

'Fuckers,' muttered the father as he turned away from the hall. 'Damn you! Damn you, witch!' he shouted before his voice was muffled by the wind.

'They have no souls,' mumbled Elspeth before surrendering to an unannounced vision of death. Before White closed the door, she stood, horrified and helpless, watching a dumb show of cadavers stretching to a dark, smouldering horizon.

Chapter Twenty-Seven

THE BROTHERS
Banff

The three men met a packman who purchased a tame jackdaw from Birdman. In his cups he was adamant that a woman answering to Elspeth's description was running a dame school in Banff. 'Some size of a woman they say, with an eye for the men. They a' fall in love wi' her. Magic powers. She says Jesus Christ's her brither.'

The brothers rested on the outskirts of the town. They needed to savour the possibility that this time they would find Elspeth. Endless disappointments had taken their toll, and they were reluctant to prematurely embrace the next one. Nevertheless, the expectation was to be enjoyed. They rested against a hay rick and looked at the distant sea and the vast sky. Birdman stood with his face upturned, a joyous expression crossing his features. He was simultaneously watching the ascent and descent of five larks at different points in the sky. He had set his traps. A brace of larks would command a goodly sum at the market.

'She will be fair pleased to see us,' said James rubbing his leg that still swelled at the end of each day.

'Aye, that she will.'

'What do you mean she's no here?' Mathew's fierceness frightened the small child who ran away down the hill. 'She was an auld witch, a bad woman,' the boy shouted defiantly from a safe distance. 'The deil skelped her erse and took her soul doon to hell wi' him. Tae Glasgow.'

The brothers pushed their way into the schoolroom. Childish chalk drawings of animals and spiky suns still adorned the plaster walls. A dominie's slate snapped under Mathew's tread. James stepped into the adjacent workroom thick with clay dust. He stooped to pick up a small pottery angel. Birdman impersonated the distressed call of a lapwing.

Chapter Twenty-Eight

THE ATTACK

The sick child died in its mother's arms before they reached Thornhill. The incident fuelled the rumours already poisoning the village. At worst, the Buchanites were satyrs and witches cavorting in a contaminated cesspit of indulgence and lust. At best, they were a cabal with rituals and practices that would shock Auld Nick himself. Something must be done.

As the leaves fell and the hills turned from green to ochre, there were fewer occasions for work and more for gossip, and indeed, doubt. The relentless rain dampened the fires of belief, while the claustrophobic hall bred restlessness in the hearts of those for whom labouring in the fields had been quietly satisfying. The apprentice boys passed most days playing cards. The Wifies slept for hours on end. Mrs Gibson and Margaret White quietly shared their disapproval of how their children were being treated by the others. Amy Johnson fretted about the plight of her now fully-grown pig, which although tethered, had been left to fend for itself in the increasingly harsh elements. James Stewart, unable to work in the leaking lean-to, had migrated to a corner of the hall where the constant tap of his hammer played on the nerves of everyone in the room.

'For the love of our dear Lord and Saviour,' said Davy McConville, normally the most patient of men. 'How many pairs do you think we will need? Are you making them for the angels now?' The cobbler looked ruefully at the small barricade of shoes behind which he seemed to be hiding.

White paced up and down the hall. No-one made eye contact, fearful lest they were summarily punished for some misdemeanour of which they were not aware. His patience finally snapped when the youngest Hunter child twisted his sister's arm until she howled. The boy had been a source of disruption and discord since the flight from Irvine. When not whining for food, or stealing, he would follow Amy Johnson around the hall pretending to be a pig. White grabbed him by the scruff of the neck, effectively lifting him from the ground, and threw him at the feet of his bewildered mother.

'Take this boy and kill him! Hurl him from a cliff, drown him, bury him alive if you like. But kill him!' Mrs Hunter cradled her son in her arms. She looked in vain for Humphy but he was nowhere to be seen. 'These are not my words alone. It is what the Lord Mother wishes. You have heard her preach. Children have no souls. They are worth nothing. Kill him!'

Mrs Hunter held her son tightly. She knew what White was capable of. The freckly apprentice boy was not the first source of rumour. In the early days, Paul, the infant son of a farm labourer and his chilpit wife, had disappeared from the barn after a long period of illness characterised by violent coughing fits. White had explained to the distraught parents that the boy must have sneaked undetected out of the hall and wandered off into the night where some misfortune must have befallen him. Mrs Hunter still heard the cries of anguish that greeted this explanation. White would not harm her son.

Elspeth was increasingly preoccupied. On the rare occasions she ventured out into the yard and looked at the sky, she found it harder to believe that soon, the same clouds would be sundered by the bright shaft of God's light. Had He forsaken her?

Her lethargy irritated White. 'You must lead and inspire. Our people need you,' he hissed so that his words would not be overheard. She looked away.

'I want to go home,' said Elizabeth to Alan. 'I cannae sleep in this room. I need the fresh air. I want to lie wi' you in the fields again.'

'And get a wet erse?'

'I'm serious, Alan. I feel that I'm suffocating.'

The simmering discontent was felt most strongly by the younger members of the society for whom the novelty of communal living was wearing thin.

Every day seemed to bring new causes for discontent. To make matters worse, the Wifies had recently embarked on a competition to decide whose infirmity was the most painful.

'I've got lice in my privates,' grumbled Emily, squirming.

'My bowels have turned to stane,' grumbled Kitty.

'I'll stick a weasel up your erse, if you dinnae stop complaining,' shouted Davy McConville wondering if he could move his mattress away from the moaners. 'That'll mak you shit.' The oldest Gibson child stopped picking his nose while he considered the logistics of the overheard threat.

Elspeth tried hard to dispel the lethargy infecting the society. 'You must be patient; you must strive to have faith.' Even to her own ears, the words sounded empty. They stuck in her throat as she was enveloped in a familiar bleakness. Knowing that she was sinking fast, she retired behind the curtain and covered her nose, mouth, and ears with her hands. There must be no orifice through which the visions could enter and scald her. But her efforts were in vain. She gasped as she saw a young man approach, distant then closer, straddling a cockerel, a skull, and a sword. He held a burning fuse with a flaming tip. Every inch of his flesh was marked with the letters from a demonic alphabet, the tight squares of a portcullis and musical notation from a vile anthem accompanying the damned into hell. Elspeth shook her cheeks loosely and fast like a horse shaking water from its head. The image splintered sending sparks into the sky where they quietly died. Not daring to breathe, Elspeth stayed still.

In the main hall, two of the youths after a lengthy period of niggling and minor provocation resorted to blows. They writhed and swore for several minutes before staggering into the Wifies who fell like tavern skittles. 'Stupid galoots!' said Kitty who had spilt her broth. White separated the boys. Choosing to make an example of the physically smaller of the two, he marched him out of the hall. Inspired by curiosity and apprehension in equal measure, the Buchanites followed them over the fields. White, aware of his audience, waded into the burn and pushed the boy's head under the water. Only when the struggling stopped and the thin necklace of bubbles ceased, did he let his victim splutter his way to the bank. With his authority reasserted, and feeling magnanimous, White led the return to Buchan Hall but not before a quick headcount to make certain that no-one had escaped.

White reluctantly embraced his role as arbiter, settling disputes over the allocation of food, accommodation, and the occasional accusation of theft which was usually directed at Tam. Mrs Gibson, still smarting from the loss of her children to Ann and Agnes, almost summoned the courage to state her case. On balance, she decided that White might exercise the wisdom of Solomon and order the oldest child be cut in half and divided equally between the competing factions.

For several weeks Elspeth had spent most of her days in seclusion behind the dividing screen. She could be heard talking to herself as she wrote letter after letter to correspondents, sincere and vexatious, who made contact seeking advice or guidance on matters spiritual. White grew increasingly impatient with her. 'They need a sign,' he said poking his head through a gap in the curtain. 'You can't forsake us now.'

'All in God's good time,' she replied. 'Remember I am the Lord Mother.'

Unable to sleep because of the sickness in her belly, Elizabeth was still haunted by the expression on the face of the rejected young mother. She had nudged Alan, but he wasn't for waking. For two weeks, she had denied the evidence of her own body. It must have been the berries in the hedge that made her sick. Toiling hard in the fields had induced cramps. Her craving for sweetmeats was easily explained by her hankering for the life she had known before she abandoned her father's hearth. She dared not tell Alan.

Joseph Gabriel, who had fought at Derby and took the credit for an orderly retreat from the battlefield, took charge of the operation. They met at the Brownhill Inn on the Thornhill Road and over significant quantities of ale, plotted their assault on Buchan Ha'. The local minister had discreetly let it be known that people much more important than himself would applaud any action they were to take. Rumours that a dying infant had been refused shelter was the final provocation.

'Burn the thatch,' suggested Mockit Willy, 'and hit the critters wi' mallets when they flee.'

'Poison the well, let their inners rot and their entrails come oot o' their arses,' was Israel's main contribution.

'Visit them with a biblical plague,' suggested the landlord who prided himself on his familiarity with the scriptures.

'And what form might that take?' asked Joseph Gabriel. 'No many locusts round these pairts.'

'Na. Rats. Hunners o' them. Empty a sack o' rats doun the lum while they shag each other.'

Eventually the wisdom of the Derby veteran prevailed. 'The air is changing; sna's coming. Wait 'til it lies thick on the ground.' The others nodded in appreciation of their companion's wisdom, and an attack was planned for Christmas Eve, when according to Gabriel, the Buchanites would be least prepared.

Buchan Ha' leaked. The sleet snuffed out the fire in the hearth. The wind rattled the windows and spread its chill through the rooms. White, swaddled in sheepskins, busied himself putting the final touches to *The Divine Dictionary*. He was completely indifferent to the news that several of the faithful were becoming unwell. The Wifies, touched by the ague, shivered. Elspeth held them both in her arms, reassuring them that 'All shall be well.'

'And all manner of thing shall be well,' they replied, gazing in rapture at the woman who would soon lead them into paradise.

Intimations that all might not be well were passed on by the factor at Closeburn Hall. Impressed by the Buchanites' industry, he had asked Hugh White if they had a dry stane dyker in their midst as one of the estate's perimeter walls was on the point of collapse. White, recalling that young Alan had been serving his apprenticeship in the trade, offered his services. A deal was struck and, for a sum of money not disclosed to Elspeth, Alan and three other men set to and repaired the wall. Eager to return the favour, the factor passed on the rumours that he had heard in the Brownhill Inn. White was grateful and readily accepted an invitation for him and the Lord Mother to take refuge in

Closeburn Hall when the attack was imminent.

After discussion with Elspeth, a stratagem was agreed. All that remained was to explain the plan to the society.

When the plates had been cleared and thanks given to God, Elspeth, having waited for silence, approached White and slapped him hard across the face. Emily Turnpike dropped her cup and the others gasped. White's temper was well known, as was the increasingly fractious nature of his relationship with the Lord Mother. A terrible storm was about to break. After staring at Elspeth for an interminable time, White turned the other cheek and smiled. The tension was broken.

Eager to show off, Andrew Innes took to the floor. 'But I say, do not resist an evil person! If someone slaps you on the right cheek, offer the other cheek also... ' Seeing that Elspeth was approving, he continued. 'Look I am sending you out as sheep among wolves. So be as shrewd as snakes and harmless as doves... furthermore... ' White indicated that he had said enough. The pantomime was the prelude to an agreement that in the event of an attack, the Buchanites, without Elspeth or White who would be in a place of safety, would sit in passive silence to confuse and confound their assailants.

The snow had been falling for almost a week when the factor fought his way over the fields from the Brownhill Inn to warn White that the attack was imminent. Before mounting the assault, the villagers were fortified with drink from the complicit landlord who had long harboured resentment that the Buchanites never frequented his tavern.

White ordered every man and woman, including those still lying unwell in their beds, to sit quietly around the table while he and the Mother departed with the factor for the warm sanctuary of Closeburn Hall. Amy Johnson briefly fretted about the wellbeing of her pig until silenced by a threat from Davy McConville who said that if he heard another word about the wretched pig, he would personally slit its throat. The shutters were tightly closed, and the wait began. Alexander Gillespie said that he would not join them at the table. He would instead observe proceedings from a distance so that he could provide the Reverend White with a detailed account of whatever was about to occur.

Andrew Innes slipped out of the door, shivered as the snow gusted into his face, and surveyed the darkness for signs of the expected attack. After a quarter of an hour spent beating his arms against his overcoat, he saw in the distance the guttering light from many lanterns. The pattern of pinpricks suggested that the villagers were struggling to make headway through the drifts that lay deep on the hills.

Innes re-entered the hall, pursued by a flurry of snow and raised the alarm. Most of the Buchanites were already sitting as if waiting for food to be served. They were quickly joined by the others who had been hiding their possessions as best they could in the spartan room. Emily and Kitty, who had rallied after the Lord Mother's ministrations, sat together and held hands. Davy McConville, who had struggled with the notion of passive resistance, held tightly to the hammer in his lap. Ann and Agnes, having corralled the younger children and pushed them under the table, urged them to be still and silent. Their exhortations proved pointless as there was much more fun to be had irritating Mrs Gibson by taking turns to run their fingers up her legs.

The gun shots, although muffled by the snow, were sufficiently loud to raise the level of fear in the room. To rally the others, Margaret White sang the first words of her husband's latest composition, but no-one joined in, and her voice trailed away. Elizabeth cradled her stomach to protect the tiny child within.

Outside, Joseph Gabriel was in his element. Once more, in his own eyes at least, a bold soldier of fortune, he flailed his arms, signalling that the assault could commence. Unable to see the human windmill in their midst but equally unable to wait patiently much longer, the villagers hurled their rocks at the door and shutters.

'Dear God,' said Kitty.

'Save us a',' echoed her friend. John Gibson put his fingers to his lips and stared at them.

When the rocks bounced off the shutters, Davy McConville rose from his seat clutching his hammer until restrained by the others.

In Closeburn Hall, the laird listened entranced as Elspeth described the fresh pastures of paradise. 'The scent of flowers will intoxicate; the melody of birdsong will soothe the breast and rekindle love for the gracious God who shares with us His bounty and goodness... '

The laird signalled for the factor to put another log on the fire and to replenish Hugh White's cup.

'When the angels pass, the movement of their wings will spin subtle melodies that fill the heart with joy unbounding.'

White sipped his whisky and wondered when it would be safe to return to Buchan Hall.

The Thornhill blacksmith inserted his crowbar into each shutter in turn. Once his fellow villagers added their weight, the planks sprung apart. It was now an easy matter to break the glass. Kitty was horrified to see a spittle-flecked face grinning at her. The face then winked before being replaced by a much angrier countenance that mouthed a threat that was mercifully incomprehensible. More windows were broken; the cold air and the battle cries chilled the room. The Buchanites, most of whom were holding hands beneath the table, derived a collective strength from each other. 'The Lord Mother will not forsake us,' whispered Andrew Innes.

'Never,' repeated the others in turn. 'Never.'

By now the door had been wrenched from its hinges and the villagers burst into the room. The foremost paused and grew silent. The others crowded forward and were also soon rendered speechless by what they beheld. The Buchanites sat, their heads bowed and as still as if carved from stone. This was not what the invaders had expected.

A shout of 'Hang the witches!' from the innkeeper broke the spell. The others rallied. It had been agreed that they would each drag one of the Buchanites out of the room into the snow where they could treat them as they saw fit.

A large man grabbed Andrew Innes and holding him easily under his arm marched him outside. 'Pick on someone your ain size,' said Kitty Buckie before she too was bundled into the snow by a tall youth with exceedingly bad breath.

The apprentice boys proved less acquiescent than the others until they were soundly cuffed for their pains. Davy McConville proved particularly uncooperative, holding himself stiff, refusing to change his posture. It took three men to carry him bodily outside, still in a sitting pose.

The villagers' planning had not extended to what they would do with their captives once they had removed them from the hall. Eventually they all assembled on the Thornhill Road where they stood, prisoners and guards alike, in the freezing cold. For the villagers, the excitement of the chase had been replaced by a sense of anti-climax, and perhaps embarrassment. For the Buchanites, their initial fear had been replaced by a growing defiance. Kitty kicked her captor hard on his shins. He clutched his leg and looked at her reproachfully. 'Why did you dae that, ye mad witch?'

'Because you are my new best friend,' said Kitty pulling herself up to her full height.

'Is it true that you all lie wi' each other?' asked a ploughman from the neighbouring farm.

'Aye,' said one of the apprentice boys. 'A different lassie each night.'

'Can onybody join?' asked the ploughman.

Eventually the villagers left and returned to the Brownhill Inn, leaving the Buchanites, sore and dispirited, to trudge back to the hall where they were greeted by Alexander Gillespie who emerged from a cupboard clutching his journal.

The room had been emptied of all their possessions and the furniture broken beyond repair.

'My poor love!' shrieked Amy Johnson, rushing to stem the flow of blood from the neck of her dying pig.

The children were found under the far end of the table where they had moved to avoid the advancing pool of pig's blood. Ann and Agnes crouched down to persuade them to come out. The mood among the returning Buchanites was muted as they congratulated each other on still being alive.

'Look,' said Kitty holding out a leather purse. 'His money, I took it from his pocket as he dragged me through the sna. Big stinkin' brute of a man. I telt him, get your filthy hands aff of me or I'll… ' She mimed a vicious kick at the space between herself and the door before emptying the contents of the purse onto the table. 'Four pounds siller,' she said.

'Hide it, hide it,' urged Emily. 'Before White spies it.'

Elizabeth and Alan held each other. 'Are you unhurt my dearest?'

'Fine, fine,' she said. Soon she must tell him about the child.

Andrew Innes knocked his hat back into shape before he started issuing orders. 'Mend the door,' he said to Jas Logan, a relative newcomer to the group who had previously worked as a carpenter on a local estate. 'You lads,' to the apprentices, 'nail planks over the windaes until we can mend the panes.'

He interrupted Mrs Muir who was rubbing ointment into a nasty wound on Davy McConville's arm. 'Leave that the now. Get some rags and mop the flair.' Amy Johnson sobbed as three of the men dragged her pig into the snow which turned crimson in the dawn.

Davidson, whose dreams had been peppered with the sound of gunfire and shouting, had missed the attack. He now stood in the doorway taking stock of what had passed. 'They will pay,' he said. 'They will pay.'

At midday, Elspeth and White reappeared to a rapturous reception from the society.

'Praise be the Lord Mother.'

'All praise to her who will lead us out of the wilderness,' said White through gritted teeth.

Had there been a fatted calf it would have been slaughtered. A dead pig wasn't quite the same.

Before they departed, Lord Closeburn had given his guests several bottles of strong spirits, one of which White now dispensed liberally among the followers. Tam threw back his dram and presented his cup for a second time. To his surprise it was replenished.

On the short journey back from Closeburn Hall, White had composed a new hymn which he now sang with gusto.

'The people in Closeburn parish residing / Came often our sermons to hear, / And rudely they questioned our words, tho' most pure / Our persons they threatened to tear. / They often with batons and cudgels combined, / With billets of wood combined, / But He who has power all men to control / prevented them breaking our bones.'

Humphy Hunter, who still looked back fondly at his finely composed reports to the Irvine parish council, thought it was probably the worst hymn he had ever heard. Even so, he joined in and by elongating several vowels managed to make the words match the tune. He too was pleased to see the Lord Mother return. In truth, he had been less ill-treated by the villagers than many. Seeing his hunchback, his attacker, a simple youth with few words, had quickly let him go, and ran off into the night, fearful that deformities such as his were contagious. What would his girl say if he returned with an extra limb growing from his back?

By now the fire had been rekindled in the hearth and they all took their turn to stand three in a row to warm their bones and dry their clothes.

Elspeth moved among them, embracing each in turn. 'We will triumph against all adversity. We must be patient. Soon our time will come, and we will rise to see His glorious face and bask in His eternal favour.'

'Amen,' said the Wifies.

'Amen,' said the menfolk.

'Amen,' said the young lovers.

When Elizabeth eventually fell asleep, White stalked her dreams. Wielding blood-soaked forceps, he invaded her womb and dragged out her child.

Chapter Twenty-Nine

LIGHT AND MUSIC

The Buchanites worked steadily at repairing the hall. John Gibson travelled to Dumfries to secure the services of a glazier prepared to bring his cart and tools to New Cample. During his brief stay, the glazier enjoyed a dalliance with Meg Dowie who embraced the opportunity to make the apprentice boys jealous. She also wanted to signal to White that he had not been forgiven for his unwanted approach. So agreeable did the tradesman find his sensual sojourn, that he seriously considered leaving his wife, several children, two dogs and considerable personal debt to join the Buchanites. However, Hugh White, having developed a growing dislike for the man, told him in no uncertain terms to pack his tools and return whence he came.

Equally unwelcome was the return of Mrs Innes who had never recovered from the decision of her remaining children to join their older brother. Since their departure from Muthill, she had carefully nurtured her wrath, denouncing the Buchanites as fornicating charlatans who had seduced her beautiful offspring.

When she arrived in Buchan Ha' the room was comparatively empty as the men were toiling in the fields. Mrs Muir was passing on her weaving skills to a small group of women while, at the far end of the table, Elspeth and White were sketching the outline of a new chapter for *The Divine Dictionary*.

'Where is the hoor? Where's Satan's ain fadoodler? Where's the deil's favourite harlot? What hochmagandie has been gaun' on?' She filled the open doorway, but was only visible in fearsome silhouette against the bright sun. 'Gie me ma bairns back. Where are ye? Come tae yer mither. Come hame wi' me!'

White put down his pen.

'Let's be having you! You weak-kneed, weak-spirited, deluded fools.' She paused while she searched the room for Elspeth. 'There you are, Satan's plaything! Come and fecht if you're hauf the woman you say you are!' She swung her cudgel in the manner of a chapbook ogre. Elspeth backed away as Andrew Innes emerged from under a blanket and attached himself to his mother's leg. The Gorgon barely broke her stride, completely unaware that her son was trying to halt her progress. She eventually glanced down and recognised him. 'Andra, Andra,' she said laying her weapon on the table. 'What has that sorceress done to ye? Come hame with me. Bring your brothers and sisters.'

Andrew, smothered in his mother's bosom, struggled for breath.

Mrs Innes approached the startled knot of weavers. Snatching one of the bobbins from the frame, she poked Mrs Muir hard in the ribs with her improvised weapon.

Hearing the commotion, White rose from the table, grabbed the broom resting in the corner and attacked the intruder who, deciding that retreat was the wisest option, fled out of the door and over the fields. The men paused and looked up. 'It's oor mother again,' said Andrew Innes placing a protective arm around Joseph. 'Dinnae say anything to your brother and sister, it'll only upset them.' Together they watched White chase her as far as the Thornhill Road, then shrugged and returned to their labours.

Once the plates had been cleared from the table, the group watched Elspeth expectantly. 'Mother, tell us again about heaven,' said Emily Turnpike. The others looked surprised. Normally the topic for discussion was chosen by Elspeth, and occasionally by White. This was unusual. How would the Lord Mother react?

She reacted well. Smiling at Emily, she paused before launching forth.

'Who do you miss in the dark of night when the owl hoots and the mice come out to play? Whose arms no longer hold you? Whisper their names in your heart.'

'My ain Dougie,' whispered Kitty.

'William,' muttered Emily.

'Yes,' said Elspeth, her voice growing deeper. 'Beloved husbands and wives. If you could speak to them one last time, what would you say?'

'I found the keys,' said Mrs Muir to her long dead husband who, before he collapsed from apoplexy, blamed her for losing them.

'Oor laddie got marrit,' said Jeannie Watt whose spouse had always maintained that no woman in her right mind would ever marry their son with his withered hand.

'Dinnae leave me,' sobbed Mrs Young. 'No yet.'

'And lovers...' continued Elspeth making eye contact with Davidson who had joined them for the meal. Embarrassed, he thought of Nancy, the chambermaid who had to leave the Brownhill Inn when he made her pregnant. Where was she now? Did she have the bairn? Did it look like him? And how did Elspeth Buchan know about her?

'And children...' Several of those present stifled a sob as a multitude of stillborn infants crowded into the room. Thomas Neil's shoulders shook as he, once more, removed his son from the scaffold.

Elspeth, skilfully reading the mood in the room, altered tack. 'And friends who left...'

Davy McConville thought of his pal Jamie who, rather than face trial for poaching, escaped and went to sea. Not a word since.

'You will see them all again,' declared Elspeth, moving among the society and touching each in turn on the shoulder or arm. 'They will be waiting for you. Husbands, wives, the children who never got to grow. The friends who left forever. All there.'

'I'll gi' him a piece of my mind too,' said Kitty smiling contentedly.

'Heaven awaits,' said Elspeth to a rising chorus of amens.

Elizabeth stood and closed the door. She feared that the child in her belly might die of heat. She hadn't yet found the courage to reveal her condition to Alan as she knew he would be distraught. Elspeth had frequently made clear that there was no room for any more children in the hall.

Despite her best efforts, Elspeth was aware of the discontent infecting the society. 'You must be patient,' she urged during her evening address. 'You must strive to have faith.'

'We try, Mother, but sometimes it is hard,' said Mrs Dunlop. White looked at the dumpy woman who had spoken. He had not noticed her before but would keep an eye on her from now on in case she was the one spreading disharmony. If so, he would soon teach her how to have faith.

'Dear brethren, I understand. Like the disciples before you, you need a sign of His greatness. On this occasion, I will provide you with a demonstration of His powers.'

White looked on bemused.

Elspeth beckoned to Mrs Dunlop and, snatching a cloth from the table, indicated that she should accompany her. As they stepped outside, the others clamoured to follow. Elspeth held up her hand, making it clear that they were not to step beyond the low wall that marked the extent of their property. Meanwhile she led Mrs Dunlop towards the hill that she had earlier identified as the site of the inevitable Great Translation.

Once they reached the crest, she unfolded the cloth which they then held between them.

'Keep it tight,' urged Elspeth, 'lest we let fall the golden coins which will soon tumble through the sundered sky.' She looked upwards. The wind was raw and her eyes smarted. 'Come, Great Christ, and visit us with your bounty. Reveal to us your munificence.'

Mrs Dunlop also squinted at the sky but saw nothing. In a small gesture of impatience, Elspeth shook the cloth sending small ripples towards her companion. It occurred to Mrs Dunlop that if God missed His mark, she might be injured by coins falling from the very heights of heaven.

'It is your lack of faith that is to blame.' Elspeth screwed up the cloth and flounced down the hill with Mrs Dunlop in her wake. When they reached the knot of observers, White took the cloth from her and carefully unfurled it onto the earth. As he did so, the others gasped at the sight of the gold guinea nestling in one of the folds.

'God be praised,' said William Lindsay who had, until that moment, been sceptical about miracles.

White was dumbfounded. Had it not been for his quick thinking and his sleight of hand, the Lord Mother would have been exposed in the eyes of her followers. In that moment, the full extent of Elspeth's vulnerability was laid bare, and he was repulsed by what he saw. She was a mountebank peddling false hope and deception. She was not the woman clothed with the sun and the moon as foretold in Revelations but a woman like any other, weak, and deserving of punishment. Unable to vent his anger on Elspeth, he settled on Mrs Dunlop, propelling her out of the door and into the barn where he took a flail and beat her. The frightened woman howled as the blows rained on her head and back. Her tunic was soon stained with blood.

No-one spoke when he re-entered the hall. The message was clear: they must have faith. They must fear not only their all-knowing God, but also Hugh White, His representative on earth.

It was one of the English newcomers who brought the book. He offered it as a gift to the Lord Mother. 'You are not the first,' he said presenting her with the new translation of John Engelbrecht's *Divine Visions of heaven and hell; The New Heavens and the New earth, The Mountain of Salvation, and the Three States – Ecclesiastical, Political, and Economic.* Elspeth ran her finger over the soft leather. Yes, she had heard tell of the German tailor from Brunswick.

She read the small tome avidly, increasingly excited by the encounter with a long dead mystic who, like herself, had been granted visions into other realms. Her finger followed each word and her mouth shaped them noiselessly.

The Buchanites welcomed the change in her. She became animated once more; on occasions exclaiming with joy at a passage that resonated. One evening while striding across the hall and declaiming loudly, she walked into the beam that sloped down in the upper chamber. Mrs Young staunched the blood from her forehead but still the Lord Mother read on.

'Listen my love, listen.' She was desperate to share her insight with White who showed complete disinterest. The last thing he wanted was a revival in her spirits. He knew that if Elspeth regained her previous enthusiasm, he would again be forced into a subservient role.

Elspeth stood on a stool and exuded a radiance not seen for many months. 'This evening we will feast as if we had obtained our destination.' The announcement prompted murmurs of anticipation. As the men left for the fields, their high spirits were evident. The womenfolk knew that the weaving would have to wait if they were to fulfil the Lord Mother's wishes. Andrew Innes, without consulting either White or treasurer Gibson, visited Davidson to negotiate victuals and drink. The farmer was more than willing to oblige. Having been rebuffed by Jean Gardner, he had turned his attentions to Annie Buchan who was turning into a fine-looking young woman, tall and sensual like her mother. He produced poultry and meat from the cold store adjacent to the well, in addition to a porter that he had kept aside for an occasion such as this.

Both Emily Turnpike and Kitty Buckie had, in earlier times, worked in the kitchens of various Ayrshire lairds and they relished the chance to use their skills for the greater glory of the Lord Mother. The apprentice boys and their mistresses worked with the old women in Davidson's kitchen while his wife complained about both the intrusion and the expense. Together, they produced a beef pie, a ragout of pigs' ears and feet, a roasted hare with bread sauce, boiled duck with onions, several braised ducklings, a boiled calf's head, and broccoli in butter.

Thanks to Mrs Muir's expertise with needle and thread, most of the Buchanites, apart from Tam who consistently stank of the charnel house, had a change of clothes. The climax to the ritual preening and grooming was the appearance of the Lord Mother. She was wearing the red dress last glimpsed on the retreat from Irvine and, to the delight of all present, a crown fashioned by Andrew Innes from tree bark, incorporating several stars cut from leather. All stood as she and White took their places at the table.

After the feast, silence descended as the Lord Mother rose from her seat then swayed waiting for the spirit to enter her. She held aloft the copy of Englebrecht. 'Brethren, I have been to hell.' The intake of breath was audible as she opened the book.

'I there saw, in the spirit a dreadful great and thick darkness; there was such a smoke and vapour, such a thick nasty fog and stench, such an horribly bitter stench that I did not know how to compare such a stench as this was with any other stench in the world. Amidst the darkness, I heard a multitude of dreadful hideous howling voices… '

Kitty clutched Emily's arm. Davy McConville regretted taking the last spoonful of syllabub as it rose again in his throat. This was not what they had expected.

'Aye such a multitude of hideous dreadful voices that I am in no ways able to utter or express them. Their cry was this, 'Oh ye mountains fall on us, oh ye hills cover us that we may by no means further endure this torment."

White fiddled with his spoon. What was she doing now, for God's sake?

'Immediately the darkness vanished, the stench was gone, the voices were hushed and still… '

This time the relief was palpable. Kitty let go of Emily's arm.

'And the holy ghost, appearing to me in the shape of a man in white, placed me upon a chariot of gold and conveyed me into a radiant and splenderous light of the divine glory; into that bright light, whereof the apostle speaketh. The chariot of gold sped me away from the darkness and from the strong stench and loud cry into the radiant lustre of the divine glory.'

'Amen, amen,' said Amy Johnson who had recovered from her shock of seeing a set of pig's ears on the table.

Humphy Hunter assumed it must be a poor translation. What else could explain the overlong sentences?

'I saw there the choir of the holy angels, the choir of the prophets and apostles who with heavenly tongues sang around the throne of God.

'Indeed, I love with all my heart to hear earthly music; because no sooner do I hear any earthly music but it brings the heavenly music to my resemblance.'

Elspeth shut the book and placed it on the table.

Her audience were enraptured. She opened her arms wide and declaimed, 'We need light and music if we are to savour a taste of the pleasure that will be ours on the day of the Great Translation. O! O! O!'

'Light and music. Light and music,' repeated the Buchanites rising from the table, eager to do the bidding of the Lord Mother.

White, who had recently urged that in the interests of economy, the quota of tapers and candles should be halved, watched askance as Amy Johnson scurried through the hall placing tallow in every corner. William Lindsay followed her with a brand from the hearth which scattered small dervishes of light across the room.

Andrew Innes re-entered the hall holding two large lanterns which he had rescued from the outhouse where they had also been banished on the grounds of unnecessary expense. They too soon cast warm light into dark corners.

'Music. Music!' shouted Elspeth. What did she mean? Previously White would only let them sing hymns, and then only if they had been composed by himself. What did the Mother want?

She nodded to Thomas Neil who, when he thought he was alone in the fields, had been known to produce his whistle so that he could summon his hanged son with his melancholy tunes. 'Fetch your pipe, make us dance.'

Neil complied with her wishes and shook the spittle from his instrument. He was soon joined by Davidson who returned from the farmhouse with his fiddle. 'Lady Ramsay's Fairy,' he announced. The Buchanites sprang into life. Chairs were thrown aside, and a space cleared. The Wifies forgot their ailments. Andrew Innes forsook his hat. The dancers bowed and threw their partners in a reclamation of their old lives and forgotten joys. Dust was shaken from the joists, small hibernating creatures were shocked awake, the cups rattled on the shelves. The children, aping their elders, danced together. The dogs howled.

After a raucous and exhausting couple of hours, the revellers said their farewells and climbed the ladder into the bed space. Annie Buchan took Davidson's hand and led him to the corner where she slept. Andrew Innes was one of the last to leave the lower chamber. After snuffing out the candles, he quietly whispered to Katie Gardner who to his delight had danced enthusiastically with him earlier. She had even removed his hat and kissed the top of his head. Perhaps... just perhaps...

Elspeth too hoped that softened by the music and laughter, her

Manchild would again possess her as he had in the early days, but for White the physical act had but one purpose: to reinforce his dominance, his innate superiority, his absolute power. He needed to hear her cry out in pain.

Chapter Thirty

THE BROTHERS
Leith

After their latest failure to find the Mother, Birdman and the brothers trudged through the barren sheriffdoms of Banff, Cromarty and Fife. They rarely spoke. All three were dogged with sickness. They were robbed on two occasions and were forced to beg for food. In the Mearns, a polecat found its way into the cart and killed half of the birds before James grabbed its tail and beat its head against a rock.

Their spirits improved after they joined a team of fish packers in Leith and spent their days shovelling salt into barrels destined for the West Indies where the contents would feed the slaves. Unbeknown to the others, Mathew would hide twists of tobacco among the fish. He liked to imagine the surprise on the face of the negro, stripped to the waist and glistening, as he found the small gift.

Birdman proved popular with the owners as he could lure the gulls away from the herring heads heaped on the quay. He confessed though that he had little affinity with the scavengers from the sea. He far preferred the small, gentle birds that lived in the fields and hedgerows. He had a repertoire of their songs: the wistful, crystal tinkling of the robin; the rattle of the wren; the nasal flourish of the chaffinch with which he could silence a crowded tavern. The tame jackdaw on his head attracted the mischievous attention of a passing drunkard who tried to swat it away. 'The birdie's nae daein' any harm,' said his companion in drink. 'Sorry pal,' he said, 'he disnae like birds.'

Eventually the brothers staggered into view. They were none too sober, having visited various hostelries asking for information about the Mother.

'Success,' said James punching Birdman on the shoulder and scaring the jackdaw into flight.

'Look what you've done. The birdy's feart.'

'No, listen, listen,' said Mathew. 'She's somewhere near Thornhill in Galloway. We met this man who had been in her company. He mentioned the special blessing. It was her, nae doubt.'

'Nae doubt,' echoed Mathew brushing the feathers from Birdman's coat.

Chapter Thirty-One

A FIRE AND A FAST

Elspeth's euphoric mood continued for several weeks. Her followers, convinced that the end of the world was nigh, discussed their new life in the clouds. The apprentice boys were confident that God, like the Lord Mother, would also turn a blind eye to their libidinous behaviour. The alternative, a celibate life dedicated to praising the ruler of the universe, held little appeal. Mrs Muir enjoyed her work as seamstress and felt anxious at the thought of having no clear purpose in life. On the other hand, perhaps angels lost the occasional feather which needed to be retrieved and stitched back into place. White took comfort from the fact that the Bible described a pleasingly hierarchical heaven. A man of his organisational skills would quickly rise in God's favour. Tam looked constantly worried; he had heard tell that strong liquor was not to be found in paradise. Andrew Innes had complete confidence that God, in His infinite wisdom, would quickly anoint him to the important role of first servant to the Lord Mother, a function that he would happily fulfil throughout eternity. He purred with pleasure.

It was Innes who first noticed the fire. He had gone outside to relieve himself when he saw that the farmstead of John Stitt, a mean-spirited man who owned the land beyond Davidson's, was ablaze. Pausing in mid-stream, he looked in astonishment as the sky turned red. He rushed inside, without bothering to tie his breeches.

'The end of the world has come!' he declaimed. 'Let us hasten to the Translation.'

The cry was taken up by the others. 'Oh! Hasten Translation and come resurrection / Oh! Hasten the coming of Christ in the air.'

White waved his copy of *The Divine Dictionary*. 'Behold, the day of the Lord comes, cruel, with wrath and fierce anger, to make the land a desolation and to destroy its sinners!'

Innes stood on a chair. 'They gathered the Kings together to the place that in Hebrew is called Armageddon!'

'Our bairn will be born in heaven,' said Elizabeth.

'What?' asked Alan.

The Buchanites tumbled down from the garret in a tangle of limbs. They went outside to stare at the red skies and smell the burning. Agnes and Ann clung to each other. Amy Johnson thought briefly about her dead pig. At least he would not be reduced to crackling in the imminent conflagration. James Stewart patted his pockets, checking that he still had his awl and leather shears.

Elspeth strode across the yard towards the source of the fire. She would find Satan and strangle him. She would release the tortured souls whose only transgression was matrimony. They would rise again and learn once more the pleasures of the flesh. As she neared the conflagration, a flaming lintel crashed at her feet. White dragged her back. 'This is folly! For the sake of Christ, desist!'

As if waking from a dream, Elspeth let herself be led back to Buchan Ha'. The others followed meekly. John Stitt pleaded with the Buchanites to help him put out the flames, but White pushed him away. The farmer watched his livelihood burn. He wept.

For her evening talk, Elspeth chose the theme of unreadiness.

'Christ's patience is limited. He will not wait for ever. His favour is not without bounds. If you are harbouring sinful thoughts, then you are to blame for the delay in our Translation. If you still hanker to hold your children...' she stared pointedly at Mrs Hunter who shuffled her feet and looked away, 'then you are responsible for our failure to escape this veil of tears. If you cling exclusively to the flesh of another,' she glanced at Ann and Agnes who stopped holding hands, 'then your selfishness will keep us prisoners. Our bodies, like our souls, are held in common.'

White stood apart, observing but not listening. He was thinking of making a low offer for Stitt's land. The man was hardly in a strong bargaining position. He glanced at Elspeth. Something in her demeanour made him uneasy. What was she saying?

'Moses was there with the Lord forty days and forty nights without eating bread or drinking water… '

Surely not, thought White. Surely not. Gradually his worst fears were confirmed. "Return to me with all your heart, with fasting and mourning,' said the Lord.'

White knew what was coming. Why didn't she consult with him first? Why was he always left to pick up the pieces?

'Where for forty days he was tempted by the devil. He ate nothing during those days, and at the end of them he was hungry. The devil said to him, 'If you are the Son of God, tell this stone to become bread.' Jesus answered, 'It is written: man shall not live on bread alone."

And so, the die was cast. As the 'amens' rang out, Elspeth moved among them with a large sack into which she swept all the food that had not yet been cleared from the table. She opened the store cupboard and emptied its contents: bread and cheese and potatoes and carrots and dried meat, and several desiccated mice.

'Henceforth we will feed, not by the mouth, but by our eyes and ears on the word of God.' Elspeth moved among them, lightly kissing the eyes and ears of everyone in the room.

'And the children too?' asked Margaret White exchanging an anxious glance with Mrs Hunter.

'The children too.'

Despite his doubts, White quickly composed several small hymns of praise to the benefits of purging the body and mind of all impurities. The situation would need to be enforced, and he was the man who would rule with a rod of iron. Obviously, he would be excluded from the strictures of a fast.

'Bolt the door. Nail down the windows!' Andrew Innes leapt to carry out White's orders.

Emily stroked her stomach ruefully. 'At least this auld belly might disappear… Mind, it's like a pal.'

'Some pal,' said Kitty, who had the physique of a rake. 'If I dinnae eat, ma bones'll clatter on the flair.'

Tam, appalled at the thought of fasting, resolved to search the midden for the sack that Elspeth had gathered.

'Can we eat the wee wormies?' asked the younger of the Hunter children.

'No,' said his mother, alarmed at the impact of Elspeth's edict on her offspring.

Since her unwanted and deeply unpleasant encounter with Andrew Innes, Katie Gardner felt increasingly detached from the proceedings. Her enthusiasm for a life in the clouds had waned to the point of being non-existent. Her sister had little time for her, and when their paths crossed could only talk about her poet. Katie's sole consolation was food. Only when eating did she feel safe, imagining herself back at her childhood hearth eating her mother's bread. The thought of fasting was abhorrent and reinforced her determination to escape Buchan Ha' and the insidious attentions of Andrew Innes.

Davidson was informed that the society was no longer available for work in the fields. He was annoyed for two reasons: not only would he struggle to keep the farm functioning but more importantly, he would have fewer opportunities to dally with Annie Buchan whom he frequently met in the shade of the hedgerow.

The older men grumbled at the prospect of being cooped up all day. The camaraderie they enjoyed when they rested beside the newly-dug peat was important. Davy McConville's tales from the battlefield were best enjoyed in the open air.

On reflection, White could see further advantages to the fast. He needed time and space to think about the next stage of the grand project, which might, or might not, feature an ascent into paradise. Too much of his time was taken up with solving petty disputes and allocating tasks to those capable of carrying them out. What was the worst that could happen? Some of the weaker members of the society might die, and he would be left with a rump of strong, physically able souls that he could enlist to his still evolving purpose. Such an outcome would be acceptable. At a more practical level, a communal fast would result in considerably less expenditure. He needed his war chest. As leader, he must also ensure that he had a secret supply of food.

Others too found benefits in a period of enforced inactivity. The apprentice boys had devised their own games of chance and secretly placed bets on which of the Buchanites would be the first to break the fast. 'Yon wee wifie,' said Sandy Forsythe nodding in the direction of Emily. 'She bites her lips a' the time. She's about to eat hersel'.'

'Na, I've seen Jamie Stewart chewing his ain leather. He'll be first.'

They were both disappointed. After the first days, the Buchanites chatted excitedly about how they were no longer hungry. 'You couldnae tempt me wi' a king's feast,' said Emily, secretly pleased to see that her waist might be returning. Perhaps it would be enough to tempt that Davy McConville.

'I get strange dreams,' said Amy Johnson. 'And they're no all about food. The other night ah was young again. Ah was hame in Irvine, running beside the river. Ah was no being chased. Ah just wanted the wind in my hair. Ah was happy, like. And then this big dog, a snarling beast, ran at me, and I was feart.'

Because of White's frequent reminder that married couples should not revert to the old habits of the flesh, Mrs Gibson waited until the Manchild was asleep before venturing across the room and climbing into her husband's bed. He felt the gentle touch of her breath on his ear as she whispered about better times. 'I think of our old house, John, built by your ain hands. What a job that was. The finest house in the parish.'

'Soon we will all bide in God's house,' he reminded her.

'Do you really believe that, John?' her question startled him, and the ashes of doubt lay thick on his tongue.

It was Tam who asked White what he had done with Katie Gardner.

'What do you mean?'

'She's no here. Have you expelled her?' Tam knew that he was taking a risk confronting White in this fashion but had found the courage in a bottle of spirits that he had hidden in the outhouse. Too disconcerted at the news of Katie's disappearance to punish the messenger, White went to where she slept and pulled back the bedding to reveal a body-shaped clump of straw. Angrily, he kicked the straw across the room.

Annoyed at himself for his lack of vigilance, White knew that he would need to make an early example of someone if he was to prevent any backsliding and further desertions. An opportunity soon presented itself. Realising that Agnes was taking much longer than was necessary to meet the demands of nature, he followed her out of the hall and, from a distance, witnessed a transaction with a tinker during which money and bread changed hands. Delighted with this discovery, White returned and planned his next move.

When the chatter finally subsided for the night, he pulled back the curtain separating him and Elspeth from the common gaze and tiptoed towards the corner where Agnes was lying next to Ann. He heard the unmistakable sounds of eating. With a finger on his lips indicating that they were not to disturb the Hunter children, he hauled them both out of their bed. Several of the sleepers woke. 'Has the Lord come for us?' asked Andrew Innes, equally choked with sleep and excitement.

'No. You stupid wee man. Back to sleep.'

As they were too weak to resist, the women were easily forced out of the hall and through the dark towards the burn. White cursed as he tripped on a furrow but kept his grip tight. Being of an essentially merciful disposition, he kept their immersions short. In any case his arms were getting cold. He left them weeping in the field.

Back in the hall, he snuggled back alongside Elspeth. 'Where have you been, my love?'

'Nowhere,' he said.

Chapter Thirty-Two

ANOTHER FALSE ALARM

Listless and lacking all energy, most of the company were in their beds. The air was rank. Little was said as words needed effort. The groans of hunger were involuntary. Each tried not to look at their companions to avoid mirror images of their own emaciated state reflected in the other. If the younger children cried, White threatened to take them outside and hang them unless they kept quiet. For several of the Buchanites, the line between their daily lives and their night-time dreams became blurred. The darkness was shot through by strange conversations with non-existent companions as animated slivers of past conversations escaped from parched lips.

Despite the prevailing sickness and lethargy, White insisted that the Buchanites sing his latest compositions. 'My holy words will keep your minds from your bellies.' After miming valiantly for an hour, both Meg and Rowan closed their eyes. White moved towards them and rekindled their commitment with a blow from the willow stick which served as both baton and instrument of correction.

'Oh! Hasten Translation and come resurrection,
Oh! Hasten the coming of Christ in the air.'

Elspeth stood at a distance with her eyes closed. Several of the Buchanites swore that the Lord Mother's feet left the ground as she swayed in a trance. 'She rose before me, ah'm telling you. And I saw this light around her face. God Himsel' was speaking to her.'

The others too claimed to have been visited with strange sights proving that the Almighty was close at hand. Mrs Dunlop said that she had seen several tiny angels dancing in the smoke that rose from the burning peat. 'Wee creatures, like fairies, twisting this way and that.'

Elspeth too contributed to the hunger-inspired hallucinations. Waking early one morning she saw that one of the windows was suffused with light. She left her bed and roused the others. 'He comes! He comes! He comes to reign!'

Pandemonium made its masterpiece. Bodies again tumbled down from the upper chamber. No-one knew which way to turn. The children screamed. Humphy Hunter clambered onto the table and flapped the sleeves of his nightgown as if he was a large, ungainly bird contemplating flight. He made whirring noises and circled his arms faster and faster. He looked at the roof waiting for the beams to tumble and the heaven to which he was shortly bound, to appear.

White opened the door and stared into the dawn. 'It's Davidson's lantern, you fools. He's working early.'

The excitement died. As no-one could be bothered returning to their beds, they all stood looking towards the Lord Mother for an explanation. It was soon forthcoming.

'Christ came to take us. His divine eye looked through that window and into your hearts where, to his profound sorrow, he saw doubt. He saw the doubt in your hearts. And saddened, he returned to glory without you.'

This last phrase was accompanied by an accusatory stare that missed nobody. Andrew Innes sobbed loudly. 'I was ready, mistress, I was ready.'

'Even you, Andrew, need to harden your faith.' Her tone mellowed. 'Even you.'

'I will try, mistress, I will try.'

After this latest false alarm, the mood was subdued. Alan, who had failed to persuade Elizabeth to raise herself from her bed during the premature Translation, stayed at her side. She was restless and preoccupied. He had noticed her distended stomach but chose not to mention it for fear of upsetting her. He knew it was a result of her hunger. He had seen sheep suffering with the bloat. The Wifies grumbled the days away. Emily was disappointed that her waist, for which she had such great hopes, had reverted to its pre-fast enormity. So much for attracting the attention of Davy McConville. He wouldn't look at a ball of lard, that was for sure. James Stewart tapped endlessly at the threadbare piece of leather stretched onto his last until one of the apprentice boys threatened to stuff it down his gullet. Thomas Neil, haunted once more by visions of his son's body swinging on the gallows, had taken to crouching in a corner of the hall, rocking silently.

John Gibson put his arm around his shivering wife. 'It's not the cold,' she explained. 'It's the badness leaving my body. The Mother told me the tiny demons escape through the pores of the skin, wriggling their way back to Satan.'

'You have not a bad bone in you.'

'No, John, I am bad. I crave things. I'm hungry but more than that, I miss our friends. I want to sit in our ain pew in the kirk, nod to our neighbours and sing the old hymns. I started singing one of the old hymns yesterday, one of the tunes we shouldnae sing because they belong to the bad old days. Just quietly, like, under my breath, but the Reverend White heard me and had a word. He said I would be left behind when the great day comes... I dinnae want to be left behind, John.'

'Shhh, my love. I will take you in my arms and hold you tight when the day comes.'

Hugh White had spent a very pleasing night with Rowan Dowie who had proved much more accommodating than her sister. He was pulling on his clothes when he saw his wife staring at him from the other side of the room with tears in her eyes. Exasperated, he approached her. 'Stupid woman,' he said. 'Stupid woman, this petty jealousy has no place in our lives now. Don't you understand?' She clearly didn't. White walked out of the hall and into the fields. He needed fresh air.

Why did he tolerate these fools? Why did he spend his days with these simpletons, these stupid souls? A heifer with large, mournful eyes blocked his path. He approached it, intent on punching it to the ground if necessary. The beast started and ambled clumsily out of harm's way. He walked faster in a vain attempt to clear his head. What was the point? Why should he live, surrounded by imbeciles deadened with hunger? He was a renowned preacher, the doyen of the reformed Relief Kirk. He had sacrificed everything to follow the woman who might just be a charlatan. He paused and stood for a while, shocked at having, for a second time, given shape to this most heretical of thoughts.

He snorted as he watched a blackbird attempting to fly with a twig bigger than itself in its beak. It was a feeling he knew well. His own flight was proving more difficult than he had anticipated but the journey would still end with him sitting in paradise on God's right hand. It was his destiny. He would be given power over the angels and would happily help God weigh his infinite mercy against the just deserts of the countless sinners who should by rights perish in the flames of vengeance. He might even, on occasions, urge clemency. After all, he was not a cruel man. Yes, he could thole the present challenges. And there were undeniably compensations. His thoughts returned to Rowan.

He was approaching Closeburn Hall. He knew that for a guinea, the factor would let him enjoy the freedom of the laird's larder.

As he walked down the servants' corridor and towards the kitchen, he was overcome by the smell of roasting meat. Pushing open the door he stared at the mutton chops, beans, barley, peas, trotters, liver and lights, and a syllabub which the cook had intended for her beau. He approached tentatively, then dipped his fingers into the boiling pots; he scraped and scoured the platters; he scooped handfuls of hot food and thrust them in the general direction of his mouth. The chicken was succulent. The juices dribbled into his stubble. The cheese was probably the best he had tasted. The salted beef was a bit too tough for his liking but was nevertheless palatable. After a few moments of ecstatic dribbling, his stomach rebelled, and he vomited copiously into the yard beyond the scullery. The laird's dogs howled and strained at the leash. Subsequently, the cook, on the factor's orders, dismissed the maid, accusing her of insolent gluttony and theft.

When he returned to the hall, Elspeth was calling out random numbers to John Gibson who was struggling to make any sense of them. 'Four hundred! The number of days between God's fulfilling of his pledge to Abraham and the children of Israel leaving Egyptian bondage… ' She paced slowly, deep in contemplation. 'Fifty! Fifty days after God told the Israelites to weave a sheaf composed of the first fruits of their harvest, the feast of the Pentecost begins! No, no. Twenty-five. Jehoshaphat ruled for twenty-five years.' John Gibson screwed up the piece of paper and tossed it over his shoulder. 'And… ' she said with mounting excitement, 'Peter counted one hundred and fifty-three great fish in his net.' John Gibson sighed. 'The date,' she said.

'Who kept a tally of the days since our flight?'

'I did, mistress,' said Andrew. 'There is a notch on my staff for every nightfall since we left the sin pit of Irvine.' He scuttled to his sleeping place and returned with the stick. 'Forty-seven,' he said triumphantly.

'And the fast?' asked Elspeth.

'By my computation and calculation, allowing for disagreements over the precise hour of the commencement... '

'Well?'

'Twenty-seven.'

'There we have it! The date of our glorious Translation. Thirteen days and thirteen nights before we rise through the clouds.'

John Gibson put down his pen. The others, aware that something significant was happening, had moved closer to the Lord Mother.

'Thirteen!' they echoed. 'Thirteen!' Even those barely able to move joined in the clamour. White too seemed pleased. The end was in sight. Thank the Lord.

Elspeth ordered that the door be thrown open to dispel the foul air. She was also eager that the Buchanites should take turns to gaze at the sky and the cloud formations for evidence that God was preparing their path.

Andrew Innes revelled in his role of tallyman as he carefully carved a notch in his new stick. He then waved it above his head as a signal for a quick verse of the hymn whose relevance grew with each passing day.

'Oh! Hasten Translation and come resurrection,

Oh! Hasten the coming of Christ in the air.'

The Wifies, pinched and emaciated, had never lost their appetite for gossip.

'Yon Rowan looks done for,' observed Emily Turnpike.

'She aye needs a rest,' suggested Kitty. 'The puir critter's walking wi' a limp these days.' Her friend cackled happily.

Thomas Neil had been thinking aloud. 'Of course, my son's a man now. Tall and strong. I'll have to gi' him a piece of my mind for causing me and his mother such pain, but then I'll hold him and forgive him. He was young mind when it all happened.'

Only James Stewart seemed less than happy. He had recently heard that angels didn't wear shoes. Did they even have feet? He wasn't certain that he could manage an eternity of enforced idleness.

Seven days before the agreed date of the Great Translation, Katie Gardner unexpectedly returned. Andrew Innes was overjoyed. She was well received. She had been popular, and her friends were delighted that she too would ascend with them through the clouds. However, ascent in any shape or form was not at the forefront of her mind. White placed a hand on the back of her neck and pulled her towards him so that he could kiss her cheek. Glancing down at her belly, he realised she was with child. He recoiled from her and pointed an accusatory finger.

'Aye,' she said. 'And dinnae think you're going to take my baby up the fields and bury it.' White took a step back.

'Bairns are no welcome here until they have souls… you know the views of the Lord Mother.'

'I dinnae care a tinker's toss about your rules. I want that wee toad of a man in the corner to tak responsibility.' All eyes turned towards Andrew Innes from whose face all blood had drained.

'It wasnae me.' The sentence died as he recalled the most precious moment of his life. 'A moment's madness,' he stuttered. 'It was dark, she didnae ken who she was lying wi'.'

'Ye wee shite!' said Kitty Buckie. This view was echoed by the others, many of whom had long resented his special, and in their eyes, utterly undeserved, position in Elspeth's affections.

'How could you lie with that feckless scrot?' asked Davy McConville who had long admired Katie. 'Aye, a wee scrot.'

Innes' dreams, when they came that night, made him twitch and fit in his sleep. His father, despairing at his inability to master even the rudimentaries of stone masonry, was threatening to have him apprenticed at the poor house on the outskirts of Mutthill. 'You're useless, you cannae guddle for a fish, you cannae hud a tune, you cannae strike a stane.'

His mother joined in. 'Nane of the lassies will look at you. A gelding. A wee puppet of a man who will never leave his ma. An encumbrance!' She was pleased with the word which the minister had used the previous Sabbath and stared triumphantly at her cowering son.

His mother mutated into Katie who had offered little resistance when he joined her in the dark. He hadn't meant to hurt her, but she had cried in pain. Perhaps it had been joy. He tried to convince himself that was the case. 'Be still, my lovely,' he had pleaded, running his hand through her hair until she rudely removed it. Afterwards she turned her back on him, and he lay there listening to her breathing. The finest moment of his life.

Subsequently she had ignored him but that was because she felt such strong emotions; she didn't want to be overwhelmed by her love for him. And she is carrying his child. Katie's face gradually merged into the glorious countenance of the Lord Mother who would never forsake him. His expulsion was only temporary. He would rise with her in glory. He was the most blessed man on earth.

Appreciating this heaven-sent opportunity to get rid off the irritating and potentially mutinous Innes from the society, White acted quickly and formally announced his expulsion. The news was greeted by several gasps. Elspeth tried to intervene on Innes' behalf. White gripped her by the elbow and propelled her behind the curtain. 'The wee man's a liability,' he hissed. 'The Gardner woman has every right to seek redress from the law. Do we really need another warrant? More snooping? More questions?' Elspeth sighed and nodded her acquiescence.

White surveyed the small human sack of bones shivering in distress. There was a real danger that Innes, who had observed the fast in every detail, would collapse and die before he had left the environs of the hall. An emaciated body lying in the road would certainly attract the attention of the authorities. It was a risk worth taking.

'Horrible wee man,' muttered Kitty as Innes took a sorrowful farewell of his former friends.

Katie watched him leave. 'Guid riddance,' she said. She knew that Innes' departure made it less likely that she could raise an action against him. She also knew that Buchan Ha' was not the place for a pregnant woman and resolved to return to her parents in Stevenston to think matters over.

'Don't forget me,' sobbed Innes with his arms around Elspeth's waist and his head nestling upwards into her bosom, ' ... when the clouds part and the angels come. I will always… ' Unable to finish his sentence, he broke away to gather his few possessions. Shortly after, he left Buchan Ha' and the imminent prospect of eternal life.

Your Lordships,

I have much to report. The mad Buchan woman has decreed that the society of deluded hypocrites and fornicators must undertake a fast to demonstrate their readiness to be translated into heavenly realms. I realise that this behaviour beggars both belief and understanding, however, as I also appreciate that your Lordships have an interest in all scientific endeavours, I have decided that I too will undertake full abstinence so that I can faithfully record the detrimental impact such behaviours will have on the humours and provide a detailed account of the physical decline that must accompany any such undertaking. If, subsequently, your Lordships wish to publish a learned tract for consideration by the Royal Society based on this intelligence, I would be flattered and would seek neither remuneration nor indeed, acknowledgement. I am, when all is said and done, your Lordships' humble servant, and offer this diary for your consideration.

Day one. The announcement of the fast is met with universal acclaim and excitement by all apart from Hugh White who seems angry. He strides through the hall seeking quarrels.

Day two. The group is more subdued excepting the children who whine and girn about their empty bellies. They are eventually subdued by their mothers, fearful lest their offspring be punished if their complaints continue.

Days three and four. A strange mood of elation takes hold. All boast of how the pangs of hunger have retreated. A phenomenon they attribute, erroneously, to divine intervention.

Day five. All complain of unwelcome flux as the body rids itself of all residue nourishment and gaseous content. The stink is hellish. I am approached by White who offers me surreptitious quantities of food in exchange for helping him exercise due vigilance over the company; he is fearful of defections and tells me he needs my eyes. I reluctantly agree as I will need sustenance if I am to be a faithful recorder of these events for the benefit of your Lordships.

Days seven and eight. The nights are punctuated by hideous groaning as the members of this hellish sect wrestle with their dreams. On waking, they share tales of apparitions, goblins and sprites coming to take their souls. Many are visited by phantasmagoria of dead relatives.

Days nine and ten. White takes it on himself to console the younger women in the party by visiting their beds. In the main they are too weak to resist his advances.

Day eleven. ~~The Lord Mother.~~ *Apologies my Lordships, I have inadvertently deployed the heretical mode of address favoured by the Buchanites towards their demonic leader. The Buchan woman, possessed of a strength that is not of this world, rises from her bed and moves to each of the company, administering words of comfort, and sips of water mixed with honey. She approaches me and tells me that although I am not what I seem, I too can rise to glory with her. I am, of course, horrified by these hideous words and refuse to engage with her.*

Day thirteen. A small commotion occurs as the young woman who earlier effected an escape from the hall, returns. She is with child and names the obnoxious Andrew Innes as the father. (This strange coupling would, of itself, furnish an interesting scientific paper.) White, who makes no secret of his profound dislike of the ~~Lord M…~~ *apologies again… the Buchan woman's most loyal acolyte, dismisses him from the company. I took advantage of Innes' imminent expulsion to glean from him further intelligence concerning the Buchanites. I asked him if it was true that White removed babies and infants from their mothers and that said children were never seen again. He agreed that at least two infants had disappeared overnight from Buchan Hall. He claimed they had wandered into the dark and had either fallen into the nearby well or met with some other misfortune. He had witnessed neither abduction nor burial. He became animated at this line of questioning and declared that this was a false calumny perpetuated by the enemies of the society. The notion that White murdered unwanted offspring was preposterous. My Lordships, he does protest too much. He is blinded by his loyalty to the demonic leaders of this abomination of a religion. I hereby undertake to be ever more vigilant until I can gather sufficient evidence to ensure that the 'King Herod of Dumfries' is hanged from the scaffold.*

In conclusion I would urge that your Lordships bring this whole sorry episode to an end by whatever means are at your disposal. As an interim measure, a spell in a debtor's prison could precipitate the dissolution of the society. Should that stratagem fail, recourse could be made to the kirk session and a charge of blasphemy levelled against this fiendish, deluded, and dangerous cabal.

Your devoted servant,

Alexander Gillespie

Postscript: further evidence of collusion with the devil:

THE WOMAN CLOTHED WITH THE SUN

1) A rat crept into the hall and made its way to where the Buchan woman slept. As it approached it was suddenly stricken by apoplexy, twitched and died on the spot.

2) I watched from a window as a sheep from Davidson's field nudged its face against the locked door of Buchan Hall. As it turned away, I saw blood streaming from its eyes.

Chapter Thirty-Three

OH! HASTEN TRANSLATION

White, appreciating that Elspeth's premature and unplanned demise could ruin his plans, had persuaded her to eat. Initially she had resisted and only succumbed when her Manchild knelt by her bed and whispered into her ear, 'The Lord said to Moses, 'I have heard the grumbling of the Israelites. Tell them, 'At twilight you will eat meat, and in the morning, you will be filled with bread.'' 'Fetch me bread,' said Elspeth.

As her strength returned so too did her certainty.

'We must be ready. We must be prepared. Rejoice!' Her enthusiasm infected her followers who stared at her through eyes enlarged by famine. She spoke to everyone individually. 'Soon, soon,' she said to Thomas Neil. He knew she was referring to his son. Soon they would be reunited. She raised Agnes and Ann from their bed and, holding their skeletal hands, led them slowly in a jig. She tugged at Davy McConville's straggly beard. 'The angels will think you are a prophet escaped from the pages of the good book.' He smiled weakly. She even had a kind word with Tam, reassuring him that ambrosia was a far finer drink than the whisky he now craved. Elspeth smiled when Amy Johnson reached up to her and asked if God kept pigs. 'All things are possible,' she said.

White looked on. He still believed in the Translation to come. His own virtue and strength would ensure a destiny denied to other mortals. He believed too that the Lord Mother was, for the time being at least, God's chosen familiar. If she were to betray weakness, then God's plans might change. Accordingly, he must be ready to take her place. In the meantime, keeping order, enforcing discipline, explaining away some of Elspeth's more obscure pronouncements, all took effort and energy. There were other complications: Rowan was becoming increasingly possessive and sulked whenever he forsook her for another. Lately too, Margaret seemed to be hankering after their previous intimacy. Why was life so complicated?

Unable to consult Andrew Innes, Elspeth insisted that John Gibson compute the precise number of days that had passed since Hugh's spiritual rebirth as her Manchild. After much sighing and crossings out, Gibson scratched his head and declared that it was somewhere between nine hundred and eighty-nine and one thousand. This last number was the one, above all others, that she longed to hear. Clapping her hands, she decreed that every evening they would all walk to nearby Templeton Hill and keep a vigil until the moment of the Great Translation arrived.

Mrs Muir, as proud custodian of the only pair of scissors in the hall, was told to fashion top knots on everyone's head. The Buchanites formed an orderly queue, waiting to add their share to the growing pile of human hair covering the floor. 'The angels need something to hold onto,' explained Elspeth sweeping the hair to one side with her foot. 'You wouldn't want to be accidently dropped when you are halfway through the clouds.' Emily and Kitty nervously fingered each other's hair which had been pitifully thinned by the lack of nourishment. 'No, Mother,' they murmured. James Stewart, who had been completely bald before the onset of the fast, needed reassurance. 'Borrow a bonnet from one of the Wifies,' suggested Mrs Muir, 'and tie it firmly beneath your chin.'

White led the way holding a lantern while several of the others held candles. One of the locals making his way to the Brownhill Inn watched intrigued as the pinpricks of light undulated over the fields. He rushed into the inn to pass on the news. His drouthy neighbours left the nappy and tumbled into the yard where they watched the lights and listened to the sound of singing.

'Oh! Hasten Translation and come resurrection,
Oh! Hasten the coming of Christ in the air.'

The Buchanites huddled together on the hilltop staring at the sky. They shivered, and several candles were dropped by hands shaking uncontrollably. The fact that the clouds were moving quickly across the moon was interpreted as a good sign. 'Look, look!' Amy Johnson pointed animatedly. 'An angel. Look!' The others stared but the heavens had reformed and hidden the celestial being, briefly glimpsed. Ann put her arm around Agnes' waist. The Wifies held hands. And then it started to rain. None of the Buchanites had considered rising into heaven through a drizzle. White shook his head. They had been forsaken. This wasn't the hour. The Brownhill drinkers returned to the warmth.

No-one spoke as they dragged themselves back to the Hall. When they had hung up their wet clothes, James Stewart and William Lindsay approached Elspeth who was lost in thought. 'Excuse us, Mother,' said the cobbler clutching his damp cap. 'Perhaps we were too far fae heaven.' She looked at him quizzically. 'The angels didnae see us.'

'To them we may have looked like sheep in the dark, no the chosen people.'

'No the chosen people,' echoed James Stewart.

'What can we do?' Elspeth was fond of these two honest men who, in several respects, reminded her of her former husband.

'We'll build a scaffold,' said Stewart.

'A tower.'

White, who had been listening to the discussion, couldn't resist flaunting the biblical knowledge for which he had been awarded the Aitken medal at the Theological College of Pennsylvania.

'They said, 'Come let us build for ourselves a city, and a tower whose top will reach into heaven, and let us make for ourselves a name, otherwise we will be scattered abroad over the face of the whole earth.' The Lord came down to see the tower which the sons of men had built.'

'Very well,' said Elspeth. 'But be quick. For certain He will come tomorrow.'

Before they settled down for the night, Elspeth addressed her disappointed followers. 'We must believe with our hearts and minds. We must trample doubt and stifle all longings for the things of this earth. Only then will Christ come for us, only then.' Her words were greeted with murmurs of agreement, and a small shout of delight from one of the children who had succeeded in capturing and eating a large spider he had stalked through the hall.

At first light the Buchanites gathered wood that could be used in the construction of the platform. They prised planks from Davidson's byre leaving the dung to leak and dribble into the soil. They also dismantled the small outhouse where White had been storing food for himself and Elspeth. They looked askance at each other as James Stewart pulled back the cloth covering the leg of cured ham from which much meat had been sliced.

Davidson was undecided whether to join his tenants on their imminent ascent to heaven. Much though he believed in the Lord Mother, he was reluctant to forsake the land that had nurtured his family for generations. When wrestling with this dilemma, he had compiled a list of the things he would miss if he let himself be dragged through the clouds to eternal bliss. It was the smells that convinced him to stay. Newly turned earth, the breath from his cows, his own sweat at the end of a day's labour, the smell of the mutton pies at the Brownhill. There would be none of these in a doubtless fragrant heaven. Furthermore, he realised that the main attraction of Annie Buchan was not just the joy of her flesh, it was also the illicit and secretive nature of their liaison; the frisson in the fear of being caught. His wife was intrigued by the ingenuity of the excuses he could conjure to explain his sudden absences from their hearth: a fox in the henhouse, the sound of someone opening a gate, a cow in distress. On reflection though, did he really want to lie with Annie for an eternity? Now and again was fine but once the novelty of her body had worn thin, would God let him sow his seed elsewhere? He doubted it.

White donned his canonicals for the second vigil. What had he been thinking of? He must never forget his own importance. The pristine white gloves felt good as he stretched his fingers into them. He tightened the belt on his gown. He handed his boots to Emily and told her to clean them. Now he was prepared.

The others followed his example and dressed in the best clothes that they could muster. Mrs Muir sewed and cut until her fingers were raw. 'It feels like a wedding,' said Kitty.

The hours passed in a fever of expectation.

As this was their last night on earth, there was no point in being parsimonious over the distribution of candles. John Gibson lit the first from the smouldering peat and the flame was passed down the line.

The singing of hymns was impressively lusty given the malnourished state of the choir. The sky was clear; this was also interpreted as a sign. An owl swept low over them. The dogs in Davidson's yard started to howl. Mrs Gibson swept a large moth away from her face. It was the gentle touch of an angel's wing. With all due solemnity, White took Elspeth's hand as she lifted her skirt and climbed onto the flimsy platform. The others stood and gazed at the holy couple.

To the faithful, the gentle breeze was also a portent. God needed to harvest the elements and submit them to His control before the ascent began. They chatted excitedly about the activity beyond the clouds: there were mansions to be prepared; rooms to be decorated; feasts to be cooked; roasted hogs, sides of beef, turkeys, ducks, venison, snipes, duck, pease soup, sweetmeats, puddings and syllabubs, cheese and pickles. But no fruit, God wouldn't permit fruit, everyone knew that fruit causes plague and indigestion.

Elspeth stood, arms outstretched and shouted at the moon. 'Dear Christ, we wait for you, yearning to see your face... ' The others mouthed their amens. 'We are ready to submit our lives to you. Take us in your arms now.' She stood on tiptoe, desperate to touch the outstretched hand of God.

White felt sexually aroused by the thought of concupiscence unbounded, lustful indulgence for all eternity, endless new flesh to be explored in heaven.

The breeze grew stronger. Something was happening. Soon the clouds would be torn asunder; they would be drowned in the glorious light of His salvation. His chariots drawn by celestial stallions, breathing purgative fire, would plunge towards them in a flash of thunder.

The breeze grew stronger, mutating into a gust. The gust grew stronger. The platform buckled and collapsed.

The Buchanites screamed. Elspeth plummeted, her arms flailing, her skirts over her head. Tam was knocked unconscious by a plank. The Wifies fell in a heap. The children cried for their mothers.

Apoplectic, White marched back over the fields towards Buchan Ha'. After they had recovered from the shock, the others followed at a snail's pace muttering to each other.

White threw a pot at Elspeth. 'You betrayed us! You lied! You are the arch deceiver.'

'Wait, love... ' she pleaded. White despatched a fusillade of plates which smashed against the wall, firing splinters and shards into the room.

'You are a fraud. A charlatan!'

Although disappointed, the Buchanites were shocked by this disrespectful tirade from White. It wasn't the Lord Mother who was to blame; it was themselves. Despite her exhortations, they had failed her with their lack of preparedness.

White held Elspeth by the throat and bent her backwards over a chair. 'The woman clothed with the clouds and the moon, the third person of the trinity, my arse! The mother of God in Scotland! Lies and deception. You are a witch! I will burn your feet and tear out your fingernails!'

Davy McConville threw himself at White. They struggled briefly until White slumped to the floor. McConville stood over him, breathing hard.

No-one spoke until Elspeth broke the silence. She was bleeding and held a cloth to her face. At first her voice was tiny, and the Buchanites strained to hear her words. 'Be strong and courageous. Do not be afraid or terrified for the Lord, your God, goes with you. He will never leave you or forsake you.' She took the bloodied cloth and held it in turn to the lips of those nearest to her. On receiving this benediction, each of the Buchanites fell into a faint.

A pantomime. A charade. Stupid deluded souls. Simpletons. Folly and weakness. White touched the lump on the side of his face, a consequence of his clumsy fall from the platform. Needing space and time to think, he closed the door on the prone, simpering crowd of fools and walked into the fresh air. As he crossed the field, White saw

Elizabeth was lying on the stubble. Alan was crouched between her legs, holding a blood covered infant.

'In the name of Christ!' said White.

'Praise be to His name,' said Elizabeth with a look of terror on her face.

'The thing's dead,' said White, stooping to take the newborn from Alan who was too shocked to understand what was happening.

'Give it to me.'

'It's no dead.'

'This child will never suck at your breast.' White took out his knife and cut the umbilical. Still kneeling, Alan held out his arms in supplication as White walked back into the hall.

Chapter Thirty-Four

DESERTERS

Even though the fast had been abandoned, some of the company were still too weak to take any sustenance. The trek to the hill and the return to the hall had almost proved fatal for the weaker members. Fearful of being held to account for multiple deaths, White took it on himself to force food through the parched lips of those most at risk of dying. 'Drink, you stupid cow! There are enough bones out there without me adding yours.' Kitty Buckie convulsed briefly before retching the thin gruel back into White's face. He drew back his hand to strike her, but just managed to restrain himself. Elspeth, having observed the attempt at forced feeding, took Kitty in her arms and held her.

There were no more joyous prayer meetings, no more sensual benedictions, just a mood of growing despondency. Squabbles broke out. Old rivalries and resentments between the apprentices were revived. Two of the boys came to blows and were only separated when Davy McConville emptied a pail of night soil over them. Squealing like cats, they rushed out of the hall towards the burn. Mrs Muir, suffering from an acute attack of the spleen, refused to mend any of the clothes that were brought to her. Tam lay drunk on the floor, and nobody cared.

For White this was a defining moment. The old vision had died; a new order would emerge. Although misguided and seriously misled by the Lord Mother, God had helped him see the error of his ways. If he were patient, the way forward would be revealed. In this mood he was sanguine about the defections. The door was left unlocked, and Gillespie was informed that he could relax his vigilance. The weak and treacherous could leave. He would not stand in their way.

The first to leave were Alan and Elizabeth. In the days preceding the failed Translation, Alan conjured images of their son waiting for them in paradise. 'Look, he's smiling. He's holding out his hands. The bairn recognises you.'. Elizabeth stared blankly at him. There was no hope, nothing. As they left the hall, Alan shook hands with several of their friends before leaving their lives forever.

Elspeth was powerless to stem the tide and smiled wanly at each departure. White sneered dismissively as the defectors bade their farewells. Before leaving, John Gibson demanded that White produce the strongbox containing the society's wealth. He argued that as prime contributor, he was entitled to what was his.

'Whore of Babylon!' White's words flicked spittle onto Gibson's face. 'We owe you nothing. Judas! How many pieces was it? Thirty? I wouldn't give you thirty shits!'

'Give me what is rightfully mine. You are the betrayer, not me, not that good woman over there.' He nodded in Elspeth's direction. 'You are the Antichrist who has hidden like a canker in our midst.' White snatched a poker from the hearth and held it under Gibson's nose, then moved it slowly towards his eyes, then to each of his ears, then held it close to his lips until the skin blistered. The tableau lasted a full minute before Gibson knocked the poker from White's grip. Emily stamped out the burning wisps of straw where it landed.

Rubbing his lip, Gibson turned to his wife and calmly told her to gather their goods, chattels, children, and broken hopes. She shook her head. 'No,' she said. 'I must stay with the Mother.' Her husband looked at her. His mouth opened but the words wouldn't come. He raised a hand to emphasise an emotion he couldn't articulate. He turned his back and left. Alexander Gillespie followed him down the path, put an arm around his shoulders and engaged him in conversation. White assumed his second in command was trying to dissuade Gibson from leaving.

White considered his next move. Half of the Buchanites had deserted. Among them were Elspeth's two daughters. The burden of having a mother who recently declared that she was Christ's sister was too much. Speaking for them both, the younger had asked, 'Does that mean that we are God's nieces?'

White knew that Gibson could resort to the law to reclaim his money. His solution was to instruct Davy McConville to bury the strongbox in the corner of a field under cover of darkness. He then decided that everyone who had stayed at Buchan Ha', either through loyalty or inertia, should be put back to work, thus ensuring a steady flow of income. He was still a leader of men, more than capable of making important decisions in the face of weakness. He was a learned man, far more intelligent than his peers. What other clergyman was familiar with the theories of Richard Cantillon and his essay on *The Nature of Commerce in General*? Rational self-interest was the way forward. Even a fool could understand that wealth was found not in trade but in human labour. Heaven could wait.

He believed that it was his wisdom and leadership that accounted for the gradual revival in the spirits of those who had chosen to remain. After being confined for the duration of the fast, the able-bodied enjoyed once more the shock of fresh air at the start of each day, and the comforting sensation of long-neglected muscles being stretched again. White insisted that they feast like kings after labouring in the fields. Yes, a semblance of normality had been restored. If only the Wifies had taken the hint and left.

The unexpected reappearance of Jean's poet almost interrupted this period of calm.

After being chased off the property, Burns chose instead to keep his distance from Buchan Ha' and contented himself with watching the women working in the fields. By crawling on his hands and knees through the stubble, he could spy on them undetected. He yearned for the hot days when the younger ones would remove their upper garments as they toiled in the heat. How he enjoyed the sight of their breasts swaying with the rhythm of the scythes. The memory inspired several short pieces of bawdy doggerel, and one song called *Noo the hurdies*.

As he shaded his eyes from the spring sun, he could see that the Buchanites were dispersed across several fields. He crept closer and looked for Jeanie, but she was nowhere to be seen. There were others though, and he soon recognised the tall, slim Dowie sisters, whom he fondly remembered kissing on the banks of the Irvine. By crouching behind the stane dyke, he was able to get close to the girls who were sharing a flagon of water.

He undressed silently. Could there ever be a better moment to flaunt his attributes? Unable to repress a shout of pure bravado, he leaped over the dyke. Not expecting to be disturbed by a jubilant satyr, both girls shrieked. By the time they recognised the owner of the exultant member, it was too late. White, on general supervision duties, had heard the commotion and strode towards its source. Sensing imminent danger, Burns hopped on one leg as he tried to dress, leaving himself unbalanced and vulnerable to the imminent assault.

'You wee, sleekit toley,' said White. Holding the half-dressed poet by the ear, he marched him towards the Thornhill Road where he administered several strong kicks to his bare backside and sent him on his way.

Further annoyance was provided by the unexpected return of Andrew Innes who pushed open the door and stood on the threshold with Katie holding their child.

The remaining Buchanites were pleased to welcome back the prodigal son and his new family. Unbeknown to White, Elspeth had written to her acolyte telling him that he was free to return, reassuring him that, 'Your act of faith puts an end to all former unbelief.' In truth she had been growing ever more fearful of her Manchild, and increasingly suspected that, sooner or later, she would fall victim to his rod of iron. Wee Andra would at least keep an eye out for her.

'A bairn. They have a bairn,' hissed White who was already plotting its speedy removal. The ill-featured runt looked sickly; perhaps nature would spare him the bother.

'She's called Curtis,' said Katie.

Innes described how he had failed to obtain employment in his own parish, how his mother had insisted that he join Katie in Stevenson and make an honest woman of her, and how he had reluctantly agreed to this course of action. 'Ah kept my fingers crossed during the whole ceremony so it wouldnae count. Ah ken it's against the rules,' he looked at White for reassurance which was not forthcoming. Elspeth though, quickly forgave this violation of a cardinal rule.

'There was no intent,' she said, rubbing his sleeve. 'And since the traitors left, there is more room.' She indicated the bare boards. 'And remember, Andrew, your child belongs to us all and will be raised by us all.' Andrew nodded eagerly. Katie looked horrified and held her daughter closer to her bosom.

After her initial delight at Andrew's return, Elspeth turned her face to the wall and lay there for two days. Wondering if she might in fact be dead, White shook her awake. She stared at him, her eyes unfocussed. She was still watching the latter stages of a recurrent dream.

'I don't understand...' Elspeth shook her head. White noted that he had been sanguine about the possibility that she might have died. This was indeed an interesting development.

'What?' he asked distractedly. Her incoherent speech included references to pottery angels and dead rabbits. Annoyed by her gibbering, White was disinclined to comfort her.

Alexander Gillespie opened the door and nodded to the constables who were in possession of a warrant in respect of monies owed to a John Gibson.

Chapter Thirty-Five

DEBTORS' PRISON

The cell was crowded and stinking. It already had seven occupants prior to the new arrivals.

'There's nae room, ye erse!' shouted an older man stripped to the waist. 'Nae room.'

'Haud yer wheesht,' replied the jailer, slamming the door after him.

'Mair flesh, mair flesh,' said the priapic simpleton, pawing Elspeth's chest until White pushed him against the wall.

'You'll be less fou o' yourself efter a day on the crank,' said a woman as she mimed turning an imaginary handle.

'Step oot o' line and the'll nail yer lug tae the wall,' White turned to the speaker, an unnaturally elongated soul with a missing earlobe.

'Jesus Christ,' he said. Elspeth stepped back as one of the younger residents relieved himself against the back wall.

'Show us yer pisser,' said the simpleton.

White slumped down and put his head in his hands. Elspeth closed her eyes.

'This is all your fault. Why did I listen to you with your lies and deceits? 'The witch woman of Irvine' indeed. And I fell for your tales and calumnies, your duplicity, your connivances.'

White's tirade attracted a small audience from among the bored inmates. 'Big words,' commented the bare-torsoed man, tugging at his chest hair. He moved towards Elspeth with a view to adding a small injury to the insults heaped on her by White but, to Elspeth's surprise, her Manchild defended her.

'Leave her! This is none of your business.' The man muttered and instead vented his annoyance on the simpleton by grinding a fist into the side of his face.

Sleep proved impossible given the endless interruptions from new arrivals and the occasional departure. The food was inedible, and the water fetid.

White watched with bored indifference as Jake, the tallyman, scratched his latest computations on a bare patch of wall. For those inmates who shared their bread with him, he provided a personal service, calculating and recording each passing day of their sentence. On arrival, they would mournfully disclose the length of their incarceration which would be translated into neat sets of vertical marks, each set denoting a week. The sound of the nail scratching its way through a mark was a source of satisfaction for the inmates. Jake provided other services. He was sole arbiter in the ongoing competition to kill vermin. Rats merited three scratches, mice one.

'Jake,' asked Elspeth. 'How many days before the righteous God returns to this veil of tears?' The cell was unusually still, and the quiet authority and low pitch of her voice drew the attention of the other prisoners.

'Ah dinnae ken,' said Jake picking at his ear with the nail. 'Ah dinnae ken.'

'He will come. The sun will be darkened, and the moon will not give its light; the stars will fall from the sky, and the heavenly bodies will be shaken. At that time, the sign of the Son of Man will appear in the sky… '

The inmates stopped what they were doing – flicking at fleas, chasing crumbs across a bowl, muttering to themselves – and listened to the tall, frail woman with wild eyes.

'Who are you?' asked a gaunt man who spent his days crouched in a corner. And then he remembered. 'You're that Buchan woman. Yon mad woman. You a' spend your days shagging, lying wi' each other. Aye, that's you.' Pleased with himself, he retreated to his corner.

'I am the woman clothed with the sun, and the moon under her feet, and upon her head a crown of twelve stars.'

White shook his head. This wasn't the time.

'Save me, mother,' said an elderly woman who approached and fell to her knees in front of Elspeth.

'All shall be well, and all shall be well, and all manner of thing shall be well.' Elspeth lightly touched the woman on the forehead causing her to faint. The others gasped.

Despite White's worst fears, the moment proved to be a turning point. Both he and the Lord Mother were subsequently treated with a near obsequious degree of respect. Several of the inmates insisted on sharing their bread with the 'Holy Couple' as they were dubbed. One of the jailors approached Elspeth when the others slept and asked if she could remove the curse placed on his wife that had made her barren. 'Rub her stomach with ewe's milk mingled with dew,' said Elspeth. The jailor thanked her profusely and left the cell, walking backwards, bowing as he went.

Andrew Innes had been busy. In the absence of his leaders, he had appointed himself as principal custodian of the Society, a role which he fulfilled by chastising and cajoling everyone who crossed his path. He tutted and fussed his way through the hall, finding fault at every opportunity. He cursed Mrs Muir for leaving an untidy skein of thread next to the fire. 'The flames could catch it.'

'Boil ye heid,' she told him, singularly unimpressed by his new-found authority. Innes did his utmost to reassure the others that their leaders' absence was only temporary, but their mood was dark. They had been promised a blissful ascent into paradise, yet nothing had happened. The Translation seemed like a chimera, retreating ever further over the horizon. Days were still marked by the dull thud of James Stewart's hammer against the leather stretched on his last. The pile of shoes grew and grew. Kitty Buckie was now permanently bedridden, and the others feared for her wellbeing.

'It's no going to happen,' said Kitty.

'Whit?' asked Emily.

'You ken, the great event, the day of wonder we've been promised.'

'Dinnae speak like that. It's heresy agin the Mither. She will soon return to save us.'

Kitty made a harrumphing noise which ushered in a coughing fit, the severity of which alarmed her friend.

Thomas Neil's nightmares were depriving the others of sleep. He claimed the shade of his hanged son regularly visited to rebuke him for not cutting him down sooner. Thomas also said that he couldn't live with the pain any longer, and that if the Translation didn't happen within weeks, he would take matters into his own hands. He owed his son a death he said.

As most of the younger girls had left with the apprentice boys, Tam had turned his unwanted attentions to the older women who did not respond as he might have wished. When he muttered something revolting into Amy Johnson's ear, she poked a spurtle into his groin. 'Wash yer mooth out,' she told him. 'Or next time, I'll cut that thing aff.'

Meanwhile the children behaved ever more badly, and to the consternation of their elders, had devised their own secret language by which means insults were shared and otherwise forbidden observations given tongue.

This was the environment into which White and Elspeth returned. Word of their incarceration had reached Davidson. Since their departure, his life had felt empty. To her acute annoyance, his wife frequently found him standing in Buchan Ha' staring into the middle distance. The least he could do was to alleviate their present distress by settling their debts. Feeling generous, he deposited a sum of money far greater than that required for the early release of the prisoners.

The Buchanites shrieked with joy as Elspeth appeared on the threshold.

'Ah telt you, ah telt you!' Emily jabbed a finger in Kitty's direction. The Lord Mother was welcomed fondly by Amy Johnson who made her sit while she removed her shoes and rubbed ointment into her feet.

White's return was acknowledged by a few sullen nods of recognition. 'Get back to your work!'

Your Lordships,

I have much to tell you. You may have heard reports of the failed ascension into heaven. If however you have been too busy with affairs of state, I would be honoured to provide you with an account.

The Buchan woman, convinced that the day of 'The Great Translation' was at hand, encouraged her deluded followers to make preparations. Words are inadequate to describe the pathetic sight of emaciated bodies, of skeletal cadavers mumbling their gratitude, singing hymns and dressing so that they might more easily be dragged by angels through the clouds. An accurate depiction of the resulting fiasco requires a writer more skilful with words than your humble servant. It is a task that would tax the skill of Henry Mackenzie himself.

After their abject failure, mutiny and recriminations took hold. Your Lordships will be delighted to hear of the likely dissolution of this aberrant society. White has taken to abusing the foul prophetess; he threatens her with violence. While some of her foolish adherents have fled the floundering ship like vermin, yet many remain steadfast in their belief in their 'Lord Mother'.

Your Lordships are to be congratulated on supporting John Gibson in his claim for financial recompense. Unfortunately – and this I report with heavy heart – your lordships' efforts were undermined by the intervention of their former landlord, Davidson, who stood surety, and the obnoxious couple were released from debtors' prison back into the arms of their followers.

Perhaps the time is ripe – and I have no wish to teach your Lordships how to peel an apple, if you will excuse the platitude – to bring a charge of blasphemy against the wicked charlatans. Should this stratagem fail, then your Lordships may wish to invoke the Poor Law.

Further Evidence of Satanic PracticeS:

1) A fledgling blackbird fell down the chimney and immolated itself in the burning fire. When the ashes were raked from the hearth the following morning, the bird took flight and circled the room several times.

2) A woman whose steading is close to Buchan Hall reported that the dugs on her cow had withered and the beast produced a pail of blood. Furthermore, her hens behaved strangely and spat out small bones.

I must close now, I believe the privations I have endured in your Lordships' service have provoked a fever which means I cannot easily control my pen.

Your humble servant,

Alexander Gillespie

Chapter Thirty-Six

CHARGED WITH DEBAUCHERY

The drunk, the unwashed and the piously prurient filed into the kirk session. It was a long time since so many charges of wickedness had been being brought against anyone residing in the parish. The occasional charge of fornication was only to be expected. Indeed, Sam the Gelder, who was at the front of the expectant queue, was still rebuilding the kirk dykes, his punishment for being caught in flagrante with Morag from the Steadings. Each nudge of the stones had reminded him of his lover groaning in the throes of their carnal encounter. How he longed to hear every detail of the Buchanites' debauchery.

Jamie Currie, the gravedigger, had thrown his spade onto the heap of black earth and hastened to the parochial house. The dead could wait a little longer. The previous year his wife, Molly, had been convicted of casting a spell on their neighbour's cow and turning it dry. Fortunately, the clerk, like the cow at the centre of the dispute, had fallen under Molly's spell and commuted her sentence. Jamie remembered how his good wife smirked and winked her way through her three appearances in sackcloth before the pillar next to the pulpit. There would be no mercy today. They were all guilty as Satan.

'Silence!' roared the kirk officer, red in the face from bellowing. 'Wheesht,' he said as the crowd finally settled on their benches. Both Sam and Jamie rubbed their hands in anticipation.

George Teale, the current session clerk, peered over his spectacles to great effect. Purchased from a merchant in Edinburgh, they sat on the bridge of his nose like an exhausted spider. However, no amount of peering enabled him to locate either Hugh White or Elspeth Buchan, the principal accused. White had reacted with scorn when the writ was delivered to the Hall. When he showed the document to the Lord Mother, she too had scoffed. Let them do their worst.

After a brief consultation, Teale decided that they would be tried in their absence. He called the first witness. James McPhee wrung his cap nervously as he approached the bench to ironic cheers from his audience. McPhee was a well-known keeker, a peeping Tom whose reputation ensured that no farmer's auld wife or young daughter would undress before checking that the curtains were tightly closed.

'I was walking o'er the fields when I saw the lichts fae the hall where they wicked, sinful Buchanites bide.'

'What reason did you have for walking over the fields?' asked Teale.

'Ma dug had no been weil, your honour, your worship. The skitters. He needed the air.'

'And why did you approach the Hall?'

'Ah was like a moth… a wee moth attracted to a flame… ' Delighted by the ingenuity of his own reply, McPhee glanced proudly at the gallery.

Teale adjusted his spectacles. 'Proceed.'

'And ah was sair affronted by the sicht that met my een… '

'Well… '

'A' these bare erses, men's hurdies… ' A pleasurable murmur swept through the crowd. This is what they wanted.

'Silence! Continue.' The spider resumed its former position on the bridge of Teale's nose.

'Humpin', yer worship! Fornication!' McPhee had never used the word before. 'Fornication!'

'And the accused, White and the Buchan woman, did you see their … erses?'

'No M'lord but I saw his tadger. A big hairy, great walloping thing!'

The crowd collapsed into laughter.

'Silence!' Teale removed the spectacles and wiped his eyes.

Andrew Innes rushed home to break the news that, in their absence, the kirk session had no alternative but to refer the whole matter to the presbytery.

Alexander Gillespie shook his head at this unwelcome development.

White received the news with equanimity, 'When Pilate saw that he was getting nowhere, he took water and washed his hands in front of the crowd.'

Kitty's health was deteriorating. Emily nursed her through the incoherent ramblings that punctuated both her sleeping and waking hours. Fixated with her dead husband, she would plead for his forgiveness for hours on end. 'Jock, ah was no a guid wife. Gi' me another chance.'

'Shush, you were a good wife. He didn't deserve you.'

'Jock!'

Emily placed her hands on her friend's shoulders and gently pushed her back down into the bed.

Each week another Buchanite turned deserter. William Lindsay and Ruth were the next to disappear under cover of darkness. Increasingly burdened by doubt, William had packed their bedding, leaving in its space some truffles he had gathered from the forest, several coins and the disbound Bible that had been handed down through generations of his family. White picked up the Bible and tossed it into the burning hearth.

The Lord Mother rarely emerged from the alcove where she slept. Her followers became anxious. Eventually, when White was away on business, Mrs Muir plucked up the courage to peer behind the curtain. She informed the others that, while still living, Elspeth failed to acknowledge her presence, had a deadly pallor, and would only stare into the distance.

Amy Johnson prepared a poultice from herbs gathered at dawn and decided to use her powers to hasten Elspeth's recovery. Her invalid offered no resistance as the concoction was rubbed into her temples. After the third application, Elspeth gripped her hand. 'I have such dreams,' she murmured. 'They frighten me.'

'Dinnae fret, Mother.'

'I'm in a deep grave, suffocating, unable to breath. But this can't be. I am not destined to lie in the cold sod. Christ has spoken to me. He has chosen me. I will rise in glory.'

'This is Satan's work, Mother. He is tempting you to despair.'

'The rats, they gnaw at my flesh. I keep my eyes tightly closed when they come near. I try to shout but my mouth is full of earth. But I am not alone. Someone is with me. His body is pressing down on me.'

Elspeth tried to rise from her bed, desperate to escape from her nightmare grave. 'Be still,' said Amy Johnson. 'This too will pass.'

'And then, from my grave, I hear the trumpet sound. It is the end of time. I open my eyes, there are glimmers of light. The resurrection is at hand, but I can't move. I can't move. I am pinned under this weight, the burden of another's body. And all goes dark again.'

White too felt that he was suffocating. In his case, it was not under the imagined burden of another's body in a dark dream, rather the stultifying paralysis of life in Buchan Ha'. The insidious creep of autumn contributed to his sense of restlessness. The chimney stack was inefficient. He should never have trusted John Gibson with its design, or Andrew Innes with its execution. Folds of smoke bellied their way back into the room. White was sick to the teeth with the constant coughing and wheezing from those who slept closest to the hearth. Tam was the worst. If he once more dredged the phlegm from the back of his throat and spat onto the flagstones, then White was prepared to scour his innards with a hot poker. He knew this situation was only temporary, and that soon the Great Translation would put an end to his suffering, but he was losing patience. God too must be displeased with Elspeth, hiding in her bed from noon to night. Why should He communicate with her when she made such little effort? Perhaps God would soon see the error of His ways and speak directly to him. Meanwhile, he was bored, trapped, and frustrated. He even thought of renewing a degree of familiarity with his wife. Margaret may have been a tame lover compared to Elspeth in her prime, but she could still cater for some of his needs. After all, they did have children in common, and their lad was turning into an agreeable young man who could be of use to his father.

Ever keen to replenish the society's coffers and put his economic theories into practice, White instructed Mrs Gibson to share her weaving skills with Jean Gardner. The fruits of their labours were impressive. At least ten shawls were now neatly stacked in a corner of the hall. He also secured several hides from Davidson, which the cobbler happily transformed into simple buckleless shoes.

White loaded the merchandise onto the cart. He was in better spirits having decided that Jean Gardner would accompany him to the

Dumfries fair. He had looked at her through different eyes of late. She was, when seen in the right light, quite a good-looking woman, and who knows, after a quart of small beer, she might appear even more so.

Jean had become increasingly obsessed with the young poet for whom lust proved stronger than cowardice. Despite his beating, he had continued to pester her. Although alarmed by his persistence, Jean came to believe that he represented her only chance of ever being rescued from the Buchanites. Davidson, despite occasional thoughts of wooing Jean himself, had agreed to convey letters between her and the man on whom she continued to pin her hopes. When she realised that White was amassing goods to sell at the fair, she easily insinuated herself into his plans. She also arranged to meet her beau.

White packed several copies, newly printed by Robert Jackson of Dumfries, of *THE DIVINE DICTIONARY or a Treatise indicted by Holy Inspiration, Containing The FAITH and PRACTICE of that PEOPLE (by this world) called BUCHANITES, who are actually waiting for the second coming of our Lord, and who believe that they, alive, shall be changed and translated into the clouds, to meet the Lord in the air, and so shall be ever with the Lord. Written by that SOCIETY.*

He had unwrapped the parcel of books with great pride. Now his name could be added to those of the four evangelists. He had decided against showing a copy to Elspeth. She was already in a world of her own, which almost certainly precluded appreciation of this wonderful book. Indeed, he considered that her contribution had been minimal; his were the words, his was the vision. He opened one of the tomes and sniffed the new, clean pages before tucking several copies under the heap of shawls. He didn't want them to get wet.

The morning was crisp and agreeable. The reins felt cold, but the horse was responsive. As they approached Dumfries, they were soon overtaken by several score of other riders competing to be the first to reach the booths. Prospective buyers would be watching the charge over the hills, and each horse's position in this unofficial race would determine the price paid for the animal. Their glistening flanks stirred White's blood.

It was a long time since he had seen so many cattle in one place.

'How the beasts groan! The herds of cattle wander aimlessly because there is no pasture for them... ' He was very pleased to have dredged the quotation from the back of his mind. Joel 1:18, if he remembered correctly. He had certainly deserved that theology award. He pulled Jean towards him and kissed her on the top of the head. Yes, she would do, unless he found someone comelier, of course.

As they approached the main thoroughfare, the horse and cart became bogged down in the much-churned mud, but White was in no rush. They could relax and listen to the vendors' cries and the sound of the fiddles. Somewhere a pig was being roasted. He thought of Amy Johnson and snorted.

His business was concluded with the sale of the final shawl and four pairs of shoes to a packman from Glasgow. He patted the breast pocket of his coat and felt the satisfying bulge of the money through the cloth. All that remained was pleasure.

He paused in front of the trickster hiding a coin under one of three cups. But he couldn't fool White who tapped the cup hiding the coin. Refusing to accept that he had been wrong, he considered hitting the smirking fraudster but instead responded to a tug on the arm from Jean who told him that she was thirsty. Striding past the peasants dressed for the day in tailored coats and vests, he took her hand and led her into the booth selling ale. He glanced at his companion for the day and appraised her breasts swelling beneath her bodice. Yes, she would suffice. He struck up a conversation with a farmer feeding scraps to an old dog beneath the table, failing to realise that this was the same man who, during a recent visit to the hall, had been unable to contain either his mirth or incredulity as White declaimed his heretical views.

'Has He no come for you yet?' asked the farmer. As recognition dawned, White rose to leave, but his new companion beckoned him to stay. 'I've thought on your words.' White relented, took off his coat and placed it next to Jean. 'Can I join your society? Can I be with you when the living Christ pushes His hand through the clouds and hauls you into His hoose?'

Failing to see that he was still being mocked, White sensed a chance to further impress Jean with his wit and erudition. Since arriving at the fair, he had walked with a copy of *The Divine Dictionary* tucked ostentatiously under his arm. Rather than answering the farmer directly, he opened the Buchanite bible, bent back its spine until it gave a satisfying crack and read the opening and undeniably masterly words from the preface.

'As one who has obtained mercy in place of guilt, the friendship of God, for the society of worldly men, the fullness of the Godhead, for the penury and want in the first Adam's family, the light of God, for the unmixed darkness of this world; a separation from sin, death, devil, self, world, in place of close attachment to all these abominable ... ' he paused for breath. Yes, it was a long sentence, but powerful nonetheless. As several of the drinkers were now paying incredulous attention, he stood up a little unsteadily to better address them. Wiping the foam from his lips and failing to see that the farmer was now convulsed with laughter, he continued. 'Where was I? Yes... abominable, and hell-leading connections, the waiting for a new heaven, and new earth, in place of wishing a prolongation of this present old world... '

Jean slipped her hand into his coat, withdrew the money, and left.

The publican had heard enough. 'Get oot o' my tent, ye snivelling God-bothering, bible-thumping turd!'

White thought of standing his ground, but after appraising the size of his adversary, picked up his coat and left. The landlord picked up *The Divine Dictionary,* tore off the spine and tucked the pages behind a lamp where he thought they might serve as tapers for lighting candles.

'Rab, tak me away wi' you.' Jean held out the stolen money. Although newly engaged to another Jean, he was certainly tempted. On reflection though, he decided that his life was too complicated. The last straw had been his mother's servant, Elizabeth Paton, turning up on his doorstop in Mauchline with a mewling brat which she claimed was his. No, life was too complex. They could though perhaps spend time in the adjacent field. For auld acquaintance sake. Jean was having none of it and threw the money at Burns who picked up the notes, shrugged and moved out of her life, but not before blowing her such a perfect kiss that she looked for it, hovering in the air.

'Where is the money, hoor?' Angry and drunk, White found Jean at the edge of the fair. She was weeping. 'Ye thievin' wee shite. Give me the money. Stinking hoor!' He grabbed her arm and dragged her back past the booths and the queues, the animals, the bartering, and the singing until they reached the cart. Fearful of being beaten, Jean lowered her face and climbed into the seat.

'No you don't, poxy minx.' White hauled her down onto the road and roped her to the back of the cart.

'I didnae mean any hairm. It must ha' been the deil got into my soul.'

The horse responded to White's whip and Jean stumbled onto the hard-trodden surface that flayed her legs. White drowned out her cries with a loud and bitter rendition of *Oh! Hasten Translation.*

Chapter Thirty-Seven

A GLORIOUS REUNION

In their absence Kitty had died. As he approached Buchan Hall, White was irritated to see that the door was wide open. The place was cold enough.

'Have you taken leave of your senses?' he shouted, standing on the threshold in a flurry of leaves. While he waited for an answer, Jean Gardner slid past him and collapsed onto the nearest mattress.

'We had to let Kitty's spirit go,' explained Emily. White grunted and motioned for Mrs Muir to remove his boots.

It was Andrew Innes who took control of the matter. Davy McConville was sent to negotiate a supply of coffin wood from Davidson. Emily Turnpike was told to wash the body, while Amy Johnson was sent to inform Elspeth that one of her followers, unable to wait any longer for the final trumpet, had made an early departure.

Elspeth raised herself from her pillow, trying to make sense of what she had been told. 'Puir rabbit,' she said. 'Puir critter… puir doggies… '

'Are you following me, Mither? Kitty's deid.'

Elspeth pulled her shawl about her, opened the curtain, and moved towards the cluster of people tending to Kitty. Her unexpected appearance surprised and delighted in equal measure. Emily moved back to let her come closer. Elspeth knelt and took Kitty into her arms, cradling her as if she were a child. 'So cold,' she said. 'So cold.' She held Kitty's face and breathed into her mouth. The others watched expectantly, wanting her to open her eyes and tell them to stop fussing. She did neither. Elspeth rocked the tiny corpse faster and faster until Andrew Innes calmed her and lay Kitty back on her bed.

Tam had been ordered to dig a grave near the boundary line between the edge of the Buchanites' land and Davidson's property. The ground was hard, and he cursed as his spade rang on striking yet another obstacle. The feeble sun had dropped behind the hill, and he desperately wanted the drink he had been promised by White if he completed his task. Seeing there was no alternative but to wrestle the stone with his hands, he leaned down into the hole and gripped it hard. It moved easily, and he lifted it onto the edge of the grave. He then shouted out in terror.

'A wee bairn,' he said on re-entering the hall. 'A bairn's bones. Just lying there, asleep, puir mite.'

White, who had been looking through the ledger by the light of the fire, dropped the book and clamped his hand over the man's mouth. 'Be quiet you drunken fool.' Because Tam was choking, he moved the restraining hand down to his throat and propelled him back out of the hall. Only then did he release his grip. 'If you say one more word, it will be your last.'

Tam cowered in the half light. 'No a word, master. No a word.' White left him simpering and walked over to where the turf and topsoil had been removed. What he saw startled him. What malign force had directed Tam to that very spot? It was beyond his understanding. He used the spade to pick up the tiny body and dropped it into the adjacent ditch. Not wanting a further confrontation with Tam, White dug Kitty's grave himself. He was unused to manual labour and the sweat ran into his eyes. He consoled himself with the certainty that soon he would be free of this earth, the vestiges of which defiled his hands and dirtied his cuffs.

The others kept a night vigil over Kitty. She was buried in the morning. White had reacted irritably when Innes asked if he would say some prayers at the graveside. Apart from anything else, his back was aching, and he had completely failed to clean the soil from under his nails. 'These heretical practices are not ours,' he said. 'The chosen people do not die.'

'Was Kitty not chosen?' asked Emily. White ignored her.

To the delight of everyone apart from White, Elspeth appeared at the graveside as the coffin was lowered into the ground. The mourners were overjoyed to see that she was wearing the red cloak. She seemed transformed and radiant in a way that they had not seen for a long while.

She opened her arms wide. 'Our sister has gone to see that God's mansions are prepared for us. She will swoon before the scent of flowers in every room. She will throw open the windows and gaze on beautiful meadows and see the light sparkling on the running burn. She will ache with pleasure as she listens to the birds singing the praises of our great God. She has already been made young again.'

'She was aye a good looker,' said Emily.

'She has met her man again. He too is young, tall and in love with her. They went for a walk along the river, then rested in the meadow. The angels came by and rubbed her feet with unction…'

'She aye had trouble wi' her bunions.'

James rested an arm on his brother's shoulder as he stood on one leg and used a stick to prise the mud from his boot. 'That's the place,' he said nodding towards the farmhouse. The brothers had witnessed the funeral from a distance but had not wanted to intrude. Birdman whistled the shrill song of the linnet.

Elspeth threw her arms round first James, then Mathew, then both at once as she pressed herself into them. 'Thanks be to the great God who has brought you here.' She ran her hand over each of their faces then blew into their mouths. She smiled at Birdman and stroked the lapwing on his arm.

The other Buchanites gathered round, curious and delighted to see such a transformation in the woman who would soon lead them out of this increasingly tiresome world. Elspeth introduced her new guests to each of them. 'Tell us your tales,' she said, leading them to the trestle next to the hearth.

'After you left,' said James, 'we fought.'

'We each blamed the ither for your leaving,' exclaimed Mathew. 'We fought in the docks.'

'We fought in the taverns.' James pointed to his heavily lidded left eye. 'Nearly gouged out,' he said. Mathew opened his mouth which was largely toothless. 'Knocked out,' he explained proudly.

'And then we got tae work, dredging the river.'

'Filthy work,' echoed Mathew. 'Buckets o' sludge and shite. And dark as the devil's erse in the stank.'

'And it was in the dark that you spoke to us.' White, who had been listening, raised an eyebrow. 'I heard you first, Mither,' said James.

'No, it was me that heard you. Maist definitely.' The young men looked at each other. Elspeth placed a hand on both of their shoulders, and they relaxed.

'You telt us to find you.'

'Dinnae forget the jail,' prompted James.

'Aye,' continued Mathew. 'Imprisoned for nae fault of ma ain.'

'Mistaken identity.'

'And then there wis the press gang.'

'But you were aye there for us in our darkest hours,' said Mathew. Elspeth kissed him on the cheek.

'And dinnae forget yon mad woman... '

'We heard tell of a woman who cried hersel' a prophetess.'

'In Manchester.'

'It took us three weeks to find her.'

'It wisnae you, Mither,' said James. 'It wis a snivelling auld crone wi' a stutter. It wis Mother Lee.'

'The wrang mither.'

Losing interest, White turned away. He didn't like the look of the boys and found Birdman repulsive. He would do his utmost to ensure their stay was as short as possible.

Elspeth raised her arms. 'Bring the fatted calf and kill it. Let us have a feast and celebrate. For these sons of mine were dead and now live again; they were lost and now they are found.'

'Amen, amen.'

White scowled. He was angry at the reception given to the brothers by Elspeth. They didn't belong. He was equally annoyed at the announcement of a feast and watched helplessly as the remaining supplies of food were ransacked without his permission. Three hams were produced. A pot of pickles was opened, and Mrs Muir dragged a sack of potatoes into the room.

'Sheer folly,' muttered White before retiring to the alcove with one of his many unsold copies of *The Divine Dictionary*. He had to make amendments.

Elspeth went to the far corner of the room where Alexander Gillespie was lying sick and spoke to him at great length.

The night of raucous celebration that followed erased the memory of Tam's drunken story about a dead bairn, and there was a consensus that Kitty would have wished to be remembered this way. At the end of the evening, Elspeth beckoned the brothers into the alcove. Birdman fed corn to the jackdaw.

White crumpled up the letter from the Kirk session clerk. He knew this summons was different. They had collectively thumbed their noses at the accusations of degeneracy and debauchery, but the threat of being evicted from Thornhill under the provisions of the Poor Law was not to be dismissed so lightly.

'We will have to attend,' he interrupted Elspeth who was talking to Mrs Gibson about the likely physical sensations of being translated through the clouds.

'We answer to different laws,' she reminded him, before turning back to the older woman who had expressed her fear of being frozen to death on the journey to heaven.

'Listen to me for God's sake! Unless we can demonstrate sufficient funds to avoid being a burden on the parish, we will be evicted.'

'God will provide.'

'Jesus wept! Stupid women!' Mrs Gibson looked at him askance; this was no way to address the Lord Mother.

White's fears were well founded. He and Elspeth had no alternative but to swallow their pride and appear before the session once more. Andrew Innes accompanied them, having convinced White that he was familiar with the provisions of the law in question as he had seen his own family evicted from Muthill when he was a young man.

After an hour of forthright questions from the session clerk and unsatisfactory answers from White, Innes strutted to the bench and peered at the official.

'Codicils,' he said. The clerk eventually located Innes in the well of the court.

'What?' he asked, unused to being addressed by a dwarf.

'Codicils in perpetua,' said Innes smugly. White glanced bleakly at Elspeth who was smiling fondly at her loyal acolyte.

'What?' repeated the official, annoyed at being spoken to like an idiot by someone much more deserving of the title.

Innes puffed out his chest. 'In manu reliquae. Need I say more? I rest my case.'

'You will all appear before the Justice of the Peace court to be convened in Brownhill on January 1st in the year 1787. If you repeat such nonsense I am confident that not only will you and your degenerate tribe of Buchanites be banished from the parish but that you wee man… ' he peered down at Innes, '… might well be horsewhipped into the bargain.'

White's foul mood soured the final days in Buchan Ha'. Part of him wanted to shake the Lord Mother until she came to her senses. Why was she not communicating with God? Didn't she understand that their days in this place were numbered? The Justices' ruling had been unambiguous. They would all leave the parish on or before the 12th of March 1787.

Irritated by the sound of laughter, White tore open the curtain, only to be met by the defiant stares of James and Mathew, who were lying under the blanket with Elspeth. She smiled at him enigmatically. She had other protectors now, and he was powerless. As White strode to the far end of the hall, he stood on Jean Gardner's hand as she lay asleep on the floor and savoured the small crunch from her fingers.

As it seemed increasingly clear that God had other and possibly greater matters on his mind, White turned to Davidson for advice. The farmer had been saddened to hear that their departure was imminent. He had benefited from their labour, and in an odd way, had come to like this strange tribe who had become an important part of his life. After all, he had enjoyed frequent trysts with several of the younger women. At heart a generous man, he wanted to make some further recompense to the Buchanites. He was also haunted by the possibility that perhaps Elspeth really was the Mother of God, or the third person of the Trinity, or whoever it was she claimed to be. Either way, it made sense to be in her debt in case there came a time when, standing alone at the gates of heaven, he needed someone to vouch for his essentially good nature.

After discussions with White, Davidson agreed to stand security if they could find other premises outwith the parish boundaries.

When White returned from an abortive attempt to find alternative accommodation, the hall was deserted apart from Tam who, too drunk to move, had been left to his solitary ravings. White stepped outside and scoured the horizon. Where were they? The sound of singing made him focus on a distant field in the shadow of the hill. He and Innes walked across the frost-hardened furrows towards the Buchanites who were holding hands, standing naked in a circle.

'For the sake of God and all his angels.'

'Amen,' replied Innes assuming White's exhortation had been a spontaneous prayer and not an expression of incredulity.

All of the Buchanites were present. Alexander Gillespie had risen from his sick bed to join them. Elspeth stood in the middle with Mathew and James. Their clothes lay like abandoned silage. Innes ran towards them, removing his clothes as he approached. For a moment, he hopped precariously as his leg was trapped in his breeches. 'Wait for me.' A gap appeared in the chain, and he was admitted to the circle.

'Soon, great God, you will appear. Soon you will lift your servants to glory.' Elspeth was in the grip of a rapture that in the eyes of the faithful, lifted her bodily from the ground. 'We who failed you in the past, have grown stronger.' A nearby sheep bleated its agreement. White shook his head.

Now back on terra firma, Elspeth embraced James then Mathew. The others broke into pairs and did likewise, the physical proximity transmitting much needed heat to the entwined bodies. Their mingled breath rose as from cattle in a pen. White shook his head.

After strong drink and a dish of mutton, Davidson and White agreed to secure a recently abandoned farm at Lower Auchengibbert, some thirty miles distant. Although reluctant to surrender the funds that he had secreted, White knew that this was the best way forward.

Paradoxically, the last days in Buchan Ha' were some of the happiest. Elspeth had sloughed off her melancholy. Her rediscovered enthusiasm and certainty communicated itself to the others. James and Mathew, delighted at their reunion with Elspeth, spread further joy and nonsense through the community. Mathew was a good mimic and readily conjured a whole host of characters. His impersonation of Tam attempting to fondle the nearest woman resulted in a slapping from Emily whose mock outrage then became the object of his jesting. Even Innes smiled as Mathew knelt on a pair of shoes and shuffled his way across the floor while singing *Oh! Hasten Translation.*

White too was in better humour. The society had become moribund since the fast. Joy had gradually leached into lethargy; anticipation had dribbled into the soil. They needed to move forward. They needed a change. God may have grown frustrated with Elspeth, but He knew that White would not fail Him. She undoubtedly had gifts which he, Hugh White, was best placed to harness. With this new certainty, he threw himself into the task of preparing the society for its last resting place on this earth.

Rumours of the imminent departure had emboldened the locals into open provocation. The Buchanites' tools were stolen. One of their horses was mutilated; the beast's tail was hacked from its body and stuffed into the chimney. A straw effigy of Elspeth was found burning on a pole outside of the hall. The carcass of a dead sheep was left to float in the well, an act that obliged Davidson to remind the culprits that he had to live on the land after the Buchanites had left.

Davidson soon gleaned from his informants at the Broomhill Inn that plans were afoot to ambush the society as they left. In their cups, the locals concocted ever more fanciful plots to ensure their departure would long live in the collective memory of the community. Elspeth featured large in their fantasies: her erse would be flayed with a broomstick until she would be obliged to turn on her tormentors, seize the besom and fly off on it towards the sea; her ears would be sliced off and nailed to the door of the kirk.

Special humiliation was also being devised for White, several of the regulars having witnessed his cruel treatment of Jean Gardner. He too would be stripped naked and shackled to a wagon. The horse would be whipped faster and faster until the flesh from his legs stained the road, and his bones flew into the hedgerows. Wisely choosing not to mention this particular detail, Davidson suggested that they take evasive action. Memories of the flight from Irvine were still sufficiently vivid for White to devise alternative plans. The flitting would occur under the cover of darkness.

At midnight on the 10th of March the moon gracefully colluded by remaining hidden behind the clouds. 'The Lord Mother had a word,' observed Mrs Muir who had spent the proceeding hours neatly folding several quires of cloth.

Davidson lent a second horse and several carts to his former tenants. Emily told the others to go on without her. 'I'll bide here. My old legs'll no carry me. You can send for us when the clouds part.'

Her offer was music to White's ears. The older members of the community were a drain on the society's limited resources, and he would willingly leave them to rot and die.

Andrew and Mathew both knelt with their backs to the old woman. 'Choose your horse,' said Mathew. After pretending to inspect the teeth and the flanks of both men, Emily climbed onto James' back.

'Light as a feather,' he said. 'It's like carrying a paddock.'

'Enough of your cheek,' she said tickling James' ear with her words. 'Or I'll get my whip out.' Her beast of burden snorted and set off at a fair pace to catch up with the others.

The society's tools, cooking accoutrements and a few items of furniture had been loaded high. Alexander Gillespie had worked tirelessly to prepare for the flitting and only now agreed to rest. Birdman draped a cloth over his cage. Andrew Innes spreadeagled himself on top of the foremost cart to prevent its load tumbling into the road. From his lofty perch he whistled *Oh! Hasten Translation* which was soon taken up by the others once they were out of earshot of their former neighbours and detractors. Tam walked at the head of the procession holding a lantern that illuminated an irregular pattern of hedgerows and shadows. A fox's eyes briefly reflected the light. There was an air of subdued excitement as the Buchanites put the miles between themselves and Buchan Ha'. Elspeth followed Tam on horseback. She knew they were being guided not just by Tam but by angels. Every now and then she caught sight of them showing the way with gracious sweeps of their wings. She heard them conversing in strange seraphic whispers.

After the cramped confines of Buchan Ha', the farmhouse seemed light and airy. A spirit of renewal was abroad. Andrew Innes skilfully resolved all disputes over the allocation of rooms. He subtlety acknowledged the latest couplings among the Buchanites by letting both new and established lovers sleep together. Katie Gardner left him in no doubt that she was still his lawful wedded wife and expected to be treated as such. Furthermore, he must spend more time with their daughter who had taken to crawling into Mrs Muir's clothes chest. She needed a father's love. Innes agreed.

White needed a new audience. As he was one of the world's finest orators, he craved a congregation that would marvel at his verbal prowess, his sophistry, his peerless biblical knowledge, and his irresistible charisma. He ordered the menfolk to build a platform in an adjacent field from which he intended to address his flock. In response to the posters nailed to trees on the road to Castle Douglas, his flock duly arrived in considerable numbers, before leaving to chew on a line of neeps left out for that purpose. White surveyed the empty field before storming back into the farmhouse where he vented his anger on anyone within reach.

Elspeth too felt the stirring of renewal. Their time was close. She knew that God was noticing them again and was pleased with what He saw. Their tribulations would soon be over, and they would all be lifted into paradise. Her disciples were thin, chilpit. She was the Lord Mother, and all mothers had to feed their families. She looked at those nearest to her as if she were seeing them for the first time. Even Mathew and James had an unfamiliar lean and hungry look. They all needed to be fed.

She returned from the field giggling like a schoolgirl as she emptied her apron onto the floor, spilling the neeps that had been left half-chewed by the sheep. Despite White urging restraint, she plundered the sack of meal they had brought with them and instructed Amy Johnson to scour the hedgerows for herbs.

A delirium of expectation swept through the room as Elspeth ladled the thin gruel into the bowls proffered by the Buchanites who said they had never tasted anything so fine in all their lives. 'He rained down manna for the people to eat, he gave them the grain of heaven,' declared their celestial cook.

'Grain of heaven,' repeated Davy McConville wiping his lips. White looked on increasingly irritated.

They begged for more, holding their bowls high as if they were chalices waiting for the life blood. They slavered and dribbled. Their eyes rolled in ecstasy as they patted their stomachs.

'A blessing! A blessing!' someone shouted.

'Gather round,' said Elspeth. 'Come near.' Soon she was surrounded. Much as they wanted to touch and hold her, the Buchanites held back out of a sense of reverential wonder and collective unworthiness. They seemed to be pushing against an imaginary wall that separated them from Christ's representative on earth. Standing in the charmed circle, Elspeth closed her eyes, swayed slightly, and crooned a tune with words in a strange tongue. The crowd watched silent and awestruck as Elspeth slowly undressed, dropping her clothes on the floor until she stood naked in their midst. With her arms pointing straight ahead, she moved towards the door, her eyes closed as if sleepwalking. Innes lifted the latch as the Lord Mother passed through and into the night. Unerringly she made her way to the side of the farmhouse where a ladder lay against the wall. The others followed, now increasingly agitated and fearful for her safety. Slowly she started to climb. Mathew ran towards her holding a coat, but the others held him back. Hand over hand, Elspeth climbed the ladder until she stood on the eave. She briefly turned, her arms outstretched as if about to dive headfirst into the arms of her followers. Her face was lit by the moon. White observed the events from a distance. For the briefest of moments, he thought of intervening and putting an end to this manifest nonsense. Then he paused, gripped by the most deliciously treacherous of thoughts: if she were to die, he would inherit the earth.

Elspeth turned again and, on all fours, started to pull herself up the slope of the thatched roof until she reached the ridge. 'Take care, Mother,' shouted Mathew. 'Stand still and I'll come for you.' Before he could make good his offer, Elspeth stood upright, and balancing like an acrobat, she made her way to the chimney stack. Searching for a toehold, she slipped and slid back down the roof. Her audience cried out. Flailing, Elspeth continued her slow-motion descent before toppling off the edge and falling to the ground.

Chapter Thirty-Eight

INDUSTRY AND INTRIGUE

Her fall was broken by Mathew who managed to wrap her in his arms before he was felled by her weight. They lay entwined on the cold earth. Mathew groaned but Elspeth lay silent. Eventually White pushed his way through and issued orders that she be carried back inside.

Davy McConville announced that Mother Buchan had broken her leg and that he would devise a splint to ensure a speedy recovery. He had in the past carried out a similar procedure on one of his dogs. Despite his neighbour urging him to drown the creature, Davy had ignored him and was subsequently vindicated when he removed the splint and watched as the animal hobbled away to join its brothers and sisters in the byre.

Elspeth eventually agreed. It was Andrew Innes who suggested that if the end of the world were to come quickly, she must be in a fit state to lead her flock towards whatever hilltop God chose for the Great Translation. Humming as he worked, Davy whittled a section of broken hoe handle until it perfectly matched the contours of his patient's leg. While the other Buchanites were solicitous of their injured Mother, White was less impressed. At least, he argued, a broken leg would keep her out of harm's way while he mapped out the society's future. It was a future in which Elspeth would play no part.

White knew that his experience of life in America would prove invaluable as he charted the way forward. When not proselytising from his pulpit in Philadelphia, he had observed with envy as the leaders in his community made themselves rich on the efforts of others. 'Hard graft and guile' was the catchphrase with which Abe Dunlop peppered his discourse during those wonderful, Bourbon fuelled evenings spent in White's study. The sweating businessman would pat his corpulent belly and pronounce, 'I have feasted on the bones of the poor and inherited the earth.' What else had he said? Yes, it all came back to him now. They had spent the day fishing on the banks of the Idaho. Abe had gripped the line in his fist and torn the hook and guts from the throat of the twitching fish. 'Show no mercy,' he said. 'Show the fuckers no mercy.' Hugh had learned lessons from that man. He would show these naïve and deluded shirkers what it really meant to be ruled with a rod of iron.

White decided that certain modifications were necessary to ensure that their new abode reflected the new hierarchy within the society. He told Elspeth that it would be more fitting if she no longer maintained distance between herself and her acolytes; she would improve morale if she lived and slept more communally. 'Christ slept with his disciples,' he reminded her. 'Do you really think he raised a net between himself and the other fishers of men when they lay on the shores of Galilee?'

Margaret White was delighted when her husband announced that they could share the room at the front of the house, and that their children could join them on occasions. 'Things are changing,' he told her.

Fences had to be built to contain the cattle. White supervised the work and chastised the labourers when they paused to improvise a prayer of homage to the Lord Mother. 'Pick up your tools, the job is not finished.'

Andrew Innes pulled himself up to his full height and, to the surprise of the others, confronted White. 'Render to Caesar the things that are Caesar's; and to God the things that are God's.' White pushed him in the chest and laughed as he toppled backwards.

Over the next few days White spoke to each of the Buchanites separately. He explained that things had indeed changed; there was a new order. He was determined to run the commune with ruthless efficiency and would not tolerate stragglers or backsliders. Tam was told to pack his bags and leave as he contributed nothing to his fellows. He was a drunk and a lecher.

'And you,' said Tam, revealing a previously unsuspected way with words, 'are an erse; a stinking turd, a useless toss pot, a cretinous toley and a leach.' White, impressed by his victim's unexpected loquaciousness, smirked, and turned away. Elspeth, hearing the raised voices, moved to calm Tam.

'Don't interfere,' said White.

'One last blessing, Tam.' He held the Lord Mother tightly after she breathed in his mouth for the final time. The others, in defiance of White, stood in the doorway and watched as Tam trod wearily over the field towards the road. Someone waved and shouted, 'God speed.' Tam turned, bowed slightly and then hurled an empty bottle towards the farm where it broke on the flagstones.

'Get back inside,' said White who still had business to attend to.

It was agreed that Mathew and James would lead a party to enclose four hectares of land to contain the two cows. Mathew looked towards Elspeth who nodded her agreement. They would take orders from her but not from her bullying Manchild.

Duncan Robertson confirmed that, if given time, he could fashion several spinning wheels. He would need a supply of seasoned wood. White told him to remove the two hogsheads he had seen resting near to the well on the adjacent land. Once dismantled, they would provide him with all the timber he needed. 'Hide the hoops,' he said. 'We will put them to good use later.' It was agreed that Mrs Muir would supervise the older women as they reacquainted themselves with the art of spinning. White's own children would learn to card the wool. James Stewart took a risk and showed White the stockpile of shoes he had produced, fearful that he would be punished for working surreptitiously. In truth, shoemaking was as crucial to his existence as breathing. He swelled with pride as the master put his hand into a particularly fine boot that he had recently finished. White put it to his nose and inhaled the smell of newly fashioned leather. 'Well done, well done. We must get these to the market.' Thus, the seeds of industry were sown, and the coffers filled.

Elspeth had offered little resistance when White made it clear that the Buchanites' labour could no longer be hired cheaply; those days were gone. To his surprise he heard himself repeating to her Andrew Innes' words about Caesar. Elspeth placed her arm on his, 'You are right. Soon we will go to a better place. The time is coming. I know it.'

White pulled his arm away. 'Yes,' he said without any conviction. 'Soon.'

He was more than happy to delegate tasks to Andrew Innes. Despite finding the man deeply irritating, he had his uses and could still be relied on to carry out instructions. For some reason Andrew Gillespie was keeping his distance.

Whenever White was absent on business, the Buchanites would temporarily forsake their tasks and gather close to the Lord Mother. 'Speak to us of the Translation,' said Mrs Muir spreading a newly woven green shawl over Elspeth's knees.

'Firstly, the skies will darken, noon will become night.' The group were utterly attentive. 'The beasts in the fields will howl in fear. Dogs will slip their leashes and hide. The bull will lower its head and slaver in terror at what is to come. The sinners will claw the clothes from each other's bodies, seeking blind respite in lust. But their drooling kisses will scour the flesh from the skull. Parents will strangle their children and drown their infants to save them from the cinders gusting in the furnace wind.'

'And what of us?' asked Andrew Innes, aware that some of the listeners were becoming terrified. 'What of us?'

'We will feel a stillness, a calm. The peace that passeth all understanding will enter our hearts. God's grace will flow like the summer sun on a meadow. We will follow the larks climbing, higher and higher into the skies until their joyous songs become our own. Our pain and sorrow, our regrets and disappointment will drop from us and tumble down towards the distant burning earth.' Birdman smiled at the reference to the larks.

The Buchanites breathed again and smiled reassuringly at each other. 'Will I see my son?' asked Thomas Neil.

'You must be patient. Your son is busy in the heavenly realm preparing to welcome his father. He will strew flowers on the path to your door. I see him clearly,' said Elspeth. 'He's wearing a shirt of silk…'

'His mother made it for him,' said Thomas. 'He was courting, you understand. We sold a stirk to buy the cloth. He looked grand, grand.'

A tremor of anxiety passed through the group. White had returned and was tying his horse to the fence. Elspeth's followers made a show of resuming whatever tasks they had abandoned.

White filled the doorway. 'I will not tolerate sloth.' James Stewart tapped guiltily at his empty last. 'Ah,' said White, 'shoes made from invisible leather. A gift for the angels perhaps.'

The Buchanites were expected to keep regular hours. Efficiency, discipline, and economy were the order of the day. In his earlier life, White had witnessed at first hand how the American entrepreneurs had tamed, then harnessed the labouring classes until they worked in harmony, obeyed their masters and felt privileged to be provided with board and victuals. It was a model to which he aspired.

The spinning operation at Auchengibbert was potentially the most profitable, but after a few weeks, the women started to complain about the quality of the wool. Feeling threatened by the emerging competition, the local mills discouraged the farmers from supplying the strange band of women who had settled in their midst. The solution was staring White in the face. How could he not have noticed before? Abel Shrive, a quiet nondescript member of the community, revealed that he had been apprenticed to a tinsmith before he had fallen under the spell of the Lord Mother. White secured a small quantity of the metal from the mine at Wanlockhead and was soon marvelling at the delicacy of Abel's handiwork. Delicate filigree broaches, small boxes with exquisitely worked clasps and utilitarian drinking cups were conjured with ease.

Davy McConville was ordered to construct two packs such as those carried by pedlars as they trekked across the country selling their wares. The Gardner sisters were then instructed to take to the highways and byways with orders not to return before they had secured at least a quire of wool with the proceeds of their sales. Andrew Innes had protested that his wife, who frequently suffered from delirium, was not in a fit state to undertake such work. White called him a snivelling runt and suggested that he should hide in Elspeth's skirts and tell her his woes.

Innes stood his ground. 'If Katie leaves, she might be absent for the Translation. I have no wish to ascend to paradise without her.'

'Talk to the Mother. I'm sure she can reach an accommodation with God if you ask her.'

Katie was pleased to spend time away from Andrew who increasingly struck her as odd and erratic. Had it not been for their child, she would have left him long ago. She also looked forward to spending time with Jean even if she could talk of nothing other than the poet who had scorned her. She had heard that Rab had sold a volume of his verses to a publisher in Kilmarnock who had promised to make him a rich man. Perhaps they could be reconciled, and she could help him spend his fortune.

White knew that the society's arrival had not been universally welcomed in the neighbourhood. Rumours of their unconventional lifestyle had followed them. So too had tales of infanticide and witchcraft.

Realising that he could benefit from some powerful friends and allies, White wrote to several local dignitaries. Overblown and obsequious, his missives were read with a mixture of disbelief and mirth by the ministers from neighbouring parishes who, understandably, were eager to see for themselves the strange community in their midst.

Dr Lamont of Kirkpatrick-Durham was the first to visit. As White was away on business securing an order for spinning wheels, it was left to Elspeth to greet the clergyman. As was now the established pattern, she grew into the space whenever White was absent. Temporarily unconstrained by his criticism, she sought out each member of the household and imparted words of comfort and encouragement. The Lord Mother assured Emily that she would soon be reunited with Kitty who had much to tell her. She told Amy Johnson that God had several piglets. She put her arms around Mathew and James and asked to hear their news. When Dr Lamont appeared smiling nervously on the threshold, Elspeth assumed that he was a new potential convert and held him in her arms. 'God in His infinite wisdom has brought you to us. Praise be to His name.'

'Praise be to His name,' muttered the confused Doctor of Theology once he had extricated himself from Elspeth's passionate embrace. Misinterpreting his breathless reticence as awe and admiration, she decided to bestow her special blessing on this most deserving of men. Squeezing his cheeks with one hand, and opening his mouth, she breathed long and deep into him. Shocked and helpless, her reluctant convert made an odd gurgling noise that Elspeth assumed was a sure sign of incipient ecstasy. Determined to complement his spiritual joy with physical consummation, she thrust her hand down his breeches and grabbed his cock. Dr Lamont of Kirkpatrick-Durham, minister of the Associate Anti-burgher congregation of Thornhill, and professor of divinity, shrieked and fled.

White thought he recognised the man who brushed him aside as he lifted the latch to the farm. The silence with which he was greeted told him that something was amiss.

'What have you done?' he asked throwing his hat on the table.

'Nothing.'

'What do you mean, nothing?'

Andrew Innes intervened. 'The minister proved unexpectedly resistant to the Mother's blessing... '

'What in God's name did you do? What did you do?' Elspeth said nothing.

'You most stupid of women... ' He paused, aware that everyone in the room was listening shocked at how he was addressing the Lord Mother. 'Stupid... stupor... God's stupor... it's a sacred state of mind.' His tone changed as he sought to extricate himself from what had started as an unforgivable verbal assault on the Mother. He put a hand to his brow. 'It means overwrought with the power of spiritual insight, a vision... '

The others drifted away and resumed their business. White knew that the present situation was untenable. He had to act decisively if he was to be rid of the Lord Mother.

The situation was complex. He had always believed that the end of time was indeed approaching; the Great Translation was imminent. He accepted too that the Lord Mother was in touch with powers beyond the ken of mere mortals. In truth, the society would not exist without her. Her followers worshipped her. He thought briefly, with an undeniable sense of loss, of those early carnal days when they lay entwined and sated. Had he ever known such pleasure? Her smell, her taste, her sheer invention. The angels must have covered their eyes. He was feeling roused by the recollection. But all that had changed. The fast had been a mistake. He shuddered at the memory of how faith had stripped the flesh from the bones of their followers; grown men and women reduced to wraiths, groaning through the night. It had been hard to lose himself in lust amid the cloying scent of famine. And then the farce of Templeton Hill. He could still taste the disappointment and hear the derisive laughs from the incredulous witnesses. What humiliation. It was unconscionable that a man of his standing and intellect should be treated like a buffoon, duped by a mad woman. A mad woman. This was the first time he had considered that, despite her spiritual calling, Elspeth Buchan was fundamentally insane. This in turn suggested a course of action. White was so overwhelmed by his own logic that he had to leave the farmhouse and walk abroad in the fresh air.

It was so obvious. He had been part of Christ's conundrum which he now had solved. Delighted with his insight, he kicked at a clod of earth that was in his path, stubbing his toe in the process.

It took White the best part of a day to reach the asylum. Having arranged to meet with the superintendent in the morning, he retired to an inn for a meal of roast beef and potatoes. In his room, White moved the candle across the desk until it illuminated the blank page which he straightened with the back of his hand. Next to it was a letter he had received from Dr Lamont of Kirkpatrick-Durham in which the learned cleric had expressed disgust at the reception he had received at Auchengibbert. The man's handwriting was distinctive with several loops linking otherwise unconnected words, and a penchant for unnecessary use of capitals. It was easy to copy. The supply of ink lasted just long enough for White to forge Dr Lamont's signature. He read over his handiwork. The tone was good; civil but firm. He had visited the abode of the Buchanites where a certain Elspeth Buchan had attempted to bestow a 'blessing' on him which the depraved woman must have learned from Satan himself. Yes, White was pleased with the letter; it had the right resonance. Furthermore, Dr Lamont had subsequently learned that the aforementioned lunatic had recently attempted to fly from the rooftops under the illusion that she was about to visit a heavenly realm. Predictably, the venture had ended with injury to herself. It was therefore the minister's considered view that the person in question represented a significant risk to herself and the community, and should accordingly be forcibly removed from her abode and contained in an asylum until such time as her wits returned. It would be wise, thought White, to hold out the possibility of recovery at some undetermined time in the future. It smacked of compassion.

After a hearty breakfast of eggs and muffins, White rode towards the asylum. The morning was fresh and smelled of possibility. As his horse slowed on climbing Parker's Hill, White took stock of his options. It was important that he distance himself from any forcible attempt to remove Elspeth from Auchengibbert. If he were to assume sole control of the society, its finances and future direction, it was crucial that he be perceived as Elspeth's protector. He must not, on any account, be seen to be colluding in her apprehension. He would easily convince the superintendent of the need to act speedily in the interests of public safety, and he would of course be absent from the farm when the officials forced Elspeth into the padded confines of the windowless cab. Then he would truly launch the Buchanites as a model community: efficient, hard-working, and pious. Yes, religion must still feature in their way of life. Indeed, they must be prepared for all contingencies including, he admitted, the Great Translation. The ideal scenario would be for him to make a success of life on this earth as well as in the next life.

As his horse ambled amiably between the hedgerows, White thought about the need to inject new blood into the society. Perhaps the old women would die soon, and he could replace them with... he thought of the girl he had spoken to at the local mill. She had winked at him as he left, he was sure of it. Perhaps she would bring her friend, the buxom one with the red hair. He loved the secret red hair on a woman. He could introduce his own blessing. Not as public spectacle, more a private initiation...

White was jolted out of his fantasies when his horse stopped at the closed gate to the asylum. After collecting his thoughts and brushing down his coat, he stood on the steps and pulled the bell cord. The servant who answered did so with a grunt and ushered White down a long corridor leading to the superintendent's office. As he walked, he realised that he was being touched by someone behind him. He turned and saw that his pursuer was an elderly man, completely naked. The inmate pressed something into his hand. 'Take it, Sir, take it. The secrets are there. All you need to know.' While the servant chased the supplicant away, White glanced at the completely blank piece of paper.

After formal greetings, the superintendent took a moment to peruse the letter. He muttered to himself as he read. White thought it prudent to interrupt and prevent an overclose scrutiny of the contents.

'I realise, Sir, that there is an important distinction between those you classify as imbeciles and those who merit the term lunatic. I think I can assure you, Sir, that the subject of the letter meets the criteria for the latter category. I am confident that her malady is essentially temporary. Perhaps of only a few years duration under your enlightened ministrations.'

The superintendent paused briefly to glance at White before returning to the letter. 'Has Dr Lamont suffered an accident?' he asked. White was disconcerted by the question. 'Has he perhaps fallen from his horse, and landed badly?'

'I don't follow your drift.'

'Has Dr Lamont damaged his hand? Or been afflicted with a palsy in the short interval of time since I dined with him?'

'Not that I am aware...'

'This is not his handwriting, Sir. This has been penned by an imposter, a charlatan.'

White decided to meet suspicion with aggression. 'How dare you impugn my honour?' He stood up and towered above the superintendent. 'You haven't heard the last of this!'

'Perhaps, Sir, you would like me to exercise my authority and have you detained in my establishment until the question of your own lunacy or imbecility can be resolved to our mutual satisfaction.'

At that moment, the servant re-entered the room and led White back whence he had come. At the entrance he pushed the unwanted visitor down the steps and closed the not insubstantial door behind him.

Murder was completely out of the question. Although White knew full well that the commandments were for the guidance of fools, there was no ambiguity about the prohibition against killing. Infants and young children were an obvious exception: they had no souls.

White delegated the day-to-day management of the workforce to Andrew Innes. Serious issues had arisen that required his undivided attention. As he was the only scholar among them, he would find a solution.

He would need a degree of seclusion and ordered James Stewart to clear the outhouse used for the storage of tools and then make it wind and rain proof. He would need a comfortable seat, a desk, a bed, and a plentiful supply of candles. Three days of intensive study should suffice. He chose two of the younger women, Agnes Short and Fiona Murdoch, with whom he had not yet lain, and allocated to each the days on which they were to bring him food and tend to any other of his needs. His reconciliation with Margaret had been short-lived. He had forgotten how boring she was, and soon tired of her endless talk of their children. In addition to a considerable supply of paper, he would need only two books, the Bible and the much more significant source of inspiration, his own *Divine Dictionary*.

Except for Agnes and Fiona, who had so far prided themselves on avoiding White's carnal attention, the society welcomed this respite from his heavy-handed rule; they had long wearied of his rod of iron. Elspeth seemed indifferent to the change. She increasingly enjoyed the solicitous attention of her followers, especially since she had taken responsibility for feeding their bodies as well as their souls. She was a gifted cook who conjured nourishing meals with few resources. James and Mathew were her self-appointed helpers in the kitchen.

'Do you mind the dog fight in Irvine?' asked Mathew while stirring the broth.

'We had to tend to your wounds,' said James.

'You still do, you still do,' said Elspeth lightly touching both of their heads.

White blew on his hands. The outhouse was cold, but he knew he would soon benefit from the heat of his own intellectual fervour. The basic question was simple: what was God's will? The candle at his elbow seemingly guttered under the weight of this insight, this clarity of mind. Was the Lord Mother the only person entrusted with understanding of His will? Might God have grown impatient with His servant's increasingly erratic behaviour? Might God have given His favour to another, more gifted, stronger messenger? In short, himself. Excited, he left his desk and paced the floor. But there was more, much more. If God were disappointed in His first messenger, how would His displeasure be manifest? Would a powerful, vengeful God tolerate apostasy? Would He countenance delay to His plans? What did God require of him? Did He want His new messenger to eliminate the imposter who had betrayed His wishes? Although this was not the first time he had thought like this, rarely before had he been able to express these ideas so succinctly.

He was interrupted by a tentative knock on the door. Fiona Murdoch stood, head bowed, offering a plate of food. Irritated at being interrupted, he glanced at the thin stew. 'It's cold,' he said. 'You may have to be punished.'

As her punishment took many subtle forms, and consumed most of the night, White was exhausted when day broke. He patted Fiona's buttocks and bid her return to the house.

Consciously moving from his carnal preoccupations to more cerebral concerns, he resumed his deliberations. With a gasp, he realised that his own words, as recorded in *The Divine Dictionary*, did indeed hold the key to his current situation. What had he written? He flicked through the much-thumbed tome until he came to the chapter headed *Concerning the Plainness of the Scriptures*. There it was, sticking out like the nose on his face: 'The person that thinks that any man can tell the mind of God more simply than God has actually done, must travel in darkness, die in darkness, and rise to inherit darkness.' Yes, yes. He must follow his instincts and trust the Lord. Obviously, he would work closely with

God, and create situations which would require Him to show His hand. Of course, he wouldn't murder Elspeth; that would be ridiculous, and would have consequences within the community, as well as destroying his credibility. He could though put the Lord Mother in harm's way, therefore obliging God to show His hand. A perfect solution. He would either save her or He would let her perish.

When he returned to the house, everyone noticed that his mood had changed for the better. He exchanged pleasantries with people he normally ignored. He dipped a finger into Amy Johnson's porridge and declared it good. He even seemed pleased to see Elspeth whom he held tight in an unexpected embrace.

'I think oor Fiona has gifts,' muttered Emily.

White realised that if he were to provide God with further opportunities to demonstrate His will, he must gain Elspeth's confidence once more. He quickly produced several doggerel hymns praising the Lord Mother and taught them to the society. He became attentive to her needs in a way that he had not done for several months. He even suggested that they might lie together again at some point. Elspeth smiled like a young woman in the first flush of courtship. She gripped his hand. 'My Manchild,' she said. The brothers looked at each other.

That evening, she chose as her post-blessing text John's tale of the Samaritan woman and her encounter with Christ at the well. 'Sir,' the woman said, 'You have nothing to draw with, and the well is deep. Where can you get this living water?'

The mention of the well struck a chord with White. He eventually recalled Elspeth telling him of a distant time when she was in service and saw a vision in the well of the large house. 'Yes!' he said to himself. 'Yes!'

White approached Elspeth as if about to take her hand in a dance. Smiling, he completed the biblical reference. 'Jesus answered, 'Everyone who drinks this water will be thirsty again, but whoever drinks the water I give them will never thirst." The company was pleased to see the Mother and White in harmony again. He held her in his arms and suggested that perhaps, they should enjoy a special blessing that evening.

The well was in disrepair and had been abandoned. The local farmers believed a sheep had fallen in and poisoned the water which was rank and fetid. The structure was also increasingly unsafe. Some of the coping stones had been dislodged while others tottered on the brink.

White held Elspeth's hand as they walked across the field. The stars were bright. He had promised to show her something special.

'Lift up your eyes on high And see who has created these stars,' said Elspeth picking her way across the ploughed furrows.

'Isaiah 40: 26,' retorted her companion, enjoying the game.

Elspeth countered with: 'He counts the number of the stars; He gives names to all of them.'

'One of the psalms... 147: 2-4?'

'I think you'll find it's 4-5.'

'Lord Mother, I defer to your superior knowledge.' She smiled, and White kissed her cheek. He thought of Judas and the betrayal of Christ. He even found himself listening for the cockcrow. No, this was not a betrayal. He was merely enabling God to make His intentions clearer.

The ground in the immediate vicinity of the well had been churned by cattle and the mud clung to their boots.

'Do you mind what you said about the Samaritan woman and her encounter with Christ? I think it was this very moment that was being foretold by John.' He placed his arm around her waist and steered her over the fallen stones towards the ring of darkness that was the mouth of the well. Pretending to peer over the edge, he declaimed the words that he had practised under his breath before leaving the farm, 'And there appeared a great wonder in heaven; a woman clothed with the sun, and the moon under her feet, and upon her head a crown of twelve stars. Look my dearest, look!'

Elspeth pulled herself further up the stones until she stood unsteadily on the edge.

'Look! Look! Don't you see?'

Elspeth lurched forward and lost her footing.

Praise be to your Lordships and your heirs,
Please forgive my tardiness in writing; in truth I have been at death's door,

infected with an ague that almost extinguished my vital humours. What I have to report may cause you to fulminate and arrive at the opinion that I have been truly bewitched by the Lord Mother. If your instinct is to consign my heretical words to the flames, I nevertheless wish all blessings on your Lordships but beg you to consider my words with an open and warm heart.

As I lay on my bed of sickness, the Lord Mother approached me; she held my hand, she soothed my breast; she brought me comfort with her sainted words. She looked into my soul and sighed at what she saw. She held my transgressions in her hand and cast them aside, and she filled the void so created with love and hope. Again, I urge your Lordships not to seethe in anger and disbelief at my words. In short, the Lord Mother made me whole. She knew my true intent was to destroy her mission, yet she forgave me and held me to her bosom whereupon my sickness left me like rain after a storm, like the sea retreating from the shore.

It is not she that is behoven to the devil, it is her foul consort, the vile White – I can barely bring myself to write his name – who is spreading dissent in the society and talking openly of schism. He wants to take those loyal to him to the Americas. I suspect strongly that the Lord Mother may suffer some terrible fate at his perfidious hand. But rest assured, I will save her!

With profound regret I must now sign myself,

Your formerly loyal servant,

Alexander Gillespie.

Chapter Thirty-Nine

OH SHAMEFUL DAY!

They walked back in silence towards the farm. Elspeth blamed herself. She must have displeased God in some way if He had, in His infinite wisdom, chosen not to share His vision with her. She heard cattle lowing in an adjacent field. They too were giving voice to the disappointment they felt in her. She must try harder, pray harder, be a better leader. Believe more.

For his part, White was furious with God who had been presented with the ideal opportunity to reveal His wishes. It had been so close. That was what made everything so annoying. Another foot or so and Elspeth would have plummeted headfirst. Of course, he could have helped her towards an earlier encounter with Christ than she might have anticipated, but who was he, a mere John the Baptist figure, to pre-empt the will of the Almighty? The episode had left him ever more certain that God had finished with Elspeth and wanted her death but why then, did He not seize the chance when it was presented to Him? He knew that God worked in mysterious ways, but...

Over the next few weeks his irritation increased. As if sensing a threat, the society were especially protective of Elspeth. They took it in turns to gather around her and listen to her ever more florid descriptions of the paradise that was waiting for them. Andrew Innes would tell her his dreams.

'The same one, Mother, but different. This time it wasnae a ladder but a rope that fell from the clouds. It was woven from golden thread. I held it in baith hands and a mysterious force pulled me upwards, past the eagles with their wide wings and bony beaks...'

Elspeth held his hand. Birdman looked confused.

'I saw souls that, lacking the strength to fly higher, fell back to the earth. I heard their disappointed sighs, and reached out to them, but to no avail. And then as the moment of divine consummation approached...' he paused.

'Yes?' urged Elspeth.

'I woke up, Mother, in a terrible fankle.'

Elspeth patted him on the head. 'Soon,' she said. 'Soon.'

Soon my erse, thought White who had overheard the exchange. He gathered his coat and left, slamming the door behind him. He needed an excuse to escape from the atmosphere of cloying sycophancy. He had been asked to visit a neighbouring farmer whose cattle were falling sick at the rate of one a day. The distraught farmer had heard rumours that the woman who bided at Auchengibbert was either witch or prophetess depending on whom you spoke to. Desperate, and willing to consider any course of action that would keep him out of the poor house, he had summoned White, hoping to persuade him to intercede with the Buchan woman. White, for his part, saw an ideal opportunity to extract money from his gullible neighbour.

As he was shown into the byre, White was surprised to see so many sick and staggering beasts. Some had already collapsed into the churned mud where they lay dying. The sweet stench emanating from the stricken cattle was strangely familiar. Soon after arriving in his Irvine parish, he had visited the sick beds of two young farmhands who had been working with cattle similarly affected. The young men had developed the same symptoms as the beasts they had tended. Both men subsequently died.

The enormity of his next thought left him overwhelmed.

'Yes,' he said quietly, 'I will bring the Lord Mother here to cure your beasts.'

As he ran back to the house, White knew that the situation had been engineered by a force far greater than him. Surely, this time, God would show His hand and make His intentions clear.

Elspeth took little persuading. Of course, she would do what he wanted.

White led her over the fields. 'I mind when we first met,' he squeezed her hand. 'You told me how when you were a child you would cure stricken beasts just by breathing on them.'

'That was a long time ago.'

'Yes, but this too is God's will.' He was grasping for a suitable biblical quote that would confirm God's limitless ambition for cows but failed. It didn't matter. Elspeth was eager to do his bidding.

The grateful farmer doffed his hat several times and led her to the byre. She walked towards the nearest cow and patted its flank. It jerked involuntarily but offered little resistance as she held its head between her hands. The beast's slaver dribbled through her fingers.

'The breath, Mother, the breath.' White watched as Elspeth's own breath visibly mingled with that of the animal. She repeated the procedure until she had ministered to some ten of the herd. Oblivious to the heavy mud and dung clinging to her skirts, she knelt alongside one of the prone animals. Its head was twisted away from her, and she had to use all her strength to shift its position until its nostrils were visible. She exhaled deeply. And then again. Unexpectedly, it seemed to revive.

'Praise be!' shouted the farmer.

White was so excited that he left without extracting an exorbitant fee from his neighbour. All he had to do now was wait.

There were welcome early signs that, this time, God was making His intentions clear.

Elspeth became lethargic. Despite Amy Johnson administering increasingly creative combinations of herbs and dubious fluids, the Lord Mother remained asleep for much of the day. She also left her food untouched. Thomas Neil made a special journey into Kirkcudbright to buy two cutlets which Mrs Muir prepared but Elspeth wasn't tempted and turned her face to the wall. The followers muttered about a second fast. The first was still a source of painful memories for many, who, despite their unflinching devotion to the Mother, baulked at the prospect of starving themselves for a second time.

James and Mathew refused to leave her side. They straightened her bedding; they sang to her. They took turns to drape a heated cloth on her forehead, a gesture that greatly affected Andrew Innes.

When she was awake, Elspeth shivered constantly and would beg Andrew to heap more logs onto the fire. Fiona Murdoch declared that she would soon be forced to wander stark naked rather than endure another moment in the cloying heat. White said that if she wished to remove all her clothing, he would have no objections. Emily fixed him with a stare that, as Kitty used to say, would curdle milk.

It was though, Elspeth's constant coughing that most alarmed the society. She was incapable of speaking at any length without her words being lost in convulsions. Andrew Innes reported to White that he had seen a speckle of blood on her pillow.

The news both delighted and alarmed White. Although Elspeth's death was an outcome that he may have fleetingly desired, he was also experiencing intimations of guilt. It would not be murder. The very thought. He was a mere vessel for God's will. He also realised that, unless he was careful, Elspeth's death could work against him. He could not be certain that Elspeth's followers would transfer their allegiance to her designated Manchild. His wish to assume control, strip out the backsliders and move in a new direction might prove more difficult than he had hoped.

'The Mother is in God's hands,' he assured the women kneeling at her bed.

'Perhaps the moment of Translation is at hand,' said Mrs Muir. The others seized on her words.

'Hasten Translation. Hasten Translation!' Chairs were upturned in the commotion. James and Mathew embraced each other. The tears streamed down Andrew Innes' cheeks as he tried to sing. Mrs Muir threw open the door to better see the clouds and any sign that they were about to be ripped asunder by the hand of God.

It was Thomas Neil who first noticed that Elspeth was straining to sit upright and speak. It took several seconds before this fact communicated itself to the far end of the hall where the words of the hymn took a while to subside. The Buchanites gathered round the Mother's bed. Unable to see because of the crush, Andrew Innes had to content himself with peering beneath Mrs Gibson's arm.

Elspeth reached out and clutched at Davy McConville's sleeve. 'Take a good look at me, Davy, that you may know me again. Did you ever see a person in the jaws of death with a countenance so composed as

I have?' Several of those nearest shook their heads, desperate to agree with her. Their faint hopes were soon dashed. 'Although it might seem that I am dying... ' Several gasps filled the space left by her attempt to catch her breath. 'I am only going to Paradise to arrange things for you. So, do not be disheartened. Hear me. If you remain pure and unalloyed in your faith, then my spirit will return to my body in six days, and we will all fly to heaven together. If you prove faithless, this will not happen for ten years. If then you are still unprepared, I say to you that I will not reappear on earth until fifty years have passed. My appearance will be a final sign that the end of the world and the final judgement of the wicked has come.'

With these words Elspeth Buchan gave up the ghost.

Chapter Forty

RESURRECTION

Although the veil of the temple was not rent in twain, the effect was similar. White knew that he had to think quickly. He had to assume control. His moment had come. 'Keep the faith!' he shouted. 'Keep the faith! We must believe.' He parted the distressed mourners clustered around her deathbed and addressed them with his back to the Lord Mother. 'We must hide our pain from the vile unbelievers and sinners who surround us. God sees our hearts in turmoil and grieves for us, not for the Lord Mother whose ascendency is assured. Trust in God!' He slowly opened his clenched fist and spread his arms in an all-encompassing embrace.

'Amen, amen.'

Collectively heartbroken, the Buchanites needed his certainty. Perhaps all was not lost. After all, the Lord Mother would never forsake them. Never. They wiped their tears and embraced each other. 'Trust in the Lord,' they muttered. James punched Mathew on the shoulder in a physical expression of solidarity and unspeakable grief.

White was expecting a visit that day from two local businessmen who were willing to invest in the community in exchange for a regular quota of tin and woollen goods. If successful, White knew that he could launch the Buchanites as a commercial collective, thereby lining his pockets for the foreseeable future. He nodded to Davy McConville. 'A coffin,' he said. 'With no lid.' The blacksmith shuffled away to find his tools. He then instructed four of the men to carry Elspeth into the barn where she would rest.

The visit was successful. White bargained hard and secured a guarantee of significant funds. 'Your workers seem downhearted,' observed one of the businessmen, wiping the beer from his lips and glancing at the Buchanites who were making a dumb show of normality.

'I forbid idle discourse during the day,' explained White, standing to block the dignitary's view. 'Distraction is the very devil.'

The mood at Auchengibbert for the next few days was febrile.

'What about my son?' asked Thomas Neil.

'What about him?' asked White, irritated at this disturbance to his train of thought. He had much to think about.

'I wanted so much to see him. And now... ' White turned away.

There was only one way forward: Elspeth must be buried. If not, her body would continue to exercise its power over her followers, many of whom were adamant that she must be brought in from the barn and reinstated in the farmhouse to await her glorious resurrection. White ignored the fanatics and concentrated instead on winning over those who had lived on the cusp of disillusion ever since the fiasco of Templeton Hill.

'We need a new start,' he explained. 'We must always carry the torch for the Lord Mother, but God's plans have changed, and we should, with humility, await His instructions. To deny her a burial is to deny God's inscrutable but immutable will.' His listeners nodded sagely.

Since her death, Andrew Innes had never been more than an arm's span from Elspeth. The previous night he had gone to the barn, climbed into the coffin and wrapped his small body around hers. He had rubbed her cheek. 'Mither, you are cold, cold and beautiful like alabaster. Remember Christ too waited in the dark cave before His power and sacred strength returned.' He stroked her brow and toyed with her black curls. 'The frost that is on you now is the harbinger of a spring that will see you rise again to inherit the earth. Be patient, Mither, be patient.' He managed to force an arm under her back and hold her in a stiff embrace. 'Here, Mither, take the heat from my body.' He was still holding her at dawn when he was gently persuaded to abandon his vigil.

Although most of the women disagreed profoundly with White over his plans for a burial, he had made it clear that he would brook no further discussion of the matter.

'It's no fair,' said Mrs Muir. 'Yon man's a charlatan.'

'Wi' no respect for the Mither,' echoed Emily.

'To put her in the grave would be...'

'Sacrilegious.'

'Aye, sacrilegious.'

THE WOMAN CLOTHED WITH THE SUN

White woke in the middle of the night barely able to breathe. The solution to all his problems was utterly simple. If he could arrange for her resurrection, he would become a rich man. He would wear Elspeth's cloak with a self-deprecating humility that would only serve to reinforce his importance as her successor. His fame would be assured. He would be asked to address learned societies. He would accept invitations – if the fee matched his own valuation of his worth. As he lay in the dark, his heart beat faster. There could be no delay. He must act now.

The most difficult part of his plan was to leave the house undetected. He achieved this by slithering out of his bed and crawling along the floor until he reached the door which, helpfully, had not been properly closed. Shivering as he reached the barn, he wrapped himself in a horse blanket and set to work. The first challenge was to bury Elspeth. After dragging her corpse into the night, he looked briefly up at the stars and breathed in the cold, clean air. Yes, this was a brilliant plan. All was well.

The chosen spot was at the edge of a neighbouring field which was well out of sight of the house. A shallow grave would have to suffice until the time was right to give Elspeth a more permanent resting place. He took an axe and a spade from the barn and caught himself whistling *Oh! Hasten Translation*. It was a good tune. He should make more time for his compositions.

The ground was harder than he had anticipated. He had to lever out several large stones with the axe before he could dig to any depth.

Before he rolled Elspeth into the hole, he remembered to remove her clothes for which he had a use. The moon emerged from the clouds and briefly cast a slither of light on Elspeth's nakedness. Were those the same legs that he had lain between?

She landed face down and he quickly shovelled the earth on top of her, remembering to replace the turf and trample it down. He covered the spot with the fallen branches of a dead tree and, pleased with his labours, returned to the barn.

The next stage of the operation was more difficult as he had to remove part of the roof to show Elspeth's route to paradise. Again, he was impressed by his own ingenuity as he dragged the large cart to the centre of the barn and tilted it until the far end was sufficiently close to the roof for him to climb up and reach the planks. Helpfully, the wood was rotten and easily removed. He then cast Elspeth's clothes on the floor in such a manner as to suggest that she had divested herself in haste, probably at the bidding of whatever angel had been sent to guide her to a better place.

As he walked the short distance to the house, he praised his foresight in having arranged for a spinning wheel merchant to visit later in the day. The innocent dupe would spread word of the great resurrection far and wide; the rumours attracting embellishment like burs on a dog.

Just in time, he caught himself whistling as he entered the house.

He had however been seen by Andrew Innis who, unable to sleep, had watched him both leave the house and return with the dawn.

White could barely wait for the morning light. How soon would the glorious truth be discovered? What was keeping them from the ritual early morning pilgrimage to pray over Elspeth's body? At last, Mrs Gibson rose and quietly crept from the house. She liked to have Elspeth to herself before the others arrived so that she could speak alone with her.

White started counting the seconds before the screaming would start. Twenty-one, twenty-two, twenty-three... And then it came. Mrs Gibson almost took the door from its hinges as she blundered back into the house. 'Christ has come amongst us!' she bellowed. The others sat up in their beds then hastened to see this miracle for themselves. White too followed them, his facial expression hovering convincingly between bewilderment and ecstasy.

'Jesus Christ!' shouted Emily, staring into the empty coffin. Mrs Muir shrieked and Mrs Gibson, feeling faint, had to steady herself.

'The Lord Mother has risen! Rejoice!'

'She has gone before us.' Mrs Muir embraced all and sundry while Mrs Gibson stood screaming. Soon all the Buchanites, apart from Andrew Innis and White, were shouting hysterically.

It was Thomas Neil who, in an instant, changed the mood from ecstatic joy to profound despair. 'She has left us!' he shouted when the tumult had died sufficiently for him to be heard. 'She has forsaken us.' He moaned and held his stomach as if it hurt.

'We are sinners.'

'We should have kept the faith, now we are forsaken.'

'Lord Mother, forgive us!'

Margaret White ran around the barn, tearing out a clump of hair that left her scalp bleeding.

With a measured pace, Innes walked out of the barn. Ignoring the pandemonium, he made his way to the field where logic told him, White must have buried the sacred body of the Lord Mother. The spot was easy to find. He pulled away the branches, knelt, and with his hands, dug in the earth until he saw the familiar black curls.

Mathew had noticed Innes leaving the barn and nudged his brother. Soon they were both standing next to Innes, staring downwards.

'O great Mother,' said James who, resuming the task that Innes had abandoned, stroked the earth from Elspeth's face. Mathew emitted a roar of pain that alerted the others.

As one, they fled out the barn tripping over rakes and flails until they came to the field. The Lord Mother was now fully exposed. Mrs Muir raised the stiff body which she then anointed anew with her tears. Andrew Neil pressed Elspeth's cold hand to his lips.

'I will tear him limb from limb,' said Mathew looking back at the barn where White had stayed to collect his thoughts. His brother rose and restrained him.

'Not yet,' he said. 'Let us choose the moment. We must stay calm.'

White sought refuge in certainty and anger. 'Of course, she must be buried. She's dead. Don't you believe your own senses? Didn't you see the maggot in her eye? Did you not smell the decay?' He prowled among the followers who sunk back as he approached. His fists were clenched, and it was obvious that he would use them if anyone were to defy him. Again, Mathew held James back. 'What were the Lord Mother's words?' continued White. "I will return in six days, or ten years, or fifty years if you are still faithless.' And you are. Six days have lapsed. Now we wait for ten years. Look into your souls for that small devil of doubt nestling there, whispering in your ears. Can you hear him?' He put his face next to Mrs Gibson's and shouted, his spittle landing on her cheek. 'Can you? Can you?' Mrs Gibson whimpered and sank to the floor.

'I am a sinner,' she said. The others took up her cry.

'You had the effrontery to doubt my words. I… ' he stabbed a forefinger into his chest. 'I, who have guided you this far. I, who have fed and clothed you.' Feeling more confident now, he moved towards Thomas Neil. Ah,' he said as if recognising a long-lost acquaintance. 'Thomas, Doubting Thomas isn't it. How is your son these days?' Neil flinched. 'Oh dear. Dead is he? Hanged, you say? What a shame!' Despite the tears streaming down Neil's face, White persisted. 'Had you kept the faith, you would have seen him again and held him in your arms. But no, you doubt my words, you question my leadership and Christ punishes you. He punishes you all!'

White milked the silence; a trick that had always worked in the pulpit. Let them wallow in his words. Give them no respite. And then Andrew Innes spoke.

'The Mither will stay in the house.'

'What?'

'She stays in our midst,' said Duncan Robertson.

'You will do our bidding,' said George Kidd.

'A stinking, plague-ridden corpse! Have you forsaken your wits? Will we collect the maggots and add them to the broth?'

Several of the women bristled at these sacrilegious words. 'In our midst,' said Mrs Muir.

'Have it your own way.' White stormed out of the house. Oblivious to the horizontal rain, he kicked open the wicket gate. He knew that his actions had profoundly disturbed many in the society. He also knew that his plans depended on cultivating the loyalty of those who might defect and follow him to a different promised land, one founded not on superstition and foolishness, but on the principles of economy and the accumulation of wealth. Let them bring in the decaying body of the mad woman if that's what they wanted. He would, in the meantime, move his bed closer to the window where the air was fresher.

Andrew Innes staggered under Elspeth's weight as he carried her back to the house, a living pieta. He refused all offers of help and eventually placed her on the table which had been cleared by Mrs Muir with a sweep of her hand causing several bowls to break on the stone floor.

'Feathers,' he said. 'We must wrap her tightly in feathers.' Mrs Gibson went into the adjacent room where the women stuffed the cushions and pillows that sold so well at market. She re-entered in a cloud of chicken feathers several of which stuck to her mouth as she deposited her light burden next to the table.

'We must keep her warm,' said Innes. 'She must rest next to the hearth.' He knelt and dug his fingernails into the lime and dirt that filled the gaps between the flagstones next to the fire. Roberson and Kidd helped him lift the flags until they revealed a space sufficiently large to house the sacred body of the Lord Mother.

To a muted rendition of *Oh! Hasten Translation*, Elspeth was lowered into her new grave, and the stones replaced. By way of a prayer, Innes searched his mind for the precise words of Luke 24. His recollection was somewhat hazy but sufficient to his purpose. 'On the first day of the week, very early in the morning, the women took the spices and went to the tomb where they found the stones had been lifted...'

'That will be me,' thought Amy Johnson who had recently persuaded a visiting packman to accept several jars of medicinal herbs in exchange for a small quantity of spice.

The Buchanites took it in turns to kneel at the hearth and pay homage to their temporarily departed leader. The individual rituals became ever more idiosyncratic. James Stewart produced a pair of shoes decorated with the moon and the stars and placed them side by side next to the Mother's resting place. Not to be outdone, Duncan Robertson put a tiny spinning wheel on the hearth, explaining, 'It will help her pass the time before she returns.' The others nodded their approval. Thomas Neil, convinced that he alone was responsible for the Mother's death, knelt at a distance from the others. Emily tried to comfort him. 'It's no your fault, Thomas.' But he wouldn't be pacified.

White knew the neighbourhood was rank with speculation about Elspeth's death. In addition, the old rumours of infanticide had resurfaced. Didn't they understand that babies had no souls? Cannibalism, concupiscence, and incest had recently mutated into accusations of murder. Elspeth's body had been given to the deil in exchange for a new supply of virgins; she had been dismembered and burnt; she had been fed to the ravens which were more plentiful and fatter than anyone could remember. He had to address the situation, or he and his plans would lie in ruins. He also understood that the authorities would need to inspect her grave and would not be best pleased to find her keeping warm by the fireplace.

'We must move the Mother… temporarily.' He was desperate for the move to be permanent but knew full well that he would face insurrection if he advocated such a thing. This was a compromise. He was a man who could find a solution for even apparently insurmountable challenges; a gift that would stand him in good stead when he started a new life in America.

Andrew Innes sobbed. 'Leave the Mither, leave her alane,' he rocked backwards and forwards.

'We must be discrete. Every kirkyard is being watched. You can see the lanterns at Kirkmahoe and Kirkmichael. They think she is a witch and cannot be buried on holy ground.' He could barely hear himself speak above the cacophony of wailing.

Sir Alexander Gordon's letter arrived the following day in which he made it clear that he would return in a week to inspect Elspeth's burial site.

'We must find a freshly dug grave,' said White. 'Lift the body and place the Mother beneath it.' Again, the solution had come to him during the night. It made perfect sense. The parish hypocrites would never permit Elspeth to be buried among the respectable, God-fearing dead. They would claw at the ground with their bare hands if it meant that her body could be tossed over the kirkyard wall and left for the dogs and rats. His plan would outwit the simpletons.

He dispatched six of the Buchanites to inspect the neighbouring parishes. It was Thomas Neil who returned with the news that Kirkgungeon kirkyard was unguarded and had, three days previously, witnessed the interment of a young farmhand who had been kicked in the head by a horse.

'Excellent,' said White. 'No plague.'

Thomas Neil and Duncan Robertson lifted the stones. Innes swept away the feathers from the corpse and wept as he uncovered Elspeth's face. He leaned into the hole to kiss her but was restrained by the others. 'Time is short,' said Robertson placing a hand on his shoulder.

The cart, filled with straw, creaked its way down the lane at midnight. The farmhand's grave was easily visible in the arc of light cast by White's lantern, and soon his coffin was once more lying on the ground next to its open grave. 'Enjoy the fresh air while you can,' said Davy McConville. Thomas Neil, who had been reluctant to accompany the party, moved to the trees where he shook with grief. The others ignored him and concentrated on the job in hand.

The farmhand's corpse was placed on top of Elspeth, and the earth replaced. Andrew Innes observed, 'If the Mither rises tonight, she'll take the laddie wi' her.'

For a full fifty years this image was burnt into his heart.

Chapter Forty-One

SCHISM

Elspeth slept well that night and was not disturbed for another two days by which time Sir Alexander Gordon had inspected the grave and declared himself satisfied that the unusual circumstances were indeed necessary to prevent the locals desecrating the burial place. He did though wonder at the quantity of feathers that still attached to the body. On balance, he understood that he was dealing with a strange community whose ways, although eccentric, were essentially harmless.

Now that the authorities were convinced that Elspeth was not only dead but well and truly buried, she was, once more, disinterred and placed under the hearth in the farmhouse.

The Buchanites' rituals became ever more protracted. In addition to the extemporised prayers and hymns, flowers and fruit were left close to the fire where they quickly withered and were replaced. Mrs Muir disconcerted the others by crawling to the sacred spot on her knees from the far corner of the room. She completed her slow journey with her hands outstretched, her face contorted from crying. Impressed by this display of pious homage, several of the others followed suit.

White was rapidly losing patience with this and other time-consuming practices. This was no way to run an efficient business. The production of woven garments had virtually stopped, Duncan Robertson had not produced a spinning wheel for several weeks, and the neighbouring farmers were starting to complain that their fields were being neglected and their crops untended.

Needing time and space for reflection, White commandeered the upper floor of Auchengibbert for himself, Margaret and their two children. Mrs Muir had been using the larger of the rooms to store the clothes produced by the weavers. She cowered as White tossed armfuls of shawls and outer garments down the stairs. James moved to confront White but was again restrained by Mathew. 'Patience, brother, patience.' Instead of pummelling White, the younger lad put an arm round Mrs Muir and led her to the hearth where she prostrated herself, calling on the Lord Mother to help them. Alexander Gillespie joined her and knelt on the flagstones. Birdman placed a shawl over his cage so that the birdsong wouldn't disturb the mourners.

Increasingly, Andrew Innes provided leadership to the Buchanites, some fifteen in number, who remained staunchly unbending in their devotion to Elspeth. He led their evening's devotions, choosing the hymn that always opened the proceedings and the text for discussion.

'Again, I repeat it out of pure love to a deluded world. Such as are crying and praying to God to save them, know not God, nor dwell in the light of God. For such as are in the light, are thanking and blessing God...'

At that moment, light was indeed an issue. Innes paused and squinted at the page, unable to decipher the next few words. Amy Johnson lit a candle from the smouldering peat and placed it next to him. He nodded and continued.

'For such as are in the light, are thanking and blessing God, that he sought them instead of them needing to seek them.'

White, who had crept down the stairs, approached the huddled group and snatched the book from Innes' hands.

'Ah! *The Divine Dictionary*,' he declaimed as if delighted to have rediscovered the sacred book. 'A demonstration that the Soul and Person is the same thing.' Like an animal scrabbling for food, he tore pages from the book and thrust them into the fire. The Buchanites gasped.

'And what is this? Concerning the Propagation of the Human Race.' He held the book at arm's-length out of the reach of Emily who vainly stretched out to retrieve it. 'What deluded vanity. What folly!' Another chapter was wrenched from its spine and thrown into the flames.

'But these are your own words,' said Innes.

'Dictated by the sorceress, now rotting under those stones.' Several of the women burst into tears. 'And another thing,' White moved to the fire, removed the red-tipped poker and stuck its red tip into the tabletop. 'Remember I am the man who rules with a rod of iron.' Mrs Muir ran from the table and threw herself on a bed in the corner of the room. 'Furthermore,' he said while continuing to scorch the tabletop with the poker, 'I have spoken to several well-connected men, well versed in the letter of the law, and they kindly brought to my attention the incontrovertible fact that none of you are signatories to the lease of this property. Accordingly, those of you who do not wish to follow me and make a new life in the Americas are hereby given notice to leave.' With that, he bowed to the company in mock deference, and returned upstairs to his wife and children.

The battle lines were now well and truly drawn. The main players in White's faction included George Hill, an estate worker from Closeburn, and Joseph Innes, Andrew's brother. The three of them slowly won converts among the members of the community, mainly men, who had never fully recovered from the disappointment of the failed translation at Templeland Hill. They gathered in the upstairs room and took tea from Mrs White, while listening to her husband extolling the delights that awaited them in the new world of America. They would, on arrival, be allocated land. They would grow rich. They would live in white clapperboard houses from the upper floors of which they could gaze on the undulating fields of wheat. They would be powerful members of the community, respected and admired by their neighbours. Of course, they would continue to pay allegiance, and indeed a tithe to White himself, without whom, they would have continued to live in penury and apostasy.

White wallowed in the devotion of his born-again adherents. Ironically, it reminded him of the heady days in Irvine when he also commanded respect. But without the distraction of a mad woman of course.

Andrew Innes, Duncan Robertson, Davy McConville, Alexander Gillespie, the two brothers and Birdman were among the loyalists who pledged never to forsake the Lord Mother whom they had failed with their lack of faith and their carnal ways. They would make amends and together wait for the moment when she would return in clouds of glory to reclaim them and make them whole again.

Innes was too shrewd to accept the brutal choice as described by White. He asked Alexander Gillespie to prepare an inventory of all the goods and chattels jointly owned by the community. He was duly presented with a list that itemised thirteen stacks of corn, seven horses in the newly built stable, seven milk cows in the byre, a large stock of black cattle on the hill and an indeterminate number of sheep and swine. In addition, all members of the community possessed two suits of clothes each with several webs of linen and woollen cloth in store. Innes nodded but was reluctant to give White any credit for the society's increased worldly goods.

Three weeks later, flanked by the large bodies of James and Mathew, Andrew Innes climbed the stairs and knocked on the Whites' door.

'What is it? I'm busy.'

'We crave a moment of your time,' said Innes pulling himself up to his full height.

'Very well, but I'm a busy man.'

White declined the offer of a chair when he joined the loyalists gathered round the hearth. He noted that the sacred stones under which the Mother was buried had been marked in chalk.

'We have a counter proposal, Mr White. Divide the assets in proportion to the numbers who wish to stay, and those who wish to follow you. We have sought advice and it appears that, although many of us are not signatories of the lease, no such caveat applies to the goods and chattels that we have in common. Furthermore, as established tenants, in situ, those of us who chose to stay cannot be easily, or speedily evicted. There you have it. I suspect that a quick settlement would be to the advantage of baith parties.'

The faithful stared in awe at their new champion. White glanced at the poker that was propped against the hearth. His instinct was to use it against the brains of this stupid little man challenging his authority. A quick application of the rod of iron would work wonders. Instead, he poked his finger into Innes' chest. 'And you, dwarf, can secure a position in a travelling show.' Warming to his theme, he gestured at his cowering audience, 'Step up ladies and gentlemen, feel free to inspect this freak of nature. Cast your eyes on the smallest cock you have ever seen.'

Innes continued. 'You may also wish to know that we have signed an agreement with the present owner of Larghill farm who will give us first refusal when the current lease expires.'

Despite his anger, White saw merit in a proposal that would get this troublesome rump out of his hair. 'Have it your own way.' He gestured to his henchmen that they were to follow him upstairs.

James and Mathew sought out a quiet corner away from the rest. 'We should join them,' said the older sibling.

'Are you mad?'

'Think, brother. Think. The Mother is dead, and we have our own lives to consider.'

'Do you really mean that we should tie ourselves to the coattails of that charlatan, that mountebank?'

'Only for a time. Let him secure our passage tae America. Let us swear our allegiance. When we land, we will leave him and his deluded followers, and make our own way.'

'We owe fealty to the Mother,' said Mathew who was still coming to terms with the loss of the woman he had loved with all his heart.

'And what do we read in the good book? 'Vengeance is mine, I will repay, saith the Lord.' And, when all is said and done, we are here tae dae the Lord's work.'

Mathew nodded as he followed his brother's drift. 'Sometimes He needs a helping hand.'

'Exactly. Let's join them upstairs.'

White was ruthless in the transactions that followed Innes' declaration. He ordered George Hill to hide four of the horses in the wood, making it seem that they had been stolen by tinkers. Several of the other men were instructed to round up the black cattle and sell three quarters of them. As their numbers had been indeterminate, it would be an easy matter to dissemble and claim that there were in fact far fewer than had been assumed. Likewise, the entire stock of woven goods was disposed of at market and the true price hidden from Innes who was outwitted at every turn.

The parting of the ways when it came, was quick. White had secured one-way tickets and two carts that nearly capsized under the weight of possessions and provisions. The true Buchanites huddled in the doorway to watch the departure of their former friends with whom they had shared mishap and rapture in equal measure.

James Stewart busied himself packing his tools into the cart. White had told him that, owing to a mismanaged quota system, the New Country was desperately short of cobblers. He could easily start his own business. 'You'll have to master the mid-calf boot and find a supplier of spurs.' Stewart nodded.

Amy Johnson was flustered. She failed to understand how anyone could leave the sacred sight of the Lord Mother's resting place. Didn't they realise that her resurrection was imminent? She could only assume that the deil was to blame, and to ward off his pernicious influence, had taken to hiding acorns in the farmhouse.

Andrew Innes stepped forward and approached Joseph. He removed his hat and embraced his brother. They had rarely agreed about very much, but both knew they would never see each other again. Joseph wept. The Gardner sisters also parted with heavy hearts. Despite her residual hatred of White, Jean had now fallen for George Hill and needed to be in a place of safety where her deranged poet could never find her. Reluctantly, Katie knew that she had to stay with her strange husband and their child.

Mrs Muir started to sing. Normally, *Oh! Hasten Translation* was sung with a joyous enthusiasm, its tempo matching the impatience of the singers to experience the promised rapture. On this occasion it sounded mournful, reproachful. The faithful stood on the path and watched as the carts and the entourage of thirty emigrants meandered out of sight. Andrew Innes closed the gate behind them and returned to the house.

The mood was sombre as the deserters made their way to Portpatrick, and from there to Newry. In an idle moment, George Hill made the mistake of humming one of White's early creations. The composer reacted with fury and stopped the convoy while he remonstrated with the innocent hummer. 'If you hanker for the dark days of deception and folly, turn back now and join the sad rump of simpletons.' Hill muttered his apologies but had to check on subsequent occasions that he was not in fact singing out loud the tune that had taken possession of his head.

White spent much of the journey in discussion with Joseph Innes. Like his brother, Joseph had a grasp on all matters financial, and confirmed that the party were leaving with substantial funds. The Buchanites who had left with White shared his view that personal wealth was not the evil that the mad woman believed it to be. Joseph mentioned that most of the emigrants had taken a leaf out of their new leader's book and siphoned off for themselves a portion of each financial transaction in which they were involved. White was silent while he absorbed this information. Eventually he told Joseph that he had heard rumours of innocent travellers being set upon in Newry by unscrupulous gangs who robbed them of the wherewithal to start their new lives. Accordingly, he would take possession of all monies held by the group for safekeeping. Joseph would of course issue receipts. Delighted with his plan, he started singing *Oh! Hasten Translation* under his breath until he saw that George Hill was looking at him reproachfully.

At Newry, the ship was being provisioned with an efficiency that impressed White. Barrels of salt fish, biscuits, beer, beef, pork and pease were hauled up the gangplanks and wheeled on their rims towards the lower decks. He breathed in the sea air and felt a small excitement at the prospect of taking America by storm with his business acumen and his gift for exploiting the men beneath him. Margaret interrupted him with the observation that their younger child was feeling poorly. 'Not now,' he said. 'Can't you see that I'm thinking?'

While the preparations continued, James and Mathew slunk away to find a tavern. The surroundings reminded them both of Greenock.

'Do you mind the dog fight?'

'Aye,' said Mathew. 'The Mother threw herself into that pit. Her blood was everywhere.'

'And then she was good to baith of us.'

'Aye.'

'Are we doing the right thing?'

'The Mother's no coming back, no matter what the others think.'

'But America's a long way.' James refilled both of their mugs from the pitcher.

White insisted that he have a cabin to himself. He was again growing tired of Margaret and was increasingly convinced that Jean Gardner, despite his treatment of her in the past, was his for the taking. Her apparent fondness for George Hill didn't fool him in the slightest. In any case, a man needed his privacy to conduct his affairs.

'I've got work to do. Plans to make. Calculations,' he told Margaret when she suggested that he might want to share with her and the children. To an extent this was true. Several months previously, he had befriended an American, resident in Dumfries, from whom he had borrowed a directory of all small manufactories in Baltimore, and the deeds of association of the local Chamber of Commerce. It was important to know your rivals. And their money. It took him a while before he could mentally convert the continental currency introduced after the revolution into real money. The fact that Spanish dollars were still in circulation was an unwanted complexity.

Each night, having checked the lock on his cabin door, he would empty the money bag bought from a saddle-smith in Portpatrick, and plunge his hands into the heap of coins, wallowing in the sensation of the metal tumbling through his fingers. He loved the music they made. He would then swirl the coins around the table as fast as he could without spilling any. The movement had to be clockwise, for good luck. This was particularly difficult when the ship was rolling in the storms like a barrel. The third part of the ritual required him to make unequal heaps of the coins so that he could guess at their number and quickly convert each pile into American currency.

White had little to do with his fellow travellers. Contact with steerage class was discouraged by the crew who had witnessed too many instances of the wealthy passengers being enticed to the lower depths of the ship under some pretext or other, before having their good nature exploited and their pockets picked. There had been rumours of murder on a previous voyage: having been forcibly separated from his rings, purse and pocket watch, an unfortunate merchant had been stripped of his clothes and, under cover of darkness and a storm, had been tossed overboard. The degree of separation suited White who had no wish to be distracted by domestic or other petty concerns. There were exceptions.

After the evening meal he sent a midshipman to summon Jean Gardner to his cabin. She arrived a little drunk, which pleased her host. He sat her down, plied her with more rum and listened with feigned interest as she shared gossip about their fellow emigrants. Joseph Innes had been visited by an outbreak of boils that had led to him being forcefully isolated from the others for fear of contagion. Mrs Dawson was endlessly troubled with nightmares about the Lord Mother and would wake screaming in the night. Eventually an exciseman, a refugee from the law, in the opinion of George Hill, threatened to strangle her if she woke him again.

White was rapidly losing interest. 'Wheesht,' he said, placing a finger on her lips before pushing her onto his bunk. He grabbed her breasts. 'So soft, my lovely.'

Rather than surrender to his wishes, Jean bit hard into the flesh between his thumb and forefinger.

'Wicked, ungrateful bitch!' He threw her onto the floor. 'How dare you frustrate the wishes of your leader?' He stood over her, sucking his wound. 'I will give you time to reflect on your foolishness, and if you do not return of your own volition to make amends for this folly, then I promise you, you will be cast into the wilderness of a foreign country that will see you for what you are, a snivelling harlot, not worth a gentleman's spit. That pathetic eunuch, Hill, will not save you.' He watched as she scrambled upright and out of the door which, accidently, he had left unlocked. White took a mental note to be more prepared next time.

The only other members of the party whose company he sought

were James and Mathew. He was still pleasantly surprised that they had found the courage to join him for a new life. They were different from the others. Strong-willed and fiercely loyal to the Mother certainly, but these were faults he was prepared to forgive. The young men had a wit about them that marked them out from the whimpering sycophancy of those who had stayed. They were also intelligent. He would need people like them if he were to fulfil his plans. Every general needed his lieutenants.

'Where will we bide?' asked James as he poured himself another drink from White's decanter.

'Newcastle in the first instance,' replied White. 'Until we get our bearings. I have letters of introduction to John McKinly, the first president of Delaware. A fine man by all accounts. Upstanding.'

Mathew nodded approvingly. 'And the others?'

White snorted. 'Some of them will be useful. We will need those capable of working without demur. Remember, we have men used to giving their labours for little return. This will stand us in good stead.'

Their discussion was curtailed by the steward knocking at the door with the order to extinguish all lanterns as the ship was heading into a storm.

On the lower deck, the brothers did what they could to console Mrs Dawson who was convinced that the devil himself was rocking the ship, tearing its planks asunder. 'What's that noise, the deil's ain laughter?'

'Na,' said James, 'that's Geordie Hill being sick.'

'This too will pass,' said Mathew, taking the old woman in his arms. He glanced at his brother who sighed. They both knew that Mrs Dawson had no place in White's plans.

Chapter Forty-Two

A CARD GAME

James had been feeding a morsel of cheese to a mouse when Mathew produced the Pope Joan box.

'Where did that come fae?' he asked, removing the lid.

'I borrowed it from the first mate. His door was open as I passed.'

The brothers spent several long nights re-familiarising themselves with the game. The sequence of the divisions on the board and their associated values was easy, and they chanted them together. 'From the top.'

'Pope Joan, Matrimony, Intrigue, Ace, King, Queen and Game.'

'Good.'

'So,' said James, 'the dealer is decided by any agreed means. Thereafter, the turn to deal passes to the left. The dealer starts by dressing the board with six counters to Pope, twa each to Matrimony and Intrigue, and one to each other compartment... '

'And then?'

'The dealer deals all the cairds round one at a time to one more hand than there are players, the dead hand remaining unrevealed throughout play.'

'But how will we get him to play?'

'Patience,' said Mathew.

Patience was in increasingly short supply. After three more sleepless nights spent in overclose proximity to two hundred other souls, the brothers were desperate to take their plan to the next stage. Propped up on their narrow beds, they watched, impervious, as a grieving family from Carlisle carried their dead relative onto the deck to be dropped overboard. James picked at the edges of the biscuit, one of several he had purchased at great cost the previous day. A worm fell onto the palm of his hand. He squashed it between his thumb and forefinger.

'Something must change. We must act soon.' A sudden swell rocked the ship and sent him tumbling sideways onto an elderly woman who had sobbed her way through the night. 'Sorry, dear,' he said.

'I was hearing that a faither took his dying son to be baptised,' said Mathew scratching but failing to locate a particularly active louse. 'He had heard that our great leader was a minister. White telt him it would cost him a guinea, so that was the end of that.'

'One more practice,' said James taking out the pack of cards. He held up several in quick succession, and then covered them with his hand.

'Ten of hearts, two of clubs, five of clubs, eight of diamonds, seven of spades and… '

'Three of hearts,' said James. 'Nae bad though. We're getting better.'

Soon afterwards the brothers took the board to White's cabin and asked if he wanted to play. Eager for distraction, White willingly agreed. 'Anything to pass the time, boys.' He cleared several documents from the table and uncorked a bottle of port.

When dealing, White slapped the cards down with a confidence that was calculated to intimidate. 'Pope Joan!' he shouted. The boys sighed as if acknowledging that they were competing with a master. 'You need a good memory,' he said tapping the side of his head.

The game progressed rapidly. White's winning streak was relentless. He whistled *Oh! Hasten Translation* as he gathered the tokens. 'You've met your match, boys. Remind me what the stakes were again.'

White refilled their glasses. 'Are you sure you have the wherewithal to pay me?' he asked slyly.

'It's all here,' said James emptying a pouch of coins onto the table.

'A most satisfactory evening,' said White holding the door open for his guests. 'Be sure to come again.'

The boys came again on at least three more occasions. Each time they lost. Each time White wallowed in his role as victor. He was feeling invincible. He had successfully broken with his old life. A new one beckoned. He would conquer America.

'We only have money for one more game,' said James counting the coins by the light of the solitary lantern permitted below decks.

'So be it,' said Mathew.

The storm had raged for two days. Below decks stank of shit and sick, and foul water sloshed across the floor. It was rumoured that the level in the bilges had risen to an unprecedented height, drowning all the chickens. An old woman shouted hysterically at intervals, warning all and sundry that the ship was descending into the bottomless pit of hell and that they must all prepare to meet Satan. Above the sound of groaning timbers, James and Mathew heard something large thumping onto the deck above. 'A mast?' asked James.

'Now is the time,' said his brother, reaching for the board. The gale howled its approval.

They made slow progress, dragging themselves almost horizontally across the deck. Mathew had been hit in the face by a trailing rope and wiped the blood from his forehead. When White eventually opened the door, his eyes were staring, and the brothers were met with the smell of strong drink.

The sight of several empty bottles pleased James. Between them the brothers had just sufficient money to buy food and drink for the remaining four months of the voyage.

The game settled into the established pattern. White ostentatiously rolled up his sleeves and rammed a pinch of snuff up each nostril. For good measure he poured a large dram down his throat. As they had agreed, the boys quickly lost the first game. 'Sorry lads,' he said, sweeping the counters towards his side of the table. Another pound Scots went the way of the first. In a rare display of what, in different circumstances, might have passed for compassion, White asked if the boys really wanted to play another game.

'Aye, our luck will turn,' said Mathew. White snorted and dealt the cards. He won again.

As he gathered his winnings, the small porthole behind them clattered open and the gale extinguished the lantern, plunging them into complete darkness. As White rose cursing from the table to find the tinderbox, Mathew took his chance and inserted an extra card into the pack.

It was the younger brother's turn to deal. White scribbled the tally in the ledger as the cards were placed face down on the table. 'Are you sure about this?'

'The Lord Mother will look after us.' White paused but chose not to challenge the remark. The dullard boys would soon be out of his sight, and he would be even richer.

'I telt you!' James turned over the Jack of hearts. 'Pope Joan has joined us.'

Aided by several subtle sleights of hand, the tide of fortune turned in the boys' favour. Initially White took the reversals with magnanimity, confident that he would prevail. As the tide grew ever stronger, his demeanour changed. 'You forget who I am at your peril. I am Christ's Manchild, whosoever crosses my path will rot in perdition!' The brothers exchanged glances; it had been many months since they had heard White make any reference to the delusions that sustained them in the past. He raised his fist, preparing to hammer it into the board.

Mathew held his wrist. 'Deal,' he said.

Shaking with rage, White dealt the cards.

'The ledger,' said Mathew who had noticed that their opponent was increasingly forgetful of recording the stakes. Snatching his pen, White grudgingly scrawled the amount in the left-hand column.

'Are you sure about this?' asked Mathew mockingly.

White snapped the quill in half, covering the board in ink.

'Careful,' said James, using a corner of his kerchief to wipe the segment nearest to him. 'You have besmirched Matrimony.'

'Integrity too,' said Mathew smudging the ink with his finger from the small compartment already piled with counters.

No longer capable of memorising the cards, White watched in a state of impotent apoplexy as his fortune drained away. James quietly assumed responsibility for recording the growing sum. On cue, Pope Joan made one final appearance.

'Fuck, fuck, fuck,' said White covering his face with his hands.

'That's no way to speak of the Pope,' said Mathew.

'Aye, and a woman at that,' added James. 'We would be exceedingly grateful if you could pay us our dues.'

'Rot in hell!' screamed White facing the brothers. James produced a dagger from his jerkin and put it against the Manchild's neck.

'Now,' he said as a thin line of blood tricked onto his victim's collar. 'Now,' repeated James quietly.

White thrust the leather bag at his persecutors. 'One more wager,' he pleaded.

'But you have nae mair money.'

'I have this,' said White producing the pocket watch that the brothers had last seen in the possession of Davy McConville. 'It's gold. Take it, and, for all I care, the clothes I stand in.'

This last offer resonated with the brothers who looked at each other. 'Very well,' said Mathew preparing the board, while James methodically recorded details of the wager in the ledger.

James refilled the glasses. White drained his and demanded another. His anger blinded him to the cards as they were dealt. It didn't matter: he was in touch with higher powers which would flay the skin from his adversaries. Mathew pulled the half hunter towards him and casually inserted a fingernail under the rim of the back plate and looked at the one visible cog jerking frenetically. Incensed, White reached for the watch and snapped it shut. As the ship lurched and the table tilted, James placed a hand over the newly dealt cards, and, for a second time, slipped the Jack of clubs into the bottom of his brother's pile.

As each card was played, the wind howled louder, then maintained a sustained crescendo as White, shaking, placed a ten of spades on the table.

'And here's our guid friend... ' said Mathew calmly. 'Pope Joan.'

The gale erupted. The cabin shook. White fell onto the floor clutching his head, then cowered, a gibbering foetus at the feet of the brothers.

'Keeps guid time, does it?' asked James, adding the watch to the bag under the table.

'Ah, Mr White... ' Mathew spoke with the good-natured cadences of an attentive servant. 'You must fulfil your side of the bargain.' White looked up bewildered.

'Your claes,' said James pulling the stricken man to his feet. With an expression of dread, White unbuttoned his tunic and handed it to James.

'And your shirt, man.'

'And your boots.' White briefly hopped on one leg pulling at his footwear. 'Sit down, man. Take your time, take your time.'

'And your breeches.'

As this last garment fell to the floor, White cupped a hand over his genitals.

'Aye, it's guy cold,' said Mathew, 'and look, yon thingy's turned intae a prune.'

Before they left the cabin, James opened White's trunk and removed all other items of clothing including the braided waistcoat and the long cane, necessary accoutrements for any man of substance intending to make his way in the New World.

Once outside, James held onto Mathew so that his brother could use a free hand to toss the clothing overboard. For a second, the wind inflated White's shirt and, together, they watched as the empty torso floated on the gale.

Chapter Forty-Three

A GIFT

Andrew Innes, a worried man, stood by the field of barley in the failing light. He plucked a head from its stalk and ran it through his fingers. He took one of the grains from his palm and tested it between his teeth. As he feared, it was small and hard. The society needed a good harvest. Despite the efforts of the weavers, and Duncan Robertson's carpentry skills, he knew that soon the bailiffs would return. He watched as the wind rippled through the crop creating small waves. The undulations brought a tune to mind, and he hummed *Oh! Hasten Translation.*

As he turned away, his foot nudged a dead rabbit. He had a distant memory of the Lord Mother telling a tale of a creature into which she once breathed new life. Their own new life would come, that was beyond doubt. By his calculations they had to wait another thousand days before she would appear among them. By then they would have waited the ten years stipulated by the Mother on her deathbed. Their faith would not fail them again. This time they would be ready. As he looked down the slope towards the farm, he could see Alexander Gillespie and Birdman in the yard, staring upwards into the dusk listening to the day's final flurry of bird song. The lanterns had been lit, and Innes was pleased to notice the thin smoke still rising from the chimney. The Lord Mother had to be kept warm. The hearth under which she lay must never grow cold.

Several of the black cattle raised mournful heads as he passed the byre. Two of the beasts had recently fallen ill and died. He shuddered at another unwanted memory and glanced at the sky where a distant arrow of birds was silhouetted against the rising moon. He envied them their flight. Elspeth often preached about the transmigration of souls.

As he approached the farm, the door was opened for him by Katie. This was unusual. All thirteen of the residents were assembled and formed a line on either side of the threshold. Bemused, he let himself be ushered towards the table where he saw the bag.

'A Mr Macrabin left it,' said Alexander Gillespie. 'A merchant. Well dressed.'

'Fae the Americas.' Katie was fingering the black leather strap.

The others crowded closer as Innes loosened the first buckle. 'Give me space,' he said lifting out Davy McConville's pocket watch nestling on top of a king's ransom of gold coins.

AFTERWORD

This novel is a fictionalised account of John Cameron's *History of The Buchanite Delusion* published in 1906. In turn, Cameron's book was a reworking of John Train's account *The Buchanites From First to Last* published in 1846. Train, who had previously written a history of the Isle of Man and a biography of Walter Scott, was fascinated by the rumours still circulating fifty years after Elspeth Buchan's death. Accordingly, he interviewed Andrew Innes, the last surviving Buchanite, and faithfully wrote down a verbatim account of their discussions as the old man relived the events that had shaped his life.

We learn little about Elspeth's childhood apart from the fact that she was born in Fatmachen, Banffshire, to the wife of an innkeeper. After her mother died, she lived with various families in the neighbourhood. She was a singular child who later confided in Innes that she was afflicted with visions during this time.

Fatmachen today is bleak and remote. It seems likely that the pile of stones at the point where a farm track meets the A714 is all that remains of the inn. There is no blue plaque declaring *This is the birthplace of Elspeth Buchan, the woman referred to in Revelations as being clothed in the sun and the moon*. Neither the sun nor the moon was in evidence when I visited, just several derelict tractors and a thin drizzle blurring the distant ribbon of sea.

We know that she was placed in service with a cousin of her father, and that the Lady of the house was engaged to a merchant with interests in the West Indies. They did indeed wait in Greenock for a ship during which time Elspeth escaped the clutches of her guardians and revelled in the dissolute company of sailors and dock workers. James and Mathew are fictional creations, of whom I have grown very fond.

She subsequently married a potter from Ayr before moving to the Broomielaw in Glasgow. It is a matter of record that her husband despaired of her debauched ways. As this is a constant theme in the novel, it merits an airing. Although it has been common practice to attribute all manner of sexual behaviour to cult leaders, there is sufficient evidence for us to believe that this was true in Elspeth's case.

Cameron concedes that the Buchanites 'indulged in indecent practises'.

Burns, who did indeed visit the society in Irvine, later wrote, 'Their tenets are a strange jumble of enthusiastic jargon. Among others, she (Mrs Buchan) pretends to give them the holy ghost by breathing on them, which she does with postures and practices that are scandalously indecent. They likewise dispose of all their effects, and hold a community of goods in common, and live nearly an idle life, carrying on a great farce of pretended devotions in barns and woods, where they lie and lodge together, and hold likewise a community of women, as it is another of their tenets that they can commit no mortal sin. I am personally acquainted with most of them, and can assure you that the above-mentioned are facts... '

Before we leave Burns, there is some interesting speculation, summarised by Cameron, that his praise for 'Darling Jean' was inspired initially, not by Jean Armour but Jean Gardner.

Burns was not the only literary figure to feature, albeit briefly, in the history of the Buchanites. In his autobiography, John Galt describes how he too was caught up in Elspeth's expulsion from Irvine: 'Many children also accompanied her but my mother in state of distraction followed and drew me back by the lug.'

Continuing my pursuit of old stones, and indeed anything that would help me connect with the strange society, I travelled down from Glasgow to Closeburn where I was able to clamber through the collapsed remains of Buchan Ha'. The current owner is apparently more than happy to collude with time and let the ruin sink back into the land. The profile of the building leaves little doubt that its sixty residents would have been obliged to live in promiscuous proximity to each other. Close to the ruins is the overgrown well which according to legend was the repository for unwanted infants. There have also been reports of farmers in more recent times unearthing small human bones.

Although my version of Elspeth's death is entirely invented and there is no evidence that White was in any way responsible, it is consistent with Andrew Innes' account. Hugh White's rod of iron ceased to be a metaphor and became a reality as he became increasingly violent towards the Lord Mother. Jean Gardner, according to Cameron, is reported to have said at a time of tension in the community, 'Hugh White is murdering Friend Mother.' There can be no doubt that latterly he saw a future in which Elspeth would play no part.

We know from John Train the identities of perhaps half of the Buchanites, most of whom feature in the novel. The others I have invented.

Although it would be satisfying to believe that some of the money that White appropriated from the Buchanites eventually found its way back to the society, sadly this too is fiction. In my defence, there is evidence that the rump of the Buchanites, under Innes' leadership, continued to thrive and eventually became significant landowners.

Appropriately, John Cameron chose to preface his account with Fabian's words in *Twelfth Night*, 'If this were played upon a stage now, I could condemn it as an improbable fiction.' And he was right. In the years following the timeframe of this novel, Andrew Innes and the remaining thirteen Buchanites were obliged to leave Auchengibbert for a remote farm in Larghill. When I visited this still utterly remote location, the farmhouse, barns and surrounding acres were completely deserted apart from the black cattle. I did though have a strong sense that I was being watched. It was here that the sacred mummified remains of Elspeth were reinterred under a new hearth where they continued to provide a focus for veneration and worship.

But this was not her final resting place. Eventually, as the society prospered, they moved several miles to Nine Mile burn, or Crocketford as it is now. Here they built a substantial home, which with a singular lack of imagination, they called Newhouse. Elspeth was installed in a small room at the top of the stairs. As she had failed to return on either of the first two dates she mentioned on her deathbed, the hope that she would put in an appearance on the fiftieth anniversary of her demise sustained the Buchanites.

As the years passed, her loyal followers died one by one and were buried in a small graveyard behind the house. Mrs Gibson was its first resident. Eventually only Andrew Innes and Katie remained alive. When his wife too died, Innes continued the ritual described in the opening paragraph of the novel. Each night he would heat a cloth and place it on Elspeth's mummified body, removing the previous day's cloth which he then placed on his own head as he sat in front of the fire.

As the fiftieth anniversary approached, Andrew was predictably excited. I will quote John Cameron's account of events: 'At last the awful hour was come! There he is – in that rough, dark cell, bending in a state of almost suspended animation over the rude 'kist' that contains all that is dear to him on earth or in heaven… he watches the shrivelled leathern features for the first signs of returning vitality. He has been keeping vigil all night long, by the dim light of his tallow candle. The morning dawns but no ray of light penetrates the windowless chamber; no ray of life lights up the withered corpse.'

Innes assumed that his own lack of faith was responsible for Elspeth's failure to return. He survived for another four years during which time he redoubled his efforts to be worthy of the Lord Mother.

Newhouse in Crocketford is virtually unchanged apart from the addition of a comparatively new extension. When I visited, developers were about to start work on the site. I knew that Dumfries and Galloway Council had insisted that the alleged burial ground be excavated before any building could start, and I spoke to the archaeologist who carried out the work. He told me that they had located one grave but, out of respect, chose not to probe further. He commented on how close to the surface the coffin was. This is not surprising given that the Buchanites assumed that they would soon be woken by the angels and hoisted heavenwards. It was a pity that he could not confirm that the coffin was resting on another.

The current site manager told me that her predecessor, a man not known for excessive sensibility, had refused to sleep in Newhouse after the repeated sight of a handprint on the wall.

Elspeth's letter to Hugh, the extracts from *The Divine Dictionary*, Engelbrecht's book, Elspeth's dying words and White's letter to Sir Alex Greenlaw are all quoted verbatim.

Cameron concludes with an account of all that he could discover about the other Buchanites after the schism.

DUNCAN ROBERTSON died in 1826 and, contrary to all

Buchanite teachings, asked to see a minister when on his deathbed.

KATIE GARDNER, INNES' WIFE died three years before her husband. To the end, although devoted to each other, they lived in separate parts of the house. When in her eighties, Katie was described as being 'extremely witchlike... shrivelled... her neck rests on her breast... her height does not exceed fifty inches.'

JOSEPH INNES, ANDREW'S BROTHER. Seems to have been one of the few to prosper in the New World, dying in 1835 worth over £8000.

GEORGE HILL. Married Jean Gardner who died soon after. He subsequently became a bookseller in Baltimore but ended his days in poverty.

HUGH WHITE. Started a school in Virginia State and occasionally preached but never referred to his earlier beliefs.

MARGARET WHITE. Died a year after reaching America.

THOMAS DAVIDSON. Died of hypothermia when trapped in a snowstorm while travelling over Leadhills.

MAGGIE BUCHAN, Elspeth's daughter, married a sailor who was subsequently drowned at sea. She eventually opened a dame school.

HUMPHY HUNTER is buried in the Old Kirk, Irvine. When he heard of Elspeth's death from a horse dealer he replied, 'Oh no, John, that is not the case, and never will be in this world!'

'Well, if she isn't dead her friends in Galloway have played her a trick, for they have buried her!'

JAMES AND MATHEW. Had they existed, would certainly have thrived in America. They would have bought adjacent farms in the Midwest, married sisters and have been pillars of their community.

STILL WAITING FOR ELSPETH